The Middle
Finger of Fate

A Trailer Park Princess Cozy Mystery
Book One

Kim Hunt Harris

Kim Hunt Harris Books, LLC
Lubbock, Texas

Kim Hunt Harris Books, LLC
3410 98th St Ste. 4-157
Lubbock, TX 79423
www.kimhuntharris.com

Publisher's Note: This is a work of fiction. Names, characters, places, and incidents are a product of the author's imagination. Locales and public names are sometimes used for atmospheric purposes. Any resemblance to actual people, living or dead, or to businesses, companies, events, institutions, or locales is completely coincidental.

Book Layout ©2013 BookDesignTemplates.com

Ordering Information:
Quantity sales. Special discounts are available on quantity purchases by corporations, associations, and others. For details, contact the "Special Sales Department" at the address above.

The Middle Finger of Fate/ Kim Hunt Harris. -- 1st ed.
ISBN 978- 1492352990

Acknowledgments

So many people encouraged me on the way to publishing this book, and they have my most sincere gratitude:

My Harvard-educated sister Kelly, who thinks I'm brilliant. She's Harvard educated. She knows these things. Thank you, Kelly, for constantly bolstering my confidence. And, you know, for being an awesome big sister.

Debbie Holt, critique partner and cheerleader. Everyone's opinion counts, but the opinion of a fabulous writer counts for a little extra. Your certainty that I am not a complete hack came at a time when I desperately needed encouragement.

Nancy Krebbs, my former writing-group buddy who is also a fabulous writer. You were the first person (besides me) to actually like this book, and I have not forgotten that.

Shirley Webb, editor extraordinaire. Writers need editors, most especially the self-published ones. Thank you for your enthusiasm, your expertise, and for telling people about my book.

And most importantly, my always patient, ever hopeful, ever encouraging husband Darryl. Without question, I would not be where I am without you. Thank you for helping make my dreams come true.

TO GET TWO FREE SHORT STORIES
SIGN UP TO MY NEWSLETTER!

I'm so excited to offer two free short stories available only to the lovely, lovely people who sign up for my newsletter.

The first takes place immediately after The Middle Finger of Fate, called Fight the Fat. The second is Get the Dale Outta Here, and it takes place between Unsightly Bulges (Book 2) and Caught in the Crotchfire (Book 3).

Just go to www.FreeBooksFromKim.com to sign up!

Please consider leaving a review for The Middle Finger of Fate on Amazon, iBooks, Kobo, Barnes and Noble and Good-Reads.com. Thanks!

Table of Contents

Chapter One

The thing about finding a dead body is, you don't expect it to look so *dead*. On television, when someone finds a dead body, the first thing they do is start feeling for a pulse. But when I found the dead woman at the bottom of the basement steps outside the First United Methodist Church, I knew without a doubt that she was deader than my split ends, and I couldn't even see her that well.

Knowing she was already dead didn't stop me from flapping around the courtyard and yelping like I needed to do something quick, when any idiot could see there was no need to hurry. I yelled these goofy, useless yelps, and hopped around long enough to see that the woman had one arm flung over her head, and her neck crooked in a very disturbing fashion. It occurred to me that she could possibly rise up from her basement resting place and look at me with her dead eyes. We were, after all, on holy ground.

Running anywhere suddenly became a stellar idea.

The closer I got to the heavy wooden doors of the church, the more certain I was that not only had the woman risen, but she was floating right behind me, *reaching out a bony finger to touch the back of my neck –*

I yanked open the door and spewed forth a string of words I promised I would never say again when I became a Christian. At high volume.

Don Chambers, the associate pastor, and Viv, my octogenarian Alcoholics Anonymous buddy, were passing down the hallway. They stopped and stared at me.

I gulped back the obscenities and focused on conveying what was most important.

"Dead body! Dead body outside! Dead!" I realized my feet were still running in place and I tried to get them to stop, but I had very little control over anything at that point. I did get one nailed down but the other stomped along by itself a couple of times. I jabbed a finger at the door. "Dead body outside."

"What?" Don and Viv said in unison.

"Dead body at the bottom of the stairs. Dead."

"Is it Merline Wallace?" Viv asked. "She looked gray last time I saw her."

Don moved past me toward the door. "Show me."

I shook my head. "Uh-uh. I'm not going back out there." My heart was beating so hard I saw spots. "You can't miss it. It's the only dead body at the bottom of the bell tower." I wrapped my arms around my waist and moved away from the door, in case there was a ghastly surprise waiting on the other side.

"Use the phone in my office to call the police," Don said before he opened the door.

"I want to go too." Viv shuffled out after Don.

My legs shook as I hurried down the hallway to Don's office. I grabbed the phone and slid into his chair.

"9-1-1, what's your emergency?"

"I'm at First Methodist Church. I need to report –"

Unfortunately, at that moment an image popped into my head of Don's face when I yanked open that door and screamed the F-word.

Now, something you should know about me: I giggle when I get nervous. And man, was I nervous. Plus, it *was* kind of funny. Not the dead body, of course, but Don's expression.

I felt the laughter bubbling up and I cleared my throat. "I found a de-he-he—"

I bit my lip to stifle the giggles.

"Ma'am? Are you there?"

I nodded, my teeth still clamped to my lower lip like I was holding back a tidal wave with a rubber band. It did no good to nod, but I knew the moment I opened my mouth I was going to really let loose. I gripped the edge of the desk so hard my nail beds turned white and I took a deep breath through my nose. There.

"I'm sorry," I said calmly. "I have found a dead – a dead...*body*." My throat closed and my voice shot up on the last word, and uncontrollable giggles overtook me.

"A dead body?" the operator asked, calm as you please. "Male or female?"

"Fe –" was all I could get out.

"And who is calling?"

I cupped my hand over the phone and fought back the giggles to catch my breath. "Salem Grimes." I stood and paced behind the desk, twisting the phone cord tight around my fingers. I bit my lip again and told myself to breathe in through my nose, out through my mouth. Or did I have that backwards? I tried it the other way and ended up snorting into the phone. "Sorry," I said again.

A fresh wave of giggles threatened to engulf me and I focused on the picture of Don's family on his desk. His blue-eyed wife and red-haired daughter, the teenage son with his foot propped on a stool behind them, one arm draped across his raised knee, his own brown hair just long enough to say that he might be a preacher's kid but he was still cool. And behind them Don stood with his arms around them all, looking like he had the best family in town.

I pictured him going home that night to tell them all about the dead body, and later whispering to his wife that Salem Grimes had been so upset she'd screamed the F-word so loud the trustees probably heard it in their meeting on the second floor.

I let out a hoot of laughter and slapped my hand hard over my mouth.

"Ma'am, are you there? I need you to stay on the line. Ma'am?"

I lifted the phone to answer but only got out a strangled noise, so I clapped my hand back over the mouthpiece and fell on my side, helpless and pathetic and just plain weird, giggling because I'd found a dead body. I'm telling you, I'm not all there sometimes.

"Police are on their way," the dispatcher said. "I need for you to stay on the line, ma'am. Are you in any danger? Salem? Is anyone there with you? I know it's scary, Salem, but I need you to stay with me."

I pounded the heel of my hand against my forehead but that didn't do anything but make my head hurt. I've learned that there really isn't much you can do when one of these laughing fits hit. It's like what everyone says about a stomach bug. You just have to let it run its course.

So I thought about Don and Viv outside, peering over the iron railing to the bottom of the basement stairs, looking at the woman below. I thought about her, wondered if she had any family.

That did the trick. Nothing funny there. I wiped my eyes and caught my breath. The operator asked me a few more questions that I managed to answer. I heard sirens outside and told her the police had arrived.

I figured as the Finder Of The Body, the police would want to talk to me, so once I'd caught my breath I went back outside. I told myself I had no reason to be nervous about talking to them. I hadn't done anything wrong – this time.

Still, it's natural instinct for me to run the other way when I see a cop uniform.

As soon as I rounded the corner, I wished I had run the other way. Of all the people I'd prefer never to see again, Bobby Sloan was at the top of the list. And there he stood, in jeans and a powder blue button-down shirt, next to a patrol officer.

Bobby was one of the reasons I had a fear of the police. Well, that's not entirely fair. The reason I had a fear of the police is because I had a history of screwing up, and the police had a history of catching me. It wasn't their fault they were better in their role than I was in mine.

I would rather have seen just about any cop in the world than Bobby, though. We had a history, too, starting with the crush I had had on him from the fifth grade through the eighth grade. Little girls really should be taught not to write notes of undying love and devotion. They always come back to haunt.

The love notes and unreturned adoration would have been reason enough for me to want to duck and hide when I saw him, but unfortunately for me, mine and Bobby's story didn't end there. Two years ago, Bobby had been serving arrest warrants and came to my house to pick me up for passing hot checks. I had been drunk and had decided to hide under the bed. It might have worked if I hadn't had a waterbed. Not one of my brighter moments, but fortunately, not one of my dumbest, either.

So there I had been with Bobby's hand around my ankle, pulling on me and laughing at me wedged up in the four-inch-wide space I was trying to hide under and hanging on for all I was worth. He tugged hard right about the same time I decided to give it up and let go.

He fell back, which would have been kind of funny, except he fell back into a big pile of dog poop from my roommate's Rottweiler, and so it was really only funny to Bobby's fellow officers. While one of them was outside hosing Bobby down and I was being led in handcuffs to the squad car, I tried to explain to him that it wasn't my dog and that that dog and his nasty habits were one of the reasons I was looking for another place to live. But the look he gave me told me he didn't really care. In fact, the look he gave me told me he hoped he would never see me again. That hurt, considering I'd pledged my undying love to him practically every day for three solid years.

Now, I just hoped he wouldn't recognize me. After all, it had been two years, and since I'd quit drinking, I'd replaced Jack Daniels with super-size french fries and gained about thirty pounds. Or forty. Or so. I used to wear my hair long and bleached blonde, but after my last arrest I let the brown grow out and stuck with an easy-to-maintain chin length bob. On a good day, I told myself I could resemble Katie Holmes' fat cousin.

Bobby took one look at me and said, "Oh no."

So much for that hope.

"What are you doing here?" he asked.

"I didn't do anything, Bobby. All I was doing was walking up the sidewalk, I swear."

"Walking up the sidewalk to a church." He crossed his arms over his chest.

"I can go to church."

"I know you *can*." He looked back over the railing. "Seriously, Salem, what were you doing here?"

"I was going inside. You'd think I was going inside a bar." Which I was actually not allowed to do. A condition of my probation.

"I would be less surprised."

I scowled at him. This was one of those times when it was better just to keep my mouth shut.

"Did you see anyone?"

I shook my head.

"Do you know her?" He didn't take his eyes off me as he motioned with his head toward the stairs.

Again I shook my head. "Why aren't you wearing a uniform?" Let him be the defensive one for a change.

"Because I'm a detective now. Stay put." He walked over to a uniformed officer and they talked for a minute.

The uniformed cop came over. He had that same passive, no-need-to-worry-I'm-in-complete-control face that every cop has. "I'm going to need for you to go back to the station with me."

I took a step backward. "Me? Why?"

"We need to get a statement."

"I gave my statement to the operator. I found a dead body. End of statement."

"We need for it to be written down."

"Fine." No need to panic. I hadn't done anything wrong. But I'd made a promise to myself that I was never going to see the inside of a jail again. "I'll be happy to give you a statement right here. I'm sure Don won't mind loaning me some paper."

He put a hand on his hip and looked back at Bobby. Bobby narrowed his eyes and lifted his chin and I knew that whatever passed between them wasn't in my favor.

The uniform turned back to me. "Ma'am, I'm going to need you to come to the station with me."

I looked at my watch, then read his nametag. "Officer Walters, I have to be at work in half an hour."

"You can call your boss from the station. I'm sure they'll understand."

I was beating a dead horse but couldn't keep from asking, "Do I really have to?"

Walters nodded. "Are you going to come willingly?"

I bit my lip and looked at Bobby.

"Go, Salem. It's just a few questions. I'll be there in a little while."

I made a face at Walters. "Fine."

"Thank you." He touched the small of my back and steered me toward his car. "This way, please."

Two more patrol cars drove up as we pulled away, followed by the Channel Eleven news van. I sat in the back of the squad car and tried to wrap my arms all the way around my body.

"So this is what these things look like when you're sober," I said.

Walters caught my eye in the rearview mirror but didn't say anything.

I have to say that, all in all, being taken in for questioning is a lot better than being taken in for driving under the influence. I didn't have to go through the whole fingerprint, smile-for-the-camera, now-blow-into-this-hose routine. I figured I would be taken to one of those little rooms with a table and four chairs and a big one-way mirror like you see on cop shows. Instead, the cop took me to Bobby's office.

"Detective Sloan should just be a few minutes. Have a seat."

I sat on the edge of the rolling chair across from Bobby's desk. "Are we going to wait for him?"

Walters nodded.

"Is that necessary? I mean, isn't there someone else who can take the statement?" Sitting across the desk from Bobby and facing probing questions wasn't high on my list of wishes at the moment.

He raised his eyebrows. "You have a problem with Detective Sloan?"

I chewed my lip and didn't answer. Yes, I had a problem, but not one I wanted to discuss.

"You'll probably want to call your boss now." The officer slid the phone across the desk.

I looked at the phone and frowned. This was all so wrong. Now I had to call Flo at Flo's Bow Wow Barbers and tell her I was going to be late because I was in jail. And no matter how much I assured her I'd done nothing wrong, I was just a witness, she would automatically think I'd been busted. That's what *I* would believe.

I raised my chin. "You do it."

Walters raised his eyebrows again. "I'm sorry?"

"You do it." I pushed the phone back toward him. "Call for me, let them know I'm going to be late because I witnessed a possible crime and you need to ask me some questions."

He looked like he was thinking about it. "You really should

handle it yourself."

"If I call, she's going to think I've been arrested and I'm making up some line to cover it up."

"Why would she think that?"

I shrugged. Why indeed.

He frowned at me for a couple of seconds, then picked up the handset. "What's the number?"

I gave him the number to the Bow Wow Barbers and he punched it in. "Who do I ask for?"

"Flo."

He handled it perfectly. Confident, courteous, in command, and yet not overbearing. I wish I could go to the police academy just to learn how they do that.

He hung up and said, "No problem."

"Maybe next time I have a head cold you could call in sick for me. Last time she wasn't terribly sympathetic."

He almost smiled. Then he bent his head over a piece of paper and got to work.

About three lifetimes later Bobby arrived. He walked through the door and Walters jumped up. They stepped out into the hallway and mumble-mumble-mumbled to each other for a few minutes. I looked around the room for an escape. If I could somehow manage to make myself half an inch wide I could squeeze through the air conditioner vent, but that seemed unlikely since I couldn't even squeeze myself into a size fourteen anymore.

Bobby came in and sat down with an old man groan, which was a little weird because he was anything but an old man. He pushed some papers around for a few seconds as if this was just a normal day at the office and he had nothing pressing to get to. He laid his arms on the desk, clasped his hands together, and looked at me.

"Okay Salem. Tell me why you were at that church."

"I had a meeting there this morning."

"A meeting with whom?"

I lifted my chin. "My AA group."

"Your AA group."

It's always a little awkward, telling people you're an alcoholic. By the time you get to Alcoholics Anonymous you're much more versed in telling people how you're not an alcoholic. Then you say you're going to AA and they get that uncomfortable, oh-that's-great-but-now-I-have-to-look-away thing. So when I tell people I'm in AA, I automatically lift my chin and start thinking of what I'm going to say to fill the awkward pause after The Revelation.

But Bobby didn't look away. He just kept staring at me with that same unreadable look. "What time did you get there?"

So that was that. Cat officially out of bag and we're moving onward. "It was just before ten." I couldn't be entirely sure because the clock in my old car was busted.

"Just before ten."

I nodded.

Bobby asked a lot of questions about who I'd seen, what other cars were around, did I talk to anyone, did I know the girl. I didn't have a lot of information to give him because pretty much the extent of my involvement was a lot of jumping up and down and yelping.

I answered him as best I could, but I have to admit there was a part of me that was inappropriately studying him. You know how you idolize someone and then you see them years later and realize they weren't anything special, just a regular person with normal faults? That was *so* not what I was feeling. In fact, Bobby seemed every bit as larger-than-life to me as he ever had. He still had that air of the supercool dude, confident, in charge, able to save old ladies and run down bad guys without ruffling his just-a-trifle-too-long hair.

Bobby studied some papers on his desk and made a few notes. It took everything I had not to ask what he was writing down.

Shouldn't he have gotten gray hair and fat by now? I added the years up in my head. I was twenty-eight, so that would make him...thirty-five. I guess he wasn't that much older than me after all. It had seemed like a lot when the seven years between us was fourth grade to twelfth grade.

Bobby didn't look older, though, just better. Those lines that bracketed his mouth were deeper, his neck was bigger around so his Adam's apple no longer stuck out like someone had thrown a boomerang through the back of his neck. He was bigger every-where, more solid and more there, somehow.

I was bigger, too, unfortunately. I felt like Jabba the Hut spill-ing out of the chair and onto the floor.

"So you walked up the sidewalk and what happened?"

"I looked down and saw the body –"

"Why did you look down?"

His sudden question made me jump a little. "I – I don't know. Don't people just look down sometimes?"

"If there's a reason to."

Oh God. Was he saying I was a suspect? My heart began to race again and I felt my fingers clench together like they do when I really *really* want a drink.

"Did you hear something that made you look down?"

"No." I didn't think so.

"See something? Some kind of movement out of the corner of your eye?"

Did I? His intensity was making me nervous. I shook my head. "I don't remember seeing anything. I just walked by and I looked down because I always look down there when I walk by."

"Why?"

"Why? Geez, Bobby, you're making me crazy! Is there some law against looking down?"

He shook his head.

"Then stop it. I always look down at the bottom of those stairs because I've always wondered where the door at the bottom of the stairs goes to, that's all."

"Then why didn't you just say so?"

"Because I found a dead body and now I'm at the police station and I'm completely freaked out and not thinking straight!" I took a deep breath and thought maybe I ought to lower my voice since I was on the verge of shrieking. I was almost out of my chair, too, so I scooted my Jabba self back.

"Calm down. Go on," Bobby said.

But I was afraid to now. "That's it. That's all I have to say."

Bobby tapped a pen on his desk and looked at me.

I tried to cross my legs but with my big thighs that's kind of hard. I settled for crossing my ankles and raised my eyebrows at Bobby as if I could sit there and have a staring contest with him all day if he wanted to.

"So you're in AA."

"Yep."

He stood. I shot out of my chair and grabbed my purse. "We're done then? Great. I have to get to work."

He stopped at the door and stepped aside so I could pass. "So how are you doing?" he asked, his voice a little softer.

He wasn't asking about my health and well-being, I knew that much. "A hundred and forty-seven days," I said. "This time."

He nodded. "That's good, Salem. That's really good." He squeezed my arm.

I am so pathetic. For me, an arm squeeze and a solemn "that's good" from Bobby Sloan is like what getting a combination Grammy/Oscar/Nobel Prize For Saving The World From Total Destruction would be for anyone else. I felt myself actually grow two inches taller the moment he said that. I mean, can anyone be so needy for praise?

But I have to admit; getting Bobby's approval was worth finding a dead body.

He asked for my phone number, and for a crazy moment I thought he was asking me out, now that he knew I wouldn't get drunk and scream at the waitress. Then I realized it was probably just so he could call me about the dead woman. How shallow am I? There's a family somewhere about to be devastated with tragic news and I'm wondering what I should wear on my date with Bobby. I felt really bad then.

Walters drove me back to my car, and since he'd already told Flo I would be late I figured I had enough time to drive through Wendy's for lunch. I was supposed to be on a diet, but after the trauma of discovering a dead body and having Bobby see all my fat, I decided I deserved a Big Classic with cheese and french fries.

I ate in my car – as I do a lot – and thought about the poor woman at the bottom of the stairs. When I left the church nobody knew who she was, or even if it had been an accident. That bell tower was tall, forty or fifty feet. If someone fell out of it, all the way to one story below ground level, onto concrete stairs, that would probably be enough to do the job. But somehow I didn't think it had been an accident. Not from the questions Bobby had asked me.

Who was she? Did she know she was in danger? Did she know today might be the day? Or was she just going along, thinking about what she had to do, matching up the days till payday against the days until the electricity was cut off the way I always was?

Nothing like contemplating sudden death to put you in touch with God. God's the only thing that makes the whole gruesome dying thing a little better. I know some people who even say they actually look forward to it because they're so excited about being with God. Myself, I'm a relatively new Christian and nowhere near that point yet. I'd still rather pretend I'm going to live forever. In theory, the idea of eternity in heaven singing God's praises sounds really good, but when I realize I have to go through the death part to get there, I'm not quite so enamored with the idea.

I was sitting at a red light about to put a french fry dipped in ketchup in my mouth when I was struck by a sudden gruesome image: dead fingers covered with blood. I stared at the fry until the car behind me honked and I realized the light had turned. I felt my stomach turn, not just because of the bloody-finger image but the whole scenario that morning, and dropped the fries back in the bag. I looked down at the burger with one bite gone and thought I was going to hurl right there. It was all I could do to wait till I got to Bow Wow Barbers and not toss it out on the street.

I gulped down bile as I tossed the food and thought that if I found a dead body every day, maybe I could finally stick to a diet.

Frank and Stump were waiting for me on the front deck when I rattled up. Frank is my neighbor and he babysits Stump for me when I can't take her to work. Yes, I know. I could leave her at home like any normal person would. But Stump has separation issues that cause her to howl and screech bloody murder and then destroy something of mine if I leave her alone. I have to pay Frank in free dinners when he keeps her, but that's okay. It's better than wondering all day what she's going to destroy.

Stump wiggled her short black body and barked hard enough to raise herself onto her back feet when I got out of the car.

"You're not going to believe what happened today," I said as I walked up. Stump flipped over onto her back so I could scratch her fat belly.

Frank is a very skinny Hispanic guy with shaggy hair and a mustache like Sonny Bono's in those old variety shows with Cher. "You killed somebody," he said.

I froze. "How did you know?"

"It was on the news. How come you're not in jail?" He didn't seem particularly worried that he was in the company of a murderer, just curious that I was on the loose.

"They said on the news that I killed somebody?"

"Yeah." He nodded. "I think so."

Frank had lived in Texas all his life and, although he spoke English, his family spoke Spanish at home. English was his second language. Sometimes he got a little crossways in his phrasing. I hoped this was one of those times.

"Someone said on the news that I'd killed someone? Or that I'd found a dead body? Because that's what actually happened. I didn't touch anyone. I swear."

"Maybe that was it, I can't really remember. Hey, Stump ate a bug today."

"Stump." I scratched her belly with both hands, which she loved. She wiggled against the deck and groaned. "You have to stop eating bugs. You're going to get one that doesn't agree with you." I looked at Frank. "What channel was the story on?"

"Eleven. Patrice Watson."

I don't watch the news much, so I didn't know who that was. I checked the clock and decided I'd better watch this, though, just to make sure Frank was mistaken.

I took a quick shower to get the Airedale slobber off me and started dinner while Frank made himself comfortable in my cracked Naugahyde recliner. He turned on one of those crime scene detective shows and I almost burned dinner because I was comparing myself to the woman on the show who was the witness to the crime. Everyone was really sympathetic to her. No one accused her of killing anybody.

After dinner I folded laundry and caught myself looking repeatedly out the window. I realized I was waiting for someone to come take me to jail. I filled Frank in on all the details and he looked sufficiently spooked.

"That's weird, man." He shook his head and his hair flopped. "I wonder what happened to her."

"I've been wondering the same thing all day." I shuddered. I'd been going to that church for less than a year, but it was weird thinking there might be a killer lurking around there.

The detective show went off and the news teaser came on.

"A grisly discovery was made today at a downtown Lubbock church."

"That's it!" Frank cried.

"Ssshh!" I ran over and turned up the volume. I expected to

see the church or maybe the police spokesman.

Instead my picture flashed on the screen. "A woman was found dead today by *this* woman..."

I didn't hear anything after that. It wasn't just any picture. It was my arrest photo from a year and a half ago. I stared at the picture and for the second time that day and said a word I'd promised I would never say again.

Chapter Two

"See, I told you," Frank said. "She said you killed someone."

A commercial came on and I dragged my attention away from the television. "She didn't say that. Did she?" Amidst the roar going on in my head I couldn't be sure. All I knew was the lowest moment of my life had been captured and splashed across the television in a completely inappropriate way. Somehow being accused of murder was no longer at the top of my list of outrages.

Why would they show an arrest photo from a year and a half ago? What did my last DUI have to do with the dead woman at the church?

I dropped back into the chair, numb and for some reason scared out of my mind. Everyone has heard stories of people being convicted of crimes they didn't commit. I'd only ever been convicted of things I was actually guilty of.

The phone rang. It was my G-Ma.

"You're on television. You told me you quit drinking."

"I did."

"Well, the T.V. station says you're in some kind of trouble. What did you do?"

Normally I don't get alarmed by anything G-Ma says because she tends to ignore minor details like facts and relies solely on impression, and that is always far to the left of reality. I was already freaking out and feeling guilty, even though I knew darned good and well I hadn't done anything wrong.

"What channel are you watching?"

"The one with the man who looks like Lee Harvey Oswald."

"That's Eleven, the same one I'm watching. Will you do me a favor and flip over to Seven and record it for me?" Maybe it was just a Channel Eleven thing. If Seven had my mug shot too, I was going to grab Stump and flee the country.

Thank goodness I'd finally taught G-Ma to work the DVR. That had only taken two years. "I'll call you back in a few minutes, I want to see what they say on Channel Eleven."

"Wait till after sports. They're going to interview the Cowboy's new running back."

So on G-Ma's list of priorities I was directly under the Dallas Cowboys. That wasn't so bad considering her fervent devotion to the Cowboys. Lucky for me it was the preseason.

The news came back on and I hung up. I had to sit through some junk about the city council meeting before they got to me. Or her, I mean.

"A gruesome discovery was made this morning outside the basement of the First United Methodist Church. The body of 22-year-old Lucinda Cruz was found at the bottom of the basement stairs by *this* woman –" There she went again with the "*this* woman" thing, and my arrest photo flashed back on the screen.

I tried to focus on what was being said, but pretty much all I could see was *this* woman. I looked...well, I looked like I'd just been arrested for driving under the influence. I looked strung-out and skanky, pale and washed out with an inch and a half of mascara under my eyes. I had been at the end of my ill-advised blonde phase, at the point when I'd quit bothering with petty details like dark roots and conditioner.

The picture stayed behind the anchor for a few more seconds, then switched to one of a beautiful Hispanic girl with long black hair and lips that a model would pay good money for. She had chocolate brown eyes and smooth skin like I haven't had since I was about five. Her mouth was open in a full laugh. She was breathtaking.

The picture switched to a bald man with a mustache, the police department spokesman.

"We're obviously very early into the investigation, but we are treating this as a homicide."

I listened really hard and didn't hear him say anything that sounded like "Salem Grimes – *this* woman! – is our prime suspect at this time."

Then the anchor went on to something about a car wreck on one of the farm-to-market roads. Something about the anchor's voice was familiar, but I was too wrapped up in feeling humiliated and terrified to play where-do-I-know-her.

"Did you catch that name? Lucinda something."

"Cruz." Frank said it with the rolling "r." Crrrrruz. I can't do that.

"Why was my picture up there?"

Frank grunted. "Because you were *this* woman who found the body."

"But they don't usually do that, do they? I don't remember ever seeing the picture of anyone else who found a dead body." I stood up and paced. In my narrow trailer house that's a three-step procedure. The fact of the matter was, I couldn't call to mind a single example of anyone else finding a dead body, but I'm sure it had happened lots of times. I didn't remember the finder's picture being shown, ever. Not once. "It makes me look like I'm the one who killed her, not the one who found her."

"See, that's what I'm saying," Frank said.

"That's not right. They shouldn't have done that. Should they?" Maybe they were just trying to give me credit or something, l

ike a screwed-up attempt at making me a hero. But I didn't think so. I switched over to Channel Seven. What were the odds G-Ma would really be able to record it anyway?

Channel Seven had a better scoop: my 9-1-1 tape.

I watched my own words scroll across the bottom of the screen. That was weird. "I need to report," I said a couple of times. Then I garbled a bunch and the screen said, "unintelligible," so I looked like a complete idiot. We finally got to me blurting that I'd found a dead body.

The anchors on Channel Seven shook their heads in sympathy. The female anchor even tssked and murmured, "Bless her heart."

"Yes," said the male anchor solemnly. "Obviously, very upsetting."

"Right on," I said to the TV. "Very upsetting." They thought I was hysterical from crying, but that was okay. I mean, different people react differently to stress, right? So I giggle. Didn't mean I didn't deserve a "bless her heart."

They ran the same clip of the department spokesman saying it was being investigated as a homicide, then they added some new information. Lucinda Cruz was one of the custodians at the church.

I mulled that news and flipped back to Channel Eleven, but of course they were on to other matters by then.

"I ought to sue them or something."

"For what?"

"I don't know." I sunk down in my chair. As far as I could tell, they hadn't said anything that was an outright lie. I probably shouldn't try to claim defamation of character, because I'd handled defaming my own character with impressive skill and expertise. Surely it wasn't a good thing for them to show an arrest photo unless it was actually connected to the story.

"Call Patrice Watson and ask her why she did it. Ask her to go out with me while you're at it. I like chubby chicks."

I studied the anchor. When I was waiting tables I worked with a lot of college girls; probably I'd worked with her years before but –

"Hey!" I jumped up and turned up the volume. "What did you say her name was?"

"Patrice Watson. I think she's French," Frank said, although clearly the girl had as thick a Texas accent as I did.

"No, she's not. She's Trisha Thompson, from Idalou!"

I couldn't believe I hadn't recognized her, but in my defense she did look way different. She'd gained a lot of weight, too, as much as I had, if not more. She was blonde now, a really pretty, natural-looking dark blonde. She had on nice clothes, of course, the kind of clothes she'd always looked at in the magazines when we were in school. We'd look at those dresses that were supposed to "take you from the office to the party with a few simple accessories." Trisha focused on the office part while all I cared about was the party look.

We'd grown up together, spent pretty much every waking moment together all through elementary, junior high and the first
couple of years of high school. Then I started partying all the
time, and she decided she was too good for me. She *was*, but still...

And she pasted my arrest photo all over the news.

"No," Frank was saying. "Her name is Patrice Watson. See?"
He pointed at the screen where the male anchor – who really did
bear a slight resemblance to Lee Harvey Oswald, I think it was
the chin – was saying, "Thanks Patrice. In other news..."

I wanted to curl up in a ball in my chair but I was too fat, so I
just sprawled there and tried to figure out what was going on. It
was like one of those times when I used to wake up in a strange
place with people I didn't know. People telling me I'd done and
said things that made no sense, and I couldn't argue with them
because it was most likely true.

I lugged Stump into my lap and scratched her ears and belly
while I tried to think. It had been ten years since we graduated
high school, but I was fairly sure I'd seen Trisha more recently
than that – within the last five or six years, anyway. But try as I
might, I couldn't come up with anything concrete, just a vague
uneasy feeling that we'd had some kind of run-in.

There was no telling what it was about. I did a lot of stuff when
I was drinking that made people mad. I have kind of a smart
mouth even when I'm dead sober, and when I'm drunk I mix in a
warped sense of humor and turn the impulse control all the way
down. It's a deadly combination.

I was still trying to remember what I'd done to make Trisha
mad when the phone rang.

"I recorded it, I think," G-Ma said. "Were you laughing?"

"Of course not. I was crying hysterically. Why would I laugh about finding a dead body?"

"You know how you get."

The phone beeped (thank you, God) and I said, "I have another call. Hang on and I'll be right back."

She wouldn't hang on. G-Ma doesn't believe it's actually possible to put one person on hold and talk to another one, no matter what nonsense the phone company was trying to peddle.

It was Les. Les is...well, it's hard to explain. He's kind of an unofficial, self-appointed mentor. He's the one who found me in jail the morning after that infamous DUI picture was taken and introduced me to Christianity. That was his calling, he told me, to find the down and out and give them hope through Jesus Christ. Since I was fresh out of hope and seriously contemplating jumping off a bridge, I latched on to him with all I was worth.

I think there's some ancient Eastern proverb about if you save someone's life, that life becomes your responsibility. Les is a solid Bible belt Christian, as far from East as West can get, but he's bought into that philosophy from somewhere, and am I grateful for that. God knew I needed someone to look after me long after that morning in jail.

"Watching the news, Salem," Les said. "What's going on?"

"Oh, nothing. I just found a dead body."

"So nothing unusual."

"Same old same old."

"Talk to me."

So I talked. I probably sounded a little self-involved, but I'd gotten wrapped up in my own public humiliation and outrage and forgotten again about the poor dead woman at the bottom of the stairs. Talking to Les made me remember that there *were* actually bigger problems on the table than wondering why Trisha would take a picture of me looking like a hag and shoot it out to a few hundred thousand people.

"Want to explain why they had an arrest picture up of you?"

Ugh. So now we were back to my problem. That was quick. "I'd love to, and as soon as I find out why that was shown, I'll let you know." I chewed my thumbnail. "I have a nagging feeling, though, that the anchor who ran that story might have a personal grudge against me, and this is how she's dealing with it."

"Why would she have a personal grudge against you?"

"I don't remember exactly. I think I might have gotten into an argument with her while I was drinking."

"I see." He did see. He'd told me stories of bar fights he'd gotten into, and the family members who still refused to talk to him because of what he'd said or done while he was drinking.

A picture flashed in my mind of Trisha, face screwed up with rage, screaming at me. She shoved me and I fell, but that's all I could remember.

"Yep," I said with a sigh. "She hates me and she used that picture to get back at me for whatever I did."

Les was silent for a moment. I hated those silences.

"Sounds like a Step 9 day to me."

Step 9 of the famous AA Twelve Steps, Make Direct Amends to People We Have Wronged. Possibly the most awkward of all the steps. "Undoubtedly. I just don't know exactly what I'm making amends for."

"One quick way to find out is to ask."

One quick and painful way, yes. "You know, what she's upset about has nothing to do with the dead body." Maybe if I steered the topic back to the dead woman I could avoid dealing with my own ugly past.

No such luck with Les, though. "I'm sure it doesn't. But think of it this way. This has given you the chance to right a wrong and heal an old wound – a golden opportunity."

"Yay."

"You could ignore it and hope it goes away."

"That's worked so well for me in the past." I groaned and slumped in my seat. "I think I'll start tomorrow."

"Good idea. Keep me posted. Are you okay?" Meaning *do you want a drink*?

I did. I'd made it a hundred and forty-seven days. Some of those days had been good and some had made me want to rip my own hair out. But I hadn't had to go through a day when I found a dead body, faced an old crush, and then was humiliated on television. So this was a new test. I had a foreboding feeling I wasn't handling it very well.

"I'm okay," I said.

"Is your house clean?" Meaning no alcohol.

"Of course."

"Is someone there with you?"

"Frank. And Stump."

"Do you want me to come over?"

"No, that's okay. I'll be fine." I decided that more than a drink, what I really wanted was to go to bed and sleep for a couple of weeks. If I kept telling myself that, it might become true.

"Call me, Salem, if you need me. I mean it. No matter what time it is."

He *did* mean it, and I said one of a couple thousand thank-you prayers to God for sending Les into my life.

"Thanks. But I think I'll be fine."

"Okay girl. Get through tonight. Tomorrow you can deal with

whatever you need to deal with."

I hung up and considered that happy prospect. My memory might be fuzzy, but I knew there was something with Trisha that had to be resolved, and it undoubtedly involved me apologizing for something stupid I'd done or said. I'd learned in AA that a big part of moving forward with life was cleaning up and putting things right with the past. Things have a tendency to cling to you till you clean them up. Especially things that stink. And this had all the markings of something rank.

But that didn't make the prospect of facing Trisha – Patrice, sheesh! – any more enticing. Standing in front of her so she could tell me what I'd done or said – or stolen, good Lord help me – to make her want to get revenge.

Frank went home and Stump and I went to bed. She curled up on the pillow beside me and shoved her big wide nose down in the space between the covers. She always slept like that. Maybe the near asphyxiation helped her sleep better, I didn't know. I measured one time and learned that the width of Stump's nose and the length of her legs was exactly the same. She was truly one of a kind. I told her every day that God made her special. No other dog I knew had such strong self-esteem.

I scratched her ears and told her goodnight. "Tomorrow is our early day," I reminded her. We opened the shop for Flo on Tuesday mornings. I hated getting up so early but I was flattered that Flo actually trusted me with a key, so I made sure I didn't screw up and oversleep or anything.

Stump's not really a morning person either, so we reward ourselves on Tuesday mornings with breakfast burritos and extra-large coffees from PakASak.

I closed my eyes and said a prayer. "Lord, thank you for...well, okay, thank you for this day. It's been a crazy one, as you may have noticed. But Les says to be grateful in all things, so I thank you for this day, weird as it was. Lord, please be with that woman's family, Lucinda Cruz." I remembered the picture of that beautiful young girl. "They're going to need comfort, God. Please be with them." I chewed my lip. "And I could really use some help, too. I know this isn't about me but I'm still finding it a little hard to deal with." I'd asked for so much help over the past year that I was in danger of wearing out my welcome. But Les insisted that God wants us to ask, and I really did need the help. "Keep me from screwing up. And please be with me tomorrow when I –" *groan groan groan* – "call Trisha. Amen."

That night I dreamed I was back in jail and this time I wasn't getting out. The judge came by and watched me through the bars, his arms over his chest and his face grim. After he stared at me for a minute, I realized it was Charles Pointer, the man that G-Ma said was my real father.

He didn't say anything, but he didn't need to put into words that I was a big disappointment to him. I wanted to hide, but of course there was no place to. So I just hung my head and wished I could die.

I woke up feeling awful, and had to remind myself that I really wasn't to blame for the beautiful Lucinda Cruz's death. Such a great way to start the day!

That's not a good frame of mind to be in when you have to face the mirror in the morning. I studied my reflection. Ugh. The weight I'd gained didn't exactly add to my overall appearance. I did still have my dimples going for me, and even with the weight gain, my skin and hair looked much better sober than they had drunk. The brown of my hair was a shiny brown, and my brown eyes didn't have those nasty bags under them anymore. But still...could I lose a quick 30 or 40 pounds before the afternoon?

Trisha had gained weight too, I reminded myself. That made me feel only marginally better, since Trisha also had what looked like a pretty expensive haircut and tint, plus a fancy newsroom wardrobe. I sported a perfectly respectable, but not exactly impressive, combination of ProCuts and Walmart.

I brushed my teeth and hair and tiptoed past Stump – snoring into my pillow – on the way to the tiny second bedroom at the other end of my trailer. I'd made a kind of little chapel for myself there. My Bibles were in there – both the King James Version Les gave me and the New Living Translation I actually understood – my devotionals, and some big fluffy pillows I'd thrown on the floor. I had a small end table with a candle tower thing I'd bought at Garden Ridge, and during the past year I'd developed my own ritual where I read my daily devotional and Bible passage, then lit the candle while I meditated and prayed about how the devotional applied to what was going on in my life.

I had to admit lots of times I'm clueless as to that part of it – how the devotional pertains to my life – except in the vaguest sense. But Les says God speaks to us through His word and I'm determined to hear something. If I was going to do this Christianity thing, I wanted to do it as deep as I could.

I took my devotional out and turned to today's date.

Matthew 5:23-24. "So if you're standing before the altar in the Temple, offering a sacrifice to God, and you suddenly remember that someone has something against you, leave your sacrifice there beside the altar. Go and be reconciled to that person. Then come and offer your sacrifice to God. Come to terms quickly with your enemy before it is too late and you are dragged into court, handed over to an officer, and thrown in jail. I assure you that you won't be free again until you have paid the last penny."

Yikes! So maybe God really *was* talking to me through his word. Dragged into court and handed over to an officer and thrown in jail? Come on!

Except I'd already decided to come to terms with Trisha. I couldn't help but think this might be a little overkill.

I flicked the long fireplace starter lighter and lit the twelve candles, taking deep breaths. That might seem a little...cosmic, lighting candles and centering my thoughts on God. But it works for me and I always feel myself become calm and focused as the candles take flame.

When they were all lit I sat back on my heels and bowed my head.

I prayed for Lucinda Cruz first, her family and friends. I didn't even know if she *had* family and friends, but I found it highly un-likely anyone that beautiful went through life alone. I hate to start my prayers with requests, but since it wasn't for me I guessed it was okay. I usually start out with thanks, though. I don't want to seem ungrateful. "Thank you for another day. Thank you for the roof over my head, a job to go to, a car to get me there." Saying that reminded me of something. "But it did get hot yesterday – the gauge went almost into the red. As you might remember I just put water in on Thursday. I don't know what the problem is but if it costs over twenty bucks to fix, I'm going to need a little help here. I've got two, maybe two-fifty in my checking account, and rent is five hundred. My check will probably be around three-fifty. So that leaves, say..."

I wrinkled my nose and tried to remember how much the light bill was. Plus I was almost out of groceries, and gas had gone up a dime a gallon over the last week, plus Flo's son was in Boy Scouts and they were selling those big tubs of popcorn and I promised him I'd buy one of the Butter Toffee Nut ones, and they were a ridiculous nineteen dollars and fifty cents. When did he say he had to turn the order in? Did I have another week?

I suddenly remembered where I was and what I was supposed to be doing. I grimaced and pictured God sitting there in his long robes, white beard down to his lap, tapping one foot and checking his watch.

"I'm sorry. I got a little sidetracked. Suffice it to say that, although at first glance it might *look* like I make decent money, things have gone up considerably since you were here. So if you could see fit to throw a blessing on either my car or my checking account, I'd really appreciate it."

I felt like an idiot, like a grownup kid asking her parents for money. My money problems were in large part due to the fines I had to pay every month, and that was nobody's fault but mine. Les assured me that if I needed something I should ask God, even if it *was* a self-induced need. Besides, where else was it going to come from?

I took another deep breath. "Okay, God. I really appreciate your reminder this morning. I already decided to go see Trisha this afternoon after work, but I suppose it can't hurt to have a little confirmation in that direction, you know? So...you might as well know I'm going to need your help there, too. I'm not exactly looking forward to this. It's going to be awkward." I thought again about the rage on Trisha's face when she'd knocked me down. The look on her face chilled my blood. Horror, hurt, betrayal. I felt sick, wondering what I'd done. "Whatever she's mad at me about, it's bad. I don't remember what it is but I know it's really bad."

I bit my lip and fought back sudden tears. I'd cried so much over the past year and a half, it was pathetic. I really did not want to get started again. But the truth was, I was afraid. And I hate being afraid.

"God, I don't want to go. I'm scared and I don't want to go."

There. I'd admitted it. And saying it out loud helped me see that although I didn't want to go, I had to.

"I don't want to see her, God. I don't *want* to know what I did to hurt her so much, and I don't want to feel guilty anymore, I don't want to think about what I've done. And I don't want her to see me so fat. So please be with me." I was really crying now, wiping furiously at tears as they raced down my cheeks. Geez, it wasn't even six o'clock in the morning yet and already I was exhausted. "Please...just, pour out some Holy Spirit or something on me and on Trisha and help us find some peace or agreement or something. Please give me a humble heart to approach her" – because whenever I thought about her using that picture I really wanted to slap her first and ask questions later – "and give her an open heart to receive me. And courage. Courage would be good right now."

I sat back and waited for that courage to sweep over me. But in the back of my mind, the clock ticked closer to opening time at Bow Wow Barbers, plus I had to stop and get a quart of oil and breakfast burritos for Stump and me. Maybe the courage would come later, when it got closer to time to see Trisha.

I started to stand then stopped. "In Jesus' name I pray. Amen." Sometimes I forget that part.

I got ready and dragged Stump – playing possum – out of bed and carted her out to my car. It started (thank you God) and we drove to PakASak. Stump woke up when we drove under the fluorescent lights at the gas pumps. She can smell a breakfast burrito at a hundred yards.

My friend Virginia worked overnight at the convenience store and she knew I'd be in on Tuesday mornings. She always had our food ready and she usually threw in an extra piece of bacon for Stump. I started to tell her I was feeling fat and maybe I ought to just skip breakfast altogether. But that burrito looked pretty good.

"Morning, Doll," Virginia rasped. I've known Virginia a long time. She used to work at this hotel bar where I hung out for a while. I even worked at the bar for a while, but I got fired, probably because I thought it was a place to hang out rather than a place to actually work. Virginia had tall blonde hair, long skinny legs, and a big round belly. Kind of like Humpty Dumpty's bar-hopping, chain-smoking aunt.

She played guitar and sang in the bar's house band. I used to crack up over her songs, except I really couldn't because she didn't intend for them to be funny. She took her craft very seriously.

She looked tired this morning. "Almost quitting time?" I asked

"Yes, thank the good Lord," she said. She's the type who actually means it when she says things like that. "I've been up for almost twenty-four hours straight. It's time for me to go home and look at the inside of my eyelids for a while." She slid a couple little tubs of salsa across the counter to me. "So what's this about you killing someone?"

"Ugh! I didn't kill anyone."

"I didn't figure you did, since you're going to work, but some people were saying last night that you were at the police station and you'd been arrested for killing someone."

"I wasn't arrested. I was taken in for questioning."

Virginia raised a penciled-on eyebrow.

"Because I'm the one who found the dead body."

"Bless your heart. Who was it?"

I shrugged. "Some girl named Lucinda Cruz. I don't know her."

" *Was* she murdered?"

"I don't know. All I know is I was walking into the church and I saw her there and I called the police." I checked the Marlboro clock behind Virginia and jumped. "I'm late."

Chapter Three

After I finished my dogs that afternoon I called Channel Eleven to see if Trisha was there. I almost didn't get an answer because I forgot to call her Patrice. The girl on the phone said she'd just gotten there. I hung up and thought about going home to change clothes. After seven hours of wrestling with dogs I didn't look or smell like I was ready to step onto any red carpets, but I knew if I went home, I'd find some excuse to put it off another day. When you put something off once, it's twice as easy to put it off again. It's the exponential law of procrastination.

Besides, God had told me that morning to go clean things up with Trisha, right? I drove across town, my mind mulling the concept of God talking to me through some story about two ancient guys I'd never met. Was he really speaking to *me*? Maybe and maybe not. I mean, who was to say? Maybe I just thought that was God speaking to me because the situation with Trisha was on my mind. Maybe that's what everyone did when they thought God was speaking to them. We all just want to believe so much that God gives a flip about the pitiful details of our lives.

I was always curious when everyday people say God told them

something. I wanted to know what that sounded like, what that felt like, how they could be *so sure*. And so far no one had been able to give me a solid answer. It made me crazy.

And if it wasn't God, if it *was* my conscience, wouldn't it be as effective to send Trisha a card? It didn't have to be face-to-face stuff, did it? Trisha was probably busy and maybe seeing me at work would only make things worse. I'd probably be disturbing her.

I almost had myself talked into a card and a little gift, maybe a gift certificate for a manicure or something, by the time I got to Channel Eleven, but I didn't go home. I pulled into the parking lot around to the side so Stump would be in the shade. I sat there and debated with myself about going in or going home until I finally turned the key and ground the gears into reverse. I backed out of the space.

Then I pulled back in. I knew that if I left now, I would spend the rest of the day arguing with myself about how I hadn't *really* chickened out, about how I was being perfectly reasonable. I've argued with myself enough for one lifetime. It's exhausting and gives me a headache and makes me want to drink.

Of course, I wanted a drink right then, too. I killed the motor, climbed out, and flapped my arms around a little to dry out the sweat and let the breeze carry away some of the dog smell. I prayed again for courage, then did a gut check.

Nope, still scared. Hmm. Courage wasn't working. So instead, I dragged up a little bit of outrage.

After all, who did she think she was, putting my picture on the news? Yes, I was there to resolve some conflict, but a part of me said that while I was there I might as well get all that was coming to me, including an apology.

That got my feet moving. I *did* make a feeble effort to remind myself to stay calm, but truth be told, I didn't try very hard. Righteous indignation is a lot more appealing than approaching someone with hat in hand, begging forgiveness. By the time I got to the front desk, I was practically stomping.

You would have thought I had asked to see the Pope or the President or something. While I was standing there trying to convince the girl behind the desk that I meant no harm – I guess the fury tactic had its drawbacks – three or four people came and went through a swinging door to my left. I figured Trisha was probably through that door.

Finally the girl paged Trisha. "She's not answering her phone," she said after a second. As if that might make me give up and go away.

I sat on the padded chair across from the desk. "I'll wait."

She looked at me like she wanted to get her fly swatter and swat me away. Then a guy with white Ken doll hair poked his head out an office behind her. "Amy, can you come in here for a second?"

"I'll be right back," Amy whispered to me.

"Okay," I whispered back.

As soon as she was gone I hopped up and hustled through the swinging door.

I followed a narrow hallway until I found a room with people in it. I don't know what I was expecting; maybe the set from All the President's Men, with Dustin Hoffman and Robert Redford types running through, dodging desks and waste baskets with their hot scoop that would ignite a national scandal. Then I re-membered that was newspaper, and this was television. This placed looked just like any other other big office, with four or five desks and people milling around.

I saw Trisha toward the back of the room, angled toward a bank of televisions that lined the wall.

"Trisha!" I said, not quite a shout but loud enough to get the whole room's attention. I wanted them all to know that Patrice wasn't her real name.

She spun around, eyes wide.

I gave her a goofy grin and a wave. "Surprise!"

Her face closed up so fast you could almost hear it slam. She crossed the floor, her lips thin and her nose in the air.

"Can I help you?"

"I don't know, Trisha. Can you? Don't act like you don't know why I'm here."

"What do you want, Salem?" She folded her arms and smirked, looking up and down my body. "The friends-join-free coupon I just got from Fat Fighters?"

"You know what I want. Do you want to talk about it in front of all these people?"

She shot a look around the room. A couple of people were watching but not exactly staring. I could change that, though, and she knew it.

She pointed back the way she'd come. "Back here."

I followed her around another corner and into a room the size of a closet, with one wall of fancy looking equipment with a few thousand buttons, switches and knobs.

Trisha closed the door behind me. "Before you begin, you should know I have the station's full support. We have unlimited resources to defend me through any legal action you might try. I was very careful to say only what I knew to be factual. You have absolutely no chance of winning a lawsuit, or of getting the station or our parent company to settle for so much as a *penny*." Her eyes flashed as she spoke.

I blinked. She actually thought I was here to threaten a lawsuit. "All I want is an apology."

She stared at me for a second. I swear she looked almost disappointed. "You're not getting one."

"Why did you put that horrible picture of me on the news? People think I actually killed that girl!"

Her teeth clenched so that she had to spit every word through her teeth. "I did it because I *could*. Because I wanted the world to see your trashy face and know what kind of person you are. And believe me, if I ever get the opportunity to hurt you again, I will take full advantage of it."

Ugh. I really wanted to hang onto that righteous indignation. But clearly the time had come to get to the root of the problem.

I took a deep breath and told myself I couldn't fix it if I didn't know what was wrong.

"What did I do, Trisha?"

Trisha rolled her eyes. "Go to hell, Salem."

"I'm serious. I need for you to tell me what I did. All I remember is a fight and you pushing me." She'd been crying then, I suddenly remembered. Red face, red eyes, tears streaming.

I was so scared. My heart thundered and I felt a little queasy. I did *not* want to hear her answer.

Suddenly I remembered something else. "Was I - was I putting my clothes on?" That had to be it. I remembered her pushing me and I fell because I had one leg inside my pants, trying to tug them on. I remembered scooting across the floor, trying to get my clothes on and dodge all the things Trisha was chunking at me at the same time.

"Give me a break, Salem." She turned and reached for the doorknob.

"No, wait." I stepped and put my hand out to stop her. She looked at my arm like she'd chop it off if she had half a chance.

"Listen, Trisha –"

"You need to call me Patrice."

It was time for another prayer, for patience and humility this time. I obviously needed it. "Listen, Patrice." The patience and humility came through better than the courage had. I let my mind go back to that time when I was a walking screw-up, when I managed to alienate everyone around me and shame myself. Humility isn't so hard if you really look at yourself. "I was messed up for a long time. I drank a lot. I was a drunk. I did a lot of things I wish I hadn't done."

"You poor thing." She crossed her arms over her chest.

"I'm an alcoholic." Man. Even now something in me wants to qualify that, wants to deny it. Even after saying it every week for over a year. "I'm in recovery now. I've been going to AA and I'm sober and I'm getting my life together. One of the steps of AA is to right whatever wrongs you can. I came here today to do that."

She opened her mouth to say something, but all that came out was this huff that said she couldn't quite believe what she was hearing.

"Trish – Patrice, I know I did something to hurt you. I remember that we had a fight or – or something. But you have to believe me when I tell you, I do *not* remember what it was about. You'll have to tell me before I can make it right."

"Make it right? Salem, there is no way to make *this* right. It's wrong and it's going to stay wrong because you're a complete waste of human flesh who destroys everything around you."

My heart thudded in my chest and I heard Les' voice, felt his hands over mine, assuring me that God's grace was big enough to cover any sin.

"Tell me," I said quietly. "Tell me what I did."

"You honestly don't remember?"

I shook my head. I was so full of dread I felt sick with it. Whatever it was, it was worse than I thought.

"And you really want me to tell you?"

Again, I shook my head. "No, I don't. Because I know when you do I'm going to feel horrible and want to crawl into a hole. But it's the only thing I know to do."

Trisha looked at me for a long time. Then she shook her head, turned and opened the door.

I stood to stop her, but suddenly she slammed the door shut and whirled on me. "You had sex with Scott!" There was murder in her eyes, and for a moment I thought she was going to slap me.

I took a step back as her words sank in. "Scott? Your boyfriend Scott?"

"Yes, you idiot. My boyfriend Scott. You whore."

"But – " I didn't even *like* Scott. "When?"

"The night before our wedding. God, you are such an idiot. You ruined my wedding, you almost ruined my *life*, and you don't even *remember* it. That's what pisses me off as much as anything, Salem." She jabbed her finger at me, stuck it hard into my chest. "You slept with the man I loved, you ruined my wedding day, you took everything that was precious to me and screwed it up just like you do everything else, and you don't even remember it. You are unbelievable." Her eyes got shiny and her voice tight. "When I think of all the sleep *I've* lost thinking about you two together, when I think of the hours I've cried over that, and to know you went on your merry way, never giving it a second thought." She shook her head, her eyes red and full of tears. "Get out of here. Get back out of my life."

I couldn't move. I remembered then more about that scene. Trisha screaming and crying and pushing me, me trying to get dressed and get away from her, hungover – or still drunk, probably – confused and scared. Scott jumping up, naked and groggy too, hair sticking up, his hands up, trying to calm Trisha down. Telling her, "Wait baby, no baby, don't Trish, don't, I love you, wait wait wait." Horror and heartbreak in his voice, regret like I've never heard, before or since.

I've done a lot of lousy things in my life. I've lied to people, gossiped to people, driven drunk and wrecked people's cars. I "borrowed" money I never intended to pay back. I let people down. I hurt people.

But I've never done anything I felt as horrible about as I did right then.

The lump in my throat and the shame in my heart were so big I could barely speak. "Trisha," I whispered, and the word felt like a hot, jagged rock coming up from my throat. "I am so sorry. I am so...sorry."

She glared at me, eyes full of rage and hot tears. Her jaw clenched, and I thought if she had a knife right then she would plunge it into my heart.

"I came here –" I had to stop and swallow. "I came here to confront you about putting my picture on the news, for intentionally humiliating me. Now I understand why you did it. I came here to try and put things right. But like you said, I can't make this right."

"No kidding. And if you try you're just going to screw it up, too."

"I can only tell you how sorry I am. I was messed up. I know that's not an excuse, but you have to know I'd never intentionally do anything to hurt you."

"Oh, I know that, Salem." She looked at me like I was a bug. "You never do anything intentionally. You just don't care. And that's all it takes."

"I didn't care. You're right. I didn't care about anyone or anything, including myself. But I do now."

"Too late."

"Please don't say that. I know I can't undo what I did, but..." But what? What do you do to make up for ruining someone's life? I was starting to understand the whole sackcloth and ashes thing.

"Scott always loved you. If he had sex with me, he must have been drunk, too."

"Of course he was drunk too. He got drunk at his bachelor party and you showed up."

"He loved you, Trisha. Patrice. Maybe you could... maybe it's not too late..."

Again Trisha shook her head. "You are the stupidest person I've ever known in my life. How do you even make it through the day?" She stuck her left hand out.

Only then did I notice she wore a wedding ring. A really nice one. Scott must have shown his remorse with diamonds. And her name was Patrice Watson. Scott Watson. Scott and Patrice Watson. Mr. and Mrs. Scott Watson. "You married him anyway? Even after I..."

"Two years after. Two years of hell and hurt and betrayal. Yes, I married him. Because he loves me and I love him. We belong together and always have. And even a train wreck like you can't stop that."

I swallowed. "I'm glad. I really am. You deserve to be happy."

"I *am* happy." The twitch in her jaw and murder in her eyes didn't exactly support that, but I wasn't going to be the one to point that out. "I forgave Scott and we moved on, stronger and more in love than ever. He's completely devoted to me. He would kill for me. I forgave him. But I'll never forgive you. So you can go back to your AA group and tell them this is one wrong that isn't going to be made right."

She turned to go, but then turned back one more time. "And another thing. This getting your life together crap. I don't believe it for a second. People like you don't change. You can go to all the AA meetings you want. But you're always going to be trouble. This morning just proves it."

"This morning?" Good Lord. What had I done this morning?

"This morning Tony Solis was arrested for the murder of Lucinda Cruz."

I collapsed into the seat of my car and closed the door. I knew it was going to be bad. But...man! This level of bad didn't even have a name. This was a level where mere depression and low self-esteem would be a giant step up.

And to top it off, Tony had been arrested for murder. Tony. My mind flashed to Tony, whirling with questions as to how he could possibly be involved.

Stump crawled into my lap and licked my arm, her little feet digging into my leg. I wrapped my arms around her and rested my forehead on her big square skull, her body warm against mine and her heart beating steady beneath my hand.

I was a sorry screw-up who ruined everything and everyone around me. I was a mistake. The very substance I was made from was tainted.

In the entire time I'd been sober, I had never wanted a drink so bad. To feel that first warm gush down my throat, feel the heat spread down into my arms, into my legs, spread out till I didn't care anymore.

I *needed* to not care for a while. I needed a break. Trisha was right. People like me didn't change. What was I fighting for? It was a losing battle. I was an idiot to even try.

It took everything I had to turn the key in the ignition, but I already knew where I was going. I wasn't supposed to go into a bar, but so what? Was someone going to stop me? Of course not. No one cared. I was the only one who thought this was a battle that needed to be won.

I drove with Stump on my lap, her head out the window, her tongue the size of a Saint Bernard's hanging out of her mouth. What the heck. I'd take her with me. I knew a little bar over on the north side of town where they wouldn't care if I brought her inside. Someone would probably give her a beer.

I couldn't get Scott and Trisha's voices out of my head. Two people in agony. Two people whose lives had taken a horrible, painful hit. A hit from me.

I barely noticed the rest of traffic as Stump and I made our way down surface streets. I couldn't see how fast I was driving because Stump was blocking the dash with her big head. And I didn't care. Let a cop pull me over. Let me have an accident.

Go ahead, God. Punish me. I asked for your help on this and what do I get? This is your idea of help? What the actual heck? Why do I have to be dragged down like this? When am I going to

get a break? Never, that's when. I get it now. You created me so I
could be miserable and try to claw my way up and get knocked
back down again. Thank you. Thank you very freaking much, you
mean jerk.

I actually thought that. I actually thought the words "You
mean jerk," to God. I didn't care. So much for trying to straighten
my life out. God was a jerk who'd made me so he could get his
grins dragging me through hell. He was a jerk and I was tired of
playing this game. I was done. He could either kill me or get out
of my way, but I wasn't going to jump through hoops for him anymore.

I waited for a lightning bolt to strike me. It didn't. Instead
smoke billowed up from under the hood of my car and it lurched
to a stop in the middle of the street, coughing and jerking like it
was having some kind of fit.

That's when I noticed the temperature gauge, solidly into the
red. For a second I considered sitting there until someone
rammed into the back of the car and sent us all up in flames. But
then a big dually pickup almost *did* rear end me, honking, tires
screeching, driver leaning out to shout cuss words at me, and I
screamed and shoved Stump into the passenger seat, put the car
in neutral and jerked open the door so I could push the car to the
side of the road.

I guess I wasn't quite as ready to die as I thought.

"I take it back," I huffed as I pushed. "I don't really want you
to kill me." Although I didn't know what I could possibly have to
live for. Still, I'd kind of had something less painful in mind than
being flattened by a dually.

I got the car to the side of the road and the flashers on, pushing
with my shoulder so hard I was practically knees to the ground.

Good thing I had a small car. Stump jumped back into the driver's seat, her front paws on the wheel, and licked my arm. It got on my nerves but I didn't have the initiative to tell her to stop. I just pushed as hard as I could and thought about how great that first drink was going to taste.

I heard *The Entertainer* and looked over my shoulder to see an ice cream truck behind me.

Les. I stood up straight, breathing hard. I'll be damned. My knight in shining armor. At least the truck was white.

He parked behind me and got out. "Car trouble?"

I thought I should at least nod. But I just stood there, feeling like I had been *run over* by a car. God sent Les. I called Him a jerk and decided to get drunk so he sent Les. And now Les was going to go on and on about how good God was, and he sure as heck wasn't going to let me get a drink.

I felt like a rat in one of those lab mazes that can never be solved. I'd finally figured out that I had no real shot of ever beating the maze, so I escaped. Except here came the lab technician, picking up my fat white rat body and scratching the back of my tiny little rat head before putting me back in the maze with an indulgent smile. I had no chance at all.

"Isn't God amazing?" Les said with that huge goofy grin. "I knew there was a reason the routes got switched around today. So I could be here when you needed me. It's a miracle."

"Yeah," I said. "A freaking miracle."

"Bad day?"

"The worst. Do you have a lighter? I'm going to set the car on fire."

"I have a tow chain in the back. We'll hook you up and tow you home."

He lifted the hood and poked around with a smile on his face, like he was rummaging through a box of possible treasures at a flea market. "There's your problem. Busted block." He pointed under the car, then back toward the middle of the street where I'd just stopped. A line of water – I assumed it was water – left a wide trail. It looked like my car had some pretty serious bladder control issues.

"Are blocks expensive?" I thought with a vague sense of hope of the little wooden blocks with letters on them.

"Oh yes," he said cheerfully. "Very." He slammed the hood and dusted off his hands. "Let's hook up the chain."

He pulled in front of me, hooked the chain to his rear bumper and my front bumper. Then the ice cream man towed me and Stump home, playing *The Entertainer* the entire way.

Les unhooked the chain from my car. "You're going to be stuck here for a while. Do you need anything? I have time to take you to the grocery store before I head back to the shop."

I shook my head. A trip to a bar was out of the question with Les, and a trip anywhere else held absolutely no appeal.

"You have anyone to look at your car?"

I shrugged. "There's a guy who lives out here, he works on cars. I can see if he'll come over this evening."

Les nodded. "Won't do you any good, it's busted beyond repair. But it's good to get a second opinion. I'm just an ice cream salesman."

"I don't have any money for a new car."

"The Lord will provide."

"Yeah, I asked the Lord for the money to fix this one and he didn't provide that."

"He obviously has something else in mind for you."

"I hope He sends it before I have to be at work in the morning."

"He will."

"How come you're so sure?" I asked, hot and tired and irritated.

Les shrugged. "Just am."

"How come you were over on that side of town this afternoon?"

"Lord sent me."

"How? How did He send you?"

"Actually the girl who does that route had a sick kid today, so I took her route after I finished mine."

"But *how* did you know that was God, Les? That it wasn't just chance?" I wanted to believe that God was good, I really did, but the evidence was just not pointing that way for me. "What did it sound like?"

"It didn't sound like anything, Salem." He took a deep breath. "He doesn't talk to me with an audible voice. He just puts thoughts in my head, and I know it's Him."

"I thought he might have been talking to me this morning when I was doing my quiet time."

"I'm sure He was, then. That's what quiet time is for."

"He told me to do something I already planned on doing, though." He hadn't exactly come through in a big way with that peace and courage request.

"That's good. He was probably confirming that you were on the right track."

"Maybe. Feels like I'm on the track of a runaway train."

"Want to talk about it?" He reached into the freezer and drew out a Push-Up for him and a Drumstick for me.

I remembered standing in front of the mirror that morning

and wishing I could lose a quick forty pounds. A Drumstick was not going to help me.

On the other hand, I also wanted to feel better. And even though it wouldn't do the job a Jack and Coke would do, a Drumstick would make me feel better than no Drumstick.

I pulled the top off and peeled the wrapper back. Did I want to talk about it? I talked to Les a lot, mostly about how much my life sucked and all the things I wished could have been different; that I could have had a normal family and my dad was really my dad, and my mom was nice, and that I was one of those people who liked to clean when they got nervous, instead of the type who liked to get drunk and start trouble.

I didn't so much like to talk about the things that were my own fault. But Les is fond of pointing out that I can't change what I don't acknowledge and keeping it bottled up doesn't mean I'm controlling it, it means it's controlling me. I think Les watches too much Dr. Phil.

"I might as well," I said. Stump was about to give herself a stroke, trying to get to my ice cream, so I tore off a little bit of the cone and let her have it. "I took your advice and talked to my friend at Channel 11."

"Pray before you go?"

I nodded. "Yeah, I prayed – a couple of times." I didn't want to admit it hadn't worked. Les was so convinced God would do whatever you asked, and I didn't want to be the one to break it to him that it wasn't always so. "I found out what I did to make her so mad, and why she hates me so much. The night before her wedding I –" Man. This was hard. Saying it out loud. Les was used to ministering to people in jail and he'd probably heard a lot worse. But not from me. "The night before her wedding I slept with her husband. Fiancé."

"That's heavy." Les licked sherbet and leaned against the truck. "Did you know he was her fiancé?"

"I don't remember. I knew she and Scott dated in high school and back then she was crazy about him. He was totally in love with her. They dated all through our last two years of school." I had been so jealous. Trisha and I had been joined at the hip since 6th grade, and suddenly she was in love with Scott and too good to be seen with the likes of me. I supposed that's probably why I did it. "I don't remember much about that night except flashes. Scott, drunk and laughing, while these two guys tugged him across the floor toward a bedroom. He was saying, "No, no, seriously, no way." But he was way out of it. I remember some guy whispering in my ear that it was just a joke, just one of those practical jokes buddies play on each other when they get married. Hey, that was Ricky Barlow. I just remembered that. I didn't say this to Les, but I'd also had sex with Ricky Barlow, too, a couple of times.

"And that's when she came in?"

"No, this all happened during the nighttime. I remember because I was standing out on the balcony watching it all through the open patio door. Trisha came in the morning; late morning, I guess, because it was already hot. I remember her chasing me outside and my feet were hot on the sidewalk."

"You haven't spoken to her since?"

"I don't think so. Not until today."

"Did you ask her forgiveness?"

"Of course." I bit through the thin cone and dropped another piece for Stump.

"Were you truly sorry?"

"How could I not be?"

"Then there's not much more you can do. Keep your heart open for opportunities to show her how truly sorry you are, but other than that you have to just let it go. She has to come to terms with things on her own time. But you can't undo it, Salem. You can't turn back time, and crawling into a bottle now won't help as much as you think it will."

"We're going to have to agree to disagree on that for the time being. Right now a Jack and Coke seems like just the thing."

"It's the wrong thing."

"So is this Drumstick."

"But you're not out of control with a Drumstick."

I held my arms out wide. "Hello? I'm as big as a house." Right now that seemed like a minor worry in light of the fact that I'd ruined so many lives.

Tony.

Man. What was going on with Tony? Was that my fault too?

"Do you have a Drumstick and pass out? Do you have a Drumstick and sleep with your friends' boyfriends?"

"I don't know." I stuck the bottom of the cone in my mouth and bit down. It was the best part because it had that chocolate plug that keeps the ice cream from dripping out. "I guess we're about to find out."

Frank rounded the corner of my trailer. He looked at the tow rope between my car and the ice cream truck. "Car trouble?"

I wanted to say something smart but I just nodded. "It was low on oil, and I forgot to put any in because I was preoccupied with all the people asking about my *arrest for murder.*" I glared at Frank like it was all his fault.

Frank, as was his custom, nodded obliviously. "Bummer." He

stuck his hands in his pockets and looked at Les. "You got any Nestle Crunches?"

Les licked his sherbet and reached through the window to hand Frank a Nestle Crunch.

"I saw on the news that they arrested the guy who killed that dead body you found."

I had a quick and unpleasant vision of Tony Solis killing a dead body. Bizarre, the way Frank worded things sometimes.

"He didn't do it."

"How do you know?"

"I just know. Tony wouldn't kill anyone."

"So, you know the guy?" Les crumpled up his Push-Up cardboard and tucked it into the little bag hanging on his glove compartment. He pulled a package of wet wipes and handed one to me.

"Yeah, I know him." I wiped the sticky off my hands and tossed the wipe in the bag. "He's my ex-husband."

I had set my sights on Tony Solis in early Fall of our senior year in high school. Tony was, or at least had been, the strong silent type, dark and brooding and really good looking. He had dark brown eyes and black hair, and I could feel him watching me sometimes. I would turn around and those dark eyes would be intense on me, and it always unnerved me. I could never tell what he was thinking. I thought maybe he was into me, but I also knew he was probably just quietly horrified by me. I was a little obnoxious back then. Okay, I was a lot obnoxious back then. I'd started the year before partying a lot, drinking every weekend, then several times during the week, and by our senior year I usually had a nip at lunch, too. I was the typical rebel without a clue. I wore tight jeans and a sullen, badass attitude and thought it was all beneath me, but I liked Tony.

He didn't talk much, but when he did he always treated me with respect. Didn't make suggestive comments or dirty jokes when I came around, and that was nice. He held the door open for me. He held doors open for all women, in fact. His mom had raised him that way.

His mom, on the other hand, hated me. She'd stare at me with those same dark eyes, but I knew exactly what she was thinking – white trash slut just like her mother, exactly the kind of girl her son would not be caught associating with. Tony was smart. Tony had a future. Tony was going places. Someday Tony would come back to Idalou in a Mercedes with his beautiful wife – who would also have graduate degrees – and their two perfect kids, and he'd build a big house there and they'd take Tony's mother on Alaskan cruises with them.

The combination of Tony's unreadable stares, his mother's very readable glares, and my own penchant for complete self-destruction – and fueled by my admiration for Tony's deep brown eyes and wide shoulders – all mixed together to make me see Tony as a challenge.

Even though we were raised in the same small town, mine and Tony's lives could not have been more different. My mom was – and still is – an embarrassing, hurtful, out-of-control train wreck of a person. I love her, but just because I don't know how to *not* love her. She's my mom. Les keeps insisting that God loves her, and that makes me feel better, somehow.

She sent me to school with half a jar of green olives and two stale canned biscuits for lunch one day when I was in fifth grade, and that was when I stomped my foot and insisted she find something for me to eat. In seventh grade, she offered the principal a sexual favor in exchange for six months' worth of unpaid school lunches. (The school secretary overheard her and passed this tidbit on to Maureen at the beauty shop, which was the equivalent of taking out an ad in the *New York Times*. My mom denied it, then later clarified that she'd actually offered a completely innocent massage, because, you know, everyone believed that.) She also showed up drunk and loud to high school football games.

Josephine Solis, on the other hand, was the model of the perfect mother. She got up at five in the morning to cook her kids a hot breakfast. They said prayers and did catechism. I didn't even know what catechism was, but Mrs. Solis acted like Tony's weekly classes were an unbreakable appointment with God himself. Tony and his sisters always wore clean, pressed clothes, their hair always trimmed and combed into place. She taught them to be polite and respectful. If Tony or his sisters ever acted up in public, Mrs. Solis turned the hairy eyeball on them, and they snapped back into line like *that*. Tony never charged his lunch or had to borrow paper or pens; Mrs. Solis sent him to school prepared. Mrs. Solis came to every school play, sat in the front row, and clapped for her son, politely thanking the teachers for devoting their time to educating her children and encouraging them to continue their education in college. She made hot lunches with fruits and vegetables and homemade flour tortillas. Sometimes she even sent warm tortillas in the morning for everyone in the class. Put a little butter and honey on those babies and it would bring a tear to your eye. I always got excited when I saw Tony carry in the little round tortilla carrier thingy. Those were the days I got a hot breakfast, too.

So, my... "family" was my family and Tony's was Tony's. But I was white, and he was Mexican, so theoretically, according to the bigoted world I'd grown up in, I should *still* have been above him. At the very least I was even with him. I decided at some point to prove how things *really* stood. I had a weird kind of admiration/attraction vs. envy/defiance thing with Tony. In my screwed-up mind that meant I had to show him how he really *wasn't* better than me.

Now, anyone with a brain could see I could never accomplish this by trying to be as good as Tony. That was not going to happen. But what I *could* do was try to make him as bad as I was.

I flirted with him. I made off-color remarks and then winked at him. I made remarks to my friends about how fine his butt looked, loud enough he would overhear.

Nothing worked. He'd give me a tolerant smile or a blank stare and go on like he didn't want anything to do with what I had to offer.

Again, anyone with a brain or a shred of self-respect would have given up and gone on. But for me, with my self-respect registering in the negative numbers, his rebuffs were like throwing down a gauntlet. That's the great thing about being me. Give me a chance to humiliate myself and make someone else miserable, and I pursue the task 110 percent.

I finally got Tony to sleep with me the night of the homecoming football game. We were all at a keg party in the middle of someone's cotton field and I was – as usual – drunk and obnoxious, dancing on a tailgate and pretending like I didn't wish I had somewhere else to be. Trisha and Scott walked by, holding hands and mooning at each other. I looked at them and I felt so low. Alone. Lonely to the point where all I could see and feel was black.

I missed Trisha so much, missed having someone to hang out with. But she'd become too good for me, and now she had a guy who looked at her like she was the only person in the world, and I didn't know how to stop my white trash tramp thing.

I climbed down from the tailgate and headed away from the fire the guys had built, away from the cars and pickups parked along the turnrows. I found a little cluster of mesquite trees, dropped down beside them and cried. I kept thinking there wasn't any point in going on with this life; it was just too screwed up.

I was there maybe five or ten minutes when Tony appeared out of the dark. He didn't say anything, just sat down on the grass beside me, slipped his arm around my shoulders and held me.

I was equally mortified and grateful. I mean, I was cool. I was tough. I did not cry. But man...I don't think anyone had ever touched me out of kindness before, not like that. I didn't know my dad, or even the man I'd learned the year before was my *real* dad, and mom wasn't exactly a hugger. Every time I got close, she said I smelled like sweat or hair or that I was making her claustrophobic.

Of course, other guys had touched me by that point. Not as many as my reputation claimed, but enough that by that night of homecoming I already knew what girls like me were good for. But those touches were rushed, harsh and selfish. Taking. Tony's touch was giving.

I sobbed against him for I don't know how long. Finally, I sat up and saw a big wet splotch on his maroon shirt. He handed me a handkerchief and I wiped my eyes and nose.

Once I stopped crying, I was really embarrassed. I was acting like such a loser, and with *witnesses*.

Tony lifted my chin and looked me in the eye. "Better?"

I looked away. This was a nightmare. What if he told someone? Anyone? *Everyone*? I was way too cool to be crying.

So I kissed him. He tried to pull away, but I was insistent and pretty desperate. I just followed right after him, kissing his lips, his neck, whatever I could get hold of. Even now it's humiliating to know he didn't really want to be with me. But I guess a 17-year-old guy isn't going to hold out too long when a girl is sucking on his neck and unbuttoning his shirt.

From that moment on, I told myself the whole crying jag was a ploy to get Tony to be with me. I wasn't sad and lonely at all. It was all just an act. I even told other people that. I'd rather people think I was manipulative and slutty than vulnerable.

I'm pretty sure that was Tony's first time. Not his last with me, though. We began what I generously called "dating" after that. He didn't want his mom to know about me, of course, so he didn't hold my hand at school or take me out, or anything like that. Mostly he snuck out of his house at night and came over to mine.

To my utter confusion, he wasn't only interested in sex. He asked about me, about how I was and whether or not I'd done my homework, what were my plans for my future, what did I want to do with my life. Of course, I hadn't done my homework, and told him as much. "You need to apply yourself, Salem," he'd say. Then I'd show him the best way I knew to apply myself, and school and grades would become a distant memory.

Tony confused me but he thrilled me, too. He treated me kindly, respectfully. In my perverse way, I was always trying to shock him, trying to get him to see how I really was and how I really should be treated, but no matter how I acted, he was always kind to me. I was flummoxed.

One night over Christmas break his mom caught him sneaking back in and all kinds of trouble broke loose. It was bad enough that he'd snuck out; when she found out he'd snuck out to be with me she just about had a stroke. She forbade Tony from seeing me again. She threatened to send him to military school or to a monastery. She threatened to file statutory rape charges against me because Tony was still seventeen and I'd turned eighteen in October.

He told me he couldn't see me anymore, but by that time, I was already pregnant.

Hell hath no fury like the woman whose prize son has been "trapped." The truth was, I had not been trying to get pregnant. We used protection, and I certainly never intended for Tony to marry me, but as soon as my mom found out, she latched onto a new reason to have a big drama and ran with it. She marched over to Tony's house and told his mom that her son had knocked me up. Mrs. Solis's eyes rolled back in her head. She mumbled something in Spanish and keeled over.

All the daughters came running and screaming. Tony stared at me with a weird mixture of fascination, horror and concern. Mom bent over and slapped Mrs. Solis on the cheeks and ordered her to get a grip. I think Mom was really upset because it hadn't occurred to her to faint, and now it was too late.

The situation quickly deteriorated into a battle between the mothers, with Tony and me being bit players who were threatened by Mrs. Solis's hairy eyeball every time we so much as opened our mouths.

Mrs. Solis wanted me to go to a home for unwed mothers and give the baby up for adoption.

"Nothing doing," Mom said. I wasn't going to be shipped off

like some dirty secret while Tony went on living his life like he'd done nothing wrong.

Well, Tony was not going to marry me. He was just a boy who had his whole life ahead of him.

What's Salem, an old lady?

Tony's going to college. He's not going to ruin his life by getting tied down to some white trash, then she said something in Spanish, I'm not sure but I think it meant *whore*.

Then Mom fainted. Well, her eyes rolled back and she fell down, but she wasn't fully committed. Half a second later she was up and trying to scratch Mrs. Solis's eyes out.

Tony held his mother back while his sisters and I dragged Mom off their porch. The neighbors called the police.

Looking back, I can't believe I let Mom get so involved in the situation. I knew whatever she did was only going to make matters worse, but I was scared. I'd never been so scared. A *baby*? What was I going to do with a baby?

I finally called G-Ma, something I should have done at the beginning. She told me to drink a lot of milk and go to bed early, and she told Mom to back off. G-Ma is the only one who could accomplish that.

In the meantime, Mom went around Idalou telling everyone I would have to get an abortion if Tony didn't marry me. I hadn't even considered that. I don't know why, because to some people it was the obvious choice, but I knew I'd never be able to go through with it.

The Solises were Catholic, and abortion was completely out of the question. One afternoon around the middle of January Tony showed up on my doorstep in a sport coat and slacks, his hair slicked down, and a terrified look on his face. He looked like a seven-year-old boy in a seventeen-year-old body.

He had a tiny ring. I knew he didn't want to marry me, and I had no idea if I wanted to marry him or not. But I didn't know what else to do. I just stood there holding the screen door open, staring at that ring, thinking there was no way it would actually work. Tony was a nice guy. He was not going to put up with me. I'd do something to screw it up within the first month.

I looked over my shoulder at Mom, standing with her arms crossed, a cigarette hanging out of her mouth, her eyes squinted against the smoke.

I thought, at least it would get me out of here.

I looked back at Tony. He said softly, just loud enough for me to hear, "It's okay, Salem. It's gonna be okay."

I don't know if he was trying to convince himself or me, but I thought, maybe it will be. He was nice, he was always good to me, and maybe I could be good to him. I mean, I hadn't *tried* to be good in a really long time. Maybe I could pull it off if I tried hard enough.

I took the ring, and two weeks later Tony and I were married in the tiny Catholic church. Tony's side of the church was full of pressed and polished, mournful looking family members. G-Ma, Mom and Mom's drinking buddy Susan were on my side, as well as a couple of friends from school. As I walked down the aisle carrying my bouquet of plastic flowers from Bill's Dollar Store, I heard Mom – as did the entire church – stage whisper to Susan, "Can you believe I'm gonna be related to a bunch of damn Meskins?"

A stellar day for the Grimes family.

Chapter Four

Frank held the door open for me. "Your ex-husband? I didn't know you had an ex-husband."

"Yeah, well, it was a long time ago." I threw my keys on the bar and scratched my neck.

"How come he was arrested?"

"I don't know, Frank."

I was trying not to be snappy, but I wasn't doing a very good job. I felt antsy and nervous and like I was on the verge of biting someone's head off. Too bad for Frank he was so handy.

Why did I have to face *two* of the worst things I'd ever done, on the same day? This was too much to deal with. Guilt and shame rolled around inside me, wrestling with pride and defensiveness. I latched onto the latter two.

After all, the thing with Scott was as much his fault as mine, right? And nobody made Tony sleep with me, either. I mean, sure, I did come on strong that first time, but he came back for more all on his own. He could have ignored me the next day the way the other guys had done. And it wasn't like I'd poked a hole in the condom. That was either a God thing or a Trojan thing, but certainly not anything that could be laid at my feet. I really hadn't wanted to marry Tony; I'd only done it because it seemed like the right thing to do. I hadn't wanted to ruin his life. I hadn't wanted to take his future and screw it up. I'd never wanted to hurt him.

I never wanted to hurt anyone, actually, except maybe myself – and Mom, on occasion.

But I *had* hurt everyone else. I screwed up my life and Tony's life and Trisha's life and Scott's life. And now Tony was being put through who-knew-what and that was probably my fault, too, somehow. I didn't know how, but I was sure that when all was said and done, somehow I was going to be at the root of this, too.

To top it all off, my car was cratered. Man!

Since I couldn't drink, I opened the fridge to see what there was to eat. If I can't have alcohol, my second choice is always Mexican food. Beef and chicken enchiladas with lots of melted cheese and sour cream. Real sour cream, too, not that nasty fat free stuff I bought one time when my pants started to get too tight. And chips. Lots of corn chips with queso. And margaritas. Six or eight of them to make me loosen up and laugh about nothing at all.

I had to settle for peanut butter and apricot jelly. I tossed a loaf of bread on the bar and muttered, "Help yourself," to Les and Frank.

Les declined, but Frank – darn his high metabolism – got a tablespoon out of the drawer and dug a good half cup of peanut butter out of the jar and smushed it across a piece of bread. He looked at the jelly jar. "Got any grape?"

I gave him a look, and he decided apricot was fine.

I thought about Trisha's sneer as she looked at me and made that remark about Fat Fighters. I dug into the peanut butter and stuck the spoon in my mouth while I spread golden apricot jelly over the bread.

"What you need is a quart of milk to wash that down," Les said.

"No, what I need is a fifth of Jack Daniels." I slapped the bread together and took a ferocious bite. I felt like my head was going to start spinning any second. "Do you ever feel like God is punishing you?"

Les nodded, which surprised me.

"When?"

"Like most people, when things aren't going the way I want them to. When I know I've done something wrong and expect to be punished."

"But what if you *haven't* done anything wrong? What if you're trying to do something right?" I tossed the spoon into the sink with a clatter. "What if all you're trying to do is live a good life and climb out of your hole, and God keeps thumping you back down? I was on my way to a meeting yesterday, for crying out loud. I did not want to find a dead body. I did not do anything wrong. I was trying to do something *right*. And not only do I get the joy of a dead body forever planted in my mind, but now I have Trisha thrown in my face, and Tony, too. I can't catch a break."

I didn't want the stupid freaking sandwich anymore, and I didn't want Les and Frank there. I dropped onto the cracked leather recliner. Stump jumped into my lap with her heavy, bony feet. I kind of wanted to shove her off, but I didn't.

What I really wanted was a drink. Just so I could not feel so crappy. Just so I could take a break for a while and figure out what I was going to do. Just to make it go away for a while, just a little while. I knew drinking was the short-term answer for a long-term problem. I knew it wasn't going to solve anything. I knew that. But at the moment I didn't care. Right at the moment all these feelings were pelting me at once: shame, regret, sadness over what I'd done to Trisha, and sadness over what had happened to me and Tony so long ago. The reason we'd had to get married, the reason we got divorced, it all made me feel really sad, and I hate feeling sad more than anything. I didn't want to do it one second longer. A short-term answer would be just fine, thank you very much.

Les sat across from me on the ottoman. He put his elbows on his knees. "You know if you make it through this one you can make it through just about anything."

"I don't care." The future loomed pointless before me.

"I know you don't, not right now. But you will."

"I doubt it."

"You will. Things will even back out and you'll be proud of yourself for being strong."

That almost made me laugh. "Believe me, I'm not strong. I'm pissed off."

"That's okay."

"I feel screwed over."

"That's okay too."

"It's not okay, it sucks."

"That's good."

"You're such a weirdo."

"I know that."

"I hate this! I don't deserve this."

"We all hate it, Salem. No one likes being an alcoholic. Nobody wants it to be this hard."

For some stupid reason, after everything else, it was the tenderness in Les's voice that put me over the edge.

The tears sprang up so fast I didn't have time to stop them. Within seconds my face was soaked and I had snot.

I gasped for air between sobs and curled up as small as I could. Les rubbed my back.

"I was on my way to Moe's," I said between hiccuping sobs.

"I know."

"I'm not strong. I'm a complete screw up. I mess up everything."

"Shhh."

"I don't want to do this anymore. It's *too* hard."

"I know."

"It's not worth it."

"You're right."

"I was happier being a drunk."

"Of course you were."

I sat back and swiped the back of my wrist across my eyes. "What kind of pillar of support are you? Where's my buck up speech? Where's my encouragement?"

"You don't need encouragement. You need a good stiff drink."

I kicked him. Ugh. I'm such a freak show.

He's just as bad, though. He stood up and kicked me back. You'd think a gentleman would have gone easy on me, too, but he didn't.

"Ow!" I rubbed my shin. "What the hell is wrong with you?"

"What's wrong with *me*? What the hell is wrong with you?"

"I'm having a very bad day! I feel awful."

"So? You feel bad. How do you think your friend felt, knowing the man she loved had sex with her best friend, the night before her wedding? Do you think she felt kind of sorry for herself for half an hour or so, and then got over it?"

"Of course not! She was devastated. It still hurts her. That's why I feel so horrible."

"Good. You should feel horrible. You need to feel that. You haven't earned the right to escape from it."

I stood and paced the room, wanting to throw him out, wanting to slap Frank for sitting on the barstool and staring at us both like we were this week's episode of a reality show, but I figured if I did, he'd take his cue from Les and slap me back.

So I folded my arms across my chest and dug my fingers into my own flesh. "I don't want to feel it."

"Of course you don't. It's not fun."

"It's horrible. I want it to go away."

"Feel it."

"I want a drink!"

"A drink would make everything all better, wouldn't it, Salem? Just one drink, and things would look a lot better. The pain would fade, you'd be back in control again. Things would be back on an even keel."

"Yes." I swiped again at the tears running down my cheeks.

"You can feel it now, can't you? Liquid warmth going down your throat, reaching out all the way to your fingers and toes. It pushes everything else back down to where it should be, out of sight, out of reach. All the bad stuff is going back down where it belongs, back down into the cellar behind a locked door."

I listened to Les, let the possibilities he described circle around in my brain. I waited for it to feel good to me.

But it didn't feel good. It felt just as bad as staying right where I was. It felt like failure. It felt like the final nail in my coffin.

I dragged my hands through my hair. "I can't get away from it."

"Go get a drink, Salem!"

"No!"

"Why not?"

"Because I don't have any money."

"I'll give you the money."

"I don't have a car."

"I'll drive you."

"No, damn it!"

"Why not?"

"Because I don't want to."

He was quiet for a long time. "Exactly. You don't really want to."

"You know, Les, as a psychologist you really suck."

"You want to get through this."

"I want to get past this!"

"I know. But guess what? You have to get *through* it to get past it. There's no bridge over it."

I rolled my eyes and dropped back down into my chair. I wanted to sink right through it, through the floor and through the ground until impenetrable darkness closed around me.

The thing about actually experiencing stuff is, I don't have a lot of practice at it. I learned early on how to daydream, how to use my mind to get away from my body. When I was a kid my daydreams looked a lot like Sesame Street: singing puppets, patient and loving adults who kept their hands to themselves – save for the occasional appropriate hug and tweak on the cheek – and nutritious after-school snacks.

I wished I could make up some world for me now. For a second

I considered using the old fantasy world coping technique, but almost immediately abandoned the idea. Right away it started taking on "Real Housewives of Sesame Street" overtones, and that was just disturbing.

I couldn't concentrate very well, what with Trisha continually popping in. I wondered if my showing up at the TV station had her as freaked out as I was.

From there my mind went to Tony, in a jail cell, I supposed, he was sitting on a metal bench with flaking burnt orange paint, arms crossed over his chest, waiting.

Frank left not long after that, but Les hung around until I finally told him I was going to bed and he was welcome to camp out on the sofa if he wanted. He didn't trust me that I wasn't going to take a drink, and if he felt the need to be my personal Secret Service guy, I didn't have the energy to fight him. He settled in to watch TV and told me he would let himself out.

Later I heard him call his wife and tell her he would be late. That woman was a saint. Les was always out helping keep somebody out of the gutter, which is nice, but can't make him the best candidate for a husband. Later, I woke for a second when he peeked in on me, then slipped out the front door.

The next morning I woke early, took my shower and got ready for work, then went to my prayer room for my morning devotional. I couldn't concentrate because I kept thinking about Tony. Maybe I could help him in some way, make up for all the garbage I'd given him. Maybe I could remember something from the crime scene that would help exonerate him.

I started to ask God to help me help Tony, but I remembered the day before, how mad I'd been at God and the entire world. The Bible says if we confess our sins He is faithful and just to forgive them, but I wasn't sure exactly what my sin was. I mean, I knew I was wrong, but I wasn't exactly sure what to confess *to*. I did a mental run-through of the Ten Commandments to see what my day had fallen under. I hadn't murdered, I hadn't stolen, I hadn't lied. What else was there? Did calling God a jerk mean I'd taken His name in vain?

"God, I'm sorry I got mad yesterday and called you...you know. I'm sorry I was rude to Les and Frank, and I'm sorry I really wanted a drink and I planned to get one. Did you send Les to keep me from going to the bar?" I suddenly remembered my car with a sick feeling. "Did you make my car break down so I couldn't get to the bar? Because if you did...well, I wish you'd thought a little longer and come up with something a little bit...not so expensive. Because you might remember, as I told you yesterday, I'm broke. I don't have money for car repairs, and I don't have money for a new car. Even a decent used one. Even a junker. I have no money. And if I have no car I have no way to work." Okay, I was getting overwhelmed again. I hated to be rude while I was in the middle of prayer, but I looked at my watch. I had half an hour to get to work. and no way to get there except to walk. It was, what...eight or ten miles away?

"Anyway, I need help. I really *want* help, and I'd really appreciate it if you'd send some help my way. Amen."

I started to get up, then went back down on my knees. "And, PS, if I can do something to help Tony, please let me know what it is. I owe him big time."

I got up and went to the front door, looking through the little rectangle window at my old junker car in the driveway. All by itself. I admit, I had kind of been hoping God was going to throw me a nice new V-6 bone with a bow on top. "Happy You're-Not-

Really-A-Total-Loser Day! Here's your band new car!"

I put on my shoes and grabbed my purse. Stump came trotting up on her little stub legs and danced around my feet. I looked at her and chewed my lip. I seriously didn't know how I was going to get to work, and I figured I should leave her at home. She was used to going to work with me except for on Mondays. Probably she didn't know it was Wednesday, but maybe she did. Maybe she'd be heartbroken if I didn't take her with me. Maybe in her despair she'd shred the entire house while I was gone.

I sighed and opened the front door. She trotted down the steps, her black bottom bumping each riser on her way down.

I locked up and said a prayer on the way to the car. "God, I would really love a new car, but if you've decided to send my miracle in the form of this car being healed, that will work, too."

I opened the car door and Stump, bless her ever optimistic heart, tried to jump into the seat. She lunged and hung, scrambling, from the doorway, until I put my hand under her butt and hoisted her up.

"This will work," I said decisively to her as I sat. "Absolutely."

She cocked her head and looked at me like she wasn't buying my BS. I said another quick prayer that was really just a, "*Please.*" I cranked the key.

Ruhr-ruhr-ruhr-ruhr. I turned it again. *Ruhr-ruhr-ruhr-ruhr.*

Stump laid her head on her paws, looking bored.

"Okay, well," I said, pulling the key from the ignition. "It was worth a shot."

I sighed and opened the door. I had to go around to the passenger side to get Stump because she refused to get out of the car. I hitched my handbag up on my shoulder, tucked her like a football under my arm, and took off walking.

We made it out of Trailertopia and onto Llano Boulevard before I started to think maybe I should have taken the gamble of leaving Stump unattended at home. Good Lord, the girl packed a lot of weight into her little body. Plus she kept squirming around, digging her rear paws into my back for traction. I shifted her from one arm to the other, but by the third block into it, I figured by the time I got to Bow Wow Barbers my arms were going to be too exhausted to lift. I stopped dead on the sidewalk.

At that moment, a car pulled up beside me.

Les was leaning over from the driver's seat, rolling down the passenger window. "Sorry I'm late," he said, cheerful as ever.

Because I was a complete and eternally grateful sap, I had to blink back tears. "You didn't have to come get me," I said, making my voice light. I had not forgotten Les's speech about getting through the tough stuff. "We were going to walk." See how full of BS I can be? I hugged Stump to me, partly to hide the shaking in my arms.

"Long way to walk," was all he said.

He dropped me off at Flo's and asked, "What time should I pick you up?"

"No need," I said. "I have a ride home." I would get one, I decided. If I had to call G-Ma, I would do that. I could not keep imposing on Les for the rest of my life, no matter how much he didn't seem to mind.

"Let me know if you change your mind," was all he said. He drove off, presumably to get to the jail so he could find other lost lambs.

I thought about Les as I went about my morning routine. He must have gotten a hefty emotional payoff, with all the helping people he did. It wasn't just me. Okay, it was *mostly* me, because, let's face it, I'm pretty much a full-time job. But still, there wasn't an hour of the day when he wasn't doing something for someone. It made me wonder what it felt like, being someone's last hope. Which in turn, made me think of Tony. If there was anyone I would love to be the last hope for, it was Tony. Also Trisha, and Stump, because I would basically do just about anything for her.

When I had two dogs left to finish, I worked up the nerve to call G-Ma. G-Ma is not the type to bend over backwards for anyone, but most especially not her beloved only grandchild. It wasn't that she didn't love me. It was just that she'd read somewhere about tough love and setting boundaries and, boy howdy, she'd taken it all to heart where I was concerned. This inconvenient attitude was aggravated by the fact that she had learned all these golden theories *after* she'd raised my mother, who had gone on to lie, steal, use, and beg her way through life. Even though I wasn't always thrilled with G-Ma's no-handouts rule, I had to admit I admired her. There were plenty of times when, if she had given an inch, I would definitely have taken the whole frigging yard.

"I thought you said you were staying out of trouble," she said when I told her what I wanted to do.

"I *am* staying out of trouble," I said. I remembered that verse in the book of James about not swearing on anything, just letting your yes be yes and your no be no. I'd spent so many years lying through my teeth that I could swear on the original stone tablet, with my hand firmly on the "Thou Shalt Not Bear False Witness" part, and it still wouldn't hold a lot of water with G-Ma. "I am staying out of trouble. I just want to go visit a friend, and my car is in the shop." See? Even when I was telling the truth, I couldn't help but lie a little bit.

"You don't need to go be seeing any friends that are in jail. You need to stay *away* from friends in jail."

"But G-Ma, it's Tony. Remember Tony?"

"Your husband Tony?"

"My ex-husband Tony. Yes, that's him."

"He didn't do anything." She said it with all the conviction of the close-minded. Like most people – most people *including* me – G-Ma believed that Tony was much too good to have married me.

"I know," I said. "I want to go visit him and find out if there's some way I can help him."

For me, G-Ma would have said no, but for Tony, she relented.

One of the things I really like about G-Ma is, she believes in having the best, whether she can afford it or not. She'll go without before she'll buy generic. I think there's an intrinsic sense of worth in her that failed to trickle down. I feel like a spendthrift if I buy Charmin instead of Walmart brand toilet paper.

The best car, in G-Ma's eyes, is a Lincoln. Not as showy and obnoxious as a Cadillac. Cadillacs are for people who just want to get attention, she says. For the discriminating person who simply wants luxury, it's got to be a Lincoln. She manages to slip into conversation at every opportunity that Lincolns cost just as much as Cadillacs.

After I finished my dogs I sponged off with the brown paper towels in the bathroom and tried to fix my makeup, then waited out on the sidewalk for the maroon Lincoln to come careening into the parking lot. I paced up and down with Stump and tried – without success – not to stare at my reflection in the shop windows. I wondered how Tony would see me. Probably he'd be too preoccupied with possible long-term prison time to notice that my bangs needed a trim and that my thighs had grown to enormous proportions.

Of course, this was extremely shallow thinking about when there were much bigger issues than the size of my thighs on the table (so to speak), but I never professed to being that deep. I tried to be deep. I wanted to be deep, but the fact was, I felt better when I fished the lipstick and powder out of my purse and freshened up a little. I also said a prayer for a thirty-pound weight loss miracle on the way to the county jail, but the Bible does say that prayers without faith don't really work.

G-Ma bounced the Lincoln into the parking lot and pulled up beside me. She hit the button and the passenger window slid halfway down.

"You're bringing your –" The window slid back up. G-Ma's not very proficient with buttons, or technology in general.

I saw her mouth the word "dog," though. I nodded.

The window slid back down.

"I can't leave her here because Flo's going to close in an hour and I don't know if we'll be back before –"

Whirr. Window going back up. I waited until it slid partway back down. "Is it okay?"

Experience told me that it *would* be okay, as long as I groveled and gave her a few minutes to complain about it.

"This is a nice car. This is a quality car. I don't want it full of dog poo."

"She's not going to poo in your car, G-Ma. She's trained and besides, she already did her poo for the day." I'd walked her after lunch; I knew firsthand the poo issue was taken care of.

"Does she get nervous riding in cars? Because getting nervous does bad things to a dog's stomach."

"She rides everywhere with me. She's never been nervous before."

"Once that smell gets in you can't get it out, you know. Doesn't matter what you use. It's permanent."

"I promise you she won't go in your car, G-Ma." I looked at Stump and mental-telepathied what I'd do to her if she made a liar out of me.

"I'd have to sell the car and I love this car. There's not another one this color within two hundred miles."

Now we were off on that fable. The guy at the dealership had fed her that line, and despite the fact that I'd seen at least five cars exactly like G-Ma's in town, she clung to the notion that she had the only Midnight Maroon Lincoln between Dallas and El Paso.

"I'll hold her in my lap," I said. "So just in case it will get on me and not the seat."

G-Ma pursed her lips and didn't say anything else, and I decided that meant she was through arguing. I opened the door and belted myself in, holding Stump tight on my lap.

The Lincoln was a V-8, and G-Ma liked to make sure all eight cylinders saw action between every red light. A lot of people grumbled when Texas made it illegal to sit in the front seat without your seatbelt on, but I was relieved to have a reason to strap myself in when I rode with G-Ma. She played a little too fast and loose with the driving rules – such as staying between the lines and using only the middle lane for turning – for my comfort.

She hit the divider in the jail parking lot and shoved the gearshift into park. I climbed out with a silent prayer of thanks for a relatively safe arrival – along with another plea for a new car so I wouldn't have to keep bumming rides – and told Stump to be good while I was gone.

G-Ma raised one penciled-on eyebrow. "It's not staying in the car."

I lifted my hands. "I can't take her inside."

"It's not *staying* in my car."

I cleared my throat and chewed my lip to push back my frustration. I was well-versed in G-Ma's looks and tones. Stump wasn't staying in the car.

I opened the door and hooked Stump's leash to her collar. She hates her leash. She screams like she's dying and fights so hard she makes herself throw up. And yet up against G-Ma's stubbornness, the leash hooked to the bike rack in front of the jail became the path of least resistance.

Stump began to whine and gag as soon as the leash was attached. Never mind the fact that the collar around her neck was exactly the same size as it had been five seconds before, and that absolutely nothing was restricting her air flow in the least. She detected a leash, and she wasn't having it.

Be firm, I told myself as I sat Stump down by the bike rack and looped her leash over the bar. Just act like it's no big deal; you're the parent here.

Before I could figure out a way to get the leash knotted, she'd tugged it off the pole and was barking furiously at me.

I gave her the hairy eyeball but, as usual, she was unfazed by that. If I ever had kids I would have to learn how to be more menacing.

I tucked her, squirming, under my arm and unhooked the leash from her collar. She stopped wriggling immediately and licked my jaw. With my free hand I looped the leash over the pole, threaded the clip end through the looped handle, and pulled the clip back up. I clicked it back onto her collar and sat her down on the sidewalk before she knew what happened.

She looked at me with outrage burning in her big brown eyes, looked at the leash wrapped securely around the bicycle rack, and began to gag.

"Give me a break," I said. "I've had a bad week. I have enough drama of my own to deal with. You can be the drama queen next week, okay? I promise."

She lay down on her side and wheezed loudly. The slack in the leash pooled onto the sidewalk.

G-Ma laughed. "Would you look at that? I believe that dog's playing possum."

"She's playing Meryl Streep on her deathbed," I said. "She passed possum a long time ago."

I asked the girl at the front desk if she'd look out every once in a while, and make sure my dog was okay. She wrinkled her brow and looked at Stump. "Is it okay? It's lying in the sidewalk. It looks like it's gasping for air."

I scooted over away from the door where Stump couldn't see me. "Now what's she doing?"

The girl drew her head back. "She's up now. Her tail's wagging."

I nodded. "She'll be fine." I asked if I could see Tony.

The girl checked a computer at the desk. "He was bonded out this morning. He's probably –" She turned and looked at the clock behind her. "You might be able to catch him at the back door. Go back out this way and around to the west side. That's where they're let out, but you'll have to hurry, because they started letting them go ten minutes ago."

"G-Ma, will you grab Stump and meet me around there? I

don't want to miss him."

G-Ma protested but I pretended I didn't hear her. Now that the time had come, I was nervous about seeing Tony and realized I could dawdle and have the perfect excuse for not having to talk to him, but I hurried anyway, maybe just so I'd be able to pretend I was really disappointed when I missed him.

I didn't miss him. Mrs. Solis was walking with him toward her car when I rounded the corner.

I recognized him immediately, even though he'd changed. He was bigger now, not fat, but solid, stocky. A man. He'd been a boy when we were married. His face was broader, harder. His d eyes pierced mine when he saw me.

I wondered if he'd recognize me, but I didn't have to once our eyes met. As usual, I couldn't read much of what was going on behind his dark gaze, but he definitely recognized me.

He stopped at the front of the car and waited as I hurried up to him.

Now that I was here, I had no idea what to say to him. "Hi," I said. I swallowed. "How are you?" *Salem, your word for today is 'inane.'*

He nodded, not pointing out that he was under suspicion of murder.

"I'm sorry," I said. "Stupid question. I'm just...are you okay?"

"What do you think?" Mrs. Solis said, gesturing wildly. "He's been arrested for murder. Maybe for you that's a normal everyday thing, but not for my family."

I wasn't going to let her divert me from the mission at hand. I'd come to see if there was anything I could do for Tony, and I was going to at least try.

"I heard that. I came to see if I could help you somehow."

"How are you going to help him? Oh, I know. You're a lawyer now," she said with a sneer. "You're going to defend him in court and keep him out of prison. You went to law school and now you're here to save the day."

I took a deep breath. "I'm not a lawyer, of course. But –"

"Oh, I know, you're a detective. You're going to find the real killer and exonerate my son to make up for all the trouble you've caused in your miserable life."

"I – I'd just like to help –"

"We don't need your help. We need to find Lucinda's real murderer because the police department is obviously not going to do it." She glared at the cop standing in the doorway. The cop didn't respond. "Come on, Tony. We need to go."

I looked at Tony. "I don't really know what I can do, but I wanted you to know..." What?

"Thank you, Salem," he said softly. He looked tired and worried, but still his eyes held kindness for me.

I heard a scuffing noise behind me and looked back, prepared to see G-Ma dragging Stump on her leash. Instead I saw a reporter and a cameraman, coming straight at Tony.

"Mr. Solis, did you kill Lucinda Cruz?"

"Of course he didn't!" Mrs. Solis snapped. "He's being persecuted by the police, targeted, racially profiled. He's innocent and they're railroading an innocent man while a killer walks freely through our streets!" She waved a hand in the air and tossed her head back.

"Who do you believe is guilty of the murder of Lucinda Cruz?" the reporter asked.

"Do I look like a detective to you?" Mrs. Solis snapped. "It's not my job to solve mysteries, that's the detective's job." She took two furious steps toward the reporter, who took three steps back just as quickly.

"But I suppose that's what I'll have to become, or else the police department will send an innocent man to prison for the rest of his life. That's the situation we live in. Innocent men go to prison, and killers walk free!"

"Mom," Tony said. "Let's go."

Mrs. Solis nodded sharply and jabbed her keys at the camera. "We're going, but the people in this city should know what kind of justice system we have. If my son can go to jail for murder, no one is safe!"

"You're Tony Solis's mother?" the reporter said. They say there's no such thing as a stupid question.

"Of course I'm his mother," Mrs. Solis snapped as she lowered herself into her seat.

"And who are you?" The reporter whirled on me so quickly I didn't have time to think.

"I'm his ex-wife," I blurted.

"His ex-wife? And do you believe he murdered Lucinda Cruz?"

Oh geez. The camera was pointed at me and I felt majorly uncomfortable. "No, no. Not at all." I shook my head at the last second, as if that would add credibility. As if Tony's freedom depended on my performance.

The cameraman shifted. "Hey, aren't you the girl who found the dead body?"

Uh-oh. I froze.

"You are, right? The girl who found the body? And you're his ex-wife?"

"Uhhh," I said.

Mrs. Solis pulled her car back, then circled back so the passenger side was closest to me. Tony rolled down his window. "She had nothing to do with it," he said. "And she's not my ex-wife."

"How do you know she had nothing to do with the murder?" the reporter asked. "Do you know who did it?"

"I'm not your ex-wife?" I asked, stunned.

Tony shook his head. "I never had the marriage annulled. We're still married." The window slid silently up and the car pulled away.

Chapter Five

G-Ma, thank God, rounded the corner just then, holding Stump on stiff arms as far from her as she could manage. Stump flopped like a twenty-five pound catfish.

"I have to take care of my dog," I said. It was a poor excuse for a reprieve, but since it looked to be all that was forthcoming, I latched onto it. I grabbed Stump and feigned great concern for her. "You're okay, girl," I crooned as I scurried back to G-Ma's car. "It's okay. Don't be scared of the big bad camera."

Of course, now she was perfectly fine. G-Ma hurried to keep up with me. "What was that girl asking you? Was that the girl from Channel Eleven? She's too skinny. She doesn't look so skinny on TV. She needs to eat something. Probably got that disease that makes you too skinny."

Frankly I've always subscribed to the theory that you can't *be* too skinny, but I was too busy freaking completely out about Tony to respond. Still *married*? How was that even possible? I'd gotten the divorce papers years ago.

I climbed in and tucked Stump on my lap. I shot a quick glance back the way we'd come, but the reporter must have decided I wasn't worth chasing down. *Thank you, God.*

"So did you get to talk to him? I missed everything. That dumb dog went running out into the street and I barely caught her before she got squashed by a cop car. What did he say? Did he do it? What was his mamma saying? She looks older than me, don't you think? She's probably twenty years younger, but she looks older. It's all that gray hair."

Mrs. Solis had probably a dozen strands of gray hair mixed in with the black. G-Ma dyed her hair a solid red that made it look like a Kansas City Chief's football helmet, but there wasn't a strand of gray in it. That was important to her. She thought it made her look young. Whatever gets you through the night, I guess.

Still *married?* Ugh.

"What happens if you're married in the Catholic Church and you get divorced?"

"You don't get divorced in the Catholic church. No such thing."

"But I got divorce papers!" It was enough to make me wish I still cussed.

"Not from the church."

"No, from somebody official."

"Catholics don't divorce."

"But that's crazy."

"Well, Catholics aren't always the most logical people."

Unlike the Baptists in my family who never actually *went* to church, *Catholics* aren't logical?

I leaned back and closed my eyes. I couldn't get Tony's face out of my mind.

God, I started to pray., for Tony, for guidance, for hope, but all I could think to say was, *God, really?*

I tried to imagine Tony doing anything to hurt anyone, but it was just not possible. I knew that under the right circumstances, people are capable of almost anything. I knew that it had been a long time since I'd been around Tony, and it was possible he'd changed. But...no. He couldn't have killed anyone.

Please help him, I silently prayed. *Please do something to help him.*

How are you going to help him? By finding the real killer? Mrs. Solis had said. Mocking, as if nothing could be more ridiculous.

I wish I could. I wish I could find the real killer and give Tony his freedom back.

As if. I couldn't even figure out how I was going to get to work in the morning.

"Did I tell you I'm going to open the restaurant back up?" G-Ma asked.

Oh no. G-Ma owned a seedy motel on the Clovis highway that catered to anyone who'd ruined their credit so much they couldn't get a room in even the scariest real apartments. The side of the building advertised Daily-Weekly-Shower rates. Bless her heart, I think G-Ma really believed that people rented a room by the hour because they needed to take a shower.

When she had inherited the place from her third and last husband, it had had a coffee shop that provided maybe half of the motel's income. A bad bout of food poisoning had put them out of business. She'd tried to reopen it as another coffee shop, an Italian place (I had told her she needed more than canned spaghetti and red checked table clothes for that to work), a burger place, and a donut shop. I had gained fifteen of my extra forty during the donut phase.

"Are you sure you want to do that?" Heaven forbid if I seemed unsupportive, but I was of the opinion that G-Ma had all she could handle with the motel. "Remember how much work that was?"

"I remember, and that's why I'm not the one who's going to do it. Mario is."

"Mario? Seriously?" Okay, I was getting a little excited now. Mario had a booming and only slightly illegal business making tamales at home and selling them to local businesses. He went around all morning carrying an insulated case over his shoulder, moving in and out of offices and through warehouses with lightning speed. He always came to the grooming shop on Thursday morning and, sad as my life was at the moment, it was one of the highlights of my week.

"He's going to quit the delivery?"

"Not exactly. The stupid health department said he couldn't cook out of his kitchen at home anymore. He has to get a professional kitchen."

"Can't they just inspect his home kitchen? You know it's probably cleaner than a lot of restaurants."

"I know it. But they said it was against the law and they couldn't keep looking the other way."

"They couldn't keep looking the other way while they had a mouthful of his tamales."

"So he's going to just cook there but keep up his route?"

"He's planning to open the dining room, too. He's going to hire his nieces to work there and another nephew to help him with deliveries. He said he figures he could easily double his delivery if he had more help."

"I didn't know he was even looking for someone to help him."

I loved my job, but let's face it – getting to eat the Mario's leftovers would be a pretty awesome fringe benefit.

Stump's little feet were digging into my thighs, and I shifted her on my lap. I remembered that I wouldn't be able to take her with me if I worked for Mario. So I supposed I would stay at Bow Wow Barbers.

"Do you need to go anywhere else before I take you home?"

I did a mental inventory of my cabinet: half a box of dry spaghetti., no sauce, a can of green beans, four or five slices of bread and a quarter of a jar of peanut butter.

Then I did a mental inventory of my checking account. Next to zero dollars and zero cents, with the promise of impending arterial bleeding in the cash department, thanks to a busted block, whatever the heck that was.

"Just take me home," I said. I could eat the peanut butter and bread, and cook the spaghetti to eat plain if I had to. I didn't have the energy to lie to myself and say I was going to eat the green beans.

Although I asked God one more time for a miracle, the stupid car was still sitting in my driveway when we got home.

I opened the door, and Stump shoved all twenty-five pounds of her weight into my thighs as she launched herself, barking, up onto the front deck.

A brown cardboard box sat beside the front door.

"What's that?" I asked. As if G-Ma would know.

"It's not yours?"

I shook my head and got out.

"Wait! What if it's a bomb?"

"Why would there be a bomb on my front deck?" But I stopped.

"Maybe people hate you since they think you killed that woman."

"But I didn't touch her!"

"I know that, but you saw that news story."

Stupid Trisha! "Stump, get back!" Of course, Stump didn't listen to a thing I said unless it contained the words "treat" or "eat" or "go" in the sentence. "Stump!"

Stump jumped up on the box and tilted it over. G-Ma and I both screamed.

Nothing exploded. Stump didn't get blown through the air. Instead, a ham rolled out of the box and onto the deck.

G-Ma clutched at my shirt. "What is it? Do you hear ticking?" She comes from the era when bombs actually ticked. I'm not sure but I think they beep now – the age of technology.

"It's a ham," I said. I climbed the steps and rescued the ham before Stump pounced on it. I leaned over the box and saw four or five boxes of different kinds of food, potatoes and RiceARoni, canned tomatoes, and more green beans – okay, okay, so I'd eat the green beans – and a loaf of bread. There was also a box of cereal, a box of dry milk, and a package of Jerky Treats for Stump.

I pulled out a white piece of paper. *I didn't know if you'd have a way to get to the grocery store so I brought a few things by. Call me if you need a ride anywhere. Les*

"People are giving you food?" G-Ma frowned. "You shouldn't let people give you food."

"I wasn't here to stop him."

"Still, you need to give that back. You're not some out-of-work welfare case."

I unlocked the door and carried the box in on my hip while I tried to decide whether or not I should argue with that one. I was still trying to decide when I put the box on the table and one of the boxes inside tipped over.

"Are those chocolate covered cherries?" G-Ma reached into the box and pulled them out. "Wow. That was really nice of him to bring you chocolate covered cherries."

Although she was right, I'm not a big fan of the chocolate covered cherry. I much prefer chocolate covered chocolate. I couldn't help but notice how quickly her tone changed when she saw something she liked.

I shrugged and took the box back from her. "Yes, it was nice, but you're right, I probably shouldn't be taking food from them."

"Well..." She looked at the box. "Sometimes it is hard to swallow your pride, but you know, God doesn't like pride."

"That's true, but shouldn't we try to be self-sufficient?"

"Of course, of course, but like you said, it wasn't like you *asked* for your car to break down." She reached a hand out for the box of chocolate and then drew it back.

"No, I didn't, and I could really use these groceries. I don't have much, and I hate to keep asking you to drive me all over town." *And* there was a big box of Little Debbie Star Crunches in there. I could live on Little Debbie Star Crunches.

"I'd be happy to drive you anywhere, but you're right, you can't keep asking me to do that." She didn't elaborate on why not, exactly.

"Besides, he went to all this trouble and it would be rude to refuse it." Which one of us was going to rip into the chocolate first?

"Ungracious."

"Ungrateful. I know you can take care of yourself just fine, but sometimes it helps people if you let him help you, you know what I mean? It's better to give than receive, I've always said, so in a way you're really helping them. Can't give if there's nobody to receive, right?"

She gave up the effort and reached for the cherries. I waited till she was ready to rip through the cellophane wrapping before I stopped her. "G-Ma, are you sure? I'd hate to be accepting charity."

"Salem." She tucked the box under her arm and took my hand between her two. "I'm sure. You need to do this. For Wes."

"Les."

"Les. Exactly. He needs for you to accept this."

I nodded, echoing her solemnity. "You're right." No way was I going to tell her this wasn't the first time Les had brought me a box of food. The first time I had gone through the whole routine of trying to refuse his help, but G-Ma – despite her self-serving motivation – was right. Les liked to give. It was his gift.

Me, I hadn't discovered yet what my gift is. I'd like to give, if I wasn't always so busy just trying to keep my own head above water. I'd like to have a huge chunk of money to give away, but since I couldn't even pay my own bills, giving didn't seem to be in the works for me at the moment.

What are you going to do, find the real killer?

I unpacked the box, so caught up in that thought that it took Stump actually jumping on my foot for me to realize she was trying to get my attention. I opened the package of Jerky Treats and tossed her a couple.

What if, crazy as it sounded, I *could* actually do something to find the real killer? I mean, I was sure the police knew what they were doing, but it didn't hurt to have a fresh pair of eyes, did it?

I'd been thinking of my "help" in terms of maybe watering Tony's plants and bringing books when I visited him in prison, but wouldn't it be cool to be the hero for a change, instead of the one who screwed everything up?

I heard footsteps on the deck.

"Hey," Frank said as he came through the door. "Something smells good."

Unbelievable. Frank can smell good food even while it's still in the box.

"We're having fried ham steaks and broccoli cheese rice," I said. "Why don't you stay for dinner?" I knew he was already planning on it, but since Les had been so generous, I could pass that spirit on and let Frank get off without having to ask.

Since I worked on Saturdays, I had Thursdays off. I liked to sleep late, but that Thursday morning I woke up early fantasizing about being the one to bring Lucinda Cruz's real killer to justice. I would exonerate Tony. Trisha would cover the story for the news, and once it was all over, she would come up to me with tears in her eyes and tell me how much she admired what I'd done. Even Mrs. Solis would wrap her petite, iron-strong little hands around mine and thank me for returning her son to her. In my fantasy, I was the hero, and somehow I was back to a size six.

In reality, I was about triple a size six and didn't know anything about the victim except her name. I had no idea why the police thought Tony did it, nor how she'd been killed. So much for cracking the case.

And one big ol' honking question remained: was I really still married to Tony?

I rolled over and pulled the covers over my head. I did not want to think about that. Being married all this time meant that not only had I lived a life of wild debauchery for the past ten years, but I'd also committed a fairly horrific amount of adultery.

Of all the things I had on my plate at the moment, that one was the one that I couldn't even bring myself to look at fully. Well...that and sleeping with Scott. Breaking Trisha's heart – I would just as soon I'd never heard about that one.

"God," I whispered. "There's so much pain I've caused, and I feel like I'm drowning in it. I am truly, truly sorry. I want to find some way to make things right. I can't stand this horrible guilt, and I need to do something, but I have no idea *what*. Please show me something I can do."

I lay there quietly and waited for God to answer me. Here's the thing that's been driving me crazy lately. I've been reading all these Christian romances that Les's wife gave me, and in them when the people pray, God answers them, in all capital letters. They know it's God, they hear His voice in their heads, and they know exactly how to respond to it, because there's no question in their minds God is speaking to them. He talks to them in all caps.

God *never* talks to me in all caps. He doesn't talk to me in all caps or all lower case or even in Morse code. I pray, I ask, and I hear as much as I do when I hold a conch shell to my ear.

I listened harder. "Anything, God," I said. "Anything I can do to make things better. Anything at all." I waited.

Stump jumped on my shoulders and stuck her cold wet nose on my neck.

I sighed and shoved myself up. "Thanks, God. That's clear as mud."

I fed Stump and took my shower, going through options in my mind about how I could make things better for both Trisha and

Tony, but everything I came up with involved large sums of money. Like hiring an ace private detective and attorney for Tony, and sending Trisha and Scott off on a two-week tropical getaway. I told God if he'd send me a winning lottery ticket, I would definitely do both those things, but I wasn't exactly rooted in faith that He would. Although I hadn't read it in the Bible yet, I don't think God looks all that favorably on gambling. Granted, there are a lot of parts I hadn't gotten to.

I got ready and did my prayer time, but I couldn't concentrate. I kept wondering, "What if I'm really married right now? What if Trisha went home after our talk and had a big fight with Scott? What if Tony is convicted of this murder and spends the rest of his life in jail?

"I'm sorry, I can't focus right now, God. You know what's on my mind." Give it to God, Les always says. "I give it all to you, God. Except...if you could just send me an idea of how to help, I'd really appreciate it."

I got up not feeling one bit better. Where was that peace that passed all understanding? My stomach was still in knots, and only a Little Debbie Star Crunch would make it better. That helped, but then I felt fat.

I wasn't going to be able to chill out until I did something, I decided. I was a person of action. I decided to get over myself and call Bobby Sloan. After all, I'd found the body. It was perfectly normal that I'd be interested in the case.

I made some toast to fortify myself for the call. I'd spent so much time avoiding law enforcement, it seemed weird to actually be calling one of them voluntarily. The more I thought about it, the more nervous I became. So I made some more toast and put peanut butter on it.

That actually made me feel better, so I made one more piece and then looked up the number.

During the ensuing runaround to track Bobby down, I polished off the toast and the Star Crunch I promised myself I would save for lunch. Thinking of Elvis and searching the refrigerator for anything else I could stuff in my mouth, I was caught off guard when he actually picked up the line.

"Sloan."

"Umm." I swallowed the croutons I'd bought to go on the salads I never made and cleared my throat. "Bobby? This is Salem. Grimes. From the – the you know – I found the –" What did they call them? Deceaseds?

"Yeah, Salem, of course. Did you remember something?"

"Oh, um, no. No, I didn't. I just wanted to check and see if you'd made any progress on the case."

"Why?"

"Why?" What kind of question was that? "Because, you know, there's a murderer loose and all. Plus stupid Channel 11 ran my picture with the story and I – well, that's made me kind of nervous, that the killer would link me with it all, somehow. So I just thought..." Actually, since Trisha's story made it sound like I *was* the murderer, the worst the killer was likely to do was send me a thank you card. But still...

"Well, I don't think you have anything to worry about. We have a suspect. "

"Look, Bobby, I know you arrested Tony Solis, but he's innocent. He's not the guy."

"What makes you say that?"

"Because I know Tony, and I know he wouldn't do anything like that. Really." *Go ahead. Take the word of a girl with three*

DUIs and a couple of bad check charges.

"I'm sure the jury will take that into consideration, Salem."

"Bobby, seriously, he couldn't have done it."

"When was the last time you talked to Tony?"

"Yesterday afternoon."

"What did you talk about?"

"I just asked if there was anything I could do to help him."

"And what did he say?"

"I don't remember. His mother was ranting, and Tony said we weren't really divorced. That's when I freaked out and left."

"You're not divorced? What do you mean?"

"Tony and I were married a long time ago, while we were still in high school, but I got divorced, and evidently he didn't. It's a whole Catholic thing." Uh-oh. That sounded kind of anti-Catholic, and I didn't mean for it to. "You're not Catholic, are you?"

"No, I think I'm Presbyterian. So you're married to our main suspect?"

"No – well, yes, but...why do you think he killed that girl?"

"You don't really think I'm going to talk about an active investigation, do you?"

"Not to just anyone off the street, no, but I did find the body. That entitles me to something, right?"

"Wrong. When was the last time you talked to Tony before yesterday?"

I thought for a second. "I guess it was when I moved out."

"And when was that?"

"Ten years ago in June."

Bobby was silent for a long time. "You haven't spoken to your husband in over ten years."

"It sounds weird, I know."

"Not for you, Salem."

"Thanks."

"I'm going to need you to come back in and answer a few more questions."

My heart thumped. I *knew* it was a mistake to call. "Why?"

"Because that's what happens in a murder investigation. We ask lots of questions."

"I answered them already."

"Maybe you'll think of something new when I ask them again. Can you come in this afternoon?"

For the first time I was actually grateful for the busted block. "My car broke down, and I don't have a way up there."

"I can send a patrolman –"

"I know what I'll do," I interrupted. "I have a friend who's coming by later this morning to help me with some errands. I'll have her drop me off there. I'm not sure what time it'll be. Probably between two and three."

I hung up in a panic. Send a *patrolman*?

Poor Tony. If his freedom was depending on me, he was in big trouble.

I walked around a while and decided I might feel a little less awful with clothes on. But then I faced a new hurdle. I could not get my pants zipped.

"Stupid cheap crap dryer. Got too hot and shrunk my pants," I said to Stump.

She looked back at me solemnly, her expression clearly stating that if I needed to lie to myself, she wouldn't call me on it. She's supportive that way.

I heaved a great sigh and collapsed on the bed. Defying all the laws of physics, I lay flat on the bed, raised my knees and tugged until I got them zipped. I tried three times to sit up before I made it all the way upright. I sat on the edge of the bed, breathing hard and counting the red spots that swam around in front of me.

"This is not good," I said to Stump. "I think I've hit an all-time high."

She blinked at me and yawned.

I shoved myself off the bed, already feeling cramped from stuffing my internal organs into a space they were not meant to occupy, and I had to grab the wall to keep from keeling over. I made my way down the hallway to the bar in the kitchen.

Tony had an aunt named Sylvia that I hadn't completely alienated. In fact, she brought her brown poodle into Flo's so I could groom it. We were almost friends, but I think that was mostly because she didn't like Mrs. Solis (old sisterly grudge) and being friendly to me was her way of being defiant. But still, I could use that to my advantage. I looked up her number and called her.

"I'm really worried about Tony, and I'm trying to think of some way I can help him," I said when Sylvia answered the phone at the laundromat she owned.

"I know, sweetie, we're all worried. I went to church and lit a candle for him last night."

"That's good," I said. *I was thinking of something a little more concrete.* Unfortunately, nothing more concrete seemed to be forthcoming. I gave her my cell number and hung up.

I had to get out of the house and do something. Not knowing what else to do, I returned to the scene of the crime. Maybe a clue would jump out at me.

I whistled for Stump.

"Remember yesterday, when we went for the walk? We're going to do a little more today." Church was probably three miles away. I wanted to lose weight, right? Maybe this broken block thing would end up being a great blessing. On the plus side, if I did manage to make it all the way to the church, I would be only a few blocks from the police station, so I could follow through on my word to Bobby. Yay.

"We're going to walk to the church and talk to George," I told her, trying to sound cheerful so I could psyche myself up. George was the man who ran all the maintenance services for the church. The church contracted a private cleaning company – Tony's company, as it turned out – but they worked through George.

I knew George because one time at my AA meeting I'd remarked that the coffee was a little strong. I swear, that's all I said. But word got back to George, and he was waiting outside our meeting room the next week, telling me that he'd talked to the staff and they'd tried to make it a little less strong. He wanted me to taste and see how I liked it. He looked nervous, like a concierge in a five-star hotel like he was anxious to please the temperamental penthouse guest, except I was a down-on-my-luck drunk at an AA meeting, and all I'd done was say the coffee was a little strong.

Every week after that, George acted as if his chief job in life was keeping me from going off on him about the coffee. I swear all I did was say it was a little strong. From the fallout you would have thought I'd thrown chairs and threatened to jump off the building. I wonder how he would react if I *really* pitched a fit about something. Like how freaking hot it was in that room in the winter.

Carrying Stump was, again, like carrying a twenty-five-pound sack of flour, but cuter. She watched the traffic go by and occasionally yawned contentedly, as if she got lugged around all the time, which she did, I guess.

I was determined not to get frustrated. I kept thinking that I wanted to be more like Les, upbeat and happy, no matter what was going on. I would just do that. I got to choose how I felt, right?

I would be like Les. Les had told me that morning when he visited me in jail that if I turned my life over to God, I would be so filled with the joy of the Holy Spirit that I would want to shout it from the rooftops. I would sing God's praises and my heart would fill to overflowing with love for Him. I couldn't *help* but be happy all the time. He said those exact words, and he had such a big ol' grin, I believed him.

Naturally, all that sounded like such a good deal to me. In fact, I thought even now that if I could choose between a winning Power Ball ticket and that overwhelming feeling of joy in my heart, I'd probably take the joy. Probably. Maybe I could negotiate a 5-out-of-6 Power Ball *and* the joy.

Despite my mind-over-matter attempts, I hadn't had either so far, and it was starting to bug me. God's love was supposed to be there for everyone. I checked my heart. Nope. My mind just spun with thoughts about Tony, about Trisha. I felt no overwhelming feeling of joy, no assurance that God loved me and was there for me; just worry and guilt and the itch to do something to make it stop.

I looked down at Stump. Now there was someone who knew she was loved no matter what. She had her pink tongue sticking out, watching the traffic go by as if she was queen of the world. She wasn't worried about the electric bill, or how we were going to afford a new car, or what was going to happen when the food in Les's box ran out. She didn't have to feel bad about something she'd done ten years ago.

"God," I said out loud, not really caring that I looked like a looney-tune walking down a busy street, carrying a fat dog and talking to myself. "I don't even know what to pray for anymore. A little help. With anything. Money. A new car. And you know when I say 'new car' I'm not actually expecting a *new* car, I just mean something new to me, something dependable. I don't care what it is. And some way to make things right for Tony and for Trisha. I'm not expecting you to make things right for me, God. I know this is my responsibility, and I want to be the one to make it right. I'm not trying to shirk my duty, seriously I'm not. But I need you to *show* me how. Throw me a bone, God. Anything. Just a little something to let me know you're in my corner."

I heard a screech of tires and a horn blaring right behind me. I jumped to the right just in time to keep from being mowed down by Viv in her big green Cadillac.

She pulled to the curb and rolled the passenger window down. "You heading up to the church?"

I wasn't sure if I should tell her the truth or not. Viv was only slightly safer to ride with than G-Ma, maybe not any safer at all.

On the other hand, I was still a long way from church, and an hour trip could turn into five minutes.

"Ummm," I said, still hesitating.

"Get in, I'll give you a lift. I'm going to choir practice."

I supposed it would be okay. Stump could serve as an airbag.

"What are you going up there for?"

"I want to talk to George and see if he knows anything about the murder."

"Good idea!"

I really liked Viv. She'd been coming to our AA meeting for a couple of months. She reminded me of G-Ma, only more fun. Our church was big and had three services, and Viv went to "big church" – a big beautiful sanctuary with a few dozen stained glass masterpieces and the biggest organ within four states. That was the service where the doctors and bankers and politicians went. I went to the little church that meets in the Family Life Center (i.e., a gym with folding chairs set out), where we sing to guitars and bongos, and the preacher has a ponytail. We call it Groovy Church.

Viv seemed to have a lot of enthusiasm for things that didn't really concern her. My hunch was, she was bored. She'd told us at the meeting that she'd been married five times, and from a few of the things she let slip I thought a couple of them had a lot of money. She had some interesting stories, but unfortunately most of them involved drinking to excess and then doing something either stupid or completely unbelievable.

The cool thing for me, though, was that Viv seemed to like me. When I talked at meetings, she always smiled and listened and acted really supportive. I needed all the support I could get.

It occurred to me it might be good to have Viv in my corner when I talked to George. He might be willing to open up a little more with Viv than he would with me. Viv had that same dogged determination and inability to take no for an answer that G-Ma had. Sometimes it's good to have someone like that around, as long as you're not the one trying to tell them no.

She'd been watching the news about Lucinda Cruz, too. Seeing someone's dead body makes you form some kind of connection to them.

"You know the guy they arrested? He's my ex-husband." I didn't feel like going into the whole ex-or-not-ex issue.

"You're kidding!"

"He couldn't have done it, though. I mean, I know everyone says that about people they know, but seriously...if Tony didn't kill me while we were married, he's simply not capable of killing anyone."

Viv laughed and slapped the steering wheel. "Know what you mean! I gave a couple of mine a decent case for justifiable homicide, myself. Why do they think he did it?"

"No idea. That's what I'm trying to find out." I told her about the cleaning company that Tony owned, and how Lucinda worked for him.

"Oh, I know. I watch the news."

Of course she did. I nodded and felt like a goof.

"I guess it's got something to do with their working relationship, then," I said lamely.

"I'm sure. It's a double shame if he is innocent. That kind of accusation can ruin a person's life, even if they are *exonerated*." She took her hands off the wheel and made air quotes. The car shot to the right and almost clipped the curb before she swung it back to the left edge of the lane. "How do you think this is going to affect his relationship with the church, or with *any* of his clients, for that matter?"

I frowned as I hung onto the armrest for all I was worth. I hadn't thought that far ahead.

"Do you think people in this church are going to stand for an accused murderer working up here after hours, with keys to all the rooms? What about the offices and banks he cleans? Who's going to trust his company after this?"

"He cleans offices and banks, too?"

"That's what *The Journal* said."

Well, that was why she knew more than I did. The *Lubbock*

Journal cost fifty cents, whereas television – where I got my news – was free.

"What else did *The Journal* say?"

"Just that the girl, whatever her name is –"

"Lucinda Cruz."

"Right, Lucinda, it said she came from Mexico about six months ago, and went to work for Solis' company about six weeks ago, cleaning offices and the church and a couple of other places."

So, I hadn't destroyed Tony's life too completely. It sounded like he'd found a way to be successful, despite my interference.

"Did the paper say anything about her? The girl? Like if she had any enemies or anything? What she did before she went to work for Tony?"

"I don't think so." She pulled up in front of the church and barely grazed the sidewalk with one tire. A successful landing.

"Do you still have the article?" I was really curious about Tony. I'd seen different people around, emptying wastebaskets and shampooing carpets. I wondered why I'd never seen him.

"I'll look. I hope Louise Murtz hasn't been messing around with my music again. She always goes in there and fiddles with my stuff till I can't find a blasted thing."

I got out of the car and hefted Stump with me.

"Cute dog," Viv said. "She's good natured. I like dogs."

"Maybe you could tell my grandmother that. She thinks Stump is constantly on the verge of doing something stinky."

Viv clucked and rubbed Stump's ears. Stump thumped her leg, which was a bit awkward for me since her leg was against my ribs at the moment. "Nothing stinky about this sweetheart."

"Viv, would you mind doing me a favor?" I asked as we walked up the sidewalk. "If you're not in too big a hurry, I mean."

"Of course."

"Would you mind talking to George for me? He doesn't seem all that comfortable with me –"

"It's just because you got so irate about the coffee."

"All I said was it was a little strong."

Viv raised an eyebrow.

"I swear. Anyway, would you mind asking him if he could show us around where the police were looking? I'm afraid if I ask him he'll think I'm up to no good."

"Mmm-hhhmm. And what are you up to?"

I sighed. "I don't even know. Trying to figure out a way to help Tony. I'm worried about him and I want to find some way to help him."

"Well, I'll admit I'd like to have a look myself, just for curiosity's sake. If there's some reason we can't, George will just tell us no and that will be the end of that."

She marched to George's office with me following in her Shalimar-scented wake, wondering if the pantsuit she wore actually cost as much as it looked like. She tapped on George's door, and within twenty seconds we had the go-ahead to go into any room in the church except the offices. George looked taken aback when he saw that I held Stump.

"I hope it's okay if I carry my dog with me," I said. "It's too hot to leave her in the car. I won't put her down."

George looked uncomfortable. "Well...'

"Of course it'll be fine," Viv said. She patted George's arm. "If anyone asks, we'll just say she's a seeing-eye dog. Where do we start?"

"Ummm," George said. "Yes, well..." He looked from me to Viv, then back at Stump, lying like a slug in my arms. "Okay, yes.

First, we'll go to the storeroom."

He led us to a squeaky elevator and pushed the down button. I was a little dismayed. I didn't go to the basement much because it was creepy and cavernous, and I knew myself well enough to know what places I need to avoid if I didn't want to give myself a heart attack. I wasn't comfortable being down there even with Viv and George right beside me. I hugged Stump and she grumbled. George eyed her as if she was about to attack him.

He led us down a few dark linoleum-tiled hallways and around dark corners. "The police were in here a lot, of course," he said as he stopped at a solid metal door and pulled out a large ring of keys. The door opened onto a room full of equipment: floor buffers, carts with wastebaskets and cleaning equipment, electrical cords, and mops and brooms.

I wasn't sure what I was looking for. A murder weapon. A clue that would be obvious to me, but that the police had overlooked. I knew, of course, that was unlikely. In my experience, only the police in movies are that dumb.

Viv and I walked around the room for a minute, as if we knew what we were looking for. I started to get depressed again, and shifted Stump to my other hip. I hoped Tony's cleaning business clients included some good lawyers.

"Where all did the police look, George?" Viv asked, poking her way around a floor buffer.

"Oh, the whole building."

"That must have taken a while."

He shrugged. "A couple of hours. I went with them and unlocked all the doors as we went. Most of the time they were in here and then out on the stairwell." He nodded toward another sturdy metal door on the opposite side of the closet.

I hadn't realized we were on the other side of the wall from where the body had been found. "Can we – can we go out there? Please," I remembered to say, so George wouldn't think I'd demanded it.

He shrugged again. "That detective told me they had all they needed and we were free to go, so I suppose it would be okay." He pulled the key ring from his pants pocket again.

"The detective, was it Detective Sloan?"

George's face went slack with panic, like a kid who'd just been called on in class for an answer he didn't know.

"Tall, dark hair, nose a little crooked?" *Chest like a marble slab? Cute dimples that stretch an inch-and-a-half long when he laughs?*

George nodded. "Yes, that was him!" He breathed a sigh of relief.

I smiled brilliantly at him and I wished I had a gold star to put on his forehead. It wasn't as if this was revelatory information, since I already knew Bobby was working this case, but he seemed so pleased with himself for being able to answer.

Stump was getting heavy again, and I wished I could put her down, but I was afraid poor George would have a stroke. I shifted her again and rubbed her ears. "Did he talk to you about the investigation at all?"

"Well, ummm, ahh, no, no, not really. Not much. Just, 'What's through that door?' 'Who uses this office?' Stuff like that. They asked for the surveillance tapes and what we knew about the, ummm, the girl." He inclined his head toward the door. Then he brightened, as if remembering something. "But I did hear him telling another officer that it looked like the murder had taken place in this room and then she'd been dragged outside, because there were marks in the dust or something."

I nodded. Everything looked clean to me, but I supposed the crime scene guys knew how to find clues.

I shook my head. "I don't know why, but I had it in my head that she was thrown from the bell tower."

"I'm so sorry," George said. "I don't believe that's – well, as I *understood* things that's not the way it happened, but of course the police might be wrong, they are sometimes, you know, but from what I *heard...*" He trailed off, the panic back in his eyes. He glanced again at Stump and inched toward the door.

"I'm sure the police know more than I do –"

"Well, I don't know about *that* –"

"I just had that picture in my mind from the first, you know, because her neck was all crooked like it was broken, I suppose."

"That's funny, that's the same thing I thought," Viv said. "Shoot. I hoped we'd get to go up in the bell tower and look around."

George's eyes got wide. "Oh, you can't go up there." He snapped his mouth shut and looked at me as if he was about to cry. "I am truly, truly sorry. The trustees have strictly forbidden me from letting anyone up there. It's the trustees. Believe me, if it were up to me, I would take you up there in a heartbeat." He put his hand over his heart. "On my life, I would take you up there."

Viv stepped close and put her arm around George. "You are just the sweetest thing! Don't worry about it, hon, we were just talking. Nobody blames you."

George looked both relieved, and shocked that Viv was hugging him. He threw a glance over at me to make sure I wasn't going to pick up a mop and bean him. I smiled and nodded. Geez, what was it with this guy? I was beginning to wonder if maybe I'd done something to him when I was drinking, too.

"We'll just quit playing amateur detective and get out of your hair," Viv said. "Thank you so much for showing us around."

"Oh, anytime. As long as it not someplace that's off limits, like that bell tower, why, you just ask and I'm there. Anytime. I mean it. Any time." He blushed and backed up again, bumping into the door.

"Well, I doubt we'll need to do any more investigating. As I'm sure you can understand, this situation has been weighing heavily on our minds and we've become a bit preoccupied with it all. But it's not as if we're going to solve the mystery by looking around the basement storeroom."

"I suppose not," George said with a laugh as we left the room. "Although believe me, you're not the first ones to be preoccupied with this. As you can imagine, we've been getting all kinds of calls. It's all anyone can talk about."

I tagged after them, thanking George as we left him at his office. I wasn't ready to go yet, but Viv was right. It wasn't as if we were really going to discover anything. I'd hoped that something would have leapt out at me, but it didn't look that way.

I dragged after Viv, wondering what I was going to do with the rest of my day. I needed to see if I could get something done about my car, but I put that off because I knew there was going to be no good news in that direction. I was debating whether or not to try and hike up to Flo's so I could arrange a ride to work the next morning when Viv ducked suddenly into a dark alcove along the hallway and yanked me after her.

I yelped as I bumped into the wall behind her. "What - ?"

"Look what I got!" She held out her hand, where George's keys rested. "Can you believe it? After all these years, I've still got it!" Her bony fingers clutched around the keys and she shook her hand in triumph. "He didn't feel a thing, did he?"

Chapter Six

I blinked. "Viv? Did you –?" My jaw dropped, and I stared at the keys in her hand.

She giggled and pressed her hands against mine. "Shhh. Don't look like that, it's not as if I took his wallet, although I could have!" She giggled again, enough triumphant light in her eyes to bring a glow to the dark recess where we hid. "I'll bet anything I could have."

She heaved a great satisfied sigh and smoothed her jacket. "Well now, that felt good. I haven't had a thrill like that in years. So are we going up or not?" She leaned around me to peer down the hallway.

I was too stunned by the revelation that she was a pickpocket to grasp what she was asking.

"Going up where?"

"To the bell tower, of course. Why else would I have lifted his keys? You heard him yourself. He would let us in any other room in the building."

I wasn't quite sure what to say. I wanted to feel around the edge of Viv's neck to see if she was an imposter with a Viv mask.

"I can't believe you took his keys and he didn't even know it. *I* didn't know it, and I was standing right there."

"Smooth as butter, that's what they always used to say about me. Buttercup was my nickname." She raised her brows and gave an unabashedly proud grin. "Come on."

"Don't you have choir rehearsal to get to?" I asked. She ignored me. Clearly, she had more interesting things on her agenda.

It only took three false starts before Viv found the right key to get us into the stairwell.

I don't know what I was expecting, something gothic and majestic, I suppose. The door opened onto a small group of rooms – two offices and a teeny bathroom, all with rotten orange carpet and used-to-be-white walls. More stairs led up to another level. Every inch within view, with the exception of a narrow path through the middle, was full of junk: old desks, filing cabinets, cardboard boxes ripped at the corner and spilling out the sides.

I looked around, disillusioned. "This is what the trustees have forbidden people to see?"

Viv was already halfway up the first set of switchback stairs. "Probably they don't want people to see what a mess it is in here."

I could relate to that.

For an old lady, Viv could scurry up the stairs pretty darned quickly. I was huffing to keep up with her. The stairs were steep and narrow, switching back every ten steps, and my tight pants were not making this easy. Every other set of stairs opened onto an identical set of offices, with a nearly identical mess.

My legs felt like logs after the third set of stairs. The third story had even more junk, if that was possible. Two long racks held play costumes – or else someone just had bizarre taste in clothes – and boxes full of fabric of some sort, blankets or draperies or something.

"Must be the stuff from the church's big musical," Viv said.

I knew they put on a play every year, but I had never gone. Tickets were forty bucks a pop.

"This place is a disaster area," I said, flipping through costumes on wire hangers. I shifted Stump and tugged at the waistband of my jeans. All the exertion seemed to be stretching them some, but they were still uncomfortable. "Someone could murder eight or ten people up here and no one would ever know."

There was another door at the top of this set of stairs, and after rattling the knob, Viv pulled out her set of stolen keys. I waited on the steps and tried to appear like I wasn't breathing hard.

It dawned on me that Viv picking George's pocket was, of course, illegal. Since I knew about it and hadn't done anything, I was either an accessory or an accomplice. Plus I was now probably trespassing; not good for someone on probation.

"Are we sure we want to do this?" I said. "I really don't need to be in any more trouble."

Viv waved a hand carelessly. "You only get in trouble if you get caught, and we're not going to get caught."

She opened the door onto a stone-walled room without interior walls. It was the same size as the office suites we'd just moved through – these rooms made up a five- or six-story bell tower – but this section looked bigger because it was open. At about every story level, window openings a foot wide and four feet long cut into the walls. The openings were covered with a wire mesh on the inside and white shutters on the outside. The ceiling hung a good three stories above us, and a single spiral staircase stretched through the center of the room. The staircase had a disturbingly rusty quality to it.

"We're going up there, aren't we?" I said, somewhat fatalistically. I tugged again at my jeans.

"I didn't pick George's pocket so I could look at old costumes from *The King and I.*"

She darted up the stairs like a squirrel racing up the trunk of a tree. I looked at Stump who, since we were so far off the ground, now weighed about a thousand pounds. She looked at me. "We wanted to do this," I reminded her, as if this had been partly her idea.

I heaved a sigh and followed after Viv, feeling even more like Jabba the Hut as I dragged one stiff leg after another up the metal risers. I had to keep Stump tucked under my left arm so I could hold onto the skinny metal handrail with my right.

About halfway up, the stairs began to sway a little. Not as if they were crashing over, exactly, but enough to be alarming. I looked down and readjusted my estimation that it was three stories. It had to be at least five.

"Kind of wobbly, isn't she?" Viv called down to me. It didn't sound like she was even breathing hard.

I, on the other hand, was certain I was having a heart attack either from the exertion or the fear of the whole staircase coming undone at the top and crashing me into one of those brick walls.

I looked up and felt a sinking in my stomach when I realized we still had a long way to go. Ever one to look on the negative side, I mentally ran through all the scenarios that could possible play out here. The stairs really *could* come loose at the ceiling and topple over. There would be an investigation, of course, which would conclude that Viv and I had stolen the keys and entered a "forbidden area," and that I had exceeded the weight limit of the stairs, causing them to come crashing down, costing the church a huge sum in repairs and landing me in jail for probation violation. Or, I could give way to the panic building inside me until I cowered, frozen on the risers, and Viv would have to call 911 and firemen would come, television crews would appear, the shutters and wire would be taken off those big openings and they'd haul me out in a cherry picker, the same way they got the big carillon bells inside. Again, Viv and I would be caught with the stolen keys, and I would go to jail.

My legs began to shake. I don't know if it was from muscle exhaustion or nerves, but it certainly didn't make me feel any more secure. Every step I took seemed to make the stairs sway more.

I thought that if I kept moving round and round quick enough, even if the stairs *did* come unmoored, my weight would keep the stairs from toppling too far in any one direction. I jogged up. Well, I jogged about three steps. Then I stopped and bent over, resting Stump's weight on the steps. I was terrified to let go of her, though, in case she went through the steps and plummeted to the floor.

"Almost there," Viv sang out.

I opened my mouth and huffed out a shaky groan.

"Are you okay?"

"I have no idea," I wheezed. I saw spots. I picked Stump back up with a groan.

"Oh," Viv said, poking her head through the landing. "I thought this was the top."

You've got to be freaking kidding me, I thought, because I was breathing too hard to speak. *We've been climbing for days. This wasn't the top?*

I rounded the last step of the spiral staircase and groaned again to see another big open room exactly like the one we'd just climbed through, except not as tall. Wind whistled through the openings and blew at the sweat on the back of my neck.

Viv walked around the room, scuffing at the concrete floor. "They really should clean up here. It looks like a flock of pigeons has been living up here."

It was pretty nasty, but I wasn't going to volunteer to bring my mop and bucket up there. I looked through the round hole above us. "This is the last flight of stairs." I saw a solid ceiling above.

Viv didn't answer.

I looked over at her. "What's wrong?"

She wrinkled her nose and looked at the stairs. "We don't really need to go all the way up, do we?"

Even though every muscle in my body screamed for me to agree with her, I said, "Are you kidding? This story is half the length of the last one. We're not going to quit now when we're this close."

"There's probably nothing up there."

Probably, she was right, but I felt this overwhelming need to go all the way to the top and see. Maybe it was a God thing, telling me how to help Tony. That's what I'd been praying for, right? Maybe there really was something up there that would point to the real murderer.

"I'm going," I said. As soon as I caught my breath.

"Are you sure? That last set of stairs made me a little nervous."

She did look nervous, I realized. She wasn't sweating or breathing hard like I was, but she did look edgy. I'd been too caught up in my own impending heart attack to think about Viv's health. She had to be eighty-something. Maybe I shouldn't be asking her to climb a bunch of stairs.

Third negative scenario. Viv has a heart attack instead of me, I have to call 911 to get help, the aforementioned EMTs come, I'm blamed for stealing the keys because – after all – who's going to blame the old lady with the heart attack?

"Are you going to be okay?" There was no way I'd be able to carry her and Stump down those six thousand spiral stairs. I didn't want to dwell on which one of them I would save if push came to shove.

"I'm fine, I just..." She wrinkled her nose again and looked up. "You go first."

"Are you sure? Because I don't know CPR."

She shooed a hand at me. "You're more likely to need CPR than I am. I just don't want to go first."

I didn't see what difference it made which one went first, so I shrugged and started back up. I kept looking down to make sure she was okay, but all I saw was the top of her curly white head. My left arm screamed and I had to stop a couple of times to shift Stump around.

I stopped as I cleared the landing. "You okay?" I called down.

Something beat the air near me, slammed into my cheek, and flew off.

I screamed and jumped up and down on the metal stairs, much like I had Monday when I'd found Lucinda Cruz's dead body. Stump scrambled in my arms and I clutched her so tight to me that she grunted.

My panicked jumping rang out on the stairs, and my scream sent several hundred pigeons into their own panic mode. The air came alive with gray and white. Below me Viv screamed, too, clutching my pants leg. Her grasp scared me again and I jumped more, terrified beyond all reason that some pigeon/boogey monster had me in its evil clutches. Every time I jumped, the stairs rang out like the bell above me and pigeon poop flew to the floor below.

"Stop jumping!" Viv screamed.

"Let go of my leg!"

"Be still!"

"Let go!"

We went back and forth like that a few more times before it dawned on me that, even if we *were* able to get through this without heart attacks for either of us, our screams were very likely to draw unwanted attention. I could still end up going to jail for trespassing.

"Okay, okay, okay," I breathed, my heart thudding from the stupid bird that had flown into me. I rubbed at my cheek with my shoulder, creeped out and fighting the heebie jeebies.

"That bird scared me half to death." I cleared the last few steps on rubbery legs.

"I knew that was going to happen. That's why I didn't want to go first."

I stepped aside to let Viv up, fighting the urge to put a shoe in her face and send her tumbling back down the stairs. "You *knew* that was going to happen? Could you have warned me?"

"Sorry, I have a thing about pigeons. They're disgusting."

"The one that just flew into my face certainly was." I moved over to the opening to let the wind knock some of the disease-ridden pigeon germs off me. I shuddered and decided as soon as we got down I was going home to take a boiling hot shower.

"This place is awful," Viv said. "Pigeon poop everywhere. Glad

I'm not wearing open toed shoes."

I turned and looked around the room. Three pipes with graduating bells stretched across the width of the small room, and one huge bell hung in front. That was probably the one that rang every quarter hour.

Viv was right. Every inch of that room was covered with pigeon poop, dripping off the bells, piled in little mountains on the floor. I would imagine murder clues would be fairly easy to find in a bunch of poop. I sagged as I realized I was not going to be able to put down Stump, something I'd been looking very forward to. At least I could shift her to the other arm now.

I stared out at the church below us. It was a beautiful building, with black slate peaked roofs and dormer windows, spires, arches and stained glass everywhere. It was about 75 years old. Five or six years ago, the church had bought the building on the next corner and then added on to it, constructing a connection between the two buildings that housed the new gym and a bunch of meeting rooms. They'd designed the new building in the same Spanish Gothic style as the old building, and they'd mostly succeeded in making the whole thing look like one humongous building. From this height, though, you could see the differences between the old and new.

"I never realized how much the building snaked around," I said as I looked out. The breeze blew against my temples and I thought, given time, I might recover enough to make the climb back down. A week, say, or two.

Viv joined me at the window. She nodded toward a courtyard in the center of everything that held a few benches and some shrubs. The courtyard sat between the old and new building, surrounded by an atrium on either side. "They couldn't build over that because that's where the tunnels all connect."

"Tunnels?" I'd never heard anything about tunnels. But then, I wasn't on all the church committees like Viv was. She was probably privy to all kinds of information including salaries, who the big donors were (since she was probably one of them) and various infighting gossip.

"Back before the old church burned down –"

"The old church burned down?" I said.

She gave me a look. "Do you ever look at the pictures on the hallway walls? Ever see the one with the burned out church? Blackened beams? Rubble?"

"Ummm," I said. Because no, I did not look at the pictures on the walls. Apparently I had missed out on some crucial information.

"The first building burned down back in the forties, and they built this one to replace it. There used to be underground tunnels that went all over downtown, but maybe thirty years ago or so they decided to close them down because some were crumbling. Four or five of them converged right there." She nodded again at the courtyard. "That's why we don't have a fountain there, either. Too heavy. Can you imagine what would happen if some of those old coots were sitting there watching the fountain bubble and the whole thing just fell in?" She cackled as if she was not an old coot herself.

"Why don't they just fill in the tunnels?" I asked.

"Too expensive. The city filled in some of them, but some of the tunnels are still in use. The city and the church got into a big battle about whose responsibility it was to fill in the tunnels, and eventually the city won." She shook her head. "In the end, the trustees decided it would be a lot cheaper to make the courtyard and avoid building over that space. Marvin Duggan was plenty PO'd," she said. "He wanted to put a big fountain like at The Bellagio in Las Vegas."

Which would go really well with Spanish Gothic, I thought. God probably put that tunnel there so a hundred years later Marvin Duggan couldn't build a Bellagio fountain in the middle of West Texas.

"What are we doing up here?" I said with a sigh, more to myself than to Viv. I walked around the room, shaking some feeling back into my left arm. I'd really thought God was leading me to something up here. I turned back to the window and looked down – *way* down, geez! – at the place where Lucinda Cruz's body had sprawled. I didn't know why I'd been so sure she'd fallen – or been pushed – from up here. Wire mesh covered all the openings and aside from a few small tears here and there, the mesh was intact. Holes big enough for a pigeon to get through, but not big enough to push a body through.

So much for listening to God, I thought sourly.

"Excellent," I muttered. "All we've uncovered is a criminal buildup of pigeon doo-doo. I don't know why I thought we could solve a mystery better than the professionals."

Viv snorted. "I'll bet we could if we had all the information and tools they have. We're handicapped because we can't get at the evidence."

"I know. I ought to go ahead and talk to Bobby again, see if I can talk him into giving me some information.

"Bobby who?"

"Bobby Sloan. He's the detective on this case."

"Salem! Why didn't you say that in the first place?" Her eyes snapped and she grinned. "You have connections."

I wrinkled my nose. "I don't know how good those connections are." Should I tell her I was supposed to meet him this afternoon?

"You're a *woman*, you can capitalize on whatever connection you have."

I tried to picture me giving Bobby a sultry pout and positioning myself to allow him a view of my cleavage. Even in the best case scenario of my imagination, it came out a little too Miss Piggy for my taste.

"I suppose I could talk to him, but using my womanly wiles is not really an option."

"Well, I can't use mine, they're all dried up."

"What do you think I ought to ask him?"

"Find out what kind of evidence they have on your ex-husband."

"I think he's my ex," I said without thinking.

Viv looked at me.

"It's possible we're still married."

"Honey, you *were* drinking a lot."

"It's complicated. It would be good to know what they've got, though."

"It's as simple as that, then."

Simple. "I actually already tried to get information from him this morning, but he wasn't talking. He did tell me to come back to the station this afternoon, though." With Viv accompanying me, it didn't seem so scary.

I sighed and turned back to the window. As much as I dreaded the thought of talking to Bobby again, I liked the idea of looking at him again. "What a mess," I said, looking out at the roof of the church. "We'd better get back before George realizes –"

BONGGGG!!!

The earth shook, and I felt my knees give way.

Viv's eyes bulged at me, then she headed for the stairs as quick as her little old lady legs would carry her.

The trip back down didn't take nearly as long, probably because it sounded like freaking Michael and all the archangels were hot on our heels. I was panting again by the time we hit the last bit of stairs.

"I wonder how we're going to get the keys back to George." She moved gingerly down the last step.

"What? You don't have a plan?"

She waved fingers carelessly while the other bony, blue-veined hand gripped the rail. "Something will present itself."

"I'm glad that you have confidence in your abilities," I hissed. "But I'd feel better with more of a plan."

"The Bible says were supposed to have faith, Salem. So have faith."

"Have faith that God will provide a way for us to get away with stealing the man's keys?" I was getting a little worried that George was going to be waiting at the bottom of the stairs with a couple of cops. Okay, a lot worried.

"You don't have to screech, Salem. If God didn't want us to be here, he would have found some way to stop us."

I could spot a dozen holes in Viv's theology, and was about to run them down for her, when Beethoven's Fifth Symphony rang out.

"Ahhh!" we both screamed. Viv stumbled against the door. She scowled while I dragged my phone from my jeans pocket and punched the "Ignore" button. Viv reached for the knob.

"Wait!" I reached out and grabbed her wrist. "What if there's somebody out there?"

"Like who?"

"Like George. With cops."

"Why in the world would George have cops?"

The woman was either very bold or just plain oblivious. Probably both.

She yanked the door open and sure enough, there was George with the cops. I saw spots and felt my knees go weak before I realized it wasn't George at all, but Don, walking down the hallway. From the wide-eyed look on his face, he hadn't expected anyone to be coming out that door.

"Don!" Viv greeted him like she hadn't seen him in years. "Do me a favor and give these keys to George, would you?" She shoved the keys in his hand before he could answer. "He really ought to be a little more careful, leaving keys in doors like that. People are forbidden to go in that tower, you know."

Chapter Seven

"Would you slow down?" Viv said when we got out the church door. "It's not like we went up there and tore the place apart."

My conscience was apparently making up for lost time. For years I did a lot of things I shouldn't have, and didn't worry about it much at all. Now I felt like I'd committed an atrocious crime when it hadn't been even an impressive prank.

"Sorry." I forced myself to slow down and tried to look not guilty, but how in the world does a person do that? The prospect alone kept my mind occupied till we got back to Viv's car.

I didn't ask where we were going, I just sat back and breathed in sweet freedom. My thigh muscles twitched from all the exertion.

"Wasn't that incredible? It's as if not a thing has changed. That was as smooth as I could ever hope for. Oh, I wish Mac could have seen that." She turned to me and slapped the seat beside me. "Mac was husband number two, and the best of the lot. He taught me to lift like that. Wasn't that a hoot!"

"Oh, yeah." I could still barely breathe. I lolled my head against the back of the seat. "A hoot."

"Did you see how smooth it all went down? That little escapade was divinely inspired, divinely protected."

"Are you kidding me?" I scooted closer to my door. "God sanctioned you to steal George's keys and go into a place you were forbidden to go? Lightning is going to strike you, and I'm going to get fried, too, because I was with you."

"Oh, hush. If God was going to strike me down, he would have done it a long time ago. I've certainly given him enough chances." She sighed with contentment as she careened the Caddy around a corner. "I believe he put into our hearts to go up into that tower. We were obedient, that's the important thing to remember here."

"If he wanted us to go up there, why wasn't there some kind of clue or evidence or something? I'm as much in the dark as I was before we went up. And now I have bird poop dust all over my shoes."

"The Lord works in mysterious ways," Viv said, white dentures flashing with her smile.

"I hate it when people say that! That's just another way of saying he makes no sense."

"Now who's going to get struck by lightning? All I know is, I was obedient, I exercised a long-dormant skill, and it has done my heart good."

I couldn't say the same. If my heart had recovered from A – the strain of strenuous exercise and B – the shock of a live pigeon flying into my face, it hadn't quite gotten over C – the bells of all hell bonging in my ears, and then G-Ma calling.

G-Ma. I grabbed my phone and called her back.

"I need you to come get your stuff," G-Ma said, not bothering with a "Hi."

"What stuff?"

"The stuff you left in the restaurant."

I didn't know what she was talking about, and I decided I didn't have the time or the energy for this. "Can we talk about this later?"

"We can talk about it when you get here. I need you to come get this stuff this afternoon."

"This afternoon? *Today*?" How was I going to get all the way out to Clovis Highway?

"Mario wants to start putting his equipment in."

"G-Ma, I don't even have a *car*. I can't come today."

"You have to, I have to get all this stuff out for Mario. He needs the room."

I knew that tone – misplaced panic mixed with stubborn determination. The gist of it was, I *would* be over there by the afternoon, if I had to walk. There was no talking to her when she decided something was an emergency.

"I'm kind of in the middle of something right now," I said.

G-Ma took a deep breath.

I also knew what that meant. That meant Give Up Now. Just give up. "I'll be over there in a couple of hours."

She was still talking when I punched the "end" button. I hoped she wouldn't call back, but with G-Ma there was no telling.

"Ugh! That is not what I wanted to deal with today."

"Luckily, I'm free and the day is young."

"You'll take me over there?"

"Sure. Got nothing else to do."

"What about your choir practice?"

Viv waved a hand carelessly. "What are they going to do, kick me out?" She flipped the lever on the air conditioner. "Now, where am I going?"

I pointed her in the right direction.

"After this, we can go visit your connection on the PD."

"You sound like someone on a TV police drama," I said. "I was thinking we could do that tomorrow or the next day."

"What's wrong with today?"

It was sooner, I thought but didn't say, and talking to Bobby was something I'd just as soon procrastinate. "Nothing, I guess." I couldn't think of anything she wouldn't shoot down. "I'll call him when we get back to my place."

Again Viv waved. "We'll just stop by the police department when we finish up at your grandma's."

"Fine," I said. "But don't say 'grandma' around her. She doesn't like it." I shoved my feet against the floor and braced for impact as Viv narrowly missed sideswiping a Lexus. Stump groaned and squirmed; I had her in a death grip.

We came to an abrupt halt in front of the motel office. It needed a coat of paint. At one point it had been white with blue and orange trim, but it was faded and chipped and just sad looking. G-Ma had changed the name to the Executive Inn eight or nine years ago, in the hopes of catching some of the traveling businessman trade. I hated to think what kind of executive would stay there.

Mario and G-Ma were inside the restaurant when we got there. "All that's your stuff over there," G-Ma said, pointing to a pile of junk in the corner. "And I can't have dogs here. This is a restaurant, not a kennel."

I looked around at the filthy, messy room. Judging by the pile of shredded paper and little black pills in the corner, and by the smell of urine, both mice and cats had been living in perfect harmony for the past several years. Stump was one of the cleanest things in the place.

"Neither one of us is staying. I'm just here to get the stuff." I rummaged through the junk. "That's not mine," I said. There was a cracked plastic pitcher with daisies, set of shiny blue and purple curtains painted with gray dolphins, and an old blanket with holes in it.

"Remember you asked me to store this stuff for you?"

I patted my leg and called Stump back from sniffing in the rat corner. Now, there are a lot of things I don't remember, but I think I would know if I ever had blue and purple curtains with dolphins on them. They weren't mine...but they did look familiar.

"This is Mom's stuff," I said. "She must have asked you to store it."

"Whatever." G-Ma waved a hand the exact same way Viv just had. I was beginning to feel dismissed. "We have to get it out of here so Mario can get to work."

"Ovens," Mario said, spreading his arms wide and looking at the space as if picturing it in his mind.

No one seemed to care that the stuff that needed to be moved wasn't actually mine.

I looked at the pile and sighed. Three big boxes and a couple of little ones. "I think I'll take it all straight to the Dumpster."

"You can't do that.. Tina will have a fit if you get rid of her stuff."

"She doesn't want it or she wouldn't have left it here. It's been three years since she moved out of that house on 22nd Street. Has this been here since then?"

"She'll want it for sure if you throw it away."

I groaned. G-Ma was right. Whatever I threw out would become Tina's most prized, beloved possession the moment she found out it was gone. There would be no end to the drama.

It wasn't as if I had lots of room to store a bunch of junk, either. I supposed I could scoot stuff around in the closet in my spare bedroom. I'd cleaned it out six months ago when I'd had a yard sale to raise money for my probation payment. I'd netted less than twenty bucks, but at least I'd gotten rid of eight-year-old clothes and books I would never read.

"Have you heard from her?" I asked G-Ma. I knew the answer but I asked the question anyway.

"You're joking, right?"

"If I knew how to get hold of her I could call and ask what she wants me to do with all this."

"Well, she's been gone, what? Three months? Three and a half? Give it another month or two and she'll be back complaining about how he lied to her and used her and how she hates being used."

My mother did hate being used, that was a fact. She much preferred being the user.

Her most recent conquest was a convenience store owner from New Mexico who promised her weekends full of skiing and camping and gambling in the reservation casinos. She'd brought him over to my trailer to introduce him one time, a skinny man named Wayne with a round belly, mostly-bald head and jeans with starched creases. Mom had gone on and on about how she was going to help him run his business. I'd kind of felt sorry for him. He had no idea she would refuse to get out of bed after the first couple of days and whenever she worked for him she would surely smoke up all his profits.

I sifted through another box. "Oh, good Lord," I said, finding a picture of my five-year-old self. My hair stuck out like it hadn't been brushed in days, and I glared at the camera.

Viv looked over my shoulder. "Ooooh, look at that frown," she laughed.

G-Ma pushed her way over and looked, too. "Yeah, she was always like that. Grumpy."

I figured it wasn't really the time to point out that at that time my father was non-existent, and my mother was negligent and had a string of low-class boyfriends, most of whom could not keep their hands to themselves. "I was not grumpy. I was...lonely and sad."

"Your own fault you were lonely," G-Ma said. "You always pushed everybody away. Never did want anybody to love you."

I frowned, put the picture back into the box, and hefted it to my hip. *What-freaking-ever,* I thought. *The kindergartner was the problem in this whole dysfunctional equation.*

I lugged the boxes out to Viv's car while Viv told Mario the story of when she worked in the pizzeria in Little Italy and learned to toss the dough in the air, and about how she'd stumbled onto a mob conspiracy to shoot the mayor of New York and she'd had to flee for her life to Los Angeles. I'd heard that one twice before, only I think one time it had been the governor of New York. Stump trotted after me. I think she was a little scared of G-Ma.

I shoved the dusty boxes into the back seat of Viv's car and said a short prayer of gratitude that Viv wasn't as picky about her car as G-Ma was. G-Ma would never have tolerated dusty boxes in the back seat of her Lincoln. I rubbed my hands against my jeans and headed back inside.

Mario was giving Viv the tour of where everything was going to fit and how many tamales he was going to make a day, and how he planned to expand his menu.

"Come up to Belle Court sometime," Viv said. "Those old people need some good healthy fat and starch in their diets. The restaurant there only serves baby food."

Mario thanked her for the tip and got back to moving junk around to make room for his restaurant equipment. My stomach growled at the thought of all that delicious food. It didn't look like there was much hope in me getting any of Mario's tamales today, though.

"I hear you," Viv said in response to the growl. "Let's grab some lunch before you go see your friend at the police department."

"You have a friend at the police department?" G-Ma asked. Her penciled-on red eyebrows made it plain she highly doubted it.

"Just a guy I knew from Idalou," I said. "Bobby Sloan. He's a detective with the Lubbock Police Department now. He's working the Lucinda Cruz case."

"I remember him. He was the hotshot basketball player and drove that car with the bird on it."

"Football, G-Ma. He played football. And yes, he drove a Firebird."

He'd had a gold one, and he'd driven it around town like a bat out of hell, and I spent about a thousand hours of my fifth grade year dreaming I was the girl riding in the passenger seat, my hair blowing loose and beautiful because he'd taken the T-tops off.

"I think he's stayed here a few times," G-Ma said, digging through a drawer. "This is all junk. Salem, why don't you carry this stuff out to the Dumpster?"

I did as I was told because I didn't want to talk about Bobby anymore, and I sure didn't want to think about him coming to the Executive Inn. I'd been staying with G-Ma one time when he came in with Carol-Anne Moore to rent a room, and it had broken my heart. I cried into my pillow so loud that G-Ma threatened to send me down to an empty room on the other end of the motel.

Lunch sounded good. I hoped Viv wanted something fried and greasy. I needed some empty calories to fortify me if I was going to be talking to Bobby that afternoon.

"Maybe you should just take your pretentious bony butt and get off my property," G-Ma was saying when I walked back inside.

Uh-oh. Old lady cat fight. I don't know what Viv said, but G-Ma apparently wasn't having any of it. She took a threatening step toward Viv.

Viv, bless her heart, laughed. I don't think she really *wanted* to get shot; she was probably just ignorant.

"I'm simply trying to give you some friendly advice," Viv said. "No need to get huffy."

Oh, this was bad. First of all, G-Ma didn't take advice, friendly or otherwise. And there was nothing she hated more when she was huffy than for people to call attention to it.

"I was gone for two minutes," I said, stepping between them. "How could you two manage to fall out in two minutes?"

"This...*person* thinks she knows all." G-Ma craned her neck around me and glared at Viv. "We've got everything under control here, thank you very much. So you can take your high falutin' advice and save it for someone who needs it."

"It's not high falutin' advice," Viv protested. "My fourth husband owned a whole string of Dairy Queens back in the early '80s. Believe me, you can pick up some grease-cutting tips in a nasty place like that."

Oh no. She really *did* want to be shot. You don't insult Dairy Queen around G-Ma. She believes Dairy Queen is the backbone of the American Heartland's economy and anybody who thinks they're too good for a Beltbuster is just a snob, plain and simple.

"Viv and I were just leaving. Thanks for giving me all that...stuff," I said, because I really *was* trying not to cuss. "Good luck with the restaurant. We'll be your first customers."

"I don't think our food will be good enough for your friend here," G-Ma said. "She can just stick with the Country Club."

Viv opened her mouth to say something else so I grabbed her bony elbow and pulled her outside. "Just let it go, Viv. There's no point."

"Your grandmother is kind of a hothead."

"Actually she's about the most level-headed one in the family. But yeah, when she thinks she's been insulted she can fly off the handle."

"And she has a chip on her shoulder concerning people with money."

"Of course," I said as I buckled myself in and wrapped my arms around Stump. "Everyone without money does. Where's lunch?"

All the talk about burritos and tamales had us choosing Taco Pete's on Thirty-Fourth Street. They had an outdoor patio that I could take Stump to. The stair climbing had loosened up my jeans, so I ordered extra cheese and sour cream on everything. Just in case I didn't feel quite fat enough to go see Bobby. For Stump I got a soft chicken taco, because her vet thinks she needs to lose some weight, too.

"So maybe you shouldn't just come right out and ask him what evidence they have," Viv coached around bites of her taco.

"There's no way this is going to work." I squeezed a packet of hot sauce onto my burrito.

"Salem, you have to think positive. Do you want to solve this case or not?"

I drew my head back. "Solve the case? What are we, the Hardy Girls?"

"If you don't want to solve the case what are you doing here? Why were we poking around in the tower looking for evidence?"

"I just want to help Tony, that's all."

"And wouldn't finding the real killer accomplish that?"

There. Somebody had said the words out loud – find the real killer. An overweight recovering alcoholic on probation and an old lady who lived in her own fantasy world were going to solve a crime that trained detectives couldn't solve.

Sheesh.

"We *could* do it," Viv insisted, pointing a tortilla chip at me. "Lots of people would talk to us who probably wouldn't talk to the police."

That could be true, but still... "It would help if I knew which questions to ask."

"The Lord will provide."

"Like he provided a way for you to get George's keys back without getting caught?"

"God is on the side of the oppressed, honey, and if your husband is oppressed and we're trying to help him, God will help us help him. I know it."

I was glad someone had faith. As for me, I'd had a few too many unanswered prayers lately to be feeling the faith thing.

"You ready?" Viv stood and rattled her keys

I looked up. I still had a burrito and a taco burger to finish.

Stump darted looks between the keys and the unfinished food on our tray, torn between her two loves – car rides and eating.

"You can finish in the car."

I pictured myself sitting across the desk from Bobby with a wiped-off blob of refried beans on my shirt. He'd have his finger over his mouth but he'd be thinking, "No wonder she's so fat. What a slob."

"What's the rush?"

"I'm motivated. Pumped. The Holy Spirit is speaking to me, telling me to move fast. Let's go free the oppressed."

The Holy Spirit should tell her to take a Xanax, I thought. I sighed and stood, grabbing a couple handfuls of paper napkins from the dispenser at the walk-up window. Since leaving food un-eaten was my other option, I decided to take my chances with the blob of beans. Stump trotted at my feet, her eyes locked on the food wrappers in my hand.

On the way to the police station, I was struck with inspiration. "The Holy Spirit is telling me to take another direction." I pan-icked the second the words were out of my mouth. I shouldn't be falsely claiming the Holy Spirit; that was as likely to get me struck by lightning as any of Viv's claims. But I decided it was still the better alternative to seeing Bobby just yet. "Tony's aunt is a friend of mine. She'd tell me more than Bobby would."

"Why would she know anything?"

"That family is really tight. Whatever Bobby and Mrs. Solis know, Sylvia knows. They don't really get along, but they see each other all the time. She'll be able to fill us in on the gossip about Lucinda Cruz, too. We couldn't get that from Bobby, I guaran-tee."

"Tell me how to get there," Viv said.

Sylvia owned a Laundromat over on 21st Street, a block or so from the church. Only a tiny blob of beans leaked from my burrito and it didn't show too bad. Stump chomped my finger trying to get the last bit of taco burger but I knew she didn't mean to.

Tango, Sylvia's chocolate miniature poodle, threw a high-pitched fit as soon as I walked through the door. He was Sylvia's baby. She couldn't stand to be away from him, and she tipped me ten bucks every time she had him groomed because I always got him in and out as fast as I could. She didn't know that I was only too happy to do so; Tango was a high-strung little pain in the butt.

"Salem, hi!" Sylvia's broad face beamed when she saw me. She wore an oversized red smock with blue and yellow parrots on it. "Tango, hush! Look, he's so happy to see you."

It was warm and humid in the Laundromat, with dryers humming and a TV blaring cable in the corner. A woman stared at the television while a toddler fished at something under a row of plastic chairs with a stick.

I faked a smile and patted Tango's curly head, trying to get my shins out of his reach. No such luck. He jumped up to my knee and began to dig with his hard little claws.

"Tango, you sweet dog you," I said through gritted teeth. Man, he was going to hit bone in a second. I bent and tried to pet him and push him away at the same time, Stump cradled once again under my left arm. She silently bared her teeth at Tango but didn't lunge, thank goodness.

"We need to ask you a couple of questions about Tony." Viv folded her arms across her chest.

I stepped in front of her. Sylvia wasn't going to be very forthcoming with that kind of approach.

"I asked Viv to bring me by here so I could find out how he's doing." I played the evil sister card. "I tried to talk to his mother, but she wouldn't tell me anything."

"That old bat. She never changes. Come on, let's go back to my office and get caught up." She led us to a small room at the back of the Laundromat.

The quickest way to a man's heart might be through his stomach, but I've found that for a woman, a common enemy works faster than pound cake.

"Have a seat." Sylvia scooped a basket of laundry off a wing-back chair and cocked her head toward Viv.

Sylvia was one of those *full of life* people. She's always the first person to talk, the first to say hello, the first to compliment you, and says your name three or four times when she talks to you. She was nice to be around, and yet it made me kind of tired, too. She was really intense.

"How sweet that you want to help Tony. I always knew you had a good heart, Salem. I hate that things went so badly for you and Tony, but I knew you had a good heart and no matter what anyone said, you never meant to ruin Tony's life."

"Ummm...thanks."

"How did Josie seem when you talked to her?"

Shrieky. Borderline maniacal. Standard Mrs. Solis. "Very upset. Scared for Tony, mad at the police."

Sylvia nodded and reached for a glass of iced tea sitting beside her chair. "I know it has to be so hard for her, dealing with this. Bless her heart, Tony's always been such a *good* boy and not given her any trouble at all, except for –" She threw me a quick glance and looked away. "She's just not used to dealing with anything like this."

I figured if anyone would be used to dealing with trouble from their son, it would be Sylvia. Her boy Rey was the same age as Tony and had been nothing *but* trouble as far back as I could remember. If something was broken or stolen or vandalized, you could bet Rey had a hand in it. If you were inclined to play a game of Compare the Kid, Josephine Solis won hands down over Sylvia.

"Of course, who would be able to deal with this? It would be difficult for anyone to believe their son was guilty of murder." Sylvia took a sip of her tea. "Would you like some ice tea?"

"No, thanks. Do you know why Tony is a suspect?"

Sylvia nodded. "Something about something of his being found there. I'm not sure what, but he was there that night, at the church. The security guard saw him go in."

"But if his company cleaned the place, wouldn't that give him reason to be there?"

Sylvia shrugged. "From what I understand, he wasn't usually there. He went there occasionally to make sure everything was being done right, but he didn't go there every day, just his workers."

"That still doesn't seem like enough to charge him."

"Well, I don't know the whole story, of course –" and she gave a look that made me think she did indeed know the whole story and a few other things besides – "but there's something about motive, like I said –a personal belonging at the scene of the murder, but I don't really know. I know it's hard to believe he'd actually do that, but you know what they say, crime of passion."

"It's impossible to believe," I said. It was kind of getting on my nerves that Sylvia wasn't more adamant in Tony's defense. Not that I wanted her to be like Mrs. Solis, but still... "Why would he have a motive to kill that girl? Why would he do that?"

"I don't know, but Tony was very fond of Lucinda. He had taken to her, you know."

"And?" And I had no reason at all to be jealous. I had never felt anything except attraction and maybe a little fondness for Tony, and certainly I didn't have any claim on him now, even if I was still his wife.

"If she rejected him, he could have been very hurt by that. People do strange things when they're hurt."

"Did he tell you he was in love with her?" I held my breath.

"He didn't have to tell me. It was plain from the way he cared about her."

"Tony's a very attentive person. You know that. It doesn't necessarily mean he was in love with her."

"And we're not really concerned with whether or not he was in love with the girl. We just want to know if he killed her or not," Viv said.

Oh, yeah. That. "Are the police saying it was a crime of passion?"

"Sweetie, I don't really know. I'm sure justice will prevail, no matter what Josie rants about. If Tony didn't do it, he won't be convicted."

"Tell that to all the falsely convicted sitting on death row right now," Viv said.

Death row. I rubbed the chill bumps on my arms. "I wish I knew exactly why they thought Tony did it. Maybe somebody could help him if they knew more..."

"Well, he does have a lawyer, and I think they have an actual investigator." She tossed a quick look from me to Viv. Did we look as stupid as I felt like we did?

"That's good," I said. Stupid-looking or not, finding proof my-self would make me feel better. As much as I didn't want to, I asked Sylvia to tell me more about Lucinda Cruz.

"The paper said she lived in Mexico until a few months ago?"

Sylvia nodded. "Actually she'd been up here before, when she was twelve or thirteen, but her family had to go back and then she stayed down there until a few months ago. Her third cousin is mine and Rosie's aunt, and she called and said Lucinda needed a job, so Josephine asked Tony to hire her."

"She'd been working for him for a few months?"

Sylvia shrugged. "I guess. Not very long."

"Was she a good a worker?"

"I suppose. I didn't really know her that well."

"You said it was clear that Tony cared about her."

"Yes, you know how Tony is, very attentive, like you said. He made sure she took care of herself and got plenty of rest, and didn't lift anything too heavy and didn't mess with any of the chemicals they work with. He was really concerned about the baby."

"Baby?"

"Didn't you know? Lucinda was pregnant."

Chapter Eight

"Pregnant?" *Close your mouth, Salem.*

"About four months, from what I understand."

"Two people were killed," Viv said. She flattened her lips.

Sylvia nodded slowly. "Exactly. Tragic."

My mind spun while I tried to find a cubbyhole in my head to put everything. Tony – the Tony I'd seen yesterday, older and more mature, steady and rock sure in the face of a murder charge, his hysterical mother and his ex-wife showing up after almost a decade – becoming "fond" of the beautiful, wide-smiling Lucinda. Lucinda, who carried a baby.

The question was out of my mouth before I could decide if it was really in my best interest to know. "Was it Tony's baby?"

"Oh, no, she was in Mexico then. That's why she came up here, because she wanted a place to raise her baby. Her mother called Josie, and Josie spoke to Tony, and he offered her a job and a place to stay."

I wiped my hands on my legs. "Sylvia, do you think that's what happened? That he was in love with her or something? That he was jealous and lost his temper?" As far as I could remember, Tony didn't *have* a temper.

That's what bothered me, I realized. The idea that Tony could have been so hurt that he'd fly into a jealous rage and actually commit a crime of passion. He hadn't lifted a finger to keep me – his wife, the girl he'd committed to being with for life – from walking out. There were no violent fits of rage, not so much as a stomped foot.

Not that I had wanted Tony to stop me from leaving, but it hurt my ego. Was I choosing to be blind to the possibility that Tony could be passionate, simply because he hadn't been passionate with me?

"Sweetie, I just don't know. I know the police wouldn't charge him unless they had some reason to suspect him. But I also know that if he's innocent, he'll be okay."

Tango pushed his cold wet nose under my hand. Don't get me wrong, I like dogs or I wouldn't hang around them so much. But sometimes I really don't want a cold wet nose sliming around my skin. I scratched his curly ears and he thumped the chair beside me. "I hope you're right. What about the baby's father?"

"Who?" Sylvia raised penciled-on eyebrows.

"Lucinda's baby's father. Is he back in Mexico?"

Sylvia took a long drink of her tea. "I have no idea. I doubt she knew where he is or even who he was."

I cast a quick glance over at Viv. Whatever Sylvia said about barely knowing Lucinda, obviously there was no love lost there.

"You didn't like her," Viv said. Subtle as a ton of bricks.

"I didn't *know* her. I don't really know what she was like. I just know what I hear and what I see and I'm smart enough to figure out the rest." Sylvia shifted in her chair.

"If she was the type of person to run around and be wild, then she was likely to have enemies." I should know. I was as wild as they came and probably a couple dozen people would have been happy to strangle me at some point.

My mind did a quick flash on Trisha and Scott. If something gruesome ever happened to me, I was sure Trisha's name would turn up on a list of possible suspects.

"We need to make a list of known associates," Viv said, apparently following my same train of thought and throwing in some lingo she'd picked up from CSI Miami. "If the police have focused in on Tony so soon, it's possible they've ruled out someone else who needs to be looked at more closely."

Sylvia stood and patted my shoulder. I got the feeling that meant it was time for me to go. "You're so sweet to want to help Tony. I'm sure he'll be very touched by it. But I honestly don't know what you could do. Lucinda had only been here a few months, she didn't have many friends here. Good luck, Salem. I hope you find something to help Tony."

"You said Tony had offered her a place to stay. Was it with him?" *Quit praying for a negative answer.*

Sylvia shrugged. "She stayed with me, actually. I let her use Rey's old room."

"You said you barely knew her." Viv crossed her arms over her chest.

Sylvia gave her a stony look and I wondered briefly if I ought to throw myself between them. Man, two near catfights in the space of an hour. Viv rubbed some people the wrong way.

I waited, though, to see what Sylvia would say. She took her time answering, and when she did she stared straight at me and spoke slowly. I was suddenly reminded that she *was* Mrs. Solis's sister. The resemblance was pretty definite in that moment.

"She stayed with me in my extra bedroom. She was quiet and kept mostly to herself. She went to work and she hung out with a few friends and she came home. I appreciate that you want to help Tony, but I don't see how interrogating his family is going to do him any good."

I squeezed Sylvia's arm. "I'm sorry if we're getting intrusive. Like you said, we just want to help. Forgive us for being nosy." I narrowed my eyes at Viv, but it was mostly for Sylvia's benefit.

It was just as well, since it was totally lost on Viv. She continued to size Sylvia up like maybe *she'd* killed Lucinda and framed Tony for it.

"I've got to hit the restroom and then we'll get out of your hair." I stood and turned to Viv, handing Stump over to her. "You and Stump can wait in the car."

Viv started for the door, and Sylvia pointed to a closed door next to her office. I turned that direction, and she said, "No, not that one, that goes down to the basement. The next door."

I scrubbed the dog saliva off my hands and wondered if Sylvia was testy because she had something to hide, or if Viv was just getting on her nerves. I had been a little intimidated by Viv when I first met her, too. She was one of those people who just looked like they have a lot of money.

I could see how that would rub some people the wrong way, like G-Ma, who's unceasingly vigilant against anyone who might think they're better than she is. And maybe Sylvia too?

Or else Sylvia knew more than she was sharing. And while I could understand why she might think it a waste of time to indulge Viv and me in our quest to free Tony, where was the harm?

There was one shred of paper towel on the roll and it wasn't

nearly enough. I opened the cabinet under the sink and rummaged around, my nose filling with a vaguely familiar scent. I
knocked over a green cologne bottle and wrinkled my nose as I
righted it. Polo by Ralph Lauren. Hello, twelfth grade. Sylvia's
son Rey used to take a bath in Polo every morning before school.
You could get high just standing near him.

I found a roll of paper towels and opened it, putting it on the
holder in the hopes that the small gesture would undo any dam-
age our questions had done to my relationship with Sylvia. I
didn't want to alienate her. She was my only friendly link to Tony
and besides, irritating or not, Tango got me a ten dollar tip every
three weeks. I couldn't afford to make Sylvia mad.

"How is Rey?" I asked when I came out. I sidestepped Tango
and reached for the door.

Sylvia was folding towels at a table, and she finished and patted the fabric smooth before she answered. "He's okay. He's coming in tonight for Lucinda's funeral."

"Tell him I said hi."

"I will, sweetie." She reached into her smock pocket and pulled
out a piece of paper. It looked like it had been torn off the back of
an envelope. "This is Tony's information. His home and business
addresses, phone numbers. You should call him."

Was it my imagination that she emphasized the word *him?*
Like, "*Call him instead of bugging me.*"

I wasn't really comfortable with that. It went against every fi-
ber of my passive-aggressive being.

"Thanks. I'll do that."

I joined Viv in the car and sighed as I fastened my seatbelt.
Thinking about Rey kind of put me in a bad mood – the slimy
creep.

Viv put the car in reverse. "She's hiding something."

"I know." I told her about Rey and the bottle of cologne I'd found in the bathroom. "I'd bet my car that was a fairly new bottle of cologne. I don't think it was eight or nine months old. But she said it had been that long since she's seen Rey."

"So it was Rey who killed that girl and her baby!" Viv slapped the steering wheel.

Okay, so apparently it was up to me to play Devil's Advocate. "I'm not saying it was Rey. I'm just saying that Sylvia seemed to be hiding something, and I think the something she's hiding has to do with Rey. I suppose the cologne could be that old. Or it might not even be Rey's, it could be someone else's."

But whatever I had that passed for intuition kept snagging on Rey. Probably it was just me wanting Rey to be guilty because he was such a disgusting jerk. When Tony and I were married, he'd come over to our little house one day while Tony was at school and tried to get me into bed, into Tony's and my marriage bed, and with me five months pregnant.

I'd been scared and furious at the same time, because Rey was a lot bigger than I was, and the look in his eye had me wondering if he was going to take no for an answer. I yelled at him and called him a slimeball, and wanted to know what kind of person would try to get into bed with their cousin's wife.

"Come on, Salem. Everybody knows there's no way you're *not* going to screw around on Tony. You are *you*, after all. I think the whole family would be relieved if it was me you were with, because at least that would keep you from rolling around with half the guys in town."

Something in his tone or the look in his eye spoke volumes to me. What he had said was true. My promiscuity had been discussed at length and in detail, probably by everyone in the county. I was *me*, after all. How could I possibly be faithful?

Ten years later I was still somewhat satisfied to remember that I'd clocked Rey right in that smug smile and split his lip. He had come at me with rage in his eyes, and I had run out the front door. He hadn't followed me far; I had looked back two blocks later and seen him spit blood onto the ground and get into his car, driving off the other way.

I couldn't have told Tony, because he would have felt so betrayed by Rey and I couldn't have borne to be the one to do that to him. In the back of my mind was the knowledge that Rey, creep that he was, had only spoken the truth. No one would ever believe that he'd been the one to come on to me. Rey had been a jerk, but I had been a slut, and that was way worse.

We were two blocks from the police station when I realized where Viv was going. "Are we sure we need to do this now?"

"You told him you were coming in, right?"

Coming in. It sounded too close to *turned herself in* for my comfort. "I don't think he was serious, though" I said. "I mean, it was more like a suggestion. Probably he would be okay with a phone call. An email."

"After we get through here," Viv said, completely ignoring me and turning into the police department parking lot, "let's find her friends. Sylvia said she had a few, but she didn't know who they were. Let's get some names from this cop of yours and see if we can talk to them."

That didn't seem like a very good idea to me. I mean, finding her friends wasn't a bad idea, but using the police to find out didn't seem like our best bet.

"Maybe we should just talk to Tony. He'd probably know more than the police would, as far as that goes." I was only marginally more comfortable with the idea of seeing Tony than I was with seeing Bobby.

"Oh, Tony's on the list – don't worry about that. But we might as well not go to him empty-handed, right?"

"I guess." I said a quick prayer that Bobby was out on a case or had gone home to bed with a stomach bug. I doubted God would smite Bobby with a stomach bug just to help me avoid an awkward moment.

I prayed anyway, but as Les was fond of telling me, prayers prayed without faith are basically a lot of hot air.

I lugged Stump up to the same bicycle rack I'd tied her to before, and she craned her neck around to glare up at me. This time she didn't bother with the dramatics, she just stared stonily at me, and I could practically see a list of my favorite things that she was planning to shred in retribution.

Bobby was walking by the reception area and saw us as soon as we came through the door.

"There she is," he said.

"Is that your ex-boyfriend? You're right, he *is* a hottie," Viv stage-whispered.

Bobby lifted an eyebrow at me.

"I never said that," I said quickly. "She's old and doesn't hear very well."

"You never said which? That I was your boyfriend or that I was a hottie?" He folded arms across a well-muscled chest.

"I – I, uh...mmmm..." Now see, *this* was why I didn't want to see Bobby.

Viv stuck her hand out. "Detective Sloan, my name is Vivian

Carson and, of course, you know my partner Salem Grimes. We're investigating the Lucinda Cruz murder." She raised her wobbly chin and spoke with authority. "We'd like to ask you a few questions."

Bobby burst out laughing. "All right, Cagney and Lacey. Come on back." His shoulders shook as he led us down the hallway to his office.

Viv sat in the chair I'd been in Monday and faced Bobby across his desk. From the way her jaw twitched, I figured the Cagney and Lacey remark hadn't set too well with her. She took a deep breath, though, and smiled. "I acknowledge that we are new to this arena, and I can imagine you see little advantage in helping us, so I want to assure you right away that have not come empty handed. We have information to trade."

Bobby did a poor job of hiding his grin. "Is that so?"

"It *is* so. We've been conducting interviews and we have a few persons of interest." Viv folded her hands over her three hundred dollar purse.

Bobby leaned back in his chair. "Now, that is interesting."

Viv gave him an indulgent smile. "Of course, we want to help in every way, and we're more than willing to share what we have. On the condition the favor is returned."

Bobby rubbed his upper lip hard, then took a deep breath of his own. "The police department is always indebted to active and concerned citizens. As I'm sure you can understand, we can't be everywhere all the time, so we rely on people like yourselves to assist us in gathering information. I will gladly listen to every concern and thought you have, and I promise every lead will be followed up on."

Viv and I both waited for the "but."

"But I can't comment on an open investigation."

"It would be strictly off the record, of course." Viv leaned forward in her chair.

Bobby fiddled with a manila folder on his desk and slid his gaze over to me. As he slid the folder into the top drawer of his desk he lifted one eyebrow as if to ask, "Where did you come up with this one?"

I quickly decided there was nothing I could do or say that would make this episode any less humiliating. I shrugged slightly and looked at Viv as if I didn't know what she was talking about.

Viv, bless her heart, appeared to be actually waiting patiently for the police detective to spill his guts to two amateur – in every sense of the word – detectives.

"You know, I think it would be extremely helpful to hear your thoughts on this investigation. You strike me as a very wise person." Bobby finally said. "I'd be willing to bet you're one of those people who can size up a character in no time."

Viv shrugged modestly. "Well, I don't like to brag, but I *am* an excellent judge of character."

"Intuition is one of the most powerful tools we have to work with. And a mature woman such as yourself has probably honed her intuition through years of experience."

"Exactly." Viv bobbed her head. "There is no substitute for experience, is there? In fact, I would dare say..." She trailed off and rubbed her chest. She opened and closed her mouth a couple of times, like a guppy scooped out of its tank. Her face flushed, then paled. "Excuse me," she croaked.

I grabbed her arm. "Are you okay?"

She nodded, still pale and now shaking. "I'm fine, I'm fine. I just feel a little fluttery."

Bobby stood. "Fluttery?"

Viv shook her head. "It's nothing, I'm sure. I just –" She stopped again and took a couple of quick breaths. "I need my heart pills."

I didn't even know she took heart pills. I grabbed her purse and was about to start rifling through there.

"No, no, they're in the car." She stuck her hand in the purse and clutched a ring of keys. "Detective Sloan, please be so kind as to fetch my pills from the glove compartment of my car. It's a powder blue Deville."

"I can get them," I said. *God, please don't let her have a heart attack here*, I prayed.

Viv turned achingly frightened, watery eyes on me. "No, please stay here. Please stay with me," she whispered. "Please."

Bobby grabbed the keys and hurried out the door. I fought the terrified pounding of my heart and the tears that rose suddenly. "You'll be okay," I said fiercely. "You're going to be fine."

Viv blinked a couple of times, then shot to her feet. "That arrogant little jerkweed. Can you believe him? Using transparent flattery to try and get us out of his hair." She rushed around his desk and slid the drawer open. "And he called me *old!* What a dipstick."

She slapped the folder onto Bobby's desk and opened it.

"Viv!" What the heck was she *doing*? I jumped up and ran to the door. "Are you insane? You'll get us arrested!"

"A *mature* woman with *years* of experience." Her wrinkled mouth pursed and her head wobbled as she mocked Bobby. "What a putz. Let's see what we have here."

"You can't do this." I did a little dance from one foot to the other, torn between getting help – which would undoubtedly only make things worse for me, since I'd been the one to bring her in there in the first place – and throttling her.

"Oh yes I ca-an," Viv sing-songed. She rifled through pages in the file. "I knew this was Lucinda Cruz's file. Did you see the way he slid this into the drawer, as if letting us even look at the outside of the folder was too much for him? Selfish. Wants all the glory for himself." She mumbled to herself as she eyed whatever was inside the folder. "Blunt force trauma to the head. Mmmmhhhmmm. I see."

"Viv!" I hissed. "Put it back. Bobby will be back any second."

"Darned straight I'm a good judge of character." She flipped through a couple more pages. "I can tell, for instance, when someone's trying to blow smoke up my –"

"Viv!" I heard voices approaching. "Someone's coming!"

She had the file back in the drawer and her head between her knees so fast I barely caught it. One second she was there, the next she was hidden behind the desk. Two uniform cops walked down the hallway and looked at me. I froze, unsure what I was supposed to do. Act like everything was normal? Were we still pretending Viv was having a heart attack?

Good thing for me Viv was on top of things. She moaned and sat up straight, one hand to her chest and the other patting her cheek. "Okay, okay. I think it's passed." She stood and moved back to the front of the desk, leaning against it and breathing hard. Her face was flushed and even a little sweaty. How did she *do* that?

Bobby rounded the corner, a bottle of pills in his hand. "This is all I could find."

"That's perfect, thank you." Viv popped the top and flipped a tiny white pill in her mouth. "I think it's passed, but the doctor told me if I felt fluttery to go ahead and take the pill just in case."

Bobby took Viv's wrist in one hand and felt her pulse. "Let's call an ambulance, just in case."

"I'm sure that's not necessary, but I'll defer to your judgment." Viv turned worshipful eyes on him and waited while Bobby counted heartbeats.

"Salem, could you grab Mrs. Carson a cup of water from that cooler around the corner? Why don't you sit back down and lift your feet?"

"Okay." Viv drifted weakly into the chair. "Really, I think I'm fine. But whatever you think is best…"

I decided maybe I needed a little white pill. My hands shook as I let the water into the paper cup and I spilled it all over the floor. If Bobby was in there taking her pulse, surely he would figure out she was faking it. And there would only be one reason for her to fake that – to do exactly what she'd done.

He would put two and two together and pretty soon we'd be in a windowless back room while Bobby and a partner played good cop and bad cop.

There was a time in my life when I might have been able to stand up under interrogation; that was during the time when I stayed in a permanent but variable state of inebriation. Now I was stone cold sober and cried during sentimental car commercials. I was ready to spill my guts as soon as I walked through the door, and I didn't even have that many guts…metaphorically speaking, of course.

Viv was on her cell phone talking to her "doctor" when I got back. "Okay, we'll be right there. Yes, yes of course." She nodded a few times and then flipped it closed. "He said that everything sounded fine but he wanted to see me this afternoon just to be on the safe side. Definitely no need to send the ambulance, though."

Bobby turned to me. "Can you drive her to her doctor's office?"

And get the heck out of here? "Sure." I nodded and shoved the half-empty cup at Viv. "Be happy to."

Viv milked the sympathy for a couple more minutes and then clung to my arm as I led her down the hallway.

When Stump saw me, she jumped up and wagged her back end before she remembered she was mad at me and flopped back down. Viv leaned on the bike rack and breathed dramatically deeply while I unhooked Stump.

My own pulse was getting back to normal, and mad as I was, I was mostly relieved it looked like we were going to make it. As soon as we got in the car, though, I let her have it.

"How dare you put me in that position? First of all, I thought you were honestly having a heart attack. You scared me half to death." I dumped Stump onto the seat between us and started the car.

"I am a classically trained actress, you know."

"No, I didn't know, and that was...it was *cruel.* I thought you were really sick." *And I believed you desperately wanted me by your side in your hour of need.* "You could have gotten me into serious, *serious* trouble by pulling that file out. I'm on probation, you know. I'd go to *real* jail."

Viv waved a hand. "It's not that bad. I suppose you ought to drive, just in case he's watching."

I decided I would throttle her as soon as I was far enough away from all the police witnesses.

"I wish you had a little cooler head. I could have gotten more information out of that file besides "blunt force trauma" and "St. Christian.""

"St. Christian? What does that mean?"

"Beats me. I didn't get a good look at it because you were having such a conniption. Watch out for that pickup!"

"What?" I swerved and honked out of reflex, then realized the pickup she was talking about was twenty yards away. "That?"

"You were headed straight for him."

"I was not. Geez, Viv, you've given me fifteen heart attacks today. Can we give it a rest?"

"I'm sorry, but frankly you're not the best driver in the world."

I pulled into Sonic and ordered a large vanilla Coke for me and a chocolate malt for Viv. "You can drive now. We're safely away from the police station."

She got behind the wheel and smiled. "There now. That was kind of fun, don't you think? Pulling one over on the guy who's supposed to have all the answers?"

"No, it was fraudulent and wrong and mean, and it didn't get us anywhere." St. Christian – that didn't even make sense. There wasn't a St. Christian, was there? I mean, weren't *all* saints Christians? Wasn't that some sort of prerequisite? "What did it say about St. Christian?"

"I don't know, I told you. I just saw those words and then you started crying and I closed the file."

"I wasn't *crying*, I was trying to keep us from being arrested. Maybe it was St. Christina. Is there a St. Christina?" And what would that have to do with Lucinda Cruz and Tony?

The girl brought my forty-four ounce vanilla Coke and I slurped down a good eight ounces of it. "Hey! Could it have been St. Christopher?"

Viv sucked on her chocolate malt so hard her eyes bugged. "Could be. It was St. Something-or-other." She gasped and sat back. "Oh no. *Brain freeze, brain freeze.*"

Stump wagged at both of us hopefully, and I opened the lid to my drink and took out a piece of ice. She chomped it down noisily.

"Tony always wore a necklace with a St. Christopher medallion on it. I wonder if that's what you saw."

Viv moaned and rolled her head back and forth on the headrest.

"Maybe his necklace was found at the scene of the crime or something."

"Maybe she was strangled with his necklace!" Viv raised up, then let her head fall back. She listlessly spooned malt into her mouth, her eyes closed. "This is what you call painfully good."

"Except that wouldn't be a blunt force trauma to the head, would it?" I shivered when I realized how casually we were discussing the death of a young woman and her baby.

"You have a brain freeze, too?"

"No, just thinking about Lucinda Cruz." And her crooked neck. If she'd died from blunt force trauma to the head, why had her neck looked like that?

"Was that an autopsy report you saw first? That had the blunt force trauma thing on it?"

Viv shrugged, spooning in more malt. "No idea. It was a form with a bunch of blanks filled in."

I almost said I wished she'd gotten a closer look, but figured she would throw her malt at me.

Viv started the engine. "It's too hot to be sitting in this car without the air conditioner running. Okay, our next stop has to be your husband's house."

I whipped my head around. "It does?"

"Of course. We have to find out if he has his St. Christina

necklace."

"St. Christopher." I *had* prayed that morning for some guidance. Now Viv and Sylvia both said I needed to see Tony. I'd secretly been hoping the Holy Spirit would guide me to a smoking gun with little effort and no awkwardness.

They were both right. If I wanted to do anything for Tony, I should actually talk to the guy, but talking to him would probably lead us to the subject of whether or not we were still married, and that was something I wasn't too keen on discussing just yet.

"Where am I going?" Viv asked as she got to the street.

I dug through my purse and found the addresses Sylvia had written down. "Home or office first?" I wondered out loud.

"Home. If I was arrested for murder I would call in sick the next couple days."

"Work, then. Tony would go to work as long as he had a pulse."

Tony's office was on the edge of town, in the industrial district. White vans with blue and green *Solis Services* logos lined up neatly outside large garage doors, and an SUV and a nice sedan sat in front of a windowless door.

"Oh, it looks like he's got company," I said, grateful for an excuse to put this off.

Viv was out the door before I finished the sentence. Good thing, I supposed, that one of us wasn't shy. Any crime-solving duo needed at least one person who wasn't a total chicken.

Viv rapped on the door, then stuck her head in.

Tony appeared almost immediately, his polite expression replaced by one of surprise when he saw me. He smiled. "Salem. What are you doing here?"

"We're investigating your case," Viv announced. "We have a

couple of leads, and we'd like to talk to you about them."

A prematurely bald man in a suit popped his head over Tony's shoulder. "You're investigating his case?" He looked at me, at Stump, then up at Tony and cocked an eyebrow.

Tony stepped back and gestured for us to come in. "This is my attorney, Craig Pharr. We were just discussing my case. Come on in."

He led us through an outer reception area and into a large office. The place was nice, and whoever decorated it had done a good job of disguising the fact that we were in the middle of a bunch of warehouses. It had thick mint green carpet, creamy vanilla walls, and expensive looking furniture. I placed Stump strategically over the refried bean stain on my shirt and followed them into the inner sanctum.

"Salem is my wife," Tony said, his face completely impassive, as if it was routine for wives to show up from out of nowhere. He reached over and rubbed Stump's head. She licked his hand and sighed.

Mr. Pharr nodded and gave me only a slightly strange look as he held his hand out to shake mine. From his expression, it looked as if the subject of Tony's "wife" had already been discussed. I shifted Stump, who groaned, and held out my hand.

"We kind of need to talk about that," I said to Tony as I returned the lawyer's handshake. "This is Viv Carson."

I'd seen Craig Pharr on the news before, giving comments about various cases he was defending. I was under the impression he was a fairly big gun in town, and was glad for Tony.

We all took seats around a coffee table on the right side of Tony's office. My legs complained as I bent to sit. I was going to be sore tomorrow, my legs from the climbing and my arms from carting Stump around. As soon as I sat she sighed again deeply, closed her eyes, and fell asleep.

Craig cleared his throat and straightened his tie. "So. You say you have a few leads? I'd be interested in hearing about them."

"They're not really leads per se," I said. Being laughed at twice in the span of an hour didn't suit me. "But we talked to Sylvia and I got a weird feeling she was holding out on me."

"Definitely holding out," Viv said. "Buttoned up tight as a drum."

Tony leaned forward and placed his elbows on his knees, his gaze on me like there wasn't another person around for miles. Geez, his brown eyes were a mile deep. "What makes you think that?"

"I couldn't really put my finger on it, but it had to do with Rey. Like she didn't want to talk about him." Now that I said it, it seemed even flimsier than I'd thought. "I mean, I guess maybe she just didn't want to talk about him, but it seemed a little weird. Remember how he used to always wear so much Polo? Does he still do that?"

Tony cocked his head. "Yes, I suppose he does."

"Polo? The cologne?" Craig cast a glace from me to Tony and I could tell he was already out of patience with our "leads."

Tony nodded. "Rey lives in Oklahoma City."

"Is this the girl's ex-boyfriend?" Craig asked.

"What girl?" Viv asked at the same time Tony said, "Yes."

"What girl? Lucinda Cruz? Rey was her boyfriend?"

"See!" Viv slapped a bony knee. Stump startled awake, glared at Viv, then closed her eyes again. "Sylvia didn't say one word about that. She *was* holding out on us."

"Lucinda and Rey broke up before she moved here," Tony said.

"Sylvia didn't say Lucinda had ever dated Rey. Isn't that kind of fishy? She just said she'd moved here from Mexico to make a new start. She said Rey lived in Oklahoma City."

"After she left Mexico, Lucinda lived in Oklahoma City for about a year. Before she moved here."

"Was he the father of her baby?"

Tony and Craig looked at each other.

Tony waited a beat. "That's what Lucinda said."

I studied him for a second. Tony was always a hard one to read, but for all his stoicism I could still tell something wasn't quite right. Either Tony had his doubts that Rey was actually the father of Lucinda's baby...or he believed it, but didn't like it.

He *had* been in love with her. The realization made me feel sad in a way I didn't even understand.

"Lie number two. Sylvia actually said the exact words, 'Lucinda Cruz's baby was conceived in Mexico.'"

I gave her a look.

"Or something to that effect. She led us to believe Lucinda came straight from Mexico to here."

"What about the Polo?" Tony asked me.

I shook my head. "It's really nothing big, but I used the bathroom at the Laundromat and there was a new bottle of Polo in there. But Sylvia said Rey wasn't coming in until tonight."

Tony and Craig looked at each other again. I was already getting a little tired of that.

"See, I told you it was nothing. Just a hunch."

"But it could be something," Viv insisted. "A good investigator could find something with a start like that. I'll bet Columbo could solve a whole case, starting with one loose thread like that."

Stump snored loudly. It was a little awkward.

Craig took a deep breath and rubbed his hands together. "Be that as it may, we will certainly look into questioning Sylvia further. And I'm sure Tony appreciates, as I do, your concern and your willingness to be of help."

Viv looked at me. "Can you believe it? He's blowing us off, too."

"I'm not blowing you off. Please, if you find any more...information, let us know. Every little bit helps."

Thankfully, my cell phone rang. I looked at the readout. Les. I sent up a quick thank-you prayer for God's timing and moved into the reception area to take it.

"Hey, girl. Got you a car."

"You got me a car?" *Hallelujah*! Wait a minute...I had no money for a car.

"My boy Cody just got a new job and they gave him a company truck. So he said you could use his car till you can get yours fixed."

"Really?" I did a little jig until I realized the door to Tony's office was still open and they could see me. "That's...that's wonderful."

"Well, hold your appreciation till you see it. It's not the prettiest car on the block, but it runs and it's fairly dependable."

"Already it's better than the one I have."

"Only problem is, I have about fifteen minutes to get it to you because my Exodus group starts in half an hour. Can you meet me somewhere?"

"Anywhere. Name the place."

He told me where he was going and I named a McDonald's not far from there. Looking like an idiot makes me crave French fries.

I poked my head back in the door. "Viv, I'm sorry but we have to go."

"Tell him about the St. Whosits thing first."

"Oh, yeah. While we were at the police station –"

"When were you at the police station?" Craig and Tony spoke at the same time.

"Twenty minutes ago," Viv said. "Pompous bunch of know-it-alls down there. It's a wonder they get any case solved."

"We – uh – well, Viv accidentally got a peek at the file on Lucinda Cruz and she saw the words "St. Christopher." I knew you always wore that necklace and thought maybe it had something…"

I trailed off at the look on Tony's face. I don't think he even realized he touched his neck. The look he gave Craig then was tinged with dread.

"Is that why they took pictures of my neck?" Tony asked.

"We'll talk about it later," Craig said. He turned back to me. "You're sure it said St. Christopher?"

I looked at Viv. She didn't even know who St. Christopher was, and she kept forgetting the name. Did I really want to hang Tony's hope of acquittal on anything Viv said?

"Eighty percent," I said with a shrug. "Sixty-five, minimum."

"Absolutely positive." Viv nodded sharply. "It also said 'blunt force trauma,' or somesuch. I didn't get much chance to look because Salem got all freaked out."

Craig pursed his lips and evidently decided he didn't want to hear any more about why I was freaked out. "That's all you saw?"

"Unfortunately."

"Please give me or Tony a call if you remember anything else."

"Sure, no problem." I tapped my foot and raised an eyebrow at Viv. "We'd better get going. Les will be waiting."

Tony followed us out to the car and held the door while I deposited Stump into the front seat. "Thanks for your help." He still looked a little preoccupied about the necklace as he held the door open for me.

"What do you think about the St. Christopher thing?" I asked. "Do you think it could be something important?"

He looked at the ground for a second. "I don't know. I'll have to talk to Craig about it." He gave me a look that I realized was shame or embarrassment or something. "Look, Salem, you might as well know, I gave Lucinda my necklace."

That necklace had stayed on his neck the entire time we were married. "You were seeing her?"

He nodded slowly.

And why shouldn't he? Good grief, how many men had I been with since Tony and I had "divorced"? Why should I be the least bit jealous or upset?

I took a deep breath. "Look, Tony, I don't really understand all this stuff about annulments and the church. I assumed, you know..." I shrugged. "We were divorced and it was over a long time ago. I signed the papers and so did you. So you don't have anything to worry about."

"But I didn't sign any papers."

"You didn't?" My heart dropped.

He shook his head. "Salem, I vowed before God that I'd be married to you until I died. That's not something you just sign off on."

Of course you do, I thought impatiently. *People do it all the time.* "So we're really still married?"

He nodded.

"In *every* sense of the word? Not just in the church's eyes?"

He nodded again.

"But that's insane! How could we be married for the last ten years and not see each other? I mean, you haven't called, or come to see me, or anything. Why would you – why didn't you – why?" I cocked my head and restrained myself from thumping him on the chest.

"God kept telling me no."

"Kept?"

He looked chagrined.

I raked my hand through my hair. "Could you have told me about this at some point? Let me know I was a married woman still?" It might have kept me from doing some of the things I did. Maybe."

"I did tell you, Salem. I sent you half a dozen letters telling you I wanted to talk to you, asking you to call me. The divorce was never my idea."

I chewed my lip. I did remember letters coming from Tony. I had thrown them out without opening them. I had been mad at him for letting me go, for not coming in person to drag me back home. I had seen those letters as half-hearted attempts at best.

No, the divorce had not been his idea. Six months into my pregnancy I had been driving down the highway when a guy t-boned my car. My arm and shoulder were broken, and my face didn't look so great for about two months.

They had told Tony and me together in my hospital room that the baby hadn't made it, but I'd already figured it out. The look the doctor got on his face when he put the heartbeat monitor on my stomach told me all I needed to know.

It was weird, feeling so sad about losing something you didn't think you wanted. I had been so scared to be a mother, to be a wife, just waiting for the moment when it all blew up in my face, knowing that destruction was inevitable. I had expected to feel relief that I was off the hook. That relief was slow in coming.

Tony, freshly turned eighteen and already fancying himself to be a mature family man, wore as always a mask of composure as the doctor told us how sorry he was. Tony had taken my hand and gripped it fiercely, had clenched his jaw and ducked his head. He nodded a few times, and then rushed from the room.

He was the one who was relieved, I realized. He was off the hook as well. Then I remembered that he was Catholic, and maybe he wasn't feeling as relieved as he was feeling totally ripped off. He'd been trapped into marrying me for no good reason, and then he was stuck with a loud, crass embarrassment of a wife.

He had never said as much, of course. In fact, he never even hinted that we shouldn't do anything but go along playing house together and pretending to be a real devoted-to-each-other couple. I got irritated, waiting for him to spring the news that he'd found a loophole in one of his catechism books that said shotgun weddings were null and void when the baby isn't produced.

He had refused to admit he didn't want to be married to me, so with the inimitable charm of Salem Grimes, I pushed him away. He refused to admit I was totally wrong for him, so I became *more* wrong. No later than a week after I was released from the hospital and we had the service to bury the baby, I had gone out with my friends and gotten completely ripped. I couldn't take it at our house anymore. Tony either sat on the couch looking morose, or followed me around asking me if I was okay. I was irritated with him, irritated with feeling sad for someone I hadn't even met, and irritated with the cast on my arm.

Looking back, I think that was a turning point for me. I'd partied before, but this had been a conscious, willful decision to drown what I was feeling. Not only did I know what I was doing – using alcohol to bury my sadness and anger – but I was all for it. I didn't have one bit of remorse, or any thought that I should handle the situation any other way. I thought, *I'm hurting and I want to feel better. Give me a drink.* It worked.

That's the thing nobody wants to talk about with alcohol. It works. If it didn't, no one would do it. Yes, the problems are still waiting for you when you sober up, but for a little while, everything's better. Nothing gives you that momentary relief when you're sober.

Saint Tony had waited up for me that night and given me a longsuffering lecture when I stumbled in and bumped my cast on the doorjamb. I had responsibilities now. I couldn't go around and act like I was still single. He understood that I was hurting and needed a way to deal with it, but things were different now and he couldn't stand by and let me hurt myself even more.

I took off my shoe and threw it at him, then went to bed.

Yet he still hadn't walked out on me. He refused. For the next three months I did everything I knew to do – short of sleeping with someone else – to get him to admit he wanted to leave. He wouldn't do it. So I left.

He had let me go. For all his talk about being committed to our marriage and his certainty we could make it work if we really tried, he didn't put up a fight when I packed my bags. He stood in the kitchen and watched me go without a word, except to tell me, "You'll always be my wife, Salem. You can't walk away from that."

I'd grown up in a world where no one kept their word, and

vows were meaningless. I'd figured if he really wanted me to be his wife, he'd stop me from going.

But he hadn't. Which gave me a convenient place to target my rage. Why not blame Tony? He sent me letters and I'd torn them up, waiting – hoping desperately, and hating myself for hoping – for the sight of him driving up to cart me back to our little frame. If only he would do that, I had told myself, I'd try. I really would. But in the meantime I would party and go wild and he could come drag me off a barstool or a dance floor if he really wanted to prove to me that I would always be his wife.

I had waited a long time. After a while I had given up and found a cheap lawyer to draw up the papers. Try as I might, I couldn't remember what had happened after that, divorce-wise. I'd moved seven or eight times since then. I'd lugged boxes of crap from place to place. I couldn't remember the last time I had seen those papers.

"We can't really still be married. I mean, there's got to be some kind of statute of limitations or something, doesn't there?"

Tony shrugged. "Sorry, that's just for actual crimes, not marriages."

I rubbed my forehead. Jeez-o-Pete. "This is crazy."

"I've actually dealt with crazier things lately."

Ugh. Right. Murder charge. "I'm sorry, we can obviously deal with this later."

"Probably Lucinda was wearing the necklace when she was found. But..." He frowned and rubbed the back of his neck.

"What?"

"The police took photos of the back of my neck when they arrested me. I had this rash back there and they took pictures of it. I didn't know why, but now I wonder if it has something to do with the necklace."

I wished I had given Viv more time with that folder. Now that I was safely away from the police department I had all kinds of bravery.

"Did they tell you why they took the pictures?"

"No, I asked, but they just wanted to know where I'd gotten the marks on the back of my neck. I told them I didn't know."

"You don't know?"

"I didn't then. I started to get a rash there and later I figured I must have gotten into something I was allergic to. That's happened before. But at the time I didn't think about that, I was just thinking about Lucinda and what had happened to her."

"Of course." I mulled the information over in my mind. If the police had taken pictures of the back of Tony's neck, obviously they thought it had some significance to the murder. "Can I look?"

He turned and dipped down. I tugged the back of his shirt away and saw a thin red line, about three inches long, across the back of his neck. "You said this has happened before?"

"Not to my neck, but a couple of times I've washed my clothes in detergent that has something I'm allergic to, and it left a rash like that all over."

"So did you use that detergent again?"

"No, of course not. But I remembered what that felt like and figured that must be what caused the rash. I haven't really given it a lot of thought."

"Try to remember, okay? If the police thought it was significant, then somehow they're using it against you."

"Why would they use an allergic reaction against me?"

"I don't know, Tony, but it matters. Are there any cleaning

chemicals Lucinda would have been using that you're allergic to? Anything she might have had on her hands when she was found?"

He shook his head. "No, it was just a certain scent, in some detergents. That scent is not in any of the cleaning solutions we use." He wrinkled his brow, then shook his head again.

"Well, I don't know what it means, but it means something. We need to find out why they were interested in the back of your neck." I remembered what he'd said about the necklace. "Do you think it had something to do with your St. Christopher? Like maybe there was some kind of DNA evidence on it?"

"Man, Salem, I don't know. This is all just...out of the blue."

"I know." I felt like I should say something about him losing his girlfriend, but nothing appropriate sprang to mind. "Listen, Tony, I meant it about helping you in any way I can. I'm really sorry you're going through this. I'm sorry...well, I'm sorry for a lot of things."

He squeezed my arm, just like Bobby had done on Monday. What was it with guys squeezing my arm?

On the bright side, maybe Tony and I had discovered the secret to a long marriage: see each other only every decade or so.

Chapter Nine

As Viv drove me to meet Les, I mulled what we'd learned and pushed to the back of my mind – or *tried*, at least – all the issues relating to my apparently-on-again marriage. Tony had given Lucinda his St. Christopher necklace, and the words "St. Christopher" were in Lucinda's file. It was probably a list of things she had on her body or in her possession at the time she was found, nothing more. Tony's first instinct had been that it was connected to the police photographing the back of his neck. Why? Why was he so quick to make that jump?

"Okay, tell me again about what you saw on that report. The words "St. Christopher", was it a list, or was it like in the middle of a paragraph?"

"Middle of a paragraph."

"A lot of commas around it? Like, for instance they'd made a list, victim was wearing blue jeans, white blouse, silver watch, St. Christopher necklace? Like that?"

"How should I know? I saw St. Christopher and then you began to pee in your pants because someone was coming."

"Someone *was* coming."

"I wish we could talk to some of her friends besides Sylvia. Maybe get a more accurate picture of what she was like."

I was struck by a morbidly brilliant idea. "Her funeral!"

"Excellent!" Viv slapped her steering wheel. "I don't know why I didn't think of that first."

"Me either." Viv averaged two funerals a week.

"I'll call Herm and find out when it is."

"What if it's not at his place?" Herman Winslow ran the big fancy funeral home where all the Belle Court residents were embalmed.

"Doesn't matter, he's got his finger on the pulse of all the deceased in Estacado County."

"So to speak."

"So to speak, exactly."

She fished in her big bucket bag as she rounded the corner at Avenue Q and 34th, swerving into the turn lane and getting us three angry honks in the process. I reached over and swiped the phone out of her hand.

"How about you tell me the number and I dial?"

I punched in the number and asked for Mr. Winslow. I tried to shut out the image of him putting down an embalming wand to pick up the receiver. He told me Lucinda wasn't at his place, but as promised, he knew all the good stuff. Funeral was tomorrow at 2:00 p.m. at Our Lady of Guadalupe Catholic Church; then the family would take her body back to Mexico. Lucinda had only a small contingency of mourners coming from Mexico, and half a dozen or so from Texas, he'd heard six one time, and one time he'd heard eight. He knew for sure they'd tried to find a high-necked dress to cover the strangulation marks, which wasn't easy to find in West Texas in August, as he was sure I could under-stand, so they had to go with a scarf.

I hung up because we were getting close to the Exodus build-ing, and I could see Les and his ice cream truck out by the curb.

"Oh...my," Viv said. "Is that your new car?"

Oh, dear God in Heaven. Please don't let that be my new car.

Les grinned widely and gestured toward what had maybe once been a turquoise green hatchback. It was now pocked with rust marks and the passenger door was held closed with wire. Viv cir-cled it slowly and we both stared in silence.

"I can't believe it actually runs."

"Me either." I hoped against hope that it wouldn't start now. "Is it too late to pretend like we didn't see him?"

Since Les was, at this point, practically leaning inside my win-dow, I already knew the answer to my own question.

Viv pulled over. "Does that thing even run?"

"Like a top. Most reliable car I've ever seen. I had this car six years and drove it all over the country – put about a hundred and twenty thousand miles on it – then I gave it to my oldest boy Randy. He moved to Houston and drove it back and forth almost every weekend. Then he got a new car and gave it to my younger boy, and he's put another seventy-five thousand just in the last year and a half." He looked at the car and beamed.

"It looks it," Viv said.

I didn't know what to say. The more I looked, the more wired-together things I saw. The passenger side mirror. The hatchback. Probably too many things to mention under the hood. There were big rust holes in the doors and the driver's side window rose half-way up and stuck out two inches. The driver's side mirror dan-gled from a foot and a half of gray wire.

"I know she's not much to look at, but she runs like a top. This car won't ever leave you stranded by the side of the road. I guarantee it."

I chewed my lip. I forced myself to dredge up some gratitude. "Les, I can't tell you how...how much I appreciate this."

Les grinned from ear to ear. "I'm just glad someone can get some use out of it. This car has been a blessing to everyone in my family and now I'm able to pass it on to my surrogate daughter."

I opened the door and crawled out of Viv's very, very nice Cadillac. I owed it to Les to at least attempt to be gracious. "It looks like it would be...great on gas."

"Exactly! With gas so high you'll save a bundle." He clapped me on the shoulder. "You keep it as long as you need to, Salem. Don't feel like you have to rush getting her back to us."

"Thanks." I leaned over to look inside. Stump growled at the car. I pointed to where the driver's seat should be. "What's that?"

"Oh, that's a twenty-five pound pickle bucket. We had to take the driver's seat out a couple years ago. Cody found this bucket and turned it upside down and bingo, just the right height."

"Bingo," I whispered.

"Oh, and I almost forgot the most important part." He reached into his wallet. "We're still carrying the liability insurance so you don't even have to worry about that."

I blinked back tears. This was my new car. The answer to my prayers.

Thanks, God.

"Les, this is truly one of the sweetest things anyone has ever done for me. I don't deserve your generosity." That much was true. Anyone who felt this bad about something that obviously made Les feel so good didn't deserve anyone to be at all nice to them.

"Well," I said. "I guess I'll just get in and...give her a spin." Gulp.

Les proudly handed me the keys.

Viv blinked back tears of her own and gripped my hand. "Good luck," she whispered.

"Thanks," I sobbed.

"And don't forget your stuff." Her sympathy already a thing of the past, she opened the trunk and back seat and stood by while Les and I loaded all Mom's junk into the hatchback and back seat. It wouldn't all fit so I put two small boxes in the bucket seat beside me.

I got in and pumped the gas, then turned the key. It started right up. I could do everyone a favor and drive it and its cargo straight to the dump ground.

"Okay, I'll just be going then." I waited for some last minute reprieve to drop from the sky. There are times when that Second Coming seems like it couldn't come too soon. When the skies remained placid and no sinkhole opened beneath me, I said, "Thanks again, Les. I'll get it back to you just as soon as I can arrange for something permanent."

"Like I said, no rush. Take all the time you need." He reached in and handed me the seat belt. "Don't forget this. Don't want to get a ticket."

I fastened the seat belt, although it was obviously a formality since my pickle bucket was, I was fairly certain, not quite up to the DMV minimum standard.

I gave a feeble wave and rattled across the parking lot onto 34th Street. The... "car" pulled hard to the right, so I had to keep the steering wheel turned twenty-five degrees to the left just to keep it on the road. The bucket tilted under me every time I shifted even a little, making my heart jump every time. Good grief, this day had worn me out.

I drove to Flo's and asked my co-worker Becky if I could switch early days with her so I could be off in time for Lucinda Cruz's funeral. She acted a little put out, but agreed. I asked Flo if I could be sure to be through with my dogs by twelve-thirty so I'd have time to get cleaned up and go to the funeral.

From there I headed home, wanting to crawl into bed and hide from the world. Frank was waiting on the front deck. He laughed when he saw me get out of the pickle-mobile.

"Where'd you find that thing?"

"I'm tired and I don't want to talk about it. Les loaned it to me, and I'm very grateful to have it." I was, at least, grateful I didn't have to walk anymore. Almost.

I sank to the deck and groaned. My legs felt like logs. "I have to go to a funeral tomorrow and I can't take Stump. Can you swing by Flo's after work and bring her home with you? I'll give you dinner."

"No prob, man," he said. "That dead body girl you found?"

"Yeah." I ran my hand through my hair. "Do we have any Star Crunches left?"

"Oh, umm..." He looked guilty. "Maybe not."

I shook my head. "No big deal," but I admit, I kind of wanted to cry.

Frank wasn't hungry and must have gotten tired of hearing me complain about how tired *I* was, because he left not long after that. I curled up with Stump and a bowl of Ricearoni, waiting for it to get late enough that I could justify going to bed. Finally, around eight o'clock I gave up and went anyway, even though the sun was far from setting. I was exhausted, and my mind was tangled. I couldn't think straight and I felt guilty that in the midst of everything, I'd still found the strength to feel sorry for myself that I had to drive perched on a pickle bucket.

I dropped down beside my bed and tried to pray, but couldn't even think what to pray for. I'd asked God for a car and I got a moving junkyard. I'd asked God for help with Tony and I got Viv committing crimes and giving me information that only confused everyone.

"God," I finally said. "I'm sorry, but I'm tired and I don't know what to do next, and I don't know if I can help anyone here so it looks like I'm just going to keep on being a mooching charity case that's fortunate to have a pickle bucket to sit on." I wrinkled my nose. "Sorry, I know that sounded very bitter. I'm just tired. I'll be more grateful tomorrow, I promise."

After ten thousand mental repetitions of the conversation between Tony and me, I finally fell asleep. All I could remember from my dreams was that something kept flashing by me, too fast for me to catch.

I woke up in the middle of the night wondering why they would need to cover strangulation marks on Lucinda's neck if she'd died by blunt force trauma to the head.

I couldn't be sure the form Viv saw was an autopsy report, and I couldn't even be sure the blunt force trauma had *been* to her head. Maybe I'd put together the words Viv read with memories from too many TV crime shows. I supposed a person could have blunt force trauma elsewhere, but "to the head" just seemed to naturally follow. Strangulation marks, though? That did not.

I got a couple more hours of sleep, then got up. My legs screamed at me as soon as I stood. "Holy mother of...!" I muttered.

I froze at the edge of my bed, not sure I could make it to the bathroom. I forced myself to move, saying "Ouch, ouch, ouch," each step of the way.

A shower helped my soreness, and afterwards I dug through my closet for something appropriate to wear to Lucinda's funeral. The pickings were slim, especially since I'd gotten too big to wear almost everything in there. Too bad I didn't have the time or money to go shopping.

I finally settled on a denim skirt I'd bought at Walmart last winter and a brown t-shirt. Not exactly your typical mourning attire, but since my only black was the wind suit pants I wore to work, I figured it would have to do.

I chewed my lip as I sifted through all the clothes I couldn't wear. There was a good twenty-five pounds jiggling between me and most of them, and more like thirty-five or forty between me and the smallest of the clothes. I wanted to cry when I looked at my skinny jeans.

I had promised to be more grateful after a good night's rest, and I approached my prayer place with resolve. I was blessed to have what I had. I was blessed with a day to do some good.

Even as I sank to my knees, though, different muscles screamed and I felt all sense of hope drain from me. Was this really doing any good at all? Was I just putting myself through pain for nothing?

"God is faithful in all he does," Les says.

I sighed and said, "Look...I don't mean to complain, but..." *But I don't really care for the way you're answering my prayers.* Was that what I wanted to say? I wasn't even sure anymore. I just knew that hoping for one thing and getting something entirely different was beginning to wear on me.

"I'm going to a funeral today. There are a lot of people in pain, and some people I care about who are scared. I'd appreciate it if you could give me some direction or something to say or... or *something*. Just something. Please." I started to ask again for a new car, but really what was the point? "And please, don't let my pickle bucket turn over while I'm driving down Slide Road." Surely that wasn't asking too much.

Turns out, it was. I left the PakASak with breakfast burritos for me and Stump, pulled out onto Slide and the freaking thing tilted into the handbrake. I panicked and kicked my legs and succeeded in knocking the bucket completely over, with me sprawling into the back floorboard. I felt the car rolling across the middle of the street, saw my legs sticking straight up into the air. My muscles screamed, I screamed, and Stump jumped into the middle of my chest and growled.

I don't think I've ever moved that fast in my life. I threw Stump back over into the passenger seat and scrambled up as fast as I could. The bucket was still on its side, and I perched on it and steered the car away from the light pole it was headed toward.

My heart thundered in my chest as I looked around at the other cars. Fortunately there were only three others on the block, and all three drivers stared at me. I pretended like nothing was out of the ordinary and headed for Bow Wow Barbers.

My heart didn't stop pounding till I was halfway through my burrito. If that had happened an hour later the street would have been packed and I would definitely have hit someone. Normally I would just chalk it up as one of those things, but I had asked God *specifically* not to let the bucket overturn while I was on Slide...man! I wonder what Les would have to say about that.

I called Viv and told her I'd need her to pick me up. I was scared to death of driving that stupid car and there was no way I was going to take it to the funeral. She said she was surprised I'd made it to work at all.

I did get a break in that none of my dogs scratched, bit, or peed on me, so I looked fairly presentable when Viv picked me up. I kissed the top of Stump's head and told her to be good for Frank while I was gone. She snorted at me and moved to sulk with her back to me in the back of her cage.

"Is that what you're wearing?" She, of course, looked like she'd just stepped out of the Wealthy Matron section of a fancy department store.

"It's all I have," I said. "I don't really want to talk about it."

She shrugged. "Been there, done that. We really need to take you shopping, though. I'd hate for you to show up at my funeral wearing that."

"If you give me six or eight months to lose some weight, I have a nice little black number that would do you proud."

"Can do. You know, I saw a coupon for Fat Fighters where two friends can join for the price of one."

The funeral was at a little Catholic church just a couple of blocks from our big church. Cars surrounded it, and I recognized six or eight people from Tony's family milling around outside. I hoped nobody would spit on me, although I did get a few dark looks. I tried to hide behind Viv as we made our way into the church, like Bluto hiding behind Olive Oyl.

In the Methodist church it's called the sanctuary; I'm not sure what it's called at the Catholic church, but it was about a quarter full. I hadn't been inside a Catholic church since Tony's and my baby died. Viv and I sat near the back and scoped out the crowd.

Viv leaned toward me and said, "I see three or four girls that age. They're going to be our best bet for good information."

Sylvia came in looking solemn, and Rey tagged right behind her. I felt my lip curl up and told myself that that was inappropriate at a funeral. I should let bygones be bygones, or at the very least put my disgust aside for the forty-five minutes or so I needed to be in the same room with the creep.

The place was small, all dark wood pews and window frames. It seemed like everything had a sponsor. This stained glass window graciously donated by the Felix Ramirez family. This pew graciously donated by the Oscar Martinez family in memory of Rosalinda Martinez.

I could read the inscriptions on four of the stained glass windows and finally found one of St. Christopher, graciously donated by the Maria Solis family in memory of their loving husband and father, Anthony Solis.

"Are all the Saints, Saints of something?" I whispered to Viv.

"Huh?" She drew her head back.

"I mean if they're a Saint, are they the Saint of something in particular?"

"I don't know. I'm Methodist."

"Aren't there Patron Saints of all kinds of different things? I remember one time it was St. Something day. He was the Patron Saint of animals or pets and all these people brought their dogs into be groomed so they could be blessed on that day."

"That's just weird."

"Shh." It wasn't cool to be insulting Catholic customs inside a Catholic church. I had thought it was sweet.

"I'm just wondering what St. Christopher is the patron saint of?"

Viv shrugged. "Hmmp."

"It could be a clue. If it was in the police report it could be important." I told her what Tony said about giving Lucinda his St. Christopher necklace.

"Maybe he's the patron saint of lovers."

"I don't think so." He'd worn it the whole time we were married, and never offered to let me try it on, but then, it wouldn't take much for him to think more of Lucinda than he had of me.

I studied the window to see what St. Christopher was the Patron Saint of, but it didn't give me any clues. A man with a walking stick carried a kid on his back. I guess both the man and the kid were Saints, because they both had those halos on their heads. It looked like they were going somewhere.

A priest walked down the short aisle sprinkling water at everybody, chanting something in Latin, I assumed. The service was kind of a blur for me because I didn't really know what was going on except when Lucinda's cousin read the Twenty-Third Psalm. The priest talked about Lucinda's promising life cut short, and the tragedy that the baby she carried would never take her first breath, but they were both with God in glory now, and the baby would also never know sadness or the heartbreak everyone there was going through. Then it was over.

"Let's corner that girl with the purple dress first. She looks like she has inside information."

"How do you figure that?"

"She's crying, so she knew Lucinda. They look to be about the same age, so they might have been friends. And, she's wearing a pretty purple dress to a funeral. She's self-centered enough to be concerned about how she looks, maybe even wants to get some attention. So we'll give her some."

Whatever. I followed Viv's lead mostly because the girl in the purple dress was going the opposite way from Mrs. Solis.

The church was set on a hill and concrete steps flanked the front, angling down to the street. Clusters of people stood on the steps and down by the parked cars. I trailed after Viv, trying not to look out of place. It was kind of hard, though. Out of thirty or forty people there, we were two of the six who were not Hispanic.

Viv angled up to the girl in the purple dress as she stood talking to one of the other white people. The girl's eyes were red and swollen. It wasn't until then that I realized the guy she was talking to was George, the building supervisor. Of course he would be at the funeral. He'd probably worked with Lucinda.

"Such a sad day," Viv said as she walked up to George. "Did you know her well?"

George shot me a nervous glance. Good grief, I tried to look as non-menacing as possible.

"She'd only worked for Solis for a couple of months, but I talked to her on several occasions. She was a sweet girl." He slid his gaze over to me as if to say, *Unlike some people.*

"Tragic, that two beautiful lives are lost." Viv turned and patted the girl on the arm. "I'm so sorry for you loss. Was she a friend or a relative of yours?"

"A friend," the girl said hoarsely. "Just a friend. I worked with her."

"I can see that you two must have been close."

The girl tilted her head and nodded. "We'd become close. She said she wanted me to be the godmother to her baby."

"You poor, poor thing. You're doubly heartbroken then, aren't you?"

Okay, Viv knew what she was doing. The girl had obviously

been waiting for someone to feel sorry for her. After that it didn't take much effort to get the girl off to the side and find out that her name was Stephanie, she'd worked for Tony for over a year, and she and Lucinda had talked about taking a trip to the beach together before it got cold and Lucinda got too pregnant to wear a two-piece bathing suit.

I tuned out for a while, thinking that a nine-months pregnant Lucinda would still look better in a bathing suit – no matter how many pieces it consisted of – than I did. I thought again about Tony and the look of guilt on his face when he'd told me he'd given Lucinda his necklace.

My ears perked back up when I heard the words "Rey" and "jerk" in the same sentence.

"She was dating Rey?" Viv asked.

I angled forward. This was suddenly quite interesting.

"Not anymore." Stephanie cast a glance of disgust over toward Rey and Sylvia. "She came here to get away from that –" She broke off and shook her head. "She came here to get away from him."

"Why?" Viv was beyond being cautious now.

"Because he's a jerk who abused her. He beat her up and called her a whore and told her the baby wasn't his."

"He what?"

She looked at me, surprised, I guess, that I was still there. "He said the baby wasn't his."

"But the baby *was* his, right?"

She glared. "Of course it was his. They'd dated for almost a year before she broke up with him and moved here."

"Do you know Rey's mother, Sylvia?" I asked.

She shrugged. "Not very well. I went over there a couple of

times to pick up Lucinda, but I never talked to her. Lucinda said she didn't talk much."

That didn't sound like the Sylvia I knew. The Sylvia I knew talked to everyone.

"Did Syliva know Rey was the father of Lucinda's baby?"

"That's the only reason she agreed to let Lucinda live with her. Rey wasn't taking very good care of Lucinda, so Sylvia said she could live with her till she got on her feet and could provide for the baby."

"So Lucinda got pregnant, Rey refused to take care of her, and Sylvia volunteered to help her out?"

Now *that* sounded like Sylvia. Always cleaning up Rey's messes.

"Tony kind of made Sylvia take her in, from what Lucinda said. Well, Tony and his mom did. Tony said he'd give Lucinda a job, but someone else had to give her a place to stay because she shouldn't be living with him since they weren't married or anything. Tony's mom said Sylvia had to do it."

Geez, he sounded like someone from Little House on the Prairie days. While Tony worried about impropriety, I'd lost count of the men I'd slept with and the girlfriends I'd betrayed, and good old Mrs. Solis, still bossing everyone around, just like old times.

"How did she feel about the baby? Was she excited about a grandchild?"

Stephanie shrugged again. "She never really talked about it much. Lucinda said she'd ask questions about how many men she'd dated, stuff like that. Like she agreed with Rey that the baby probably wasn't his."

I wondered if they had done a DNA test with the autopsy.

Would it matter who the father of Lucinda's unborn baby was?

I cast a glance over at Rey. He wore a starched white shirt, dark slacks and mirrored sunglasses. I couldn't see his eyes, but I could feel him staring back at me, the slime.

He did it. I felt in my bones that he was the one who had killed Lucinda, and then tried to put the blame on Tony.

Of course, I had absolutely nothing to back up this theory other than an intense dislike for the guy, and I doubted that would carry much weight in court.

I turned back to Stephanie. "Who do you think would have done this to Lucinda?"

She was quiet for a minute. "I don't really know. I mean, it could have been anyone, I guess. I was always a little creeped out in that church, to be honest, because it's so close to the bus station. There are always a lot of homeless people walking around. I was afraid one of them would sneak in and hide somewhere and wait for me."

"Do you think that's what happened to Lucinda? Some unstable or drugged up homeless person hiding out in the basement of the church killed her?"

She didn't look especially convinced. "I don't really know."

"Do you think it could have been Rey?"

She looked over at him.

"Don't look!" Viv snapped.

Stephanie whipped her head back, her eyes wide. "I – I don't know. Maybe. I mean, he did beat her up and tell her he'd kill her before he let anyone else have her."

"He did? Well then, that proves it, doesn't it? He killed her!" I wanted to bang a gavel.

"Hush!" Viv said. "Chill out a little."

She was right. Stephanie's second-hand account wasn't exactly proof of anything besides the fact that Rey was a lowlife, but it was something to pursue.

"Bobby needs to know this. I'll bet he doesn't even know about Rey at all. They're so busy harassing Tony they probably haven't looked at anyone else."

A hand landed on my shoulder. "Hi, Salem. You're looking..." He raked his gaze down to my feet and back up again and sneered. "...healthy."

I felt my eyes bulge as I looked up at Rey's smirking face. For a second I heard the Psycho music in my head. A cold-blooded murderer was touching me.

Then the fact that I'd been insulted penetrated my paranoid brain. I sidestepped away from him and sniffed. "What is that smell? Oh, I think it's all that stuff in your hair. How are you, Rey?"

"My unborn child and her mother were murdered. How do you think I am? What are you doing here?"

"Paying my respects. So where were *you* the night Lucinda was killed? Have the police asked you that yet?"

Rey's jaw twitched, and from the corner of my eye I swore I could see his fist clench.

"We're here to show our support for the family during this time of mourning." Viv stepped between me and Rey, bless her. "It's a tragedy and we are so sorry for you loss. We both attend the church where Lucinda was murdered, and we want you to know that we're here for you during your time of need."

I raised my eyebrow. We were?

"Salem goes to church? My, how things have changed."

Man, I really wished I had a comeback for that one. I had to settle for more glaring-mixed-with-disdain.

I kind of hoped Viv would whip out one of her zingers in my defense but she just nodded. "Yes, of course, times do change. If you or any of your family needs the church's help for anything, please do not hesitate to ask. Just call the front desk and they'll know who to put you in contact with. Please accept our condolences."

She turned again to Stephanie. "Thank you again for talking with us. We are so sorry for your loss as well. This is a very difficult time, but we're confident that Lucinda and her child are both in a better place and we know God will make sure justice prevails."

She took me by the elbow and steered me back to the car. I waited till we were buckling up before I asked her, "What was all that about? You're being nice to the killer? What's up with that?"

"That was about building a false sense of confidence. The police are not looking at him right now, so there's a possibility he's left some kind of evidence somewhere that will exonerate Tony. If we let him know someone suspects him, he'll look closer at covering his tracks."

That made sense. Still, it was morally wrong for her to be nice to someone who'd insulted me, oh, and had probably murdered someone. "Do you really think Rey did it?"

She waved a hand. "He could have. The main thing is, he is a suspect worth looking into, and if it takes the heat off Tony, then we're making progress."

Apparently for Viv, truth and justice didn't necessarily have to go hand in hand, but she was right. Rey *could have* done it. He had a history of violence and had stated that he would kill Lucinda – well, that part was hearsay, but still – and that was more than a little noteworthy. Bobby would want to have that information. It could help Tony out.

If Rey happened to be put in jail for the rest of his life in the process, so much the better.

We drove to the police station. "Please don't be having any fake heart attacks while we're in here, okay?"

"I'll try," Viv said resolutely, tucking her handbag under her arm.

Bobby was getting coffee off a stand in the hallway when we came in. "Hey, it's my favorite mystery-solving duo. How's the case going?"

"We have a new lead." Viv lifted her chin. "We'd appreciate the opportunity to discuss it with you. If you have the time, of course."

Good. She was going with the quiet-and-respectful-determination routine.

"Of course." Bobby motioned with his head toward his office. "In here."

"You feeling okay?" he asked Viv as he motioned for us to sit. "What did your doctor say?"

"He said I'm in excellent shape for a woman my age who has a bad heart. We just came from Lucinda Cruz's funeral service."

Bobby lifted an eyebrow and settled back in his chair. "Yes?"

"We were able to question a friend of Lucinda's, one Stephanie Duncan. She had some interesting things to say."

She waited for Bobby to ask what kind of interesting things. Bobby waited for Viv to spill it, refusing to ask. I got tired of this grown-up version of the game of chicken and leaned forward. "We think you need to take a look at Rey."

"Rey who?"

"Rey Ramirez, Tony's cousin. You remember him."

Bobby nodded. "Vaguely. Why do you think we need to look at him?"

"He was Lucinda Cruz's ex-boyfriend. He has a history of violence toward her, and he was heard to threaten that if he couldn't have her, no one would."

"Is that right?" He seemed singularly unimpressed.

"Bobby, come on. The guy is a snake and you know it. He beat her up, he threatened her. She was carrying his child, and she left him. He was furious and came after her. In a fit of jealous rage he killed her and framed Tony."

"Nice theory." He leaned forward and put his elbows on the desk. "But, unfortunately, I'm legally bound to work with facts, not theories, and your scenario doesn't match up with the facts we have at this time."

"Then get some new facts," Viv snapped. "The man is an abuser of women!"

"I know that," Bobby said calmly. He began to look a little worried, though. Probably didn't want to get Viv riled into another heart attack.

"You do?"

He nodded again. "We've already checked him out. The Oklahoma City PD has a couple of arrests on him for assault, but assault's not murder. He's got an alibi, Salem. He was 350 miles away when the murder took place."

Oh. Again, enough to make me wish I still cussed. "Are you sure?"

"Salem, I promise, we're doing a thorough job on this investigation." His eyes actually took on a soft look and instinctually I melted a little in my chair. "I know you want to believe your husband is innocent, and I swear to you, we'll follow every lead and go over every piece of evidence with a fine-toothed comb. If he's not guilty, he won't be convicted. Period."

Viv made a snorting noise. Bobby cast a glance toward her but remained silent. He turned back to me. "Listen. Tony Solis would not have been charged if we didn't feel we had sufficient evidence to try him. We have to look at the facts, Salem, and I've got to be honest. It doesn't look good for him."

I took a stab in the dark. "Look, I already know about the St. Christopher thing."

It was weird. It wasn't as if "that's it!" was instantly written all over Bobby's face or anything. In fact, it was as if he was trying so hard *not* to show anything that I knew I'd hit *something*. So I kept pushing.

"He told me he'd given her the necklace because he had feelings for her. That's why his necklace was at the crime scene, not because Tony was there."

Bobby was silent for a long second. He leaned back in his chair and stared at me. The carefully blank look was gone, though, so I supposed that meant if I *had* been onto something, I was off it now.

"Salem, we don't need the necklace to tie him to the crime scene. Surveillance video does that."

"Surveillance video? What kind of church has surveillance video?"

"The kind that's downtown across from the bus station, in an area that's otherwise deserted at night." He stood. "Look, I really do appreciate the fact that you want to help, but the first thing you need to do is leave the detective work to the detectives."

I stood, frustrated. "But did you hear what I just said? Tony had feelings for her. Why would he kill her if he had feelings for her? He gave her his necklace, for crying out loud. I was his wife, and he never gave me his necklace. Why would he do that if he was going to kill her?"

"Well, if she was going back to Rey and he became jealous, he might have done it," Viv said.

I whirled on her.

"What? I'm just thinking out loud!"

"Well, stop it." I took her hand and led her to the door. I turned back to Bobby. "Promise me you won't dismiss Rey out of hand. His alibi could be bogus. He could have done something to set Tony up. He's like that. Tony's not. Believe me, I know. Rey is the hothead. Did you even know Rey was the father of her baby?"

"I know we're waiting for DNA tests to prove who the father is. *That's* what I know." He held the door for us. "I do appreciate your coming to me with your information."

"Whatever," Viv said. "If you're not going to do anything with it, maybe next time we'll just go straight to Tony's lawyer."

If anything, the episode made me feel even worse for Tony. We'd found an actual lead and yet we'd gotten nowhere.

We went back to Viv's car and I sank into my seat, dejected enough that even Viv's driving didn't get my attention. "Tony is so screwed."

"He is if you're giving up that quickly."

"What else can we do?"

"Keep digging. What do we have?"

"Besides nothing?"

"We have a likely suspect."

"Who has an alibi."

"So the first order of business is to find out what his alibi is. Bobby said Rey was in Oklahoma City when the murder occurred. So we can assume that someone there vouched for him, or that he has something that supposedly proves he was there."

"So we'll just go to Oklahoma City and ask around?"

Viv chewed her lip. Little hairs on her chin quivered when she did that. "We'll think of something." Which meant she had nothing. "One thing I do know. Lucinda Cruz was murdered with that St. Whozits thingy."

"How do you know that?"

"Well, we know it's important, right? I mean, it was in the crime scene stuff. And Bobby said they didn't need it to tie Tony to the scene. And he got an awfully careful look on his face when you brought it up, which all points to the fact that it's a big deal. So *why* would it be such a big deal unless it was a murder weapon?"

"We can't just assume it was the murder weapon. It could be anything. Besides, didn't the autopsy say something about blunt force trauma? How could a little gold medallion be heavy enough to kill someone?"

I remembered then about the guy at the funeral home – Herman – and his remark about the strangulation marks. "Could there be two causes of death?"

"Don't you ever watch T.V.? There's only one cause of death, but there can be multiple injuries."

"So he strangled her and then knocked her over the head?"

"I guess. What a putz."

An idea was forming in the back of my mind. I knew someone who had some experience with murder investigations, and might even have some inside information about this crime, someone who might be able to point us in a direction that could lead to something else.

It was someone I really, *really* didn't want to talk to.

I groaned and wrapped my arms around my stomach.

"Do I need to pull over?" Viv asked.

"No, I'm okay. Do we have time to go see one more person?"

Viv looked at the digital clock on her dash. "Well, in fifteen minutes Belle Court will be serving their weekly Ice Cream Social in the Nifty Fifties Diner." She made gagging noises. "You wouldn't believe the stuff they try to pass off as ice cream. Low fat dairy-free crud. Where we going?"

"Channel Eleven. I know a girl there who might be able to help us dig up something. Trisha – I mean..." What did she call herself now? "Patrice Watson."

Viv slapped the seat between us. "Get out! You know Patrice Watson? I love her! She needs to lose some weight, though."

"Yeah, well, I knew her when she called herself Trisha and didn't need to lose any weight. And just so you'll know, she's mad at me for some stuff I did while I was drinking, so there's a good possibility she's not going to feel very hospitable toward me."

Viv shrugged. "Won't be the first time someone's not excited to see me."

The receptionist who'd try to brush me off last time was standing with her back to us, talking to someone in the office behind her. I grabbed Viv's arm, put my finger over my mouth to try and keep her quiet, and dragged her across to the swinging door toward the newsroom.

"What are you doing?" Viv jerked her arm back.

"If we have to deal with the receptionist it'll take an hour, and

I want to get this over with. I'm going to have to grovel."

Trisha – Patrice, Patrice, for Pete's sake call her Patrice! – was on the phone when we got there. She raised an eyebrow when she saw me but kept talking.

Viv wandered around the room staring at people and picking up stuff she probably wasn't supposed to touch. "Can I help you?"

"You're Mike Maloney!" Viv said to the red-headed kid who did the weekend weather. "What are you doing here? Did they let you out of school early?"

"I'm filling in for Bob Sherwood while he's on vacation this week," Little Mikey said. Geez, he looked even younger in person, not standing in front of his weather map. Did he even have a driver's license yet? Or was I just old enough that everyone looked too young to me?

On that happy note, Trisha – man! Patrice! – walked up behind us. "They're here to see me," she said. She clipped an earring on her ear. "Come on back here."

She hustled us out of there pretty quick, and I saw a couple of curious heads turn our way as we passed through. I even thought I heard a couple of whispers. I looked at Viv to see if she was catching the vibe, too, but she was too star struck to see anything but Patrice.

There. I said it.

She led us into a break room and closed the door behind us. "What do you want? I've already told you that you have no chance of winning a lawsuit. The station is behind me one hundred per-cent and is prepared to fight whatever charges you want to file. In fact, they're hoping you'll file a suit so we can get some pub-licity out of it." She crossed her arms over her chest, looking from me to Viv. "So? What do you want? A quick buck? Think you can blackmail me or something?"

Geez Louise, but Trisha had gotten bitter. I just stared at her, not believing she was going over this again. I was afraid she'd bring up the thing with Scott, but she was still on the non-existent lawsuit stuff.

I thought about how she'd rushed us in here and closed the door, and suddenly her attitude took on a new light. She was going for a determined look, but something told me this was a "the best defense is a good offense" move.

"You're suing her?" Viv looked from Trisha – good grief, I was never going to remember to call her Patrice – to me. "No wonder she's mad at you."

"I'm not suing her. I've already told her that." I narrowed my eyes and studied Patrice. "You're bluffing."

She snorted. "I'm what?"

"You're bluffing. The station's not behind you. You got in trouble for showing my picture, didn't you? They raked you over the coals and now you're all just waiting for me to file a lawsuit, scared to death."

"You live in a dream land, Salem." She turned and reached for the door.

"Trisha, I know you, and I know when you're lying. Remember when you told Coach Haney you had cramps so you could skip P.E.? You have that exact same look in your eyes. You're lying through your teeth because you know I can hurt you."

She froze for a moment, then turned slowly. "You can't hurt me, Salem. You can make me lose my job, you can destroy my reputation, you can take every material thing I have. But you can't hurt me. You've done all of that you can."

Well. There wasn't much I could say to that. If I'd had any

notion of pressuring Trisha into helping me, it flew out the window. I wished we hadn't come.

"She's not here to hurt you, you drama queen. She's trying to help you."

Trisha raised one eyebrow and looked at Viv.

"I'm serious. We're on to something in the Lucinda Cruz case. We have the actual killer in our sights. We just need to do a little investigating and gather the evidence to prove it."

I rubbed my upper lip. I really wished Viv would leave the speaking to me sometimes. I'd planned to ease our way into things a little more gracefully.

"You have the real killer, huh? Who is it, O.J. Simpson?"

"You're funny. Too bad you're not going to be laughing when we go down to Channel Seven and give them our exclusive."

"Okay, that's enough." I put a hand on Viv's shoulder. "Patrice probably doesn't care where we go with our exclusive, seeing as how we don't actually have anything yet." I turned to Tri...Patrice. "Look, I think Tony's innocent, and I'd do just about anything to help him out. We've been talking to some people and we think maybe he's being framed."

"Is that so?" She looked at her fingernails.

"I know you don't owe me anything, just the opposite. But I don't know who else to ask, and I figured in your line of work you've probably learned a thing or two about investigating things. You know, you being a journalist and all. We could tell you what we've learned, and maybe you could share with us things you know that are not public knowledge, things you've learned from being in your position. Then maybe we could decide where we need to look next."

"You're serious?" Patrice sneered a little. "You're really doing some kind of private eye thing to vindicate Tony?"

"I know it's crazy, and I know if he gets out of this horrible mess, it's probably not going to be because of us, but...well, I'm sure you can understand that there are a lot of wrongs I'd like to make right. There's a lot of hurt I've caused that I really want to make up for, and Tony's pretty high up on my list of people I want to make restitution to." I cocked my head and met her eyes, which wasn't exactly an easy thing to do. "He's second from the top, in fact."

Patrice looked at her nails some more and chewed the inside of her lip. I was pretty sure she still wanted to slap me.

"Would it help if I told your boss I have no intention at all of suing you? Maybe I could sign some kind of waiver or something?"

She narrowed her eyes but still didn't say anything.

"Can I talk now?" Viv asked.

"Not yet," I said. "Give her some time to think about it." If she said yes, maybe that would create an opening for her to forgive me. I knew it wouldn't happen quickly, and for sure we'd never be friends again – how could we be? – but if she said yes, that would mean that some part of her wanted to forgive me, or wanted to see something redemptive in me – something, just a crumb.

I found that I couldn't breathe, waiting for her to answer.

"I doubt very seriously you're going to have any information I don't already have."

"Probably true," I said. "But maybe some people would talk to me who wouldn't want to talk to someone official, you know? Since I'm just a regular person and all, I'm not a threat or anything. Not that you're a threat to anyone," I said quickly. "It's just...maybe people who aren't comfortable talking to you, might be less intimidated by me. We'll never know till we compare notes," I offered.

Patrice responded, "there's probably not much I could share with you. If I haven't used it in a story, it's because all I have is a rumor, or I haven't been cleared by the PD to use it."

I was dying to know if she already had something she couldn't tell me, but I kept my mouth shut and nodded quickly. "That's okay. You can't work off of rumors, I get that, being a professional and all, but Viv and I aren't bound by the same rules, and we can chase all the rumors we want to. We're not respected professionals."

"Would you quit sucking up?" Viv frowned at me. "We don't need her that bad."

"She slept with my fiancé," Patrice spat out. "She will never suck up enough." She looked at me. "Look, I'll help you on two conditions. The first is, you do sign a statement saying you do not hold me or this station or our parent company liable for anything in the past or in the future. And second, you tell me everything you get no matter how small or how far out in left field it seems. If this case breaks open, I want to be the one to break it."

"So you think he's innocent, too?" I wanted to heave a big sigh of relief. Finally, someone with actual credibility was agreeing with me. "I mean, Tony's not the type of person to do something like this, don't you think?"

She shrugged and rolled her eyes. "Salem, I've long since quit being surprised at the horrible and out-of-character things people do to each other. I have no idea whether he's innocent or not. I do know that if I can get a story out of it, I will."

She turned and yanked open the door, leaving us to follow in her expensive-perfume wake.

"Cold," Viv said, with a trace of admiration.

"Don't let her fool you," I whispered as we followed. "She pretends to be a hard-ass, but I remember how she cried when the 'Saved by the Bell' kids went to college. She has a soft heart."

The first thing Patrice did was type up a letter saying that Channel Eleven had my permission to use my likeness in any situation deemed appropriate by them and in any media, whether it be print, film or video – blah blah blah – that I held them blameless now and forever more for any and everything – blah blah blah –that I would neither expect nor request to be compensated in any way. Blah blah blah. I was pretty sure even *she* didn't know exactly what she was writing and that something that broad would never hold up in court, but I signed it anyway. I was happy she was willing to spend five minutes with me.

"I'm going to lunch," she announced to the room at large as soon as she'd made copies and given me one. "I'll be back in forty-five minutes."

Viv and I watched her walk out the door. We looked at each other. "That didn't really go as well as I would have hoped," Viv said.

"Me either. Are we supposed to stay here till she gets back, or just wait at home till she calls us?"

Patrice poked her head back in the door. "Hello? Are you coming or not?"

"Oh. Yeah!" Viv and I lurched behind her.

Chapter Ten

Viv drove her expensive sedan behind Patrice's expensive sedan to an Italian place down the road from the station. Apparently Patrice Watson was a regular there, because they sat her at her "usual" table near the back of the room.

I perused the menu, wondering if I could get away with ordering a bowl of soup or a salad or something. Payday was still two days away and I had less than ten bucks in my purse. The cheapest entrée was eight-fifty, and with tax and tip that would be...

"What can I get you?"

Patrice ordered a fancy fish dish with cream sauce. Viv ordered linguine with clam sauce. I closed my menu. "You know, I'm really not very hungry. I think I'll just have a glass of iced tea." My stomach growled.

"The station is paying," Patrice said curtly.

"I'll have fettuccini alfredo," I said.

"And bring us a bottle of that Merlot I had last week. Three glasses."

The waitress walked away, and I could feel Viv looking at me. She wondered if I'd told Patrice I wasn't drinking. She didn't want to out me if I didn't want to be,

but Patrice knew. I'd told her three days ago when I saw her. And from the smirk on her face, she was enjoying this little test.

I took a deep breath. "That's very generous, but Viv and I don't drink. Thanks anyway."

"Oh, come on. One glass isn't going to hurt you. We need to loosen things up in here."

"She said we don't drink –"

I put my hand on Viv's. "It's okay. Don't worry about it. Let's go ahead and get started, shall we?"

Patrice had thrown down a gauntlet, and thankfully her manipulation was enough to get me focused on winning this contest instead of on how much I *really* wanted a glass of that wine – just one glass – because everything had been so crappy lately. One glass because I'd been so good and deserved a reward. One glass because I was trying so hard and nothing – abso-freaking-lutely nothing had gone my way in a very long time. Just one glass because right at the moment I felt like I'd been a sold a bill of goods with the whole sobriety *and* Christianity thing. None of it was what it was cracked up to be, and none of it was as great as Les and everyone else kept promising me it was. I wanted just one glass.

I focused on what information we had. "We've been able to get a brief glimpse at the initial crime report and just saw a few things; blunt force trauma, and something about St. Christopher. We also know that Lucinda had bruises or something around her neck – the funeral parlor guy called them strangulation marks."

The waitress dropped a basket of breadsticks on the table and Patrice and I knocked our knuckles reaching for carb heaven. Now this, I could indulge in. To heck with the skinny jeans in the closet.

"That's all pretty much public knowledge, Salem. The official autopsy results won't be in for a few more days so we don't know which injury was the actual cause of death, but it doesn't really matter. She was knocked over the head and choked and something did her in." She slathered butter on her breadstick.

I hadn't seen the butter. I waited politely till she got through, then dug my own knife in.

"Will the autopsy results be public record when they come in?"

"Not until after the trial. If this is all you have, I don't see how we're going to be able to help each other."

"Don't get your panties in a twist," Viv said. "Give me some of that bread. All this animosity flying around is making me nervous."

"I talked to Sylvia and I think there's something worth looking into in that direction."

"Sylvia?"

"Sylvia Ramirez, Tony's aunt. Rey's mother. You remember Rey."

Patrice groaned and rolled her eyes. "Slimeball."

So she didn't know about Rey yet. Ha.

"He used to date Lucinda Cruz. She lived in Oklahoma City, and they dated for a year and a half. Then she broke up with him and he supposedly went crazy. Said if he couldn't have her, nobody could."

"Dialogue straight out of America's Most Wanted."

"So apparently her mom called Sylvia and Josephine – Tony's mom – and asked them to help Lucinda. Tony gave her a job, and she was staying with Sylvia in Rey's old room."

"Why would the girl want to break it off with Rey, then move in with his mother? Why not just break it off clean? Or stay with him?"

I blinked. When Patrice said it like that, the whole thing didn't make sense. I bit into another breadstick.

Viv, thankfully, was better at thinking on her feet. She slipped into her tough-old-broad persona. "Here's what went down. Rey knocked her up, but he's such a jealous control freak he doesn't believe that the baby is his. He hits her, accuses her of messing around on him. She gets fed up and leaves him, but she's got nowhere else to go. She doesn't want to go back to Mexico, she wants her kid born here, a US citizen, so what's the next logical step? Turn to someone who knows her, someone who might have an interest in seeing that the kid is okay." Viv leaned back in the booth and shrugged. "You know how Sylvia was always cleaning up Rey's messes. Of course she steps in to make things right."

I looked at Viv, impressed. She'd managed to make even me believe for a second that she'd known this family all her life, and I knew for a fact she'd met Tony, Sylvia, and Rey exactly once each.

"This is all total conjecture."

"We can conject," Viv said. "We're investigators, not litigators. We don't have to prove anything to start snooping around."

"Here's the weird part," I said. "We went to Sylvia's place yesterday and talked to her about the murder. She didn't say one word about Rey and Lucinda being involved. Or about the baby being Rey's."

"She was definitely hiding something. Very hostile. Secretive." Viv gestured with her breadstick.

"Maybe she was just didn't want to talk to you. Didn't want to answer nosy questions."

On that happy note the waitress brought the bottle of wine and set down three glasses.

I picked up two and handed them back to her. "We're just going to stick with the tea, thanks."

Patrice kept up the smirk while she poured her wine. "Good," she said. "More for me." She drained half of it in one drink, then sighed and said again. "Good."

I grabbed another breadstick and swirled it around the bottom of the butter dish. "Anyway, I had a funny feeling that Rey had been there recently. I could smell his cologne, but Sylvia said he wasn't coming into town until last night."

Patrice looked bored, then drank down her glass. She poured a second glass, her eyes on me as the wine ran thick and dark into the glass. I remembered the taste of Merlot, the dryness of it, how full it was. White wine or beer was for drinking when you were doing something else – hanging out with girlfriends, watching television. Good Merlot was an event unto itself.

Viv didn't seem to like the silence. "She was definitely hiding things. Why would she do that, unless she had something to cover up?"

"I'll stand by my nosy question hypothesis. And I hardly think smelling the man's cologne is proof positive of his being there. Lots of men wear cologne."

"I know, but it was the same kind that Rey wore, and really strong like he always wore it. Kind of a coincidence, don't you think?" I was sounding desperate and I knew it. I felt like I was making my way through a tunnel with my tiny key chain flashlight. "And, no, that doesn't prove he was there by any means. But all of it together, I believe, bears looking at. Rey threatened Lucinda, Rey had a heck of a stronger motive than Tony did. Rey has a history of violence. Tony has a history of being inhumanly nice. There's something wrong with this picture, and I don't see any harm in looking a little closer."

Patrice raised her glass again, her eye steady on mine the whole time. Bulldog stubbornness had me refusing to look away, but I would have been better doing so. I could taste the wine as it went down her throat.

"You're on the thinnest ice I've ever seen, Salem. This isn't a lead. This is a hunch. This is a vendetta. It's a dead end, sweetheart. All you're doing is making a fool of yourself."

I swallowed, then reached for my own glass of iced tea. Poor substitute. I debated telling her the truth: that I'd prayed and prayed for God to help me help Tony, and that Rey was the only thing that came up.

"If Rey is such a hot suspect, why haven't the police looked at him?"

"Alibi," Viv said. She waved her breadstick. "Whatever."

Patrice raised an eyebrow at me. "I can't believe I'm wasting fifty bucks of the station's money on this crap."

The waitress brought our plates then, darting nervous glances at each of us, obviously wondering what was going on. I had to admit, I wondered the same thing.

What was I doing here? Why was I asking Trisha for help when I didn't even know what help we needed? Did I really think she would give us something that the police didn't already know, something that would let me ride in like Mother Teresa on a white horse and save the day?

At least the fettuccini was good, and it was free. Was that worth looking like a fool over?

I twirled my pasta and considered that notion. The sad thing was, I'd made a fool of myself for so much less. Trisha meant to make me back down. She wanted to see me give up, but I wasn't ready yet. Maybe I wasn't *exactly* on a mission from God, but I was on a mission; a mission to redeem myself in some way.

We ate in silence and Patrice finished her second glass of wine. Either she had more control than I did, or it wasn't very good wine, because she stopped there. It was probably that first thing.

I wanted to hug Viv when she stopped the waitress. "Could you please bring me the check?"

"I said I'd get it," Patrice said.

"You were under the impression we had something of value for you. Obviously we don't. I don't want to be beholden to you."

I didn't blame her. I was beholden to a lot of people, and it sucked.

To her credit, Patrice did start to look like she felt a little bit bad for being so snarky. She had every reason to be snarky with me, but it probably wasn't making her feel as good as she thought it would. While Viv signed the check, I turned back to Patrice.

"I appreciate your time. I know this must seem like a lost cause for you. I probably am making a fool of myself." I smiled. "But, hey, it's not like it would be the first time, right? I mean, I've done lots stupider things than this, and at least this is for a good cause, even if it turns out to be a lost one." I looked at her glass of wine, at the disbelieving smirk on her face. "I've made a lot of really bad mistakes, Trish. Not just with you. I'm sure you can understand, I don't want that to be my legacy. I have a chance to maybe do some good here. It won't make up for everything bad I've done, but it would be a start. That possibility is enough that I don't care if I make a fool of myself. It's worth it to me."

I slid out of the booth. Every time I moved my muscles protested, but I gave it my very best shot at putting on a happy face. "Thanks again for your time. I'm sorry we couldn't be more of a help to you."

We turned to go.

"Salem, wait." I turned back and she looked like would rather eat dirt than tell me whatever it is she had to say. "Look, if Rey *was* in town, chances are good he would have talked to Rick Barlow."

Well, ugh. It seemed there was no end to the list of people I would prefer never to see again. Good ol' Ricky Barlow, he'd thrown Scott Watson's bachelor party and then put a drunk me and a drunk Scott into bed together.

"I thought he moved somewhere. Like under a rock in the middle of the desert."

"He's back." She didn't appear any happier about it than I was. "He and Rey got really tight after John died." John was Rick's younger brother, and had been Rey's best friend. John had died in a motorcycle accident a few years ago.

I made a flatulating noise with my lips. I doubted very seriously that Rick would give me any information at all. Had I really just said I didn't care if I made a fool of myself?

"Where can we find this guy?" Viv asked.

"He manages that big self-storage place with the stars and stripes on it, over on the Brownfield Highway."

"I know that place. All American Storage. They have a room where you can rent a gun and shoot at targets," Viv said.

"Fun," I said. Right now I wouldn't mind shooting a few holes in a paper target. Or a real one, for that matter. "Let's go."

We got back in Viv's car. "Do you want me to drop you off at your car since it's on the way?"

I groaned. I forgot about the pickle-mobile. "Not especially."

She made a funny noise and I glared at her. "Don't laugh at me! That's just cruel. You don't laugh at people when they're down."

"You do if they're driving a rust-covered pile of junk and sitting on a bucket."

I slouched in my seat. If I never had to look at that car again I would be just fine, but I didn't see where I had a whole lot of choices on my list. "It would be too far out of your way to take me back to Bow Wow Barbers after we get through with Rick, so sure, drop me off there. I'll drive the pickle-mobile out there." Why not? Rick would undoubtedly make some remark about how fat I was, and how I'd let myself go, so why not just toss in an embarrassment of a car, too?

It was getting late, but it was still hot. Too bad the pickle-mobile didn't have air conditioning.

Trying to drive in a skirt made the bucket feel even more precarious. I drove with a scream waiting in my throat. I'd almost grown used to groaning every time I moved. I had to make two turns and I knew I was going to tip over both times. By the time I got to All American Storage, I'd almost decided Tony could go to jail. I had problems of my own to deal with.

I didn't even bother to park around the corner. Let Rick see the piece of crud I was driving. Let him see how huge I was. Let him make jokes. I was beyond caring.

Except Rick didn't make jokes. He drove up on his little golf cart while Viv and I were getting out of our cars. He didn't recognize me at first – finally, somebody didn't recognize me! – but as soon as I started talking he grinned real wide like he was glad to see me. Go figure.

"Come on in," he said. "Let's get out of this heat."

He led us past a chest-high counter and into his office. "Something to drink? I've been out on that concrete cleaning up and fixing a few small things, and I'm about to have a heat stroke." He pulled three soda cans from a mini fridge behind a cheap desk and handed us each one. "Sit down, sit down. You looking for a storage space to rent?"

"Actually we're conducting an investigation into the murder of Lucinda Cruz," Viv said crisply. She raised her chin and those little hairs quivered again.

Rick gave me one of those awkward is-this-a-joke smiles. "Seriously?"

I tilted my head. "Kind of, yeah. I don't know if you've heard, but Tony Solis has been arrested for the murder. I don't think he did it, and I'm afraid the police have stopped investigating because they think they've already found their man."

Rick nodded slowly and leaned back in his seat, rubbing the heel of his hand across his chin. "Um, yeah, actually I saw on the news that Tony had been arrested for that. What a shock, huh? I mean, of all the people who'd kill somebody, Tony Solis is the last person you'd think of."

"Exactly. So that's why Viv and I are trying to do this little investigation of our own. With the cooperation of the police, of course." I guess Bobby's good-humored tolerance could be called cooperation. "Just asking a few questions, nothing major."

Rick kept rubbing his chin, nodding every once in a while like he was really listening. But I got the feeling he wasn't.

"Yeah, well...that's nice of you, I guess. I'm sure Tony could use the extra help right now, somebody in his corner. I hope you're right. Like you said, it's hard to believe he'd actually do it. But I wouldn't worry too much if you don't find anything. I mean, it takes a lot of evidence to convict someone of murder. If Tony didn't do it, he won't be convicted. I have great faith in our justice system." He scratched his ear, then let his chair fall with a soft thud and picked up a picture frame on his desk. "Since I haven't seen you in so long, I have to take a minute to brag, if you don't mind." He flipped the frame around so I could see a studio portrait of him with a young, pretty blonde woman and a little girl who looked to be about three. "This is my wife and daughter. Well, stepdaughter. But I'm going to adopt her in three more months."

"They're beautiful," I said. They were. But...were we through talking about Tony?

"She's a looker." Viv sounded surprised. "You must be proud."

I checked Rick's face, but he didn't seem offended by Viv's intimation that he'd married up. He stared at the picture in his hands as if he'd forgotten we were there.

"I'm sure they're proud of you, too," I said. "And I appreciate your words of encouragement. But it makes me nervous to just leave things in the hands of fate. I'd like to find something more concrete to help Tony."

Rick nodded but his eyes were still on the picture. He finally dragged them away and looked at me. He flipped the frame over and over in his hands, and I noticed that his leg started to wobble a little, like he was bouncing his heels. But his face remained perfectly calm.

"Of course," he said. "That's understandable."

Something was really weird here. Rick Barlow was loud-mouthed and obnoxious. I mean, that's the way he'd always been, but this guy was the picture of good manners and respect. I didn't know quite how to react to that.

"We're wondering if you've talked to Rey," Viv said.

Rick's leg bounced higher. His jaw twitched. "Rey?"

"Yes, Rey. Ramirez. We understand he's a really good friend of yours."

Rick tilted his head back and forth as if he was weighing that description. "Yeah, we're buddies. I mean, I don't see him much anymore since he moved to...where is it? Albuquerque?" He laughed a creepy, high-pitched laugh.

"Oklahoma City," I said. His leg was really going to town. "When was the last time you saw him?"

"This morning?" He squinted up at the ceiling. "He came by here before he went to the funeral."

I nodded and glanced at Viv. She had one eyebrow raised in the direction of Rick's leg.

"I'll bet he was pretty upset about Lucinda? And the baby?"

Rick nodded quickly and his jaw twitched again. "Yeah, you know, he really did care about her. And the baby, of course. It's a – well, it's a tragedy, that's the only way you can look at it. Really sad." He dropped the frame on the desk and rested his arms there. I suspected he was trying to keep his entire body from vibrating, but it wasn't working. "Really sad for everybody. Really sad." But then he laughed again. Short, almost like a bark.

I started to get nervous. He was acting weird. And I wondered for a second what would happen when the leg shake got completely out of control.

"And before that?" Viv asked. "When was the last time you saw him?"

Rick twisted in his chair and did a weird little back and forth thing with his chin. "Let's see...I can't really remember. You'd have to ask him. I'm really busy with this place and time kind of loses all meaning for me, you know? Could have been six months, could have been a year. Know what I mean?" He laughed, a kind of creepy desperate laugh.

I wanted to look at Viv but I was afraid to. Rick was freaking me out. Obviously he was hiding something. Until I figured out what, I didn't feel comfortable pushing him on it. If, for some bizarre reason, he had been the one to kill Lucinda – and for the life of me I couldn't think of a reason to believe he did – I didn't want to be around him one second longer than necessary.

Viv stood. "Well, you've been a very big help, and we appreciate your time. Please keep us in mind if you think of anything else."

She headed for the door. For a second I thought she was going to leave me there. I shot out of my chair.

"Thanks for your help, Rick. It was good to see you again." Whatever. Weirdo. "And congratulations again on your new family."

Viv had her car revving and thrown into gear before I had my bucket adjusted. I followed her down Brownfield Highway and into the parking lot of a 7-11. I opened the passenger door of the Caddy and sat down.

"That was so weird," I said.

"He's guilty of something. I don't know what, but it's something, and it has to do with this murder."

"Do you think Rick killed Lucinda?"

"I don't know, but he's guilty of something, and he started to freak me out with that laugh." She shuddered. "Did you notice that he never asked *why* we wanted to talk to him about the murder?"

Some ace detective I was. "No. He didn't even ask, did he? Hmm." Why hadn't he asked? "That in itself is a clue."

"Yes." She nodded sharply.

"To what?"

"I don't know."

I sagged against the seat. "What the heck is going on?"

"I don't know, but we're on to something." She rummaged through her purse. "Obviously he was expecting someone to come to him at some point, so he knows something, which means we keep digging." She pulled out a package of gum and offered me a stick.

"Dig where? With Rick?"

"Maybe we show up at his house and lean on his wife a little."

I chewed my gum and nodded. How, exactly, did one go about "leaning" on another person? "How's that?"

"I don't know. But Columbo reruns come on A&E tonight so I'm going home to see if I can get some ideas from the master. Call me tomorrow when you get off work."

Actually, watching Columbo reruns seemed like a fairly decent plan of action. Too bad I didn't have cable, but there were plenty of crime shows on network television, so maybe I could do some research, too.

I found myself checking the rearview mirror every few seconds as I drove home. The jangling nerves I'd gotten at Rick's office didn't want to smooth themselves out. I didn't know what exactly I was so paranoid about, but I was.

Frank and Stump were sitting on the front porch when I got home. Stump took one look at the car and turned her fat little butt in my direction. I didn't know if she was making a judgment about the car, or if she was mad at me for leaving her with Frank all afternoon, but she was pouting about something.

I stopped at the edge of the deck and scratched her on the back. She finally came around, grudgingly consenting to lick the back of my hand. "Anything happen today?" I asked Frank.

"Stump almost ate another bug but it got away. Fast mover. And I stopped at Food World and got another box of Star Crunches." He looked very pleased with himself.

"That is excellent." I groaned as I made my way up the steps. On top of the aching muscles, I felt like there was some ax just above my head, waiting to fall. Why did I feel like that?

Maybe because axes had fallen on me steadily for the past several days, maybe because I was just paranoid.

"Stay for dinner?" I didn't really want to be alone just yet.

We ate fried ham steaks and mashed potatoes and even an entire can of green beans. Then we sat in front of the television and ate Star Crunches and watched CSI. It didn't give me clues as to how to deal with the Lucinda Cruz case, since it was about a bunch of gang members who accidentally killed a storeowner and then planted his body in a freezer in another state. All I got out of it was, if you're a female detective on television, at some point you're going to have to wear a tank top, it's mandatory.

Frank went home voluntarily, and I decided to be a big girl and let him, even though I still felt a little edgy. I figured some time alone to sort out the details of our case would do me some good.

I got an old spiral notebook, a pen, and one more Star Crunch for good measure and crawled into bed with Stump. I wrote down all the facts I knew and all the hunches I had: Lucinda Cruz, former girlfriend of Rey Ramirez; approximately sixteen weeks pregnant with his child. Out to the side of that I wrote the word "maybe." Then I crossed it out and wrote the word "allegedly." I might as well be professional. Then I put Tony recorded at the crime scene. Maybe I ought to call him tomorrow and ask him about that. What was he doing there? Did he normally go to the church at night, or was that unusual? I added Lucinda both strangled and dealt some kind of blunt force trauma. Rey's alibi. What exactly was his alibi, anyway? All I knew was that he was in OKC. Well, that wasn't necessarily true. Bobby had said he was 350 miles away, but that didn't necessarily mean OKC. I could get on some Google map thing and see what else was a radius of 350 miles from Lubbock, Texas.

On a whim I went back into the kitchen and got the phone book and my cell phone. It was a little late, but not terribly late. Maybe if I caught Sylvia off guard I'd get an honest answer.

She answered on the second ring.

"Hi, Sylvia. It's Salem. Would you mind if I ask you what Rey's alibi was for Lucinda's murder?"

"What?" She laughed a little, but not the really amused kind of laugh.

"Well, I told you that we were trying to help Tony, you know." I hated to admit it, but back in my drinking days I was pretty good at snowing people. You get good at it when you have a lot of practice. One thing I learned is that if you keep as close as possible to the truth and just put a little spin on it, you can get away with a lot. That all came back to me while I was talking to Sylvia. "So we're kind of going over everything we know and everything we could find out from the police, and I asked Bobby Sloan – you remember Bobby – he used to play football at Idalou and drove that gold Firebird. Anyway, he's the lead investigator on Lucinda's case, and I heard him say that Rey had an airtight alibi. I didn't really think about it at the time, but I was curious about what the police would consider an airtight alibi? Like, does he have proof of where he was? Is he on video surveillance somewhere? I'm just curious."

I let the matter hang for a second. After way too long, Sylvia laughed. "Salem, I think you have too much time on your hands."

"You're probably right about that. It's just that I want to help Tony, and I'm kind of getting into this detective thing. Maybe I'll be a private eye."

"Or maybe you should just stick to grooming dogs. You're good at that."

"You're probably right about that, too. Stick with what I'm good at. So, what was his alibi, do you know? Or has he told you?"

"He was at work, Salem. The next state. He was *working*. His boss vouched for him, and his boss is a very well-thought of member of the Oklahoma City community. He owns several business."

"I see," I said brightly. Should I push it and ask who his boss was? From the tension in Sylvia's voice, maybe not such a good idea. "Well, that certainly makes sense. Like I said, I was just curious. Playing Nancy Drew, you know. Listen, next time you bring Tango in for a haircut, remind me to try this new conditioner Flo bought. It's just for brown hair and it really makes it shiny."

"Sure, Salem," Sylvia said. "I'll remind you."

"You sound tired. I'm sorry to bother you so late. Get some rest."

I hung up and chewed my lip. So Rey had the word of his boss, a supposedly upstanding member of the community. Was that really airtight? Someone's word, no matter how upstanding they are?

It shouldn't be, if you asked me. If it was, then Tony should be able to use my word that he would never hurt someone, except I wasn't quite so upstanding, come to think of it.

I crawled back into bed and snuggled up with Stump. Her eyes were droopy, and I heard her snoring while I was still thinking and chewing on the end of my pen, mentally examining possibilities.

I didn't realize I'd fallen asleep with the light on until it winked off. I couldn't figure out what was going on until it dawned on me that there was someone else in the room, and *that* someone had turned off the light. Still, I wasn't scared – probably because I was still in that la-la land between wake and sleep – until the bed creaked with that someone's weight.

Chapter Eleven

The bed dipped at my side. *That* woke me up. I gasped and scrambled. I tried to scream but one strong hand grabbed my right wrist and yanked me back down. Another hand shoved my chin until my head was jammed up against the headboard and I couldn't open my mouth. Hot fingers closed over my lips, digging in. Male fingers.

I grunted and thrashed. A knee crashed into my stomach and dug in, bearing me down into the bed. Icy panic clutched at me, and I was dead certain I was about to be raped, beaten, and killed.

Stump, bless her fierce heart, jumped on me and snapped at the man.

He took his hand off my chin long enough to backhand Stump across the room. She hit the wall with a sickening, terrifying yelp.

"Stump!" I screamed before the hand slammed back into my face. He covered my chin with his palm, his long, nasty fingers over my mouth, and shoved and twisted until I was looking straight up at the headboard, unable to see anything for the pillows I'd been sleeping on.

"Starting right now, you're going to mind your own business," he said, inches away from my ear, deadly calm. "You're going to go to work, and go home, and quit asking questions. You're in over your head, and you're not doing Tony any good."

I rolled my eyes around, trying to get a glimpse of something, something I could remember. But I couldn't see anything, just feel hot breath on my cheek and ear, and smell the stench of his sweaty skin in my nose.

"Tony will be fine if you'll just keep your fat nosy ass out of this. Got it? Mind your own business." He gave me one last shove before bolting off of me and running down the hall. Seconds later I heard the front door open and slam shut.

If it hadn't been for Stump, I think I would have dove under the covers and stayed there until the sun came up. I knew he was gone, but still, I was so afraid I couldn't move. My heart beat so hard I couldn't breathe, and every time I thought about getting up to turn on the light, everything in me screamed, "No!"

I forced myself to jump out of bed and hit the light switch, desperate to see Stump and terrified at the same time of what I was going to see.

"Stump!"

She was lurching toward the bed on three legs, whimpering.

I dove to the floor and snatched her up. She yelped and twisted around, trying to get out of my grasp.

"Oh, my baby, my baby," I said over and over. What had he done to her? I laid her on the bed and felt her fat little body gingerly. She held her left front leg close to her body, and she whimpered again when I ran my fingers over it.

I looked frantically around the room, not sure what to do first. Call the police? But Stump needed help now. Her leg looked like it was broken. Did I take her to the all-night vet and *then* call the police? Call them from there?

Finally, I ran into the kitchen and got my phone off the bar – an expedition that took every remaining ounce of courage I had – and dialed 911.

"Someone's broken into my house," I said. "He's gone now, but I need the police. Get Detective Sloan if you can."

"Are you hurt, ma'am?" the operator asked.

I felt my neck and chin. They hurt, but it was probably nothing a doctor could do about it. I almost said no when I looked at Stump. "Yes, I'm hurt. He choked me."

"I'll have the ambulance on its way in a few seconds," she said. "I'll stay on the line with you until they get there."

"Thanks," I said weakly, sitting down hard on the bed as the strength in my legs suddenly drained. Having her on the other end of the phone wasn't like having someone there beside me, but it would have to do.

I hugged Stump as close as I dared. "Hang on, baby," I whispered to her, stroking her head. "Help is on the way."

I watched out the bedroom window until I saw the cruiser turn into the Trailertopia lot. I realized at that second that I was wearing nothing but panties and a big t-shirt.

"They're here," I told the operator, and hung up. I laid Stump down carefully and grabbed the faded black sweats at the foot of my bed. I hopped into them on my way to the door, succeeding in knocking the heck out of my pinkie toe on the footstool as I did so. When I opened the door it was with tears in my eyes.

"You?" I blurted without thinking.

Officer Walters, the same cop who'd come when I reported Lucinda Cruz's dead body, stared back at me.

I wish I had a cop face. No surprise, nothing catches them off guard, no big deal. *I'm here and I'm in charge now, you don't even have to think.*

"What's going on?" he asked, looking down the hallway to the second bedroom and then back in the direction of my room.

I explained what happened and told him the guy had left. The ambulance pulled up while we talked and I went to get Stump while he examined the front door.

A young skinny guy came in first carrying a toolbox – the modern equivalent of the black doctor's bag. An older woman huffed up my deck behind him, overweight and windblown, with unruly curly hair and gray roots. That was me in fifteen years, I realized, if I didn't make some serious lifestyle changes.

I sat on the sofa, clutching Stump for all I was worth, while the EMTs asked me questions and took my blood pressure and temperature and stuff. She was breathing hard and even when I held her up and stared straight into her eyes I knew she wasn't seeing me.

"Can you look at my dog?" I finally asked. "The guy knocked her off the bed and I think her leg is broken.

"Honey, we're not vets," the lady said, but the young guy smiled. He looked familiar. I realized then where I'd seen him. He sometimes came into Lagoon Saloon, this place I used to hang out a couple of years ago. I didn't really know him but we'd talked a few times about nothing in particular. I wondered briefly if I'd done or said anything that should embarrass me now, then I decided I didn't really care. I had other things to worry about at the moment.

Randy, his nametag said. I looked at him and he shrugged. "I don't mind looking at her if you promise not to sue me."

"Swear," I said, handing Stump over to him.

That's when the shakes started. As long as I had Stump in my lap I was doing okay, but as soon as he took her I started to shake all over and couldn't stop. The lady let me grab the quilt that covered the holes in the couch and wrap myself up tight in it, although I really wasn't cold, just vibrating out of control.

Randy looked in Stump's eyes with his little flashlight and I didn't like the look on his face. "You're taking her to the vet soon?"

That was all I needed to freak completely out. "Why? What's wrong? Is she okay?" I jumped up and grabbed my keys by the door and shouted to Walters, "I have to take my dog to the vet this second. I'll be back in a while."

At least now the cop face was gone. Walters actually looked a trifle panicked that I'd leave. "You can go as soon as we're through here."

"But she needs medical attention this second!" I shrieked. A little over the top, I know, but hey. When in my life had I been more entitled?

"She'll probably be fine," Randy said.

"Probably?" I wondered what would happen if I just pushed past them all and left with Stump. I decided it was worth a try.

"I'm going to wrap her leg and she'll be okay till you can get her to the vet." Randy said, although the look on his face looked more hopeful than convinced. I took Stump back and shoved past him – right into Bobby.

"What's going on here?" He took my arms and steered me back into the living room.

"A guy came in and choked me and told me to mind my own business and he hit Stump and now she needs to go to the vet and this joker won't let me go and it's an emergency, her leg is broken and she's got internal injuries and if anything happens to her I'm going to sue you!" I pointed at Walters.

He raised an eyebrow at Bobby.

Bobby sighed, went and mumble-mumbled to Walters for a second. Walters' cop face was sliding fast; he clearly didn't like whatever Bobby was mumbling. He threw a disdainful glare at me and turned back to say something to Bobby between clenched teeth.

Bobby had his back to me, leaning toward Walters and I could see he was working a hard sell of something. He shot off a couple short sentences that didn't budge Walters. Finally, he said something that must have been his ace-in-the-hole, because Walters rolled his eyes, muttered something that sounded suspiciously profane, and shoved past Bobby.

Bobby said, "Walters is going to take your dog to the vet so we can finish your interview. Make sure you're okay."

"But – but..." Clearly this was the way it would have to be, but I didn't like the idea of Stump being in the scary vet's office without me.

"Just say thank you, Salem," Bobby ordered.

I handed Stump over to Walters. "Thank you. Please be gentle with her."

He gave me a look that didn't give any promises.

"Just drop the dog off and come back," Bobby said.

"You're going to leave her up there by herself?" I said. "She'll be scared..." I stopped dead at the look Walters threw over his shoulder. "Okay, okay. Thanks again."

"You'll be a hero, Walters," Bobby called after him. "Get your face in the paper."

Walters flipped him off.

"Okay, tell me exactly what happened," Bobby said, sitting on the stool in front of me. "Every detail."

I went through the whole thing again. Woke up, somebody on the bed, grabbing my wrist and yanking me down, knee in my stomach. Told me to mind my own business, go to work, go home, I wasn't helping Tony...right about then I started to feel a little weird. Like I wasn't completely there, but I didn't know where the rest of me was. Kind of floaty.

I heard my own voice talking to Bobby and felt the EMT lady pumping up the blood pressure cuff again for like the third time, but I had very little interest in what was going on. Bobby leaned in close and stared deep into my eyes. I had spent a significant portion of my middle school life dreaming of just such a moment, but right then I didn't care.

When I got to the part where he knocked Stump off me I decided I didn't really want to talk anymore. In fact, I thought, it would be a good time to go back to sleep. It was, after all, the middle of the night and I'd been through a lot. I saw black spots and thought how nice it would be if they'd just blend all together and everything would go black.

"She's going down," Bobby said with urgency, and I felt his arms around me as I slid over. That was the last thing I heard.

When I came to I was lying on the couch with my feet on the armrests.

"You're going to take her in, right?" Bobby was asking the EMT. He actually looked nervous. Probably he was concerned his star witness to the break-in was going to do a belly flop, but I indulged in a few seconds' fantasy that he was really worried about me, personally. It was almost worth getting attacked for, but not quite.

I scooted around to sit up.

"Lie down," the EMT said.

Bobby put four fingers against my chest and pushed. "Stay."

I raised an eyebrow, but I stayed. He really did look worried. Whoever had broken in must be pretty important.

"I think I'm okay," I said. "I just got a little woozy for a second."

"Have you ever fainted before?" the lady asked.

"Does drinking till you pass out count?"

She shook her head.

"Then no, I haven't."

Bobby gnawed on his lip and looked from me to the lady. He was making me nervous. I heard a racket and looked up to see Randy bringing a gurney up my front deck. Frank was right behind him.

"What's happening?" Frank asked.

"A guy broke in and choked me, kind of." I turned to Randy. "There's no way I need that thing. I don't really even need to go to the hospital. I just needed to sit down for a second."

"You were sitting when you passed out. You're going in, Salem, so give it a rest."

Bobby stood and hovered while they argued with me about the gurney until I finally got mad and stomped out to the stupid ambulance and climbed in. "Okay, I'm going, but I am not riding on the gurney." Mostly I just didn't want to hear Randy groan when he tried to pick it up with me on it.

Before they drove off, I asked Frank to go to the emergency vet and check on Stump. He was way more worried about her than he was about me, but that was okay, because so was I.

Bobby grilled the doctor so much he got on her nerves and she almost admitted me just to satisfy him. He even had me a little freaked out that there was something horribly wrong with me, even though I'd been there for the attack and I knew all the guy had done was shove my chin and knee me in the stomach. We finally got out of there right before daybreak. Bobby said if I was up to it I'd need to go to the station to give a report.

I really wanted to go get Stump first. But since she was with Frank, and he was practically family, I knew she'd be okay. I was exhausted, but it wasn't as if I was going to be sleeping any time soon.

"Do you have someplace you can go for a couple of days till we catch the guy?"

I hadn't thought about that. I didn't feel so great about going back to my place alone.

"I can find someplace," I said.

He looked over at me. "You're sure?"

"Yeah. Frank won't mind if I bunk at his place, or probably Les wouldn't mind if I stayed with him." I chewed my lip and thought I'd better call Les and let him know what happened. He liked to know when stuff happened with me. Not that anything like this had ever happened before.

Bobby was quiet for a few seconds. "Yeah, well, I guess it's good you've got so many...people you can call on to help out."

What was with him? He stared straight ahead at the road and clenched his teeth. If I didn't know better I'd think he was jealous.

I looked down. Nope, I was still fat. So that ruled out any possibility of jealousy.

So for the second time in a week I sat in Bobby's office and gave a "statement." He had me look through some books of pictures but it didn't do a lot of good since I hadn't seen the guy. I only had a vague sense of size – on the short side, and from the weight behind the knee in my stomach he hadn't missed many meals – and I thought I'd detected a slight Mexican accent. Definitely not as strong as Frank's, but the guy was used to speaking two languages.

Bobby made me repeat everything three times. Thank goodness I didn't pass out any more, but the longer I went without seeing Stump the more worried about her I got, and the more times I told the story, the more convinced of one thing I became.

"We were on the right track," I said.

Bobby chewed his lips. "Sounds like you were definitely on to something."

"I knew it. I wonder what it was?"

Bobby shrugged. "There's no telling. Who did you talk to yesterday?"

I told him about the weird way Rick Barlow had acted. Bobby remembered him, but mostly because he'd been on the scene of Rick's little brother's motorcycle crash six or seven years ago. "I remember it hit him really hard."

"I guess maybe that ordeal was what changed him. He used to be loud-mouthed and obnoxious, vulgar and rude. But yesterday he was actually polite."

Bobby gave me a funny look. "Maybe you ought to give more people a chance to be polite to you. You could be pleasantly surprised. So why were you talking to Ricky Barlow?"

"Because he was a friend of Rey's, and Trisha said if Rey was in town, Rick had probably seen him, because they're tight since John died. We just went over to ask if he'd seen Rey lately, and how long had it been?"

"Did you tell him why you wanted to know?"

"Actually, yes. We told him we were conducting an investigation into Lucinda Cruz's murder and were trying to get a clue as to where all the key players were. And you know what?"

Bobby raised an eyebrow, trying to look bored, but in light of the fact that someone had resorted to physical violence to stop me, I didn't think he could ignore the fact that I was a force to be reckoned with. Possibly.

"He didn't ask why we wanted to talk to him. It didn't even occur to him to *ask*. Obviously, he was expecting someone to come talk to him."

"Maybe he figured he really was the logical conclusion to tracking Rey down."

"Oh." I hadn't thought about that. "But he acted really weird."

"Weird how?"

"Really nice, like I said. Polite. Showed me pictures of his wife and kid. He had this very creepy laugh."

Bobby kept up the bored look.

"I'm serious. You should have heard it. Viv and I were both completely freaked out over it."

Bobby nodded slowly. "Viv. Your friend with what I'm starting to suspect was a fake heart condition."

"Hey, the woman is eighty something. And you should hear some of her stories from her drinking days. She made me look like a Girl Scout. Do you really think she's the picture of health?"

Bobby fiddled with the stapler on his desk. "Look, the issue right now is who broke into your house and why."

"You know what's weird to me? I got the feeling that we were actually working for the same thing."

"Who?"

"Me and the guy who choked me. I mean, he said I wasn't doing Tony any favors. And that Tony would be okay if I'd just leave things alone. What do you think that meant?"

Bobby sighed a deep, tired-old-man sigh and scrubbed his hands hard over his face. "I don't know, but I'd really appreciate it if you'd do what he said, at least for a couple of days. Go to work, go home. Leave this alone. You're no detective, Salem. Leave all this to the professionals."

"But we were on to something."

"And if you keep following that something you're going to get worse than a bruised neck!" He slammed his hand down so hard on his desk my ears rang. I jumped, and he looked a little shocked himself. "One girl is already dead, Salem. Have you forgotten about that? Do you want to end up like her?"

I blinked. I remembered the instant last night when I was certain I wouldn't see the light of day. "Of course not," I whispered.

He took a deep breath. "Good. Because I don't want you to, either. I'll check out Rick Barlow and see what I can come up with. If he has something to hide I'll flush it out."

"You might want to consider going to his house and leaning on his wife."

Bobby lifted an eyebrow.

"That's what Viv and I were considering. But you do whatever you think is best."

He stared at me for a couple of beats, then went on. "In the meantime, go stay with one of your friends. It shouldn't take more than a couple of days. I'll let you know when you can go back home." He sat back in his chair and swiveled back and forth a couple of times. "You ready to go get your dog?"

I would have leapt out of my chair if I hadn't been exhausted. "Please, yes."

He drove me to the vet's office, and on the way I rehearsed what I was going to say about why I couldn't pay my bill. I was pretty sure they'd let me pay it out, because they'd let me do it before when Stump ate a particularly evil-looking bug and I freaked out and thought she would die. Plus, I was a fairly steady customer with Stump's shots and heartworm pills and stuff. Still, I would have preferred to just write out a check and know it wouldn't bounce from here to kingdom come.

Dr. Porter's office is in a little Colonial-looking cottage just off of Slide Road. It's completely out of place for West Texas but cute still. I was a little surprised when Bobby got out of the car with me.

He shrugged at the questioning look I gave him. "I want to see how the dog is."

I looked through the diamond-paned window of the front door. An unfamiliar face was on the phone behind the counter.

"Uh-oh. I don't know that girl."

"Is that bad?"

"Hopefully not, but don't be surprised if I have to resort to a few tears to work out a payment plan on my bill."

As it turned out, no theatrics were necessary. Dr. Porter himself told me Stump had been taken home already, and was resting comfortably. She'd sustained – his words, not mine – a hairline fracture to her back leg. She would need to stay still for at least a week and then would need to wear the bandage on her leg for another two weeks. At that point she'd come in for another x-ray, but he expected her to make a full recovery and be good as new.

"She'd benefit greatly from losing a little weight," he said, looking sternly at me.

"Wouldn't we all," I replied.

"I'm going to keep saying it until you take it to heart, Salem. Clearly you love your dog. You could show it by keeping her on a healthier diet."

"You want to be the one to tell her she can't have any more bugs? Believe me, I've tried."

"It's not the bugs and we both know it." He raised an eyebrow at me. "How does she like the special low calorie food I sent home with you last time?"

Should I tell him about the hysterics Stump threw when I poured that dry stuff in her bowl? The moping, the whining, the pitiful, watery eyes she'd turned on me? The way she'd choked and fallen prostrate, letting the dry nugget roll out of her mouth and onto the floor, one eye on me to see if I was getting the picture?

I took one look at Dr. Porter and knew he would not have the compassion for Stump and her drama that I did. That's why God sent her to me. I understood Stump; I could relate to her. I *was* Stump, in human form. Well, my legs were longer, but we carried around similar baggage, both figurative and literal.

"She loved it," I bald-faced lied. "Unfortunately it costs more to buy her food than it does mine. So we're back on the regular stuff from Wal-Mart."

"That's not the best, but it would suffice if you limited her diet to strictly that. No table scraps, no human food of any kind."

"Listen, I can barely afford to feed myself, and if you haven't caught on from my own girth, I don't leave a lot of leftovers. Speaking of which, I'm going to need to work out a payment arrangement for my bill." (Like a dollar a week for a few hundred weeks).

But the bill had been paid. In full.

I glanced at the new girl behind the counter. She nodded.

I knew right away it was a mistake. Frank didn't have any more money than I did, and even if he did he wouldn't pay Stump's vet bill. Not that he was stingy, it would simply never occur to him to do so. Maybe, I thought, this was God's way of giving me a little break. I didn't feel like standing there any longer with my middle-of-the-night hair and baggy sweats to argue with them. I made the follow-up appointment, thanked them both and left.

"One of your boyfriends pay your bill for you?" Bobby asked as he pulled out of the parking lot.

See? There again he sounded jealous. Weird.

"Sure, one of the legions of suitors I have lined up outside my door paid it for me. Else the new girl made a mistake, and I'll be getting a bill in the mail in the next couple of days. Smart money's on the second scenario."

My yard looked like a used car lot. Les's ice cream truck and Viv's Cadillac were in the drive, and a car I didn't recognize was parked at the curb.

"Popular girl," Bobby muttered. His phone chirped and he mumbled something when he looked at the readout. "I've got to get this. Check in later this morning and let me know where you'll be staying. I may have more questions."

I saluted smartly as I climbed out and thanked him for the ride. He barely acknowledged it, swinging the car around and roaring down the street. Obviously he had important cop things to do, but I couldn't help but think that his mother would be appalled at his manners.

Poor Stump was crashed in a cardboard box by the couch, a white bandage wrapped around her left front leg.

"The doctor gave her some good drugs, and she's out, man," Frank said.

I was so glad to see her I had to duck my head so nobody would see the tears in my eyes, my poor innocent, fierce baby. I rubbed her fat little tummy. She snored loudly, and her good leg stretched to its limit.

"Dr. Porter said she had to keep quiet and still for a week. I don't think Stump's going to be okay with that prescription."

"Just keep her on the knockout drugs," Frank said. "She'll be a happy camper."

It wasn't until then that I noticed Tony sitting on my couch, staring at me, his face hard.

I drew my head back in surprise. "Tony."

"I heard what happened. I wanted to see if you were okay."

"Oh sure," I said, waving a hand. "No big deal."

"Maybe not to you," he said. He didn't look like he had much of a sense of humor about the whole thing.

"How did you all hear about it?"

Les spoke up. "Viv heard your address on the police scanner."

"It was three in the morning. What were you doing listening to the scanner at three in the morning?"

"I couldn't sleep," she said.

"So she called me, and she and I met here just as Frank was getting back from the vet's."

"And I knew it had something to do with his case, so I called him."

Frank leaned over and whispered loud enough for everyone to hear, "He called the vet and paid your bill for you. Just gave them a credit card number right over the phone. Like Donald Trumpet or somebody would do."

"It's Trump." Viv scowled at him. "And anybody can do that."

"Yes, but one guy actually did. Thank you, Tony. I'll pay you back. I don't know when, but it'll be sometime during this lifetime."

Tony waved the topic away, rose and lifted my chin, checking out the bruise that ran from my chin to my neck. His face got darker.

"Who was it?" he asked.

I shrugged. "You've got me. Someone I'd prefer not to see again."

"What did he want? Did he rob you?"

I gave a short laugh. "No, I've still got both my dollars."

He looked like he wanted to ask another question. I finally caught on to what it probably was. "He didn't do anything, except give me this bruise and tell me to mind my own business. He said I wasn't helping you any, and that you'd be okay if I just went to work and went home and kept my fat nosy ass out of things. A real charmer, that guy."

He got a weird look on his face.

"What do you think that means, Tony?"

He didn't answer.

"I mean, it sounds like someone who was here on your behalf."

"I didn't send someone to rough you up!" he barked.

"Of course you didn't. I didn't say that. But doesn't it sound like someone who knows something important and helpful that I don't? That's the feeling I got. And seeing as how it was my house that got broken into and my fat ass being insulted, I think I should be privy to any hunch you might have that could shed some light on this."

"Salem, if I knew who it was, believe me, I'd be pounding him down right now." He spoke softly, but his eyes blazed with a fire that had me thinking I didn't want to argue with him. "You can't stay here." He straightened. "Why don't you stay at my place for a few days until this gets worked out?"

I blinked. "At your place?"

"Yes, I've got an extra bedroom and I'd feel a lot better knowing you were safe."

"So would I," Les said.

"Well, so would I, but...don't you think that will be a little...awkward?"

Tony actually smiled. It was a distracted, somewhat sickly-looking smile, but a smile nonetheless. "Why would it be awkward? We are married."

"Yes, see, that's exactly why it would be awkward. This whole we're-still-married thing." I looked to Les for help.

He shrugged. "I'm sorry, but my son's apartment is being fumigated and he's asked to stay with us for a few days, or else I'd offer his room."

"Well, you can't stay with me in the old folks home. Management frowns on overnight guests."

I looked at Frank, but he just stared back blankly, totally clueless.

"You'll have your own room and you can come and go as you want. Please, Salem. I've got too much on my mind right now to be worried about someone coming after you."

"You know I have a dog," I warned.

"She'll get along great with my cat. Go ahead and pack up enough stuff for a couple of days. I'll bring you back if you need anything else."

So, I was going to Tony's. My husband's house. Which, in a weird way, might make it my house? I decided I was too tired to think about that very long. I threw some clothes in my old gym bag while Viv sat on my bed and watched, and we discussed what we might have found out that we weren't supposed to find out.

"It was that Rick guy," she insisted. "He was a strange one."

"I think so, too. I told Bobby about him, and he said he would follow up." I tossed my toothbrush and toothpaste in the bag, along with my hair dryer and curling iron. I put a hand on my hip. "I feel like I'm going to be babysat."

"No kidding." She leaned over and looked down the hallway. "He looks like a guard dog. Way too serious. But I'll bet that's because of the whole murder investigation thing."

I shook my head. "Nope, he was way too serious when he was seventeen and the world was his oyster." I scratched my head and sighed. "I'm not altogether sure I want to do this."

"Do you want to stay here?"

As if on cue I felt again my bed dipping under me as the guy knelt beside me. I didn't think I was ever going to be able to sleep on that bed again, and for sure not for another dozen years or so. "No."

"Where else can you go?"

I picked up my cell phone and called G-Ma's motel. "Someone broke into my house last night and I'm kind of creeped out about staying here. Do you have a room I can use for a couple nights?"

"Sure," she said cheerfully. "I just got new bedspreads and I put up some pretty little shell soaps in the bathrooms. You'll like it."

I breathed a sigh of relief. "Great. Thank you."

"It's only forty-seven fifty for the night, or you can have the entire week for two-fifty."

"You're going to *charge* me?"

"Of course I'm going to charge you. That's what motels do. They charge rent for their rooms."

"You probably have at least half that are empty."

"Not for long. Mario is almost ready to open his restaurant, and once that happens this place is going to be at full capacity every night, I guarantee you. I have people coming by here two or three times a day asking when we're going to be open."

"But still..." I started to launch into an impassioned plea for sympathy and family support, but I knew it was going to be a waste of breath. I might be able to talk her into giving me a break on the price, but even that would come at the much higher price of having to tolerate G-Ma's company. "Never mind. I'll stay with friends."

"Suit yourself, but you know you're always welcome as long as there's a vacancy, sweetie. 'Bye."

I thumbed the phone off and tossed it back in my purse. "So I'm staying with Tony. No big deal. We've lived together before."

One look at Tony's place had me wondering why I'd put up any fuss at all. He lived in a nice older neighborhood with big oak and elm trees everywhere, large ranch-style brick homes and basketball goals in every other driveway. It was the kind of solid middle-class family neighborhood where I'd dreamed of living when Mom and I were moving from one rental shack to another.

The grass was like a golf course, and plants in clay pots of various sizes lined the front walk. Inside was somewhat sparse but neat as an army barracks. I cast a glance down at Stump, asleep in the cardboard box that Tony carried. Maybe I would just keep her stoned on the happy pills the whole time we were there. She was housebroken, but I just *knew* this would be the place she regressed to puppyhood. An alarm would probably go off.

Tony showed me to a small bedroom with its own bath. "Let me know if there's anything you need," he said, opening the blinds. "I can get whatever."

"Thanks," I said, sliding my bag to the floor. "It looks fine." I chewed my lip and wondered what I was supposed to do next.

Tony hovered in the doorway for a minute.

"You were right. This is not at all awkward," I said.

He smiled. A real smile this time, and I remembered those times when I was seventeen and I'd managed to make him smile. It was a thrill for me then. I was a little surprised to find that it was still a thrill.

"Told you it wouldn't be. It's no big deal."

I nodded. "No big deal. It's just for a few days, till things blow over and I can go back home."

"Exactly. And in the meantime, I have some work to do here at home. You can get some rest or read a book or something. There's a whole library in the den. There's food in the fridge and towels in the bathroom if you want to take a shower. Make yourself at home."

He darted a quick glance at my neck and that dark look came over him again. "You're sure you're feeling okay?"

I nodded. "I'm okay Tony, really. Thanks a lot for...for everything. You really don't owe me anything, and I appreciate your stepping up like this."

He took a step back. "Yes, well...I haven't been able to take care of you the way a good husband should, so I'm glad I can do something."

He gave a little wave and headed off down the hallway.

I stepped to the bedroom door. "Tony."

He turned, one eyebrow raised.

"Why did you go up to the church that night? When Lucinda was killed?"

He only hesitated a second. "She asked me to. There was something wrong with one of the floor buffers. But when I got up there, I couldn't find her. And the floor was cleaned, so I figured whatever it was, she got it worked out." He cleared his throat. "I—uh, I called her back but she never did answer her phone, so...so I just left her a message and went home." He rubbed his forehead, hard. "I thought I could hear her cell phone ringing, but it was really faint, you know, and I wasn't sure. I wish I'd stayed, of course, and kept looking for her."

"Did you tell the police all this?"

"Yes, of course."

"And your lawyer?"

"Sure."

I didn't know what else to say to that, so I nodded and moved to step back into the bedroom. Then I said again, "Tony?"

He gave me a patient smile. "Yes?"

"Seriously. Why didn't you sign the papers?"

"I told you. I made a vow."

"I know, but no one would have blamed you for doing it anyway. The church would have given you an annulment, on the grounds of abandonment or something. Surely you wanted to, sometime during the last ten years."

He was silent for long enough I was sure he wasn't going to answer me. Finally he took a deep breath and said, "God kept telling me no."

Again with the *kept*. He was stuck with me.

Most people would have gotten a different God.

I wanted to ask what that sounded like, how could he be so sure it was God talking to him and not just his conscience, the voice of an overly-strict nun in his past coming back to haunt him. How did he know for sure God kept telling him no? Instead I asked, "Did He say why?"

Tony kind of laughed. "Not specifically. He's not always so anxious to justify His reasons to me. But it was something about giving you some time."

Oh. I didn't like the sound of that. That made it sound as if there was an actual marriage waiting for us on the other side of all of this.

I didn't really know what to say about that, so I just nodded like it made perfect sense to me. *Sure, I'll bet that's what it was. God says stuff like that to me all the time.* "Okay, well, I'm going to take a nap, then."

Tony cocked his head. "Your turn first."

"Okay."

"Why are you so sure I'm innocent?"

"I don't really know. *Are* you innocent?"

"Yes, but you don't really know that."

"You're not the type."

"Anyone can become the type. You haven't seen me in ten years. Anyone can be capable of rage and violence, if they're passionate enough about something."

I didn't want to think about him being passionate about Lucinda Cruz, so I said, "You sound like you're trying to convince me of your guilt. Maybe God talked to me, too. Maybe He told me you were innocent, and I could make up for some of the rotten things I've done by helping you out."

He actually laughed.

"What? If He talks to you He could talk to me."

"Of course He could. But He wouldn't tell you that you need to make up for anything. God's into forgiveness and grace, not having people *make up* for whatever wrongs they've done."

"I know that," I said with a scowl, although obviously I wasn't quite so sure. "But maybe He's the one who told me to help you."

"Well if He did, I'm grateful."

"Really? I'd be hacked off, myself. A good practicing Catholic deserves a more competent advocate than I am."

"See, that's where you've got it wrong again. God likes to use the incompetent and under-qualified."

"Then I'm right where I belong." I stuck my tongue out at him. "And I need a nap. Wake me up before dinner time, please."

I closed the door behind me, my head aching from all the different dramas going on around me. I was going to lie down and think it out, but instead I fell asleep. I didn't wake up till I heard Stump whining. She'd wet her bed.

Chapter Twelve

I was washing Stump's towel out in the bathroom sink when I heard Viv's voice. Ordinarily I would have been glad to see her, but at the moment I wasn't glad of much of anything. I ached all over. My neck felt like someone had run over it a few times with a car, and the bruise on my stomach was green and purple. Plus, for some reason every bone in my body ached. I supposed it was from the stress or something, but whatever it was, it felt like I was coming off a five-day binge.

Viv poked her head around the bathroom door. "You decent?"

"As I ever am," I said, wringing out the towel. "What's going on?"

"Just checking to see how you're doing."

"Let me know when you find out, would you?"

Tony rapped on the door. "Salem, I need to go and check on a job. It'll take a little while. Will you be okay?"

I nodded, although I'll admit it was a little pathetically. "I'll be fine."

"Dinner's in the oven, I'm keeping it warm for you. Help yourself to anything else you need."

"Thanks, Tony," I said.

As soon as he was out the door Viv whispered, "I found a little more information for us to work with."

"You did?"

She flipped open a little spiral notebook. "Yes. Our suspect's alibi is his job in Oklahoma City. His boss vouched for him."

"Oh yeah, I knew that." I scooched Stump around a little, trying to make her more comfortable. She looked up at me with big, sorrowful brown eyes.

"You what? Hello? Were you going to share that information with your partner?"

"Hello?" I mimicked. "Yes, I was, but then I got a little side-tracked by being attacked and beaten up."

"How did you find out?"

"I called Sylvia last night and asked her. How did you?"

"I went to her shop this afternoon. She was really grumpy, too."

"Did she happen to say what kind of work he did? I forgot to ask."

"He sells water filters. Evidently he signed some big contract for some business the day Lucinda was killed. Couldn't possibly have been anywhere near here."

I sighed. "Unless, of course, his boss is lying."

She sat on the toilet, crossed one leg over the other and swung her foot. "Listen, Salem, maybe it's time to give up on the Rey angle."

"But I don't want to. I want him to be guilty."

"That would be fine with me. But if he's innocent, he's innocent."

"He has *never* been innocent." I groaned and stood. "My whole body hurts."

"You look awful. Your neck is green."

"Thanks."

She looked around the bathroom. "This is a nice place. You sure you don't want to be married to this guy? He's pretty hot. And he cooks." She sing-songed, "He has nice stu-uff."

"I know." The thing was, I wasn't sure if I was sure or not. I wasn't sure of anything anymore. Living on my own wasn't exactly going so great for me, what with being broke all the time and my car breaking down and people breaking into my house. But marriage...sheesh. I was even worse at that than I was at being single. "I don't know if I have much of a choice," was all I said. I mean, if God was telling Tony not to divorce me, and he was adamant about being obedient, then what chance did I have?

The thought made me feel a little trapped and lightheaded. I needed to get out of there before I hyperventilated. I picked up Stump's box and carried her to the bedroom and opened the window.

Tony's backyard was even prettier than his front yard. Three big Spanish Oak trees spread a green canopy over even greener grass. It's not easy finding shade in West Texas, but Tony had a haven out there. Flagstone lined a broad patio and a walk that curved through the grass to the back gate. If I didn't know better I'd think I was in Connecticut or something. I supposed. Never having seen Connecticut outside of television. I rested my elbows on the windowsill and wondered what it would be like to actually live in a place like this.

"You know," Viv said, "If Tony ends up going to prison he'd want someone to look after his stuff. And you *are* his wife. So this could work out okay for you."

I knew she was just kidding, but it smacked with a little too much reality for me. "Just hush," I said. "I don't want to talk about my marriage."

She sat on the edge of the bed. "Then let's get back to suspects. Who else do you not like? Maybe we could find a way to pin this on them."

"Too bad it's not that easy." I sat on the bed and leaned over to scratch Stump's ears. She was coming out of her stupor and I wondered if I should give her a pill to put her back in. "So if it's not Tony and it's not Rey, who could it be?"

"You know what Columbo would do?"

"Something smart, I'm sure."

"He'd go back and talk to the same people he already talked to."

I thought about that for a second. If either of us talked to Sylvia again she'd slap us both. I didn't want to go back to Rick Barlow's place, not without some kind of protection. So who did that leave? "Remember that girl Stephanie, from the funeral?"

"I was just thinking about her!" Viv slapped her knee. "That's got to be a God thing, or women's intuition."

"Or the path of least resistance." I stood and looked down at Stump. "Are you going to be good while I'm gone?"

She thumped her tail a couple times. I had no idea what that meant.

I looked at Viv. "Do you think we should take her with us?"

Viv shrugged. "Fine by me."

"You are so much easier than G-Ma."

"I'm easier than everybody. Where are we going?"

I thought for a second. "Probably Columbo would have gotten a phone number or address."

"Probably your husband has his employees' numbers around here somewhere."

I raised an eyebrow. "You want me to go snooping through Tony's stuff?"

"No, I want to see what kind of cook he is. Then I want to go snooping through his stuff."

You know those people who can't eat when they're stressed out? I'm *so* not one of those people. Food sounded like the best idea I'd heard in a while, and if I knew Tony, whatever he had would be hot, full of cheese and meat and probably sour cream – the real thing – and the very definition of comfort food.

"Let's go."

Stump whined when I walked out of the room so I went back and carried her into the kitchen with us. The aroma of whatever Tony had cooked lingered in the air and my stomach growled.

I eyed the kitchen table, a really cute little built-in bench and table setup. A banquette, that was what that was called. I'd seen it on HGTV. I slid Stump's box onto the table. She sniffed the air and whined.

"Settle down, girl," Viv said, patting Stump's head. "You can have some, too."

I kept my mouth shut and opened the oven. The dish inside looked so good I very nearly took the Lord's name in vain. I settled for a breathy "Oh my."

Viv appeared at my shoulder. "We need plates and forks, ASAP."

"Forget the plates," I said, grabbing a potholder off the counter. "And at this point forks aren't necessarily a deal breaker."

I slid the casserole dish onto the island and rummaged through drawers till I found the silverware. I handed a fork to Viv and dug in.

It came away covered in cheese and some kind of white sauce. I knew it would have sour cream! It was all I could do to blow on it before I shoved it in my mouth.

I had to hold back tears, it was so good. Chunks of white meat chicken, creamy just-spicy-enough sauce, thick gooey cheese, layered with soft corn tortillas.

Viv made a noise but I was too engrossed to ask if it meant if it was good or bad. Hopefully she didn't like it. That would mean more for me.

No such luck. She hooked her foot around the rung of a stool, scooted it under her bony butt, and settled in.

Eventually I became aware that Stump was whining again, rather insistently. Her nose stuck out above the edge of the box, sniffing wildly. I felt kind of bad, but not bad enough to slow down. Two more bites, I promised myself. Then I'd get her a little.

She grunted and flopped around in the box, trying to get up.

"Oh, okay," I said, my mouth still half full. "Don't mess your leg up." I fished through cabinets and drawers until I found a plastic bowl and scooped some of the enchiladas into it, blowing on them to cool them off. She whined and danced around as best she could with her poor little broken leg.

"I want you to know I'm giving you this against the express wishes of your physician."

She didn't care any more than I thought she would. She dove headfirst into the bowl and didn't come up for air.

I reached down and gingerly felt her bandaged leg. She growled, her face still buried in the bowl. I didn't know if my touch hurt her leg or if she simply wanted my hands away from any proximity to her food. Either way, I drew my hand back out and left her to her work.

"If you don't want to be married to this guy, I do," Viv said, as she slid the casserole dish away and leaned back on her stool, hands on her stomach, and groaned. "Oh, I'm going to need some Tums real soon."

Viv rummaged through the bathroom for antacid while I searched for an address book. He'd left a note on the table with his cell number on it. I *could* call him and ask if Stephanie was working that night and if so, where. If I did, he'd want to know why I wanted to talk to her, and then he'd tell me I should just stay out of things and let the police handle it. Where was the fun in that?

I found in my search that Tony was still as compulsively neat as ever. There was one change of clothes in the hamper in his closet. He had a lot of nonfiction books and biographies of people I'd never heard of. He liked jazz music. And somewhere along the way he'd switched from briefs to boxers.

"Why are you looking in there?" Viv said a little too suddenly behind me.

I slammed the drawer and hit my thumb. I stuck it in my mouth. "Some people keep stuff in their drawers."

"Yes, like their underwear. See, you do still want to be married to this guy. Let's check the computer in the second bedroom. It's on, so we wouldn't even have to figure out his password."

She took off down the hallway.

"I don't know, Viv," I said. "That seems a little intrusive."

"Since that's coming from the girl who was just digging through his underwear drawer, I'm going to ignore it." She slid into the chair behind the computer and grabbed the mouse.

"You're just a technophobe. Don't worry, it's not going to blow up on us or sound an alarm or anything."

She was right. I was a technophobe. I barely knew how to work my cell phone, and most of the time it didn't work anyway because I kept forgetting to charge it. I pulled up a chair and sat behind her. "What are you looking for?"

"Anything. If I can't dig around and find something, we'll do a search on her name."

She clicked on a few things and different screens popped up. Not having any clue what I was doing, I just sat back and watched, my mind mulling over the possibility of actually living in this house. This neighborhood had Trailertopia beat all kinds of ways. It would be nice to have someone steady to come home to every night. It would be nice to have someone besides Frank, looking for a free dinner. Someone to help me out when things went south. Someone to talk to, have conversations with, laugh with. To have someone to share a life with.

I looked around the neat home office, wondering if, when this was all over, Tony would ask me to move in. He didn't act as if my very presence repulsed him. In fact, I think a part of him still cared for me, beyond a normal concern for my welfare that most people would have for someone they'd once been married to.

What did I feel for him, though? What did I feel besides a lot of guilt over the way I'd treated him in the past, and guilt in knowing that if we *were* still married I'd been disgustingly unfaithful to him, I had a lot of admiration for him as a person. Tony was a stand-up guy, solid and dependable, rooted in his values. Did I know anyone else like that? Well, there was Les. Les was like that, and irritatingly cheerful, besides. But Les was also twice my age and in love with his wife – not a good marriage candidate for me.

Marriage candidate – sheesh, get a load of me, sizing up the qualifications of my own husband. I blinked and felt a little dizzy. Husband.

The thing was, yes, I had been sober for a while. A hundred and what...fifty-two days? In a lot of ways I was doing really good, but in other ways, I felt like I was hanging on by my fingernails. I would definitely have headed straight to the bar after seeing Trisha the other day, if God hadn't intervened and made my car explode. How would I react to the pressure of being married?

Just thinking about it made me nauseated. Of course, that could be due to my overindulgence in chicken enchiladas. Still, there was no question that if Tony and I lived as a real man and wife, I would completely freak out and start to over-think every little thing I said and did. I'd obsess about details and then I'd get irritated with Tony for being so calm all the time, and then I would pick fights with him and use that as an excuse to drink. Possibly.

So, maybe Trailertopia wasn't such a bad place after all, as soon as I could feel reasonably certain no one was going to break in and chop my head off or anything.

I thought I ought to pray about it, but I was afraid to. After all, God hadn't exactly been speaking volumes to me like He was other people. It would be just my luck that He'd choose this moment to speak, to tell me I had made a vow to Tony and my duty as a wife was to get myself back with him and be the best wife I could be. I wasn't a big theologian, but I thought God was pretty big on husbands and wives being together.

"Honey, you *do* want to be married to this guy," Viv said. She pointed to some numbers on the screen. "Here's his profit and loss statement from last year."

I didn't really know what I was looking at, just numbers with a lot of zeroes. "Is that, umm...profit or loss?"

"That's profit, honey. My fourth husband was in his sixties before he was worth that much, and by then he didn't really like to spend it. Not that I'm complaining. He saved enough for me to get a swanky place at Belle Court."

I stared at the numbers. I guess I really could cross guilt over ruining Tony's oyster off my list. He'd done extremely well for himself. I thought he had a small operation, cleaning a few office buildings and places like the church, but judging by the numbers I was looking at, he must be cleaning half the town.

"Why are we looking at this? There are no names and addresses on here."

"Same reason you were looking in his underwear drawer," Viv said without apology. "I'm curious."

"Well, close that and find Stephanie."

"I saw a folder marked 'Schedules.' We'll look at that first."

The next thing she opened was a spreadsheet of different names, times, and business names. No wonder Tony was doing so well, I thought as I scanned the list of restaurants, office buildings and business. He even had the new big movie theatre on the north side of town.

The grid was set up with the business name across the top, times down the left side, and names inside boxes throughout the screen. But they were all first initial, last name.

"Do you remember her last name?" I asked.

"I don't think she gave it."

"Some detectives we're turning out to be. We're going to have to learn to be more observant if we're going to make a living at this."

"I know what. She said she and Lucinda worked at the church together, right? So we'll look for anyone with the first initial S under their list." She pointed with a long maroon fingernail to the column under FUMC. L. Cruz was there, along with L. Clark, T. Johnson, T. Thompson, S. Patz and S. Hidalgo.

"Hey, look at that." Viv scrolled across the row of dates. "The night Lucinda was killed, she wasn't scheduled to work. S. Hidalgo was."

"Is S. Hidalgo Stephanie?"

"Get a load of this." She clicked on S. Hidalgo and a smaller box opened up with Stephanie Hidalgo's full name, address, phone number and Social Security number, along with what she'd made so far that year and how much she'd paid in taxes. "Fancy program with cross references."

"I wonder why Lucinda worked for her that night."

"I wonder why Stephanie didn't say anything about that when we talked to her."

I was struck by a thought so powerful it rocked me back in my chair. "Oh my gosh! Lucinda and Stephanie are both Hispanic."

Viv raised an eyebrow. "You're just now catching on to that?"

"No, I mean, they're both young Hispanic women, close to the same age. They both have – *had* long hair. They're about the same height, give or take an inch or two."

"You know, you're getting that same look in your eye Columbo gets when he's on to something. Of course, he's got that one lazy eye and you don't, but –"

"What if it was meant for Stephanie? I mean, what if whoever killed Lucinda thought they were killing Stephanie?"

Viv stared for a second, then the other eyebrow shot up. "Hey!

I never thought about that!"

I jumped up. "I'll bet the police haven't either! I'll bet they never even asked." I fished through Tony's drawer and found a Post-It note and a pen, writing down Stephanie's address and phone number.

"This chart says she's supposed to be working at this office building right now," Viv said.

"We'll go there first. But if we can't get in we'll just wait at her house."

I lugged Stump out to Viv's car and we drove a couple miles to the small office building on the address. The place was deserted except for a little purple hatchback. Evidently Stephanie liked purple.

The front door was locked, of course. "I'll go around and check for a back or side door," I told Viv.

The building was long and skinny, with an outside door half-way down. It was locked, but the back door stood open.

I looked in and saw Stephanie carrying a couple of small plastic wastebaskets. She set one inside an interior door and moved down the hall away from me. I lifted a hand and called out to her, but she didn't acknowledge me. That's when I saw the cord for the headphones she wore.

I was a little hacked off at her for not telling us about the switch in schedules when we talked to her at the funeral. Of course, it's possible she had other things on her mind at the time and she hadn't really taken our "investigation" all that seriously, but still...I couldn't help but think she was hiding something, just like Sylvia was hiding something. Everyone was hiding something. It was starting to get on my nerves.

So that was probably why I was a little bit mean when I tiptoed down the hallway, sticking to the side away from her. Sometimes, I admit, I have a little bit of a mean streak. Just a little bit.

I wasn't actually going to do anything, except get right up behind her and say, "Stephanie!" really loud, maybe grab her arm. I'd say it was because she had the headphones on and didn't hear me the first three times I called her name.

When I was five yards from her I heard a horrendous, ear-piercing wail from outside.

I knew that sound. That was Stump, in the throes of acute separation anxiety.

It had made me jump, though, probably because I was on edge anyway, and because I was trying to be quiet to sneak up on Stephanie. I jerked back and shouted, "Stump, hush!" before I could stop myself.

Stephanie gasped, jumped through the nearest open doorway, and slammed the door.

Well, crud. I stood there a second, looking at the closed door. Then I heard what I thought were whispers, so I tiptoed up and put my ear to the door.

"Hurry!" Stephanie said. She sounded desperate. "He's right outside the door!"

I lurched back and looked around. He who?

I looked both ways down the hall and didn't see anyone. I looked into the office behind me, certain Rey or some other killer was bearing down on me. Nothing.

I put my ear back to the door.

"I don't know. No, I left the back door open because I was carrying out the trash. I just saw him sneaking up behind me and I ran in this office and locked the door. Please hurry!" I heard only panicked, heavy breathing for a few seconds, then, "No, I didn't see a weapon or anything. But he was a big, hulking guy."

I stepped back and scowled at the door as it hit me. Hulking, huh? That was it. I was joining Fat Fighters if it took every dime I had.

I pounded on the door. "Stephanie!"

She screamed.

"It's just me! Salem Grimes. We met at Lucinda's funeral."

Silence. I put my ear back to the door.

Mumble mumble.

"I just want to talk to you," I said. Crud. Double crud. The police were on their way. Should I run or stick around and try to explain? "Tell the police it was a mistake."

Something tapped me on the shoulder.

I screamed. Usually I wasn't so much of a screamer but nothing was usual in my world at the moment.

When I screamed, Stephanie screamed.

"What in the world is going on?" Viv shrieked. She was carrying Stump, who flailed around in her box. She shoved the box at me.

"I don't know!" I shrieked back, hefting Stump. "But the police are on their way, and I'm going to lose some weight if it's the last thing I do."

It would have been true irony if the responding officer was that guy Walters. It wasn't. Some blonde lady cop who clearly hated me on sight came first. Walters showed up three or four minutes after her.

The next twenty minutes were lots of fun. Stephanie didn't seem to believe me, nor did Walters or the lady cop. I think even Viv was beginning to believe I was making up something. I'd had a lot of experience trying to convince people I'm telling the truth when I wasn't. It was hard. For some reason, though, it was even *harder* when I was telling the truth. The female cop kept giving me these disdainful looks and walking a few feet away to murmur to Walters. She'd turn to talk into the radio handset clipped to her shoulder. Then she'd give me another look. I started to wonder if maybe I'd slept with her fiancée, too.

Stephanie stuck to Viv as if the old lady were her lifeline. She gave me doubtful looks while the police decided what to do with us.

"We just wanted to talk to you, I swear," I told Stephanie. "I'm really sorry I scared you."

She shook her head, edging closer to Viv. "It's okay, I'm sorry I panicked. I just...I saw you out of the corner of my eye and it looked like you were sneaking up on me and then you yelled and I've kind of been on edge ever since Lucinda..." She shrugged.

I felt like a jerk. I didn't feel bad enough to come clean and admit I *had* been sneaking up on her, but enough to pat her arm and tell her I was sorry again. That was pretty big for me; I'm not much of a toucher.

"That's why we wanted to check up on you. We wondered if maybe you'd considered the possibility that Lucinda wasn't the intended target for the killer..." Viv raised a penciled-on eyebrow.

Stephanie nodded. "Oh, yeah. I've considered that a lot. I mean, I was supposed to be the one to work at the church that night, not her. So I wondered...we're about the same size and we're both Hispanic and everything."

I felt myself deflate a little. Okay, so maybe I wasn't as ahead of the game as I thought I was. "Did you tell the police that?"

"Of course." She looked at me like I was crazy. I was getting a little tired of all the different looks I was getting. "I told that Sloan guy, the cute one...hey, there he is."

Bobby pulled up and got out of his car. He tilted his head at me. "What are you doing now?"

I just lifted one palm and settled Stump against my hip with the other. I'd let him draw his own conclusions.

He talked to Walters and the blonde hatemonger for a couple of minutes, then he sent them on their way. He walked over and squeezed the back of my neck.

"What would happen if you tried to go an entire twenty-four hours without causing trouble?"

"We just came up here to talk to Stephanie about Lucinda's murder," Viv said. "There was a misunderstanding and we're getting it all worked out. No need to worry."

"Still hot on the case?" Bobby said to Viv. He gave me a look that said he wasn't exactly thrilled.

"We're concerned for Stephanie's welfare, since we learned that she was supposed to be working at the church that night instead of Lucinda." Viv pierced him with a look. "You were aware of that, were you not?"

Bobby folded his arms across his chest. His jaw twitched a little, and he tried to look amused but I thought a part of him also looked a little called-on-the-carpet. "As a matter of fact I was. Which is why her call was responded to so quickly. We're keeping an eye on her just in case she's in any danger."

See, I *thought* it hadn't taken them very long to get there, not nearly as long as it took them to get to my house the night before.

Bobby took my elbow and led me over to Viv's car. "How are you feeling?"

I nodded and slid Stump back into her cardboard box. She looked up at me with those liquid brown eyes and whimpered. I thought it was mostly for Bobby's sake, but I scratched her ears anyway. "Not too bad, a little sore and achey, but not bad. I slept all afternoon."

He stared darkly at my neck for a second. "Did you find a place to stay?"

"Yes, Tony's letting me stay with him. He's got an extra bedroom."

Bobby froze. "Tony."

"Yes. You know, my not-so-ex-husband?"

"Yes, I know Tony. Accused murderer Tony."

"Bobby, come on. He's innocent and –"

"You're staying in the home of an accused murderer?" His voice rose and he leaned his palm against the roof of the car. "Salem, tell me this is a joke."

"Why? You're not going to laugh."

"Salem, come on! What are you thinking?"

"That he's my husband and I trust him and he's the only one who *asked* me. You know I couldn't stay at my place."

"Couldn't you find someplace to stay that doesn't have killers?"

"He's not a killer! He's being very nice to me."

"He was very nice to Lucinda Cruz, too."

"You're being ridiculous."

"Me?" He raked his hand through his hair and did a little pace-back-and-forth thing for a couple of seconds. "Salem, don't you – couldn't you – " He groaned and I thought for a second he was going to throttle me.

"What is your deal? Why do you care so much? And do not

look at me like that! I'm sick of people looking at me like I'm an idiot."

"You're acting like an idiot. Running around town getting yourself involved in who knows what, hanging out with murderers and getting yourself attacked – "

"He didn't do it!"

"He didn't attack you, but he did kill Lucinda Cruz! Salem, he is on surveillance tape going straight to the scene of the crime. He left personal possessions *at* the scene of the crime. He had a romantic relationship with the victim, and he has defense wounds consistent with other evidence found at the crime scene. He did it!" He took a deep breath and backed up half a step, lowering his voice. "Look, I'm sorry. I really am. I know you want to believe in his innocence. But honey, he's not. Stay away from him. Please."

He looked so worried. My throat got tight and for a second, I wondered if maybe he could really be right. Could I be lying to myself?

Heck, why not? Maybe I wanted Tony to be innocent so bad that I wasn't thinking clearly. Maybe I was just making a big fool of myself and Tony was going to kill me, too.

"If Stephanie was the intended target, that would take away one leg of your theory."

He rolled his lips together. Then he nodded. "One."

I chewed my lip. That left three. A stool would stand on three legs. For a moment, the image of Tony, head covered and arms bound behind his back, standing on that stool with a noose around his neck flashed in my mind. I swallowed hard.

He gave a short humorless laugh and squeezed my shoulder. "Salem, don't go back there."

"Bobby, I have to. Quit worrying about it. Believe me, if Tony didn't kill me when he was married to me, he's not going to now."

"There's got to be someplace else you can go."

"There's not. Les' son is staying with him, Viv lives in a retirement home that doesn't allow sleepovers, and G-Ma wants to charge me fifty bucks to stay with her."

I looked at him, and he looked at me, and I knew, I *knew* he was about to ask me to stay with him. I could feel it. The words were right there on the tip of his tongue. The idea both thrilled and terrified me. As ridiculous as it sounds – I mean, he was still fiercely hot and I was still borderline obese – we both knew what was going to happen if I stayed with him.

As much as I had to admit I wanted that – oh, to have someone hold me again, kiss me, make me feel good – I did *not* want that again. Not like that. Not a one-night stand, with all the awkwardness in the morning, feeling ashamed and sleazy and like I'd taken something that wasn't rightfully mine, given something that wasn't mine to give. I'd had enough of that. I'd left that life behind and I wasn't going back, even for Bobby.

I stepped away from Bobby's grasp and lifted my chin. "I appreciate your concern, but unless I'm breaking some law or unless Tony's forbidden to have me stay with him, I'll be there until I can go back to my place."

He hesitated a second, then nodded. "If that's the way you want it."

"I do." I looked back at Stephanie and Viv. They were staring openly at us. "So what's the deal with Stephanie? How do you know for sure she wasn't the intended target?"

"We *don't* know for sure. Like I said, we're keeping an eye out for her. The patrol desk has her schedule, and we're driving by three or four times every shift making sure she's okay." He turned to me, his voice soft like he was trying to break some bad news to me. "But Lucinda *was* the one having the relationship with Tony. And I have to tell you, Salem, nine times out of ten in a crime like this, it is a matter of a relationship going south. Someone's jealous or angry and loses control."

I lifted my chin. "And it's that statistic that has you so hyper-focused on Tony you can't see anything else. You just wait, Bobby. I'm going to find something to exonerate him. This is the one time out of ten, okay? And you're going to owe me a steak dinner and a big apology."

"I can't wait. Call me first when you get your proof. In the meantime, sleep with one eye open." He fished his keys out of his pocket and went over to say a few words to Stephanie. After making sure she was okay with us being there, he gave me a little wave. "I've gotta go. Got a stakeout tonight."

"Oh, can I come?" Viv asked. "I always wanted to do a stake-out."

"Maybe next time. You two stay out of trouble."

"As always, I'm not making any promises." She gave him a cheerful wave and watched with me as he drove away. "Now, the good Lord knew what He was doing when He made that man." She whistled under her breath and shook her head slowly. "If I was thirty years younger..."

She didn't elaborate, but she didn't have to. I didn't comment, but in my mind I figured she'd probably need to be more like forty-five years younger to get his attention.

"I am really sorry I scared you," I said to Stephanie.

"I'm sorry I called the police. I'm just a little on edge lately."

I didn't mention that the obvious solution to that would be to close doors behind her. "Would you mind telling us about the schedule change the night Lucinda was murdered?"

"She already told me. Lucinda texted her that afternoon and asked her to switch."

"Did she say why?"

Stephanie shrugged. "There was a guy at the other place, this office building down on Pine, he was giving her the creeps."

"Giving her the creeps? How?"

"She didn't say. Just that he was giving her the creeps and she wanted to know if I would switch with her."

"No more information than that? And this guy, he didn't give you the creeps?"

"I didn't even know who she was talking about."

"She'd never said anything to you about this guy before?"

She shook her head. "Not really, no. We talked sometimes, you know, about getting freaked out when we were working by ourselves. Those big buildings, deserted and dark, you know. You start to think you hear things, sometimes. I was glad to switch with her, because that church has always given *me* the heebie-jeebie, especially down in the basement. All those big metal doors, and who knows what's behind them. Those creaky old elevators and spooky dark hallways and stuff." She shivered and rubbed her hands over her arms. "I think something in me knew something bad was going to happen there."

Viv patted her arm. "You're very empathetic, dear. Very sensitive. I wonder if there's any other...vibes you've picked up on that might – on the surface – seem to be unrelated, but that might actually be connected to Lucinda's case."

Stephanie chewed her lip. "Well, I don't really know of anything. I mean, I guess I had a few feelings here and there."

Viv nodded slowly, encouraging. "I'll bet you did."

"Like, I think Tony liked Lucinda but I don't think she was so much into him."

"Did you tell the detective that?" I asked.

She shook her head. "I told him they'd been seeing each other, but not that part. I didn't really think about that until later, you know, when I was kind of going back over things in my mind."

"So what makes you think she didn't like him as much? Just a hunch?"

"Yeah, you know, he'd always single her out, be real attentive to her. Not in an obvious way, but he'd always check on her and make sure she was feeling okay, she had what she needed to get her job done, stuff like that. I mean, he's that way with everyone, but he'd single her out special, you know? At first I thought it was just because she was new, and then I found out she was pregnant, and I thought it was just because she was pregnant, but the way he'd look at her..." She trailed off and cocked her head. "You know how a guy looks at a girl and you know it's the real thing, not just an ordinary look. You know?"

Viv nodded happily. "I do."

"Sure," I said, although I couldn't say that I'd ever been on the receiving end of one of those looks. I thought I'd been, a couple of times, but it turned out to be too much alcohol on either his part or mine, or both. "And you're sure she didn't return the feelings?"

"I know she liked him okay. I mean, she wasn't pushing him away or anything. She talked a lot about how nice he was to her and what a great person he was, how successful and dependable. But it was always like, "Oh, he's so much nicer to me than Rey ever was." And "Oh, if Rey could see the way Tony treats me, he'd be furious. Rey would be eating his heart out if he could see how much money Tony makes." Stuff like that."

"So Rey was still on her mind a lot."

Stephanie nodded sadly. "I think so. She said she hated him, but I think a big part of her loved him still, too."

"That always sucks," Viv said.

"Tell me about it."

What all this had to do with the murder, I didn't know. It didn't look good for Tony that he loved Lucinda more than she loved him. It only bolstered Bobby's theory that Tony killed her in a jealous rage. If he loved her, and she was still in love with Rey, who knew what could happen?

It was getting late and I was suddenly very tired. My head was starting to hurt, and I became aware that the rest of me did, too. The meds must have been wearing off.

"I'm sorry, but I think I'm going to have to get some rest. Can you think of anything else?"

Stephanie chewed her lip and shivered a little. "I don't know, I just..." She looked from me to Viv.

"What is it?"

She shrugged. "It's nothing really, it's just...well, you yourself said I can be sensitive to stuff, and I keep having this feeling that..." She rubbed her arms again. "When this first happened, I didn't think there was any way Tony could have done it. But the more I think about it..."

"Are you serious? You really think he did it?" Maybe I was getting a little shrieky because the possibility was starting to sink in on me, too, and I didn't want it to. "Then why are you still working for the man?"

"Because I need the job. And because he's not in love with me, he's not jealous of me." She shrugged. "I don't think I have any-thing to worry about, so..."

"Well, he didn't do it, so you're perfectly safe. From him, at least." I gave her a menacing look but it was completely lost on her. "In fact, I'm spending the night in his house and I'm not a bit worried."

"Well, of course you're not," Viv said. "He's not in love with you, either."

"Let's just go." I stomped to the car then remembered that I might need Stephanie's help again later if I had more questions. "Thanks for your help," I said. "Sorry if I seem a little...grumpy. I'm just tired and worried about Tony."

She nodded and waved. "No problem. I understand. Lucinda was like that, too."

I watched her close the door behind her and leaned back in the seat while Viv drove me back to Tony's. I mulled over what Stephanie had told us. Lucinda was the one who switched the schedules around. I wonder if they were supposed to clear that with Tony. I wonder if she had something else up her sleeve. But what? Why would she have wanted to go to the church that night? What could she have been up to?

And what did Stephanie mean, Lucinda was like that? Worried about Tony? Tired, grumpy? Or just moody?

I turned in my seat and laid my cheek on the back of the seat. "This detective stuff is hard."

"Tell me about it. But it'll get easier as we get more experi-ence."

There she went again. "Viv, we're not going to be getting more experience."

"Sure we will. You said so yourself."

"When?"

"At Tony's house you said we'd have to learn to be more ob-servant if we're going to make a living at this."

"I was joking."

"No you weren't. Maybe you *thought* you were joking, but your heart knew this is what you really want and that's why you said it. It's a whole Freudian thing."

"My heart doesn't really want to be a detective."

"Sure it does. Just think about it. If we could do this kind of thing every day. Go around talking to people, asking nosy ques-tions, making sure good triumphs over evil."

Actually, it *did* seem kind of fun. "There's only one problem I can see."

"What's that?"

"We suck at it."

"I told you, we'll get better." She swooped her car down Indi-ana Avenue. "Do you think she was trying to make him jealous?"

"Who? What?"

"Do you think Lucinda was using Tony's affection to make Rey jealous?"

I shrugged and leaned my head back down. I was really tired. "I kind of figured she was using him as a security net since Rey hadn't worked out."

"Either way, she was using him."

"I think so. Which doesn't make her look so nice." I yawned and shifted in my seat. "I keep wondering why Lucinda would want to switch with Stephanie that night. Stephanie said Lucinda told her someone at her regular job was giving her the creeps. But if that was the case, wouldn't she ask a guy to switch with her? Not another girl who looked so much like her?"

"It sounds like one of them wasn't telling the truth. And I don't know about you, but Stephanie doesn't sound like the manipulative type to me."

I shook my head. "She's too naïve. Do you think Lucinda could have been setting up a meeting at the church? With Rey, or whoever? If there are lots of places to hide..."

"Beats me, I'm fresh out of ideas at the moment. I'm going home to do some more Columbo research. When Tony gets home pick his brain. Find out why he was up at the church that night and whether or not Lucinda told him she was going to switch with Stephanie."

"Will do." I couldn't decide how the notion of talking to Tony made me feel. On the one hand, I couldn't deny the niggling doubt that was creeping up that maybe, perhaps, he just might be guilty. On the other hand, I was really afraid to be alone at the moment. So, hopefully, if he was a killer, he'd gotten it out of his system with Lucinda.

Chapter Thirteen

Tony was home. I lugged Stump in her box up to the door and knocked.

He looked like he'd been waiting for me. He wore baggy gray sweatpants and a t-shirt. He looked tired. I felt bad because apparently I'd kept him up.

"I'm sorry," I said as soon as I came through the door. "Viv and I thought we'd go talk to Stephanie for a while."

He raised an eyebrow. "Is she okay?"

"Sure, she's fine." I carried Stump into the den and set the box on the floor. "I think I scared ten years off her life, but she was fine when I left there."

He stared at me a second.

"She's fine, really. She wasn't expecting anyone to come up there and she's on edge because of everything that's happened, so..." I shrugged. "But she was back to work when we left there." Maybe I would leave out the part about the police coming.

Tony nodded and reached over to scratch Stump's ears. Stump moaned and shifted under his hand, so he dug in a little more and cruised his hand down her neck – or where her neck would be if she had one – and down her shoulders.

Stump looked worshipfully up at him and tried to thump her leg. Doing so made her lose her balance, and she rolled back up like a Weebil and licked his hand.

See, the thing was, Stump was a really good judge of character. She was a better one than I was, as a matter of fact. She knew who she could trust. She liked Les and Frank, and she was a little more reserved around Viv. But she always growled at the man who came to read the gas meter, and he was a creep who gave me lascivious looks every time I saw him. One time a few months ago she flat-out *hated* this new girl who moved into Trailertopia. I thought the girl was really cool, and I got all excited about making a new friend, until one day she stole the money I'd left in the sugar bowl on my kitchen cabinet. That was how I ended up losing my phone and having to go completely cellular.

Right now Stump was looking up at Tony like he was the answer to every prayer she'd ever prayed. That evidence probably wouldn't convince Bobby, but it went a long way with me.

We moved back to the kitchen, and I set Stump's box on the floor at my feet. If I were home, the box would have gone back onto the banquette table, but I had the strangest feeling that Josephine Solis would somehow, some way with that hairy eyeball of hers, find out.

"I guess I should tell you I scared Stephanie so bad she called the police."

"You...what?"

"She was wearing headphones and didn't hear me come up." Even while spilling my guts I wasn't going to tell the part about me sneaking up on her. I would confess that to God and God alone. "She saw me out of the corner of her eye, and she thought

I was an intruder –" Yep, I left out the part about her saying I was a hulking man, too – "and she called the police. They were there in like thirty seconds. They're keeping a close eye on her."

His jaw twitched, but as always his face remained totally in control, totally neutral. "Well, that's good to know."

"I swear she was okay. She was just on edge, and I scared her so she called the police. They did their job very well."

He nodded. "Okay, fine."

"You'll be calling to check on her later, won't you?"

"Within the next five minutes. I was going to pretend to go to the bathroom."

"But since I've already figured it out..." I tilted my head toward the phone on the kitchen counter.

He kept the call quick. I smiled when he hung up. "Feel better?"

"About that, yes." He laughed. "You've always been...interesting to have around."

I scooted back and got comfortable in the corner of the banquette. I really liked that thing. It was stylish and functional. I liked saying the word, even just to myself in my head – banquette banquette banquette.

I felt a little woozy, I realized. Maybe I needed to lie back down for a while, but I didn't. Instead I smiled at Tony. "You're so polite. 'Interesting' is a better word than irritating, or pain-in-the-butt, or just plain horrible."

"You were never horrible."

I looked at him for a moment. "Of course I was. The whole thing was horrible. You did your very best to make it work, while I did everything I could think of to make it *not* work. It's okay, Tony. I've learned that being dishonest with myself just gets me more of what I don't want."

I remembered what Les kept telling me about being a new creature in Christ. He said that when I was born again, I was literally a new person. Sometimes I didn't feel like a new person; actually, most times I felt like the same old screw-up I'd always been. Les insisted it didn't matter how I felt; the Bible said I was a new creature and so it was a fact. I wanted to believe that. I *really* wanted to.

"I'm a Christian now," I said. I felt a little goofy saying that. Okay, a lot goofy. I was cool, I'd always been cool and the kind of person who would laugh right in the face of someone who said, "I'm a Christian now." Of course, I would be a Christian now. That's what people do when they've screwed up too hugely to fix things themselves.

Except with Tony, it felt safe to say. I knew he would be happy for me.

He was. His face lit up and he reached over and squeezed my knee. "I knew there was something different about you!"

"Oh, that's just the forty pounds I've gained."

He laughed and stood up to hug me. "No, it's not. It's you. You're different."

"Well, I'm sober too. I haven't had a drink in a hundred and fifty-two days."

"Outstanding. A miracle." He wasn't trying to be funny, either. He squeezed my shoulders and sat back down.

"Yeah, well..." I shrugged. I thought about making some smart remark like, *"Well, it's no Virgin-Mary's-face-on-a-piece-of-toast, but..."*, but that would be crass, so I only thought about it. "That's really the only explanation for it, isn't it? It's a miracle."

Tony leaned forward and cocked his head. "What is it?"

I shrugged again. "It's nothing."

He raised a brow. "You know, you've never been as good a liar as you thought you were."

I sighed. "It's just...I don't know. You're a Christian. Do you ever feel like..." I wrinkled my nose. "I don't know how else to say it. Do you ever feel like you might have been sold a bill of goods?"

He had the nerve to laugh. I'd opened up about one of my deepest concerns and he laughed. "What do you mean?"

"I mean about this whole new birth, new life, everything's coming up roses stuff."

He clicked his tongue. "Well, I'm Catholic. The coming up roses part is probably for Protestants."

I rubbed the bruises on my throat. "I just really thought things were going to be...different. Better. Like people wouldn't break into my house, and I wouldn't have to drive a pickle-mobile."

He blinked, but didn't ask.

"Les told me that when the Holy Spirit would come into my heart and would transform it. I would be made new, and I'd be filled with joy, and I'd always have the – the –" I mimicked Les' booming voice, "*The Great Comforter* with me, whatever the heck that means. Where was this Great Comforter when the guy was sitting on my stomach shoving my head into the wall? Where's the Great Comforter when I'm feeling like a complete screw-up who's never going to get it right? I mean sometimes, Tony, I have to tell you, I feel like one of those poor salmon swimming upstream, except at least the salmon actually *get* somewhere for all their trouble. I keep leaping out of the water over and over again and flopping around for all I'm worth, but I'm at the same stupid spot in the same stupid river – and no matter how hard I work I'm always going to end up right there. I thought it wasn't going to be like this anymore when I was born again. I didn't want to get born again as the *same person*." I took a deep breath because I was beginning to see spots. "Sorry. I hadn't meant to say all that. I'm really kind of woozy from the pain meds."

"What did you think it was going to be like?" He leaned forward in his chair, his brown eyes intense on mine.

"Just better."

"Better than what? Better than it was, or better than this?"

"Both. I mean, I *think* I had realistic expectations. I didn't think everything would actually be coming up roses *all* the time. I can see that life is still life and bad things still happen sometimes. But I thought more good stuff would happen, and I thought, even when it didn't, I'd have..." How could I explain it? "I wouldn't feel so *alone* all the time. I'd feel like I had someone in my corner, someone on my team, and even if things sucked every once in a while, it wouldn't be so bad because I wouldn't be alone while things were sucking. And even if I didn't have, like, you know, the *great love of my life*, I would have love *in* my life. And that would make all the rest of it bearable." I made a face. "I don't think I'm explaining it very well."

"I think you're explaining it very well."

"Les promised me in that jail cell that the spirit of the living God would be alive inside me and that I would actually be able to *feel* a difference."

"And when was this?"

I didn't really want to talk about that part, even if this was Tony, who had seen the very worst of me and still wasn't totally repelled, but there was no going back now, and he probably already knew the statistics even if he didn't know the details.

"A year or so ago, in the county jail. I'd just gotten another DUI. Les came up to talk to me. He does that – goes to the county jails around here and out to the prison and talks to people about God. Witnessing, he calls it. I was sitting on that cold metal bench thinking about how there was really no point in my even being on the planet, all I ever did was hurt people and screw things up. I knew there was no way that my life was ever going to amount to anything, even if I got out of that mess and didn't go to real jail." I hugged my arms around my waist and remembered that night. I'd had low moments before, but that night was different. "I was drunk, but not drunk enough to escape reality. I faced the facts. I was a loser. A mistake. I always had been – neither of my parents had wanted me, and my grandmother barely tolerated me. The way I saw it, I had two choices. I could accept the fact that I was a loser, get comfortable with it, and just drink myself to death because that was what was going to happen eventually, anyway. Or, I could *not* live the rest of my life."

Tony nodded slightly, remaining silent.

"And then I heard this voice beside me, saying, 'There's another choice.' I looked up and there was this guy standing over me, bald, holding this ratty-looking Bible." I remembered that first meeting and almost started to laugh. There I sat, drunk and depressed, my life a wreck, my hair bleached and ragged, my makeup smeared off, my clothes wrinkled and stained, and even then one of the first thoughts I had was that Les should just shave off those few straggly hairs he was clinging to on the top of his head. He diverted my attention quickly, though.

"He had started talking to me about how there was another way to live, one that didn't involve jails, and struggling, and always being out of control, always being disappointed in myself and always finding myself on the losing end of things. He told me there was a way to start over fresh, with a clean slate. I could take all the mistakes I'd ever made and make them go away forever. I could be a new person."

"That must have sounded pretty enticing to someone sitting in a jail cell."

"Oh, believe me, it was. He could have told me I had to donate a kidney and I would have gladly done it on the spot. I mean, be *somebody else*? Have all my mistakes completely erased? That was a heck of a deal. Then he started talking about Jesus." I shook my head and winced. The more I talked, the weirder I felt. Maybe because it was getting late, and I was woozy from the drugs. Maybe because of the situation and the weirdness of the last few days. Sitting at the banquette across from Tony, I remembered that morning a year before afresh, but from a different perspective.

"I was irritated at first. I mean, *Jesus,* seriously? Religion is for gullible losers, right? For the close-minded and simple, grasping at delusions. But then he told me about his life, before he got – got *saved,* as he called it. He had been as messed up as I was. More, maybe. He's an alcoholic, too, and he had done time in the state pen for armed robbery. He held up one of those check-cashing places with a gun, can you believe that? *I* can't believe it, but he said it was true. Then these people had come to the prison and talked to him about becoming a follower of Christ, and he had said this prayer, and..."

I tried to find words for how I felt that morning, listening to Les, but my brain wasn't firing on all cylinders. But it had seemed...real. Powerful. Les wasn't like a shouting, fire-and-lightning-bolt televangelist. He was just solid. Convinced he'd tapped into a power, convinced there was a true before and after, and he was living the after.

"Well, he made it sound really good. Like an instant, dramatic change. New person, inside and out. While there I sat, so tired of being me I couldn't even think straight. I *was* a loser, and I wanted to be gullible for a change."

"So what happened?"

"I said the prayer Les told me to say. I decided if I was going to do it, I was going to do it all the way. Go all in. So I did."

"And how did you feel?"

I leaned my head back and closed my eyes. "I remember feeling scared. Relieved. Like I was relinquishing control, and that part was terrifying, but it was a good thing, too. I didn't know what was coming next, and I was afraid I wouldn't be able to pull it off, whatever *it* was. But I also felt hope. I had another chance." I shook my head and opened my eyes. "I kept waiting for that joy to fill me, to feel that overpowering love of the Holy Spirit that Les kept talking about, but..." I shrugged.

"But you did feel hope. And just before that you were completely hopeless and not sure you wanted to live."

I nodded. "That's right. I did feel hope. But Tony...don't get offended, but I feel the same thing when I see a really good info-mercial. You know, the kind that promises to change your life with this diet and exercise video or this big rubber ball or this money-making scheme or whatever."

Tony stared at me and his jaw twitched. He was quiet for a long time. I thought I'd finally done something to make him never forgive me when he shook his head. "You're one of a kind, Salem. What exactly is it you're wanting?"

I threw up my hands. "I don't even know anymore. *Something.*

Something that tells me that I really wasn't just a gullible loser after all, that I'm *not* grasping at delusions. Something to show that it's real. Not just, you know, the Emperor's New Clothes or something."

"And a feeling would do that for you?"

I stopped. "I think so. Wouldn't it?" I was a little confused now. What else was there, besides a feeling? What would it take, for me to truly *know* it was real?

"Taking your friend's word for it – Les? That won't do it for you? Taking my word?"

I thought about it. "Apparently not," I finally said. "The thing is, I think it could, up to a point. I mean, it *has*, right? Taking Les's word for it seems to have gotten me to this point. It could get me sober. But Tony, nothing but genuine, actual power is going to *keep* me sober. Life is just too hard."

"Tell me about it," he said, shaking his head.

Once again I had forgotten I didn't have the worst problems in the room. "I'm sorry, Tony, I know you have other things on your mind –"

He stood, shaking his head. "No, no, it's okay, I'm glad we're talking about this. Let me get a book right quick." He moved into the living room to a floor-to-ceiling bookshelf and tilted out a few books, then opened up a couple more and browsed through them before he found what he was looking for. He brought it back to his seat.

"I'm sure being a Methodist you've already heard this story many times, but don't you think that's what John Wesley was talking about?" He flipped through a few pages.

The name sounded familiar. "Is that your lawyer?"

Tony looked at me, one eyebrow raised. "John Wesley? The

founder of the Methodist Church?"

I nodded. "Oh yeah. *That* John Wesley. Sorry, I'm just a little tired." And clueless. I knew I had heard something about John Wesley at some point. The founder of the Methodist Church, huh? Probably I should know all about this guy. Lucky for me I hadn't had to pass any kind of test to be a Methodist.

"I read this book about different letters he'd written. Early in his preaching career he had some major doubts, just like you're talking about."

"And he was a preacher?"

Tony nodded quickly, warming to the subject. "Yes. He knew what he was *supposed* to be feeling, but he didn't feel it." He shrugged. "He had doubts. Major ones."

"And yet he started an entire denomination?" Wow. That seemed...I didn't know. Deceptive or something.

"Yes. Obviously, there was a turning point in there. And it came at this meeting..." He ran his finger through a couple of paragraphs. "Yes, here, at Asbury. You've probably heard about Asbury before. Something happened at that meeting, and he said in this letter to his brother, 'My heart was strangely warmed.'" Tony held the book out so I could read it. "His heart was strangely warmed. He felt something, Salem. Something real. Physical. Something that made him different. And from that point on his ministry was different." He handed the book to me. "I don't think it's so unusual, Salem, what you're feeling. This guy had the same problem, and he struggled with it. He knew something was missing. But he kept pursuing it, and it came to him. Profoundly."

I fingered the book, and let that drift around in my mind for a couple of minutes. "Why would something be missing? Did I not do something right?"

Tony shook his head. "Salem, I have no idea. I'm no expert. My faith has just..." He shrugged again. "It's just always been there."

"You know more than I do. You're a better Methodist than I am, and you're Catholic."

"I don't think God's so much into splitting hairs. He's not going to withhold something important because you said the wrong word or didn't bow the right knee. Whether you feel it or not, He loves you."

"But I *don't* feel it."

"But it's there," he insisted. "God didn't start loving John Wesley at Asbury. John Wesley started feeling that love at Asbury."

I thumbed through the book. "Does it say anything in here about what happened that night to make his heart get strangely warmed?"

Tony laughed. "I don't think so, but if you do a little research maybe you could find out."

I read a couple of paragraphs and the words swam in front of me. I tried to hide a yawn, but it got completely away from me.

"You're tired, Salem. Why don't you go to bed and we'll talk about it tomorrow?"

"Thanks." I stood and tucked the book under my arm. I turned to go, then turned back. "Oh, by the way, Bobby Sloan is convinced you're going to strangle me in my sleep. You're not going to, are you?"

He shook his head. "Not planning on it."

"I didn't think so. Stump's a good judge of character, and she seems to trust you."

Tony smiled. He had a very nice smile. It was hard to imagine he would kill anybody. It was hard to even imagine that a few hours ago I'd wondered if I was safe with him.

"Sleep tight, Salem."

I carried Stump to my room and put the book on the nightstand. What a weird day. What a weird conversation. I lay down and pulled the covers up to my neck. Old John Wesley wasn't feeling the love, either. Why did that make me feel better?

Stump whined and I looked down at the floor. "You're going to have to sleep down there tonight, babe," I said. "This is how we act when we're company – like you're a pet. I know it stinks, but that's the way things are."

Stump had very expressive eyes. They seemed to say, *"Remember when I was the only one who wanted to be around you? Remember when you were lonely and sad and I was there licking your hand and making you feel okay again? Remember how you thought you'd either die or go back to drinking if it weren't for me, keeping the loneliness from swallowing you whole?"*

I lifted her up into the bed with me. "Don't tell anyone. And don't pee on Tony's sheets." She'd never peed on mine, but still, it didn't hurt to keep the expectations clear.

I picked up the book Tony had given me and thumbed through it. His heart was strangely warmed, huh? That sounded like Les talk.

Maybe I just wasn't trying hard enough. My enthusiasm, I had to admit, had taken a direct hit from all my unanswered prayers lately. My phoned-in efforts were not apt to get me a strangely warmed heart. I was much more likely to get a good case of heartburn from overeating Tony's cooking.

The whole thing was depressing. I didn't know why Les's experience was so different from mine, but I guess that fell under the "God works in mysterious ways" category. God had selected him for special work, so maybe He'd poured on the power a lot thicker than He had for me. It was obviously up to me to make up the difference, so I didn't hold out a whole lot of hope that I'd ever get to that warm heart. How about a strangely lukewarm heart, God? What can you do with that?

I fell asleep feeling overwhelmed and a little depressed, but safe, at least. That went away, though, when a noise outside my window woke me some time later.

Stump growled low in her throat and tried to stand up, her nose pointed to the window. She stumbled in the covers but stayed hard on point.

I bolted up and was on my feet before I came fully awake, shifting back and forth between the door – which would take me to Tony – and the phone on the nightstand – which would bring me the police. Tony was quicker but probably unarmed. The police would bring firepower, but they'd take a few minutes. While I was deciding, I heard a spew of foul language in a familiar voice.

I plastered myself against the wall and edged closer to the window. After a few seconds of hearing more cursing and stumbling around, I gritted my teeth and ripped the curtains back.

"Viv! What in the world are you doing out here?" I shoved the latch on the window and opened it. "I almost called the police on you."

"I keep telling you, it wouldn't be the first time. It wouldn't even be the first time today, in fact." She scowled down at the ground. "I changed my mind about you staying married to Tony. The man has an honest-to-goodness garden gnome back here. And it attacked me."

"It's a guard gnome." I leaned out the window. "What are you doing that you couldn't come to the front door?"

"I had an idea and I didn't think waking Tony with it would be the smart thing to do."

"And waking me would?"

"I keep thinking about that weirdo guy with the storage place. Whatever he's hiding is the key to this whole thing."

"Ricky Barlow. What makes you think he has anything to do with this?"

"He's the one thing that doesn't add up. Everyone else has a reason for acting the way they do. Sylvia is defensive and secretive because her son hasn't exactly exhibited the best behavior."

"True. She's always been quick to jump to his defense, bail him out of the scrapes he's gotten in to."

"So it's not really a big mystery that she didn't want to talk to us about Lucinda. If she talks about Lucinda and Rey, then she talks about how badly Rey treated her. And Stephanie told us everything she could think of to tell us. And obviously Tony's been more up front than anybody else would have been. But this guy...he made no sense at all."

I nodded. We'd been through all this right after we saw Ricky. "So what does it mean?"

"I'm not sure. But I think we need to investigate him a little further. If you remember correctly, he was the last person we talked to before you were attacked."

"Of course I remember!" I snapped. "Maybe that's why I'm not so hot to go *investigating* him in the middle of the night."

"But what if he's the one who holds the key? What if he's the one who actually killed Lucinda Cruz and the police are so far from him they'll never even look in his direction?"

"What if we go after him and get ourselves killed in the process?" I hated to be a wuss, but being attacked in my own home hadn't set well with me.

Viv stood there in Tony's garden and gave me a funny look. Finally, she patted her hip. "I've got a little protection."

I felt my eyes bug. "You what? You brought a *gun?*" The last word squeaked out.

"Just a little one. For protection. Probably we won't even need it."

"Probably. *Probably?*" I threw up my hands and spun around.

"Oh, chill out."

I took a few fortifying breaths and leaned on the windowsill, talking through my teeth. "Do. *Not.* Tell. Me. To. Chill. *Out!* I'm trying to stay safe. You should do the same."

"I am safe!" Viv slapped her hand against her thigh and screwed up her face. "That's the whole problem! I'm so safe I'm practically dead. Salem, you don't know what it's like, living in that mausoleum with all those old people. Day after day having to maneuver around their walkers and wheelchairs and the nurses with their medicine carts. I don't mean to be disrespectful, honestly, but those people are just hanging around waiting to die! I don't care what the brochure says about a place for active seniors, it's a holding tank for the almost-dead. Their lives are over; they're just hanging out till God calls their number. Salem, I'm not done living yet."

She leaned her hands on the windowsill and I noticed a shine to her eyes I'd never seen before. Good heavens, was she going to cry on me? I had no idea how to handle it if she did.

"I'm not old, Salem. I know I look old, and if you look at my birth date you'd think I was ready for the grave, but I swear on the inside I'm not a minute older than you are. I'm not ready to hang up my towel yet. I'm not through with excitement and adventure. Salem, I've danced with the Rockettes in Times Square. I've dealt blackjack to Dean Martin. I cut the ribbon on the first McDonald's in the state of Oklahoma. Okay, that last one was lame, but still, I have led an exciting life. In all my life, I've been up and I've been down, I've been on the edge of complete poverty, and I've been sitting in hog heaven. But until now, I've never, ever been bored." She shook her head and for just a second she looked older than anyone on earth. "Salem, what's the biggest challenge to your sobriety? Stress? Dealing with money and job and people?"

"Mostly, yeah. Except those days when I just want to taste it. That's the worst of all."

She nodded. "Yes, that's the worst. When you just want a taste and nothing else will do. But for me, in the day-to-day challenges, I don't have a lot of stress. Boots left me with enough money and with smart enough people to take care of the money that I don't have to stress about much. Whatever I don't like, I don't have to deal with if I don't want to. But Salem...my challenge every day is flat-out boredom. I don't want to live like this. I don't want to sit and wait for my number to be up. I'm not ready to give up. I'm not even ready to *slow down*. And every day I think, well, what the hell difference would it make if I have a drink? What if I drink an entire fifth of Wild Turkey every day of my life? I've got nothing else to do."

I've always been a sucker for a sob story. Guys found that out early on, and I handed out a lot of pity comfort before I caught on that I was being used. But I was a total sucker for Viv and her sad eyes. I was ready to jump out that window and take her wherever she wanted to go, just to make her go back to the in-your-face, always-upbeat Viv. I didn't like this sad, pitiful Viv.

"Viv, don't," I said. "You're not old, you don't have one foot in anything except a ridiculously expensive shoe. Quit talking like this."

"But Salem, this past week has been one of the best in my life. I have a *mission*. I have something important to do, something besides playing cards or writing my memoirs or learning a new stinking computer program. Something that actually matters. This week I've had something to think about. And I'm not ready to let that go."

I sighed and made a face at her. "Well, I'm certainly not up to jerking the rug out from under someone's entire reason for living, not in the middle of the night. Give me a minute to get dressed."

"Make it quick."

I turned back to her with my finger raised. "I'm bringing Stump with me."

"Fine with me. She can be our sidekick. All great detective teams need a sidekick."

I reached for my sweats and pulled them on. "I'm warning you right now. If somehow this night goes south and the police become involved, I'm giving you and your gun up first thing. I'm not getting into more trouble just because you're not taking to the mahjong thing. If you want excitement, try the county jail. It's a thrill a minute."

"You're crabby in the middle of the night. Are you still sleepy? When you get to be my age you don't sleep so well. If you want I can get you one of those flavored-up coffee things at PakASak to wake you up."

Actually, I wasn't all that sleepy. I'd slept most of the day, and besides, Viv's little speech had stirred something in me, too. The past few days had been frustrating, but it had also been exhilarating. I knew what Viv meant when she said she was finally doing something that mattered. I mean, I loved my job at Bow Wow Barbers, but lives don't exactly hinge on a dog's haircut or color of nail polish, no matter how passionate some customers feel about it. What Viv and I were doing was important. Well, it *would* be important if we actually helped Tony. It would be life and death. I finally had a glimpse of a notion of why someone would want to be a cop. Before, I always thought it was for the uptight and power-hungry. Now I realized that someone could go into law enforcement because they actually wanted to *help* people.

I wasn't tired anymore. However, Viv had offered me one of those flavored-up coffee things at PakASak. Cappuccino, in other words. PakASak had the richest, chocolatey-est cappuccino in town. It was kind of like a chocolate candy bar and a cup of coffee melted together in a cup. So I yawned. "You know, a cup of something caffeinated would help me think a little more clearly."

"Are you going to tell your husband you're leaving?"

I shook my head and tugged my shoe on. "Let's let him sleep." I didn't think he'd be too keen on any of this.

I handed Stump through the window and giggled as I threw my own leg over the sill. "I haven't done this since high school."

"See, I told you. This is exciting stuff."

We tiptoed around the house and jumped in Viv's Caddy. I heard a soft noise as we drove, and looked over to see Viv singing, "Bad Boys, Bad Boys, watcha gonna do, watcha gonna do when they come for you?" under her breath.

I was happily pouring my cappuccino when Bobby touched me on the shoulder. "Hi!" I said with a grin, right before I realized we weren't just coincidentally bumping into each other.

"What's going on?" He didn't look happy.

"With what?" Viv asked.

"What are you two up to?"

I looked at Viv. She looked at me. Clearly this was not the time for the truth.

I set my cup down and frowned at him. "Fine. But I want you to know this is completely your fault."

His jaw twitched and he glared at me.

"It is. All your talk about Tony made me paranoid. I couldn't sleep, thinking about all the stuff you said."

"So you're finally showing some sense."

"Get the smug look off your face. You freaked me out. I had to call Viv to come get me. She's taking me back home."

"I thought you were going to stay away from there till we find the guy who attacked you."

If there ever was a time for a good defense being a ballistic offense, this was it. "What the heck do you expect me to do, Bobby, sleep under a bridge? I have to stay *somewhere*. And my best choice has now been ruined by what is probably your own narrow-mindedness. Tell me what you think I should do? Just sit in my car till you finally find the guy who wants to beat me up? And what are you doing following me around, anyway? Am I a suspect or something?"

"Actually, you are." He raised an eyebrow.

Uh-oh. I'd only said that to make him defensive. I hated it when things backfired on me. "I am? Why?"

"Because suspicious things keep happening around you, Salem. You find dead bodies. You harass witnesses. You're the main suspect's ex-or-maybe-not-wife and you refuse to stay away from him even though he's clearly someone you should be nervous around." He lifted his lip with a slight sneer. "You're not making a lot of sense, Salem. And that makes you look guilty."

Viv, bless her heart, intervened before I could hyperventilate. "Enough of that, Detective. Is she a suspect or are you simply browbeating her? Because if you suspect her, you need to make it official and take her in for questioning."

Uh-oh. I was back to near-hyperventilating again.

"And if not, we'll need for you to step back and leave us alone. This week has been very traumatic for my friend, and she needs her rest."

Bobby stared from me to Viv and back again. Funny, most of the time I didn't have a clue what Bobby was thinking, but now he seemed to be thinking all kinds of things: like he really did suspect me of something but he wasn't sure what, and he really was worried about me and frustrated because he couldn't tell me what to do, and mostly he really did think Viv was a crotchety old pain in the butt.

I shrugged and put the lid on my cappuccino. "Now if you'll excuse me, I'm going home."

He didn't say a word. Just stood by the cappuccino machine and watched Viv pay for our drinks, then followed us out to the parking lot.

Two blocks down the street Viv said, "Is he behind us?"

I didn't have to turn around to see; I'd been watching in the sideview mirror. "Yep."

"Crud. What do we do?"

"No idea. I guess you'll have to take me home."

"Crud crud crud. Okay."

Chapter Fourteen

So we went to my house. Stump was glad to be there, even if it was the middle of the night. She whimpered and twisted around in her box. Finally I made a pallet from the old blankets on the sofa and let her lay down on those. She was snoring within five minutes.

I checked out the whole trailer – a three minute task – and came back to make sure Viv was comfortable. She had her keys and was moving toward the door.

"Oh, no, you're not. You're not leaving me here by myself."

"This is your house."

"So what? I was safe and snug in bed at Tony's and you came and woke me up. If I have to stay here, you and your gun do, too."

She sighed and looked out the rectangular window in the door. "Your boyfriend is still out there. I guess he was watching Tony's house when I came up."

"*I* was his stakeout. That's interesting." I collapsed on the couch. "I wish I was sleepy. I'm so wired I could tap dance."

Viv crossed her arms over her chest and plunked down on the chair. "Join the club. I never get more than four hours of sleep a night anymore. The rest of the time I stare at the ceiling and count ex-husbands."

"Do you think Bobby really believes I have anything to do with this murder? Or was he just trying to spook me?"

Viv shrugged. "Who knows? He was probably just blowing smoke."

I leaned sideways and scratched Stump lightly on the back of the neck. She groaned and shifted away. Stump doesn't like to be disturbed when she's sleeping. I drew my hand back before she decided I might be a monster she needed to take care of.

"'Probably' isn't very reassuring to me. He can't really think I'm guilty. It makes no sense."

"Salem, honey, the only thing that makes sense in this crime is that Tony did it."

I looked around for something to throw at her. But the only thing within easy reach was Stump, so I settled for a glare. "If you really believe that, why are you so pepped up about solving this crime? It's not just because you're bored."

"I didn't say I believed he was guilty. I said he's the sensible one to suspect. There are so many illogical things about this whole situation that it makes me want to get to the bottom of it. Somebody's lying here, and it's not just Tony. Lots of somebodies are lying."

"Listen to this," I said as I tugged my shoes off and dropped them on the floor beside Stump. "I asked Tony what the police had on him, and putting it together with what Bobby let slip, this is the evidence. One, Tony was seen going into the church around the time of the murder. That in itself wasn't a big deal, because although he wasn't scheduled to go there that night, it wasn't un-common for him to visit the job sites to check up on things."

"Did he say why he went?"

"He said Lucinda called and asked him to come. She was having trouble with one of the floor buffers or something, but when he got there, she was gone. He checked out the buffer, saw it was working okay, so he went looking for her but didn't find her."

"Was she already dead by this point?"

I shrugged, remembering the tightness in Tony's voice. "He said he thought he could hear her phone ringing, but it was too faint to be sure, and eventually he left."

Viv shuddered. "That's creepy." She was quiet for a minute. "So the cell phone records would back up his story that he was there because she asked him to come."

"They would show that she called him, and that he called her back. But of course none of that means he didn't kill her."

Viv frowned. "So what else do we have?"

"A strange mark on the back of Tony's neck. Remember the other day at his office when he showed me the back of his neck? The police took a picture of it when he was arrested. There was a thin red mark there, like a little scratch. Tony said it felt like an allergic reaction, and he's had a similar reaction to some kind of cleaning solution before."

"Ugh!" Viv leaned back in her chair. "None of this makes sense. You would think, if they were looking for some kind of defense wound, they'd look at his hands or his face or something on the front of his body. Like scratches from her fingernails, you know?"

"That's what they always do on CSI."

"I know! And on Columbo. What kind of defense wound would be on the *back* of your neck?"

I sat with my chin tucked into my chest, mulling that thought and also thinking that one of those Star Crunches would go great with my cappuccino. An uncomfortable thought intruded: Tony would rub an allergen like that on his neck if he wanted to cover up another, more defined mark.

I wished I hadn't thought of that. I got up to comfort myself with a Star Crunch.

"What's that look for?" Viv asked.

I told her my idea.

"What kind of more defined mark?"

"A mark that would indicate he'd been in a struggle. Just think, the St. Christopher has something to do with this, right? I was thinking, maybe it was ripped off the killer's neck during the murder. And if it was, it would probably leave a mark on the neck of whoever it was ripped off of."

"Right."

"So what better way to cover it up, than to make a bigger wound over it?"

Viv stared at me. "Now who's talking like they believe he's guilty?"

I sighed and took a Star Crunch out of the box. There were only two left. I held one out to Viv in silent offering.

"What kind of kiddie junk food is that?"

"The good kind."

"Give it."

We silently tore off the plastic wrappers and chewed while we thought. I was right; the Crunch and the cappuccino went great together, too bad it was sitting like a hot sour ball in my stomach.

"He can't be guilty," I said finally. "Stump loves him, and she's the best judge of character I've ever seen."

"She just seems that way in contrast to you. You're the worst judge of character I've ever seen."

"I hang around with you, don't I?"

She nodded solemnly. "Exactly." She leaned back and lifted the curtain. "He's still out there."

"I feel like I'm sitting here eating chocolate while Tony's twisting in the wind."

"I know. But it's good chocolate."

"What are we going to do?"

She sighed and chewed. "I'm out of ideas."

Just then I had an idea. I liked it only minimally more than my last idea. "Your car is blocking the pickle-mobile."

"What?"

"Your car is blocking the pickle-mobile from Bobby's view."

She got a look in her eye. "And?"

"And we could sneak out, slip into the pickle-mobile and go over to Ricky's place. See what we can see."

"We'll never get away with it."

I stood up and began to pace. I had to do it longways, because whenever I try to pace middle-ways in my trailer it leaves me feeling like I've just played dizzy bat. "We can sneak out the back door –"

"You have a back door?"

"Yes, in the laundry room. We can crouch down –"

"You have a laundry room?"

"It's more of a laundry alcove, actually. Listen. If he's paying any attention at all, he'll see us. We have to crouch down, get in the car, and then push it down the street in the dark."

"At the risk of repeating myself, we'll never get away with it."

"So what? So what if Bobby catches us? What's he going to do, arrest us? We haven't done anything wrong."

"That's what Tony said."

I stopped pacing and chewed my lip. I was struck by a memory I'd totally blocked, of the night I'd wrecked my car and our baby – Tony's and mine – had died. I had awoken in my hospital bed in the middle of the night. I didn't know what time it was or even what day it was, but I knew I'd been in an accident and I knew the baby had died. I'd already been told that much.

I'd heard a noise and looked toward the foot of the bed.

Tony sat on a cot against the far wall. He didn't know I was awake. He had his head in his hands and his shoulders shook. He hadn't made a sound. He just sat there and cried harder than I'd ever seen anyone cry. The sobs seemed to come from somewhere deep inside him, from his soul. He shifted and one hand clutched his chest, twisting his t-shirt as if he was trying to rip his own heart out. His face twisted hard in a horrifying grimace.

I hadn't been around very many men in my life – just the ones Mom brought home and my few "boyfriends." I'd certainly never seen a man cry before. I'd never seen *anyone* cry as hard as Tony cried. The sight of it disturbed me more, somehow, than losing the baby had.

He actually loved the baby. I hadn't realized it before then. I was shocked, confused, and yes, sad, but also maybe even a little relieved, but he was devastated.

I hadn't thought of that night since. I stopped in the hallway in front of the bathroom and thought that no one who loved someone they'd never even seen before could be capable of murder.

"You know what? I'm through going back and forth, wondering if Tony could be guilty or not. He says he's not, I believe him, and I'm going to do everything within my power to help him prove it. If that means sneaking around behind Bobby's back, so be it." I pulled my shoes back on. Determination and the Star Crunch had fortified me. "You don't have to go if you don't want to. In fact, it might be a good idea if you stay here and move around every once in a while so he'll think we're still in here."

"Uh-uh." She stood and grabbed her purse. "You'll probably solve this and leave me sitting here, left out of the glory. Nothing doing."

Stump tuned into us moving around and began to whine, swiveling around the box on her fat bottom.

"You really should stay here," I said. "I don't know where we're going or who we're going to see, so it might not be safe."

She lifted her nose and her mouth went into a little O shape that was an early indication of an ear-splitting howl.

Great. I wouldn't get one foot out the door before she'd be screaming loud enough to wake all of Trailertopia and have Bobby running to our rescue.

I shook my head. "Fine. But don't say I didn't warn you."

I switched on a lamp in my bedroom and made sure my cell phone was charged. I thought about calling Frank to ask if he'd divert Bobby's attention, but knowing Bobby, he'd catch on, and knowing Frank, if Bobby didn't catch on, he'd spill the beans.

The door to the laundry room opened on the opposite side of my house from the front door. I hadn't opened it in the eight months I'd lived there; there was no telling how long before *that* it had been opened. It didn't budge when I pushed on it.

I pushed harder. I leaned my shoulder against the door and shoved. I braced my feet against the dryer and groaned as I pushed. The dryer moved, the door didn't.

I stepped back, panting and irritated. I wasn't going to be stopped from saving the day by a stupid door.

I remembered something I'd seen Les do when his ice cream truck didn't start one day. I looked back at Viv and commanded, "If you laugh at what I'm about to do, I'll take you back to Belle Court and tell them I found you wandering the streets babbling and looking for your pet armadillo Pookums."

I put one hand on the door and took a deep breath. "Door, I'm talking to you. Listen to me. In the name of Jesus Christ, I command you to open."

I heard a snicker behind me. I whipped my head around to see Viv staring at the ceiling, her lips a very thin line.

I glared and took hold of the knob again. I turned it and with great confidence I shoved all my weight against the door.

They say God has a sense of humor. Seeing me fly through the air and thud to the ground must have been a real knee-slapper for Him.

"You've got the spirit of something in you, I'll grant you that," Viv said from the doorway.

When I got my breath back I rolled to my feet. "That Pookums thing wasn't an idle threat. You'll end up on the fifth floor with a very special friend to keep you constant company." The fifth floor at Belle Court was reserved for dementia patients. I happened to know Viv's greatest fear was that she'd end up there and lose every last bit of her freedom.

"You don't have to be such a grouch," she said, toeing Stump's box into the doorway so I could lift it out. "God finally answered one of your prayers. I would think you'd be happy." She squatted with a groan and climbed out of the door. I closed it quietly behind her, although I figured my launch into the backyard had caused at least some noise. If Bobby was paying very close attention there was a possibility he would be heading our way any second.

I decided if he was, I was just going to be honest. He didn't like me snooping around, but he couldn't very well stop me, could he? As long as I wasn't under arrest I was free to leave my own house. I tiptoed to the corner of the trailer and peeked around. From what I could tell, he was still in his car. There was a span of about five yards where Viv and I would be in open ground before we could duck behind a short bushy pine. If we made it that far, I had fairly high hopes we could get out.

I turned back to Viv. "We have to make it quick between here and the bush. Should we run together, or one at a time?"

She peeked around the corner, too, then turned big eyes back to me. "You go first. I'll wait a few seconds then I'll cross." From the excitement in her voice you would have thought we were sneaking past guards at Alcatraz.

I got down as low as I could and scurried across to the bush. It wasn't easy, lugging Stump with me. I dropped the box on the ground a little harder than I'd intended and Stump grumbled. I put a hand in to soothe her. "Shhhh. I warned you this wasn't going to be all fun and games."

Viv, however, seemed to think differently. I turned back to motion her to come on and saw her doing some kind of weird bowing, shaking thing. I realized after a moment she was laughing.

"Would you get over here!"

She bent over and lurched across the yard. There was no way we were getting away with this. She looked like that old cartoon buzzard, and she cackled as she fell against me behind the bush.

"What is your *deal?*" I hissed as I helped her regain her balance.

"This is the most fun I've had in fifteen years," she said, hooting behind her hand.

"I'm glad you're enjoying yourself. It's about to end, if you don't keep it down." I couldn't help it. I giggled a little, too.

I crept to the side of the bush and peered through. No sign of movement from Bobby. Unbelievable. Maybe he'd fallen asleep.

"Okay, you get in and make sure the car's in neutral." I said. "I'll push. Steer into the alley behind my trailer. After we get a few lots down I'll drive us out of the trailer park."

"I get to drive the pickle-mobile." She clapped softly.

We crept to the car and eased the doors open. I popped the passenger seat up and slid Stump's box into the back seat. I still hadn't taken out all those old pictures and junk that G-Ma gave me, and I had to shove them aside to make room for Stump's box. I handed Viv the key. She was still laughing. I knew how she felt; I had the same reaction to stressful situations from time to time. Still, it was kind of irritating to watch.

"Are you in neutral?" I whispered.

She nodded, unable to speak.

"Are you going to be able to steer?"

She nodded again.

I had serious doubts, but we were in too deep to back out now. I got behind the car and pushed.

I don't know why I'd thought it would be easy. I guess because the car was so small, like something that came inside a Happy Meal box. But still, it *was* a car. I shoved and my feet slid in the gravel. I almost bonked my chin on the bumper.

I considered commanding it to move the way I had the back

door, but reconsidered on the off chance that Viv and Stump would go sailing through the double-wide across the alley. I straightened and pushed again, groaning with the effort. It didn't budge.

I leaned my cheek against the back window, panting. Why did saving Tony's life have to be so frigging *hard?*

"Ooops," I heard Viv whisper. I looked in to see her putting the emergency brake down.

After that it *was* easy. The tires rolled over the gravel, and we made fairly quick time down the alley, past Frank's place, and down two more spaces, until I felt fairly sure that Bobby wouldn't hear us start the car. I came around and tapped on the door. "Okay, I can drive now."

"Please can I drive? This is fun."

I might have mentioned that Viv is not the safest driver in the world. In fact, I believed she might be the *un*safest driver, at least in Lubbock. I didn't want to think about what adding a pickle bucket to the mix was going to do. But she had this look in her eye that if I didn't let her drive, she was going to kick up a fuss. Plus, I was kind of tired from pushing.

I climbed into the passenger seat and fastened my seat belt. I kept one eye on the side view mirror, but no headlights followed us. Once we got onto the street, I watched the streetlights behind us, but if Bobby was following us with his lights out, he was too far back for me to see. "I think we actually pulled it off."

"Woohoo!" Viv gunned the motor. It made a wheezing sound and the speed increased maybe three miles an hour. "Now, where are we going?"

I should have known breaking into a shooting range would be

impossible. We stood looking at eight-foot fences covered with razor wire and padlocks, the adrenalin of our escape wearing off in the face of our ineptitude.

"What would Columbo do?" I stared down a concrete alley between storage buildings.

"He'd put two and two together and get Rey," Viv said. "I'll bet you can climb that."

"Forget it." I sighed and put one hand on the fence. It shocked me. I shouted a couple of bad words and jumped back.

"Electric fence?" Viv asked.

That made me want to cuss more. This had not been a good week for my resolution to keep only what was good on my tongue. I clamped my mouth shut and stomped back to the car, settling on the bucket.

Viv didn't argue, she just silently handed over the key. This whole thing was making me mad, and I wanted to cuss a whole lot more. I wanted to beat the steering wheel and rail my frustration and fear and go get a drink to even everything out. I shoved the gas pedal down and had to hang on for dear life when the bucket rocked under me.

Instead I drove back to PakASak and borrowed Virginia's phone book. She and Viv discussed the latest developments in light bladder control products while I hummed loudly in my head to block them out. I looked up Ricky Barlow's home address. Barlow, Richard and Cynthia, 4524 38th Street. Richard, huh? He was husband of the cheery-looking blonde Cynthia, family man and business owner, and he was bursting with pride over his pixie step-daughter. He'd come a long way from his days of playing drunken pranks on his friends.

A part of me wondered if I wanted Rick to be guilty of something for the same reason I wanted Rey to be guilty of something: I didn't like them, and I wanted something bad to happen to them. Another part of me thought there might be something bigger behind my seemingly irrational determination. I wanted to believe that I had a hunch, that I was being led by intuition or the Holy Spirit or something. I was probably just chasing rabbits, but in the absence of anything else to chase, it would have to do.

Ricky lived halfway across town, and Viv and I were silent on the drive over. Her giggling jag was far behind her, and I glanced at her as we drove under the orange glow of a streetlight. Viv didn't usually look her age. She didn't look thirty-five, like she wanted to think, but she looked no more than sixty or sixty-five. Right then, she looked every bit of the eighty-something she was. I felt a pang of guilt. I shouldn't get so wrapped up in my own drama that I forget other people had needs of their own. Viv might be bored, she might want excitement, but she was still an old lady, and I didn't have any business dragging her around in the middle of the night. I wondered if I should turn back.

I glanced over again. Her chin rested against her chest and her eyes were closed. I chewed my lip and decided that, since she was asleep anyway, I'd just drive by the Barlow's house and see if anything was up. Viv could sleep through that. She had told me she had a hard time sleeping, so best to let her get what she could, even if it was sitting up in the pickle-mobile.

I was so focused on finding 4524 38th that I almost sideswiped a parked car. I hadn't been able to read the curb number because a low-slung sports car was in the way. I drove east until I came to 4522, then 4520 and pulled over.

I twisted in my seat, then checked my watch. It was almost

three in the morning. Kind of late for Barlow, Richard and Cynthia, to be entertaining guests on a weeknight. They had the little girl, after all. But there they were, two male figures standing on the front porch, heads bent low as they discussed something. One was silhouetted in the doorway; that was probably Rick. The other was a little shorter, stockier, his hands in his pockets, nodding as Rick spoke.

Something about the guy made me uneasy. He moved up half a step, nodding still, then stuck out his hand to shake Ricky's. He clasped it firmly, his other hand on Ricky's elbow, kind of holding Rick there while he talked. Something about the way he stood, the constant nodding, the almost captive way he stood, made me think he was doing his best to persuade Rick of something.

He made me nervous. Or maybe it was just the situation that made me nervous. The guy pumped Rick's hand a couple more times then moved down the steps and toward the car parked at the curb.

He stepped under the streetlight and I got a better look at him. I didn't know him, but my blood went cold anyway. He had a paunch. The guy who'd attacked me in my bed had a paunch, too. The height was about right. The age was about right, although I was only going by the voice I'd heard last night and the feel of the body that had knelt on mine to guess at his age.

What I needed was a witness. I lifted Stump's box so she could look out the window. "See that guy? Does he look familiar to you?"

She growled. Of course, that could either mean he was the attacker, or it could mean she didn't want me picking up her box. The guy dug in his pocket for his keys, turning in our direction as he did.

Stump went nuts. She jumped up and bayed like a hound after a fox. The guy looked in our direction.

"It's him!" I yelped. I dropped the box and dove into the seat beside Stump. She growled again but didn't bark. The box of pictures and junk cascaded to the floorboard.

Viv snorted. "Wha...?"

"It's the guy who attacked me," I whispered from the backseat. The bucket rolled beneath me and I did my best – unsuccessfully – to right it without getting up. "He just left Ricky Barlow's house. I think he saw me looking at him."

She craned her neck to see down the street. "The guy getting in that car back there?"

"Yes. Duck down! Is he coming this way? What are we going to do? Maybe we should call the police. Hey, I know. Get your gun!"

"Would you relax?" But she picked up her purse and began to dig through it. "What did I miss?" She pulled out a gun that was a whole heck of a lot bigger than I expected it to be.

"Just Rick standing on the porch talking to that guy. But I think that's the guy who broke into my house."

"I thought you didn't get a look at him."

I didn't, but Stump did." I rose a little and looked at Stump. She looked scared. Well, actually she looked the same as she always did, but around her eyes she might have looked a little scared. "She positively identified him as the assailant."

Viv was too busy fiddling with the gun to give much thought to how credible a witness my dog might be. "I knew that Barlow guy was fishy. This proves that he's connected somehow." She made something on the gun click and my blood went cold.

"Wait a minute, wait a minute." I tried to rise and succeeded in rolling completely off the bucket and onto the runners were the seat was supposed to be. "Do you really know what you're doing with that thing?" The glow of headlights lit the windshield. "Oh no, is he coming? Is he coming this way?"

Viv held the gun like she shot at people every day. "You don't handle pressure very well, do you? He's going on past."

I wanted to sit up but my heart was hammering too hard. I tried to catch my breath. Obviously I wasn't quite as cut out for this stakeout stuff as I thought I was. One look at a bad guy, and I'm a basket case.

"Which way do we go?" Viv asked. "Back to Barlow's to put the squeeze on him? Or after this joker?" She waved the gun around.

I grasped the steering wheel and pulled myself up. I thought for a minute I was going to break it completely off. But I knew if I didn't put myself back into play Viv was bound to shoot something or someone.

I flopped around in the floorboard until I managed to get the bucket back in place, bruising both knees and scraping my back on the steering wheel in the process, while I decided. Rick was still speculation, but I was almost positive the other guy was the one who'd attacked me. As much as I didn't want to, I knew where we needed to go.

"Let's follow that guy," I said.

"We're probably going to lose him now, you took so long getting back up."

All the better, I thought. "I'll drive fast."

We caught up to him three blocks later. He was headed back toward the loop and it wasn't hard to fall into the sparse traffic and tail him from a quarter mile back. As I drove I focused on two things: keeping the bucket upright and wondering what we'd do if we actually learned the guy we followed was the killer. I decided I'd let the woman with the gun make the decision on that one.

He got off at Slide and drove north. I stayed back as far as I felt comfortable doing, and had a small heart attack when I saw his brake lights flare. He turned into a parking lot and Viv shrieked.

"It's the laundromat!"

My eyes bugged and I didn't know what to do. He'd turned into the parking lot at Sylvia's laundromat. Surely that couldn't be a coincidence.

We drove past and Viv shrieked again. "He's going around back. Kill the lights and pull to the other side of the building."

I did as I was told. The pickle-mobile bounced into the parking lot and I crept to a stop on the north side of the building. Viv and I opened our doors as quietly as we could and I scurried around to plaster myself to the side of the building. My heart beat so hard it was making me nauseous, but Viv looked completely in her element. Probably because she felt secure with her protection. I was definitely going to get a gun before we did this again.

She slid along the wall and peeked around. "He's banging on the back door," she turned back to whisper. She watched for a few more seconds. "He's going in now."

We stood and looked at each other for a couple of seconds. "What do we do now?" I asked, having a feeling I knew what she was going to say.

"We go down there and see what we can see."

I put a hand on my stomach. "Okay. Let's do it, then."

She crept around the building, looking again like that cartoon buzzard. She came back a few seconds later. "What are you doing?"

"My feet won't seem to move."

She raised her hands, the gun dangling from one finger. "Well don't poop out on me now. This is the big moment, our chance to shine. True adventure. Besides," she lifted her right hand and the gun swung. "What are they going to do to us? We're well protected."

That got me going to the edge of the building. I froze again there until I remembered Tony, sitting on that cot in the hospital, crying his heart out over a baby he'd never seen. That got me past three metal doors, all closed up tight, all the way to the laundromat's back door.

I'd had some vague notion that the back door would be open, Sylvia and the paunchy guy would be inside talking about how the murder had taken place, who was guilty, how we could find proof, etc, and then Viv and I would sneak back, alert Bobby from the safety of the pickle-mobile, and the case would be solved. Instead we faced a very solid, very silent metal door and a short concrete stoop.

Again Viv and I looked at each other. "Okay, what now?" I asked.

She put her ear to the door. "I can't hear a dat-blamed thing."

"Well, we tried. I guess we'll just have to call it –"

She took off down the other direction, checking the door on the next space.

I shrugged and put my ear to the door. Maybe since I had younger ears...I did hear something. Not voices, but a weird kind of moaning, high-pitched and choppy. Kind of like one of those Indian battle cries you hear in the old Western movies. It grew louder. I drew back, realizing that the sound wasn't coming from inside the building.

It hit me the same time Viv whirled around, a panic-stricken look on her face.

"Stump!" I hissed. I took off back for the car.

I heard Viv running behind me. Good grief, once Stump got going you could hear her for blocks. The sound carried a lot better at night. The unholy keening was like a siren going off.

I was two doors from the end of the building when I heard an "Ooomph!" followed by the sound of Viv hitting the ground. She dropped the gun and it went off with every bit of the volume a huge gun is supposed to make.

I screamed and ducked, sure I'd been hit. Viv raised herself to her knees, looking more chagrined than hurt. "Sorry about that."

I ran back and helped her up, Stump went silent for a couple of seconds, and then started back in even louder than before. Viv grabbed the gun and I helped her hobble to the car, all thoughts of solving any mystery lost in the urgent need to get the heck out of there.

I heard one of those metal doors slam behind us but I didn't look back to see who was following us. I shoved Viv into the passenger seat, ran around to dive onto the bucket and shoved the key at the ignition. The bucket rocked wildly under me, but I didn't let that slow me down. I jabbed at the ignition and finally got the key in when the guy rounded the building and stood, wide-legged, in front of us.

Viv and I both screamed. She raised the gun with trembling hands. It spun around in her hand and for a second aimed right at me.

"Him! Shoot him!" I said, not caring if he was really the bad guy or not, just not wanting her to shoot me by accident.

She grabbed the gun with both hands and tried to steady it; she looked like a female Don Knotts and the nose of the gun kept diving toward the floorboard.

"Here," I said, reaching for the gun. "Let me –"

My door flew open, and something very, very hard slammed into my head.

Chapter Fifteen

I saw stars. I wanted to faint, I really did, because then the pain would go away. Unfortunately, all I did was slump off the bucket. Strong hands grabbed at my shirt and dragged me onto the ground outside the car.

I tried to stand up, but the thing knocked me upside the head again, and I slid down to rest on the concrete. I could hear Stump barking furiously and Viv stuttering something between indignation and terror. Then I was being dragged by one arm around to the front of the car.

"Pull it around to the back," a voice said. It was Sylvia, I realized. Sylvia, with a voice like steel, giving orders to some unseen person who did as they were told.

I got my feet under me enough to crab walk instead of being completely dragged. Ahead of me Viv had her hands on the back of her head, her own gun shoved into her back by the paunchy guy. He led her to the back door, which stood open now, and pushed her inside. Sylvia and I followed.

Sylvia shoved me hard enough to knock me down, then went back to the doorway. "Shut that thing up," she barked. "It'll wake up the whole town."

Whoever was in the car was as powerless against Stump's fury as I was, I noted with a totally-inappropriate-for-the-mess-I-was-in sense of smugness. Finally, he came in carrying Stump in her box.

Rey. Rey the jerk, Rey the scumbag, Rey the murderer.

"Give me my dog," I said from my position on the floor.

He dropped the box and Stump landed with a yelp of pain. "Shut her up," he said.

"Hey!" Viv shouted. Rey shoved her into the same chair she'd sat in the other day when we "interviewed" Sylvia.

I looked up at the paunchy guy. "I know you're the one who broke into my house."

"Congratulations, Sherlock," Rey said. He squatted in front of me, his face nonchalant. "What are you going to do about it?"

"We're going to alert the authorities and they're going to put him in jail," Viv said.

Rey and the guy laughed. Sylvia didn't seem to see the humor in it any more than I did.

"You two quit kidding around and get this taken care of. I told you it wasn't a good idea to send him, *mijo*."

Rey shrugged. "What difference does it make now? Thomas gave her a warning, she didn't heed the warning, so now we'll go back to the original plan." He gave me a cold smile that made my blood chill. I didn't want to know what the original plan was.

I remembered Thomas now, one of the many cousins who lived in Oklahoma City who came to visit occasionally. He might have been at Tony's and my wedding, I didn't remember. He was a few years younger than Tony and Rey, the little shadow who idolized

Rey and did everything Rey told him to do. Even now he was looking to Rey for his next move.

Sylvia, on the other hand, looked completely POed. "This is completely out of hand, Rey. Things weren't supposed to go this way. If you had listened to me from the beginning this would never have happened. I told you that girl was bad news, and now look at me. About to have two more murders on my head."

"Don't, Mama." Rey rose and hugged his mother. "Don't do this to yourself. Think about your blood pressure. I'll take care of it this time."

"This time?" I blurted. I looked at Sylvia, shocked. " *You* killed Lucinda?"

"It's none of your business!" Sylvia lunged toward me, her hand raised to slap me. I scooted back as quick as I could. "This was a family matter. If you'd kept your fat ass out of it everything would have worked out fine. You had to barge in and mess up everything."

"I was just trying to help Tony. He doesn't deserve to go to prison for something he didn't do."

"You idiot. He wouldn't have *gone* to prison. Don't you know anything? Tony is squeaky clean. His record is spotless and the evidence against him is completely circumstantial. He has a great lawyer. He would have gotten off." She laughed, a cold laugh that chilled my blood. "St. Anthony the Perfect would never have served a day of prison time."

I shook my head. "You mean you *didn't* try to frame him?"

"We didn't do anything except divert suspicion away from Rey. Tony would have had his day in court, he would have been acquitted, and everything would have gone back to normal."

The fog was beginning to clear somewhat. "So, you killed Lucinda and framed Tony, and left just enough evidence for him to be charged but not convicted." I hugged Stump to me. "That's a risky game, Sylvia. There are a million things that could have gone wrong with that."

"Yeah, like a nosy fat loser sticking her nose in where it doesn't belong." Rey kicked my thigh and Stump growled.

"That's enough!" Viv said sharply. "The next person who calls her fat is going to regret it. She happens to be big-boned."

I looked at Viv. "Thanks, but right now we have bigger issues to deal with. We can tackle fat discrimination another day."

"There's not going to be another day for you," Rey said cheerfully. He looked at Thomas. "What do you think? Cut them? Or take them out and shoot them?"

"You can't make it look like a murder, *mijo*," Sylvia said. "It has to be an accident." She pursed her lips and studied us for a second. Then she reached for the door going into the shop, turning to Thomas. "You keep an eye on them. Keep them quiet, whatever you have to do. But don't shoot them."

She went into the hallway and Rey followed, closing the door behind them.

The fact that he had strict orders not to shoot us should have made me feel somewhat secure. But it didn't. It was, after all, a very big gun and although he didn't look like he *wanted* to shoot us, he looked like he could panic at the first hint of trouble and apologize for it later.

I chewed my lip and looked at Viv. Maybe she had an idea of how to get us out of this. But there weren't any light bulbs going off over her head. In the movies, this was always where the bad guy started monologuing, explaining how the crime had happened. I had a lot of questions, but mostly they were about me and how I could stay alive. Lucinda was pretty much knocked off the top of my priority list at the moment. But since I didn't know how to manage that, I settled for the next question on my list.

"What does Ricky Barlow have to do with all this?" I asked quietly.

"Shut up," Thomas said.

"I'm sorry, I'm just curious. I know he's connected because I followed you from his house. But I don't know how. What did he do?"

Thomas ignored me.

"He seems pretty clean. I mean, he used to party a lot when we were younger, but I can't figure out what he has to do with all this."

Silence.

"Did Lucinda know him?"

"You need to shut up. I can't shoot you, but I can knock the crap out of you." He raised an eyebrow. "It wouldn't be the first time."

My stomach did a somersault. "Don't get ugly," I said. "I'm just curious. This doesn't add up. He's not connected in any way except he's a friend of Rey's..." I stopped and chewed my lip. "Is he Rey's alibi?"

It was a shot in the dark, but I could see on Thomas's face that it was on target.

"But how is that even possible? He was here, and Rey's alibi is in Oklahoma City. That makes no sense."

"Maybe he went to Oklahoma City and posed as someone else to *be* Rey's alibi," Viv said.

Thomas rolled his eyes. "How stupid is that? He would have had to know in advance that Rey was going to be here and going to need an alibi for that to work, and nobody knew Rey was going to be here. Sylvia didn't even know until Rey called her from the church."

Viv and I looked at each other. So we were the stupid ones, huh?

"So, Rey went to the church to talk to Lucinda? But then things went south? And he had to call in his mommy for help?"

Thomas glared. Looked kind of pouty to me. Like he'd just lost the Monopoly game.

"And then words were said," Viv said.

"Lucinda probably insulted Sylvia's cooking." I looked at Viv and nodded.

"So Sylvia killed her," she said.

"Rey was right. You are a smart-mouthed loser. I should have done what he suggested to you that night, instead of holding back like Sylvia wanted." He gave me an up-and-down lecherous look that made it perfectly clear what Rey had suggested he do to me.

I should have been scared. Actually, I *was* scared, but the fear was making me sick and if I kept smarting off and concentrating on keeping one up on Thomas, I could keep my mind off the fact that I was probably about to die. If I thought about that I'd start to cry and the last thing I wanted was to have Rey come back in and see me crying.

"You always do what you're told, don't you, little Tommy boy? Always Rey's little shadow, following whatever orders Rey gives you."

"Shut up."

"See, Viv, we're wasting our breath with this guy. He doesn't know what happened that night. He only knows what Rey tells him to do, and he's so busy keeping his head up Rey's butt he can't even see that they're using him."

Thomas stood and leveled the gun at me. "You'd better keep in mind that you *want* me to follow orders right now."

I opened my mouth to say something, but nothing would come out. At last my big mouth was showing some intelligence.

I looked up at Viv. Her face drooped like an old hound dog's. "You know, everybody was right. We're no good at this detective thing. We never did figure it out. And now we're going to die."

"No, we're not. They wouldn't kill us."

"Sure they would. They killed Lucinda. They framed Tony to take the fall for it. Why wouldn't they kill us, too?"

Viv was scaring me even more than Thomas and the gun were. "Lucinda was an accident. And you heard Sylvia, they never intended for Tony to go to jail. They just used him to take the heat off Rey."

Viv turned to Thomas, her hands shaky and her voice pleading. "If it was an accident, then it's not too late for this all to be straightened out. Maybe Rey or Sylvia would do a little bit of jail time, but they'd get off light. Not like the prison time he's going to get for murdering her *and* us. Was it an accident? Was it?"

Thomas swallowed and lowered the gun. He shook his head. "I don't really know. All I know is Lucinda and Rey had a fight, then Sylvia said she had to step in and take care of things."

"But why did Lucinda call Tony that night?" I asked. "Did Rey break that floor buffer just to get him up there?"

"You're totally over-thinking it, Salem. Lucinda never called anybody, the buffer was never broken." Rey came into the room holding two glasses. Ricky Barlow followed him, looking sick and terrified. You'd think from the look on his face *he* was the one about to be murdered.

"Why?" Viv asked at the same time I said, "What are you doing here?"

Sylvia came in behind them, carrying a length of fabric and looking grim.

"Rey went to see her because he wanted to talk to Lucinda. Just talk. About the baby and about what they were going to do. But Lucinda never would listen." She said something in Spanish that didn't sound like a compliment. "She never knew how to keep her mouth shut. She's the one who's the troublemaker and always has been. I warned Rey about her, but he all he saw were those big innocent eyes and that body she flashed around."

She stepped behind me and pulled my arms behind my back. "Don't you judge me, Salem. You have no idea how hard it is to raise a family, and you never will. You don't know what a mother would do for her son."

As she talked she wrapped the fabric around my wrists, tying them tight enough I couldn't get out.

"Would she kill for him?" I asked.

"If she had to!" She tugged the fabric and pulled my shoulders painfully. "Don't you dare judge me! If it meant saving her son from a prison sentence he didn't deserve, then yes, she would. If she was any kind of mother at all, she sure would." Sylvia straightened and pushed her hair out of her face. "You weren't there, Salem. You have no idea what happened or what you would have done if you'd been there. All Rey wanted to do was talk to her, and she goaded him and teased him with threats of going to Tony. No one in their right mind would be able to withstand that kind of torture from the woman he loved, from the woman carrying his child. Of course he snapped."

"He snapped?" Viv asked. "How did he snap?"

"None of your business," Sylvia said.

"I did what I should have done a long time ago," Rey said. "I shut her up. I gave her a taste of what happens when you don't treat people right. She never treated me right. She used me and then threw me away."

"Stephanie said you refused to marry Lucinda."

"That's a lie!" Sylvia shoved Viv until she was perched on the edge of the chair, then snatched at her arms and began to wind the fabric tight around her wrists, too. "That lying little tramp had better keep her mouth shut if she knows what's good for her. She doesn't know the first thing about anything. All she knows is what Lucinda told her and you can't believe one single word of that. Rey wanted to marry her, *tried* to marry her, but all he did was insist she take a test to make sure the baby was really his. He was going to marry her even if it wasn't his. He just wanted to know the truth so they could start out the marriage in truth, in honesty."

I snuck a look at Rey. Somehow I didn't think the paternity test was completely his idea.

"So you hit her?" I asked quietly.

He stared at me. He didn't have to say the word yes. He didn't have to say that he'd do it again in a heartbeat, that he wasn't a bit sorry. His eyes said it all.

"But it didn't kill her. You hurt her enough for it to be serious, maybe even knocked her unconscious. You panicked, didn't know what to do. So you did what you always do. You called your mommy."

I lifted my chin and waited for Rey to hit me again. So I was a little startled when the knock to my head came from Sylvia, straight into my right temple.

This time I almost did pass out. I kept talking, because I thought if I didn't, I *would* pass out. Irrationally, I thought that if I could just stay conscious, I could stay alive. "Sylvia showed up and knew you were about to go to prison for beating up a pregnant woman and her unborn child. Maybe you even killed the baby. That's at least a manslaughter charge right there."

"A manslaughter charge he did not *deserve!*" Sylvia barked. She jerked the fabric at Viv's wrists.

"Ow, you heifer!" Viv shouted. She pulled forward. "The tunnels! Under the church! Remember, Salem? We saw them the other day when we were up in the tower. They snuck through the tunnels." Viv looked very proud of herself. "That's how they got in and nobody saw them."

"But how did you get into the tunnels?" I asked. Then I remembered the last time Viv and I had been to the laundromat to speak to Sylvia. That seemed like months ago, but it was just a couple of days. Sylvia had pointed out the door that led to the basement. There was probably access to the tunnels in her basement. Viv had said they went all over downtown.

Ricky stood in the corner, looking like he wanted to blend into the paint, and Rey walked by and hissed something at him. He looked at Viv and me and nodded grimly.

Sylvia ignored my question and answered one no one had asked. "He was goaded into it, Lucinda egged him on." She groaned as she straightened and stood. "She knew just which buttons to push to get him to lose his temper, and then she went running to the police when he did. She liked playing with him like that, liked the power she had over him. She played with him like a cat with a mouse. She was the one who deserved prison, not my son. Not my son who was working so hard to turn his life around, who wanted nothing more than to raise his child and live in peace. Not my son who'd just gotten the call to serve God, who'd just developed a passion for helping people."

I was *real* careful not to let my face show what I thought about that statement. Rey serving God. Rey helping people. Puh-leeze. I believed, of course, that people *could* change. I had to believe it, since I'd been trying so hard to be one of those people. But looking at Rey's eyes right then, I didn't think he was one of those people.

I felt sorry for Sylvia. She was right; I had no idea what it was like, raising a son. A son who disappointed you, broke your heart, manipulated you repeatedly to clean up his messes and fix what he'd broken. I had no idea. Shoot, I'd probably do the same for Stump and she was my dog, not my flesh and blood. I still didn't want Sylvia to kill me, but I did feel sorry for her.

Sylvia picked up one of the glasses Rey had brought in. What was in those glasses? Rat poison? Something that would eat my insides out?

I looked at Viv. She was coasting on her tunnel epiphany, which I had to admit, was satisfying to know. Kind of like when you finally figured out where you'd seen that bit actor before. It wasn't as if that discovery was what we needed to get us out of this mess, but it did seem to put some pep back in her.

"There is no way you're going to get away with this," she said. "You'll be charged with capital murder." She looked from Sylvia, to Rey, to Thomas and then to Ricky. Of all of them, only Ricky looked like he might be wavering a little. He also looked the least capable of helping us off this runaway train.

"We won't be charged with a thing, since you're going to both die in a tragic, fiery accident which will be entirely the fault of your alcoholic friend here. Too bad Salem, a known drunk, had to drink and drive off a cliff. Too bad gas is going to leak out and catch the whole car on fire." She brought the glass over to me and took hold of my chin. "Open up, sweetie. You're going to like this. It's your favorite."

It could have been all my favorites mixed together and dipped in chocolate and I still was having none of it. I clamped my lips together, feeling foolish but also determined to keep my wits about me. I just *thought* over the past few days that I wanted a drink. Turned out what I really wanted was to live.

"Come pry her mouth open," she ordered Thomas and Rick.

They did as they were told. Thomas twisted my nose with one hand and grabbed my jaw with the other. I did my best to writhe out of his grip, but with Thomas in front of me and Rick behind me putting a choke hold on my skull, I was pretty much out-matched. I tried to close my throat but choked and swallowed a fiery mouthful.

"Keep on it," Sylvia ordered, more in charge of her emotions now. I guess she was one of those people who, when the ball got rolling, found her stride and carried through. Goodie for her. "She'll need enough in her to make it look legitimate. How many Jack and Cokes can you handle, Salem?" She looked blandly at me, her eyebrows raised. "A drunk like you? Six or eight?"

I fought to come up for air. They were going to suffocate me before they got me drunk. Thomas was about to break my nose in his death grip. And despite everything, the alcohol was already taking effect. It was hot and liquid down my throat, filling my belly. Adrenalin shooting through me kept the relaxation from transferring to the rest of my body.

I heard a shuffle and looked up just in time to see Viv launch herself into Sylvia. They both fell across me and the glass flew out of Sylvia's hand.

"You old witch!" Rey yelled.

Sylvia rolled on the floor, squawking about how her knee hurt. She'd hit the concrete floor with all her weight on it, poor baby.

Rey kicked Viv in the ribs and I screamed at him. Stump went berserk. She came out of the box and stumbled, growling, toward Rey's leg.

Thomas kicked her. The son-of-a-pudgy-biscuit-eater kicked her for the second time and sent her skidding across the room. Filled with that superhuman strength that happens when people are put in desperate situations, I launched myself off the floor and threw myself, bound hands and all, at him.

It was pure pandemonium for a second. It didn't stop until Sylvia took the gun from Thomas and slammed it into my head. That was the third frigging time she'd hit me in the head and I had just about had enough of it. I decided if I was going to die I'd at least leave some marks on them to give the police a clue. I head butted her as hard as I could in the chin. I heard her teeth clonk together and saw her eyes roll up in her head. She didn't faint, though. She blinked a few times, then sank to the chair Viv had been in.

"Get them out of here." Her voice was thin and tired. "Take them out to the canyon and put Salem in the driver's seat. Make sure neither one of them has a seat belt on. Get a big rock and knock a hole in the gas tank." She took a deep breath, let it out, and rubbed a hand over her face. "Make sure you do it someplace they won't be discovered for a while. I don't want anyone to see the fire and come running."

"Should we kill them before they go over, just in case someone comes by, or in case they don't die in the crash?" Thomas asked.

"No, you idiot. They have to have some smoke in their lungs or the police will get suspicious. They have to be alive when the car catches fire." She stood and rubbed the small of her back. "You'll have to stick around long enough to know they're dead. If they get out alive, we'll all go to prison." She looked from one to the other. "You do all understand that, don't you? We're all equally involved now. Some of us are in even more trouble and don't need for this to get out." She looked at Rick.

He looked, if possible, worse than I felt. Guilty and horrified and panicked.

"What does she have on you?" I asked.

Sylvia slapped me. At that point I guessed she was too tired to put any heart into it, so it didn't hurt too bad. Besides, at that point what was a slap to me, someone who'd been knocked in the head and was about to die a gruesome, fiery death? But that slap told me enough.

I decided the best thing Viv and I could do was get away from Sylvia. As long as she was running the show, I didn't have much chance of talking my way out of this.

I looked at Viv. Her lip was bleeding from the scuffle when she'd thrown herself at me. Her thin hair was sticking out. Her mouth was set in a grim line. I was glad to see she didn't look scared, just mad as all heck. I hoped that would help us out.

I nodded at her, hoping to convey to her that I had a plan. I didn't, but I was doing my best to put one together. I also prayed for everything I was worth. *God, tell me what to do. Tell me what to do. Get me out of this. I don't want to die now.*

I stood when Rey put his hand under my arm. I nodded again at Viv to show her it was okay, we were going to be okay. She stood but jerked her arm away from Thomas.

"I can walk, thank you very much." She stuck her nose in the air and walked out the door like he was a slow maitre'd.

Rey frowned when he got the door open to the pickle-mobile. "It figures you'd drive this piece of crap car, Salem."

I smiled at him. "Haven't you ever driven on a pickle bucket? You're in for a treat." I climbed in the backseat and slid around on the junk back there. Rick climbed in after me, having to fold his body in half to fit, and Thomas pushed Viv in after him.

Rey and Thomas mumbled to themselves as Rey drove out of the parking lot. "Dude, I hope we don't all die in this car," Thomas said, serious concern on his face as he watched Rey try to stay up.

"You'll get the hang of it," I told him. "Just don't make any sudden moves."

I, on the other had, had to make my move soon; I didn't want to be out of town before I took action. Besides, having my shoulders pinched back like that hurt like the dickens and my head swam from the liquor.

I turned to Ricky, keeping my voice low. "I don't know what they have on you, but I guarantee it's not as bad as helping them commit murder."

He stared straight ahead, looking sick.

"Sylvia probably has you convinced you have no options, but that's not true. Viv and I will both testify that they made you do this. I'll swear on my life that you were forced to be here. I know in my heart you don't want to do this. I know you wouldn't be here if you thought you had any other choice."

His jaw worked and from the streetlights that flashed by I thought I saw a shiny spot in the corner of his eye.

"It's not too late. We can stop this now before you get in too deep and Sylvia gets you into prison. Viv and I will testify that you were blackmailed and that you helped us escape. We'll do everything we can to make sure you get off as lightly as possible. What does she have on you, Rick? What is she using to force you to do this?"

He clenched his teeth together and, barely turning his head, he looked from the back of Rey's head to me. He looked like someone caught in a trap.

"What is it, Rick? Maybe I can help you. Don't forget that you have something on Sylvia now, too. You know she committed murder. You can use that. You can plea bargain your testimony against her in exchange for a light deal in whatever she's using against you. You can do that, I know the D.A. would go for that."

"You don't know jack!" Rick whispered. "You have no idea what's going on or what to do about it."

"I know that helping them commit two more murders isn't going to help you!" I hissed back. Man, my arms were screaming and the alcohol had me fighting to keep on task. I leaned up and looked at Viv. Her face was white and her chin sagged against her chest. She gave me a look that chilled me. She looked like she'd already given up.

Rey threw a look over his shoulder. "They behaving back there, dude? Not giving you any trouble, are they?"

"Salem's about passed out and the old lady looks like she died already." Rick shot a look at me that said I'd better keep my mouth shut.

I did, for a few seconds. We were going over the flyover to the interstate now. A few more miles and we'd be exiting to head out to the canyon. Nobody would be on that road this time of night. If we were going to do something, it had to be now.

"Just think about it," I said, trying not to sound desperate. "You know more about this crime than anyone except the guilty parties, I'll bet. You can hand the D.A. a case all wrapped up in a shiny package. You can make their jobs so much easier. Of course they'll go for that. Ricky, don't you want to go home to that pretty wife and daughter? Don't you want all this to be over?"

He whipped his head toward me. "Of course that's what I want! That's all I want. That's all I've wanted for the past three years was just to have a normal life, to keep out of trouble and be a good husband and a good father. Sylvia promised me that if I helped Rey out this time she'd make sure nothing ever came back to haunt me and mess that up."

Three years. Three years Sylvia had been holding something over Rick's head.

Rick's brother John died three years ago. But he'd been drunk, the crash was his own fault.

I took a stab in the dark. "You were with John when he died?"

He shook his head. "No, I wasn't with him then. I was with him before."

I got it then. Rick and John had been drinking together before John had his accident. Possibly Rick could have been charged with involuntary manslaughter if he'd contributed to John drinking and then driving. I knew all about that kind of thing. Way more than I wanted to know.

"You know, don't you, that the deal with John isn't anything like this?"

He stared at the back of Thomas's seat and didn't answer.

"You know that a charge like that can be reduced to probation, to house arrest. It's nothing like murder, Rick. This is going to be murder, first degree –"

"I can't let my wife know!" he said suddenly. "I can't let her know about John, I can't let her know about this. She'd never understand, she thinks I'm a saint, she thinks I'm the best thing that ever happened to her. If I lose her and Kaylee I couldn't go on, Salem. I have to make this work somehow, I can't –"

A shriek pierced the air and like a gray blur Viv shot out of her seat. She thudded into Rey's back, her arms still tight behind her.

The car swerved sharply to the left, toward the median. Rey yelled a curse and wrenched the wheel back to the right. The tires squealed and we were sideways in the middle of the interstate, leaning hard toward the driver's side.

Rick and I were thrown against Viv. I heard a lot of screaming and realized most of it was coming from me, but I couldn't stop. I thought that if all our weight was on that one side of the car, surely it would have to tip all the way over and flip. I didn't know if any of us would live through that.

With strength born of desperation, I threw my body up and back, hitting the passenger side of the car as hard as I could. The car bounced back with all four tires on the ground. For once I was glad I was packing all that extra weight.

Rey was in the back seat now, tangled up with Viv and Rick. Thomas gave short little yelps as he tried to take control of the wheel. We headed up the steep embankment toward the frontage road and the bridge for 50th Street. Rey's door popped open and for some bizarre reason Thomas lunged for it. We bounced hard and he went sailing out.

Rey was like a turtle stuck on his back, lunging over and over to get up and unable to do so. Viv slid down and sat on him. He growled at her but he couldn't do much about it.

I had to give Viv credit for taking charge of the situation, but I wasn't so sure this was our best choice. Still, it was what it was and I supposed I should make the best of the situation.

I threw myself over the seat with the vague notion that I would throw myself onto the steering wheel and somehow direct it with my shoulder or chin, anything I could do to get it under control and the car stopped.

In the headlights, a stop sign appeared, impossibly close. The next moment we crashed into the pole, and my head went through the windshield.

Chapter Sixteen

When I came to, everything was bizarrely quiet. For a moment, I wondered if I was dead, if we *all* were dead, because it was so quiet. I felt the metal of the car hood under my cheek, and heard the ping and pop of the motor.

That, coupled with the sudden realization of intense pain in my head and my right leg, made me think I wasn't dead. I didn't know about everyone else, though. I thought if I could get my head up I could check.

I looked around me, but saw only the side of the hill where we'd landed. But my leg was stuck. I tried to slide down the hood to the ground, but I didn't get anywhere. I realized my jeans were stuck on the broken windshield. I tugged frantically at my legs and finally, by some miracle, I was able to get the fabric ripped off. I felt something warm on my cheek and smelled blood. I reached up and felt a big gash across my forehead and up over my scalp. My hand came away soaked in blood.

That freaked me out. I let out a strangled cry and tumbled off the hood of the car into the grass. I heard a whimpering sound, and this time it wasn't me.

Stump! I bolted up and looked around. "Stump? Where are you?"

I couldn't see her. I heard sirens now, and saw something moving through the grass. Too big to be Viv, and definitely too big to be Stump.

I couldn't see Stump anywhere. It was too dark, and my eyes weren't working so good at the moment. I clamped my hand over my head and cried like I had when I was a kid and fell off my bike. I sounded like an idiot. I didn't care.

"Stump! Viv! Where are you? Are you okay? Oh God, please help us!"

The figure moving through the grass stopped. It was Ricky, I realized when he was reflected in passing headlights. He bent over, looking at something in the grass. He threw a look back at me, then straightened again and took off running.

Let him go. To heck with him. He and Thomas and Rey could all run. I would find some way to convince Bobby they were guilty. I stumbled along the ground, calling for Stump.

The sirens grew louder, and I saw flashing lights on the other side of the interstate. I couldn't hear anymore whimpering from Stump, and that scared me. I also didn't hear anything from Viv, and that scared me too. I'm not going on record as to which one scared me more.

"Stump! Viv! Talk to me. Where are you? Are you okay?" I crawled to the back of the car, one hand still clamped against my scalp while blood leaked and ran down the side of my face, exhaustion weighing down on me. "Stump!"

Ricky stopped and looked back at me. Then he turned, walked back a step and picked up whatever he'd been looking at in the grass.

It was Stump. She lay still in Rick's arms as he carried her up the hill. I was still crying, and I cried even harder when he put her in my arms. She was alive, but she lay too still for my taste. I kissed her and prayed as hard as I ever had that she'd be okay.

The sirens chewed up the silence in the air and flashing lights strobed around us. The siren cut off abruptly, but the night spun with the flashing lights and people jumped from the ambulance and raced toward us.

"Back here!" Rick cried. "She's bleeding! She needs an ambulance."

"Where's Viv?" I asked Rick, but he was gone around to the other side of the car.

"In here, too," I heard him say. "She's unconscious."

"I'm not unconscious," Viv groused faintly. "I've been in an accident. I have a right to sit and rest my eyes for a second without everyone getting all up in arms about it. Just get that – get that light out of my face if you don't mind." Her tone stated plainly she didn't care if he minded or not. "I am fine. I just need to catch my breath."

"That's good news, ma'am," said a new male voice. "All the same, I think I'll let the EMTs take you in and have the doctors look at you. Just lie back now. They'll be here in a second."

"Well, okay," Viv said. She sounded weak, wobbly. She was giving up without much of a fight. Not a good sign.

The cop came around and knelt in the grass beside me. "Hang on, ma'am, the paramedics are on their way. Want to tell me what happened? Who was driving this car?"

"Rey Ramirez."

He motioned to Rick. "Him?" He lifted my hand off my leg and swore. "I need a gurney over here!"

"No, that's Ricky. He wasn't driving, he was kidnapped like we were. Rey ran off, and you need to call for backup to catch him and catch Thomas, too. Thomas is Rey's cousin. And while you're at it, call for someone to arrest Sylvia Ramirez. She was last seen at her laundromat on 21st Street. She's guilty of the murder of Lucinda Cruz and of the attempted murder of me and Viv, and –"

"Why don't you just lie back and save your breath? We can get a statement at the hospital."

Then he stood and spoke into the radio handset clipped to his shoulder, "Sloan, I have contact with the party you've been looking for, 50th and the Interstate."

"Bobby's looking for us?" I asked. Of course he would be by now. How long had it been since Viv and I snuck out? "Some party," I said with a half-hysterical giggle. "This has been a wild one, even for me."

When the paramedics came up with the gurney I became more concerned with having everyone's lives saved than all the stuff with Rey and Sylvia and Bobby. Another ambulance came right after, and I was a little bummed that Viv and I wouldn't be riding together. But all in all, I had to say I was feeling pretty good that the people in authority were there and we weren't on our own anymore.

The paramedics pushed Rick out of the way and put something cold against my head. I kept thinking Rick was going to run like Rey and Thomas had, but he hunched by the back of the car looking lost.

"Sir, can you hold the dog?" one of the paramedics barked at Rick. He phrased it as a question, but it really wasn't. Rick came over and took Stump gingerly from me.

"Thanks," I said, my throat thick. "Thanks for coming back. That was really nice of you." I remembered why I hadn't wanted to see Ricky Barlow in the first place, when Trisha first suggested we see him. "That makes up for putting me in the bed with Scott Watson at his bachelor party."

He just stared at me for a second, as if trying to figure out what I was talking about. "Oh yeah, I'd forgotten about that." He rubbed his face with one hand, making the front of his hair stand up. "That was a long time ago. One of a long list of things I'd prefer to forget."

"You think *you'd* like to forget it? I slept with my best friend's fiancé on the eve of their wedding. Not exactly my proudest moment."

"Yeah, but it's not as if anything happened."

It was my turn to stare. "What?"

"Please be still, ma'am," the paramedic said. He pushed me gently but firmly down onto the gurney. "Don't move a muscle." He ran back up the hill toward the ambulance.

"Nothing happened," Ricky said. "Scott passed out and you did, too, if I remember right."

"What are you talking about?" I completely violated my orders and moved several muscles at once.

"Scott passed out. Come on, are you telling me all this time you thought you two actually had sex?"

"All this time since last week, when Patrice brought the memory back into focus. I'd blocked it out up to that point."

"Yeah, she was pretty mad about that. I guess I should have told her what actually went down. Scott passed out and you just giggled and got into the bed with him. Then you passed out, too. Believe me, neither one of you were in any shape to do anything that night."

"You've got to be kidding." Part of me wanted to strangle him. Another part wanted to kiss him.

I felt like someone who'd just been buzzed by a 747. What a heck of a near miss.

The EMT came back then and got really mad at me. Two of them lifted me onto the gurney and I only worried a little bit about how fat they must have been thinking I was. Then a face appeared beyond them, looking absolutely furious and frantic all at once.

"I'm sorry, Bobby." I tried to sit up and the EMT shoved me back down. "We just wanted to talk to Ricky and so we snuck out and then we almost got killed and I'm sorry we didn't say anything –"

"Would you just shut up?" He did the old mumble-mumble thing with the EMT as they rolled me to the ambulance. While he talked he looked back at the pickle-mobile.

I got a good look at it, too, as they loaded me into the ambulance. Most of the glass in the windshield was gone. Blood smeared over what little was there, and across the hood. "Yuck," I said. "Is that mine?"

They didn't answer, just gave each other a funny look as the EMTs locked the gurney down. That look had me wondering just how messed up I was. Blood was still dripping down my face.

"Can you make sure Stump gets taken care of?" I asked Bobby. "That idiot Thomas kicked her again and then she was thrown from the car when we crashed. Make sure she's okay."

"Sure, no problem. Lie down and quit talking. You need to rest."

"Don't worry, I'm not going anywhere. I just wanted you to

know that I was right about Rick. He was connected to Lucinda's murder."

"Okay, Salem, whatever."

"I'm serious. He's connected because Sylvia was blackmailing him. But he tried to help us, Bobby. Give him a break because he was working with me to get us away from Rey when we went off the road. He's not the bad guy here."

"If you don't stop talking this second I'm going to put you under arrest." He put a hand on my shoulder, and I shut up. He was worried about me. Frantically worried, from the way his hair stood on end and his brow furrowed. I wanted to tell him I was fine, but the truth was, I wasn't so sure about that. I felt light-headed and woozy; between the several blows to the head I'd received and the alcohol, I knew that my head should hurt like crazy. But it didn't, not really. It made me wonder just how much more blood I could lose.

I finally understood why people become hypochondriacs. There's a definite payoff in people being worried about you.

The next few hours were taken up with medical stuff – x-rays and forms and stitches (ouch, by the way). One of the ER nurses was a regular Bow Wow Barbers customer, so I talked her into checking on Viv for me. She was going to be okay, was all I could discern. I decided, for the moment, that was good enough.

I woke in my hospital room with Les and Bobby on either side of my bed. Judging by their carefully guarded expressions, I didn't look so hot.

I wanted to ask about Stump first, but for decorum's sake I asked, "How's Viv?"

"Ornerier than ever," Bobby said. "Giving the nurses a hard

time and demanding a bigger room."

"Was she hurt?"

"Oh, sure. Sixteen stitches in her head, broken collarbone and broken arm. Couple of cracked ribs. Otherwise she's in good shape."

"What about Stump?" I'd held off as long as I could.

"Vet said her injury from the other night was aggravated and he wanted to keep her in the hospital for a few days. But he said she would be okay if she could stay out of the exciting crime-fighting life for a few days."

My throat closed up, and my eyes burned. I didn't know what I'd do without Stump. "I assume, since you're here, you caught Rey and Thomas."

Bobby nodded. "Rey was hiding in a dumpster a couple of alleys from the accident. Thomas showed up at the emergency room with a broken elbow and a story about falling off his roof."

"Falling off his roof? In the middle of the night?"

"He said it had happened earlier in the day, but he couldn't stand the pain any longer so he came on in."

"What a tool."

"It took him all of fifteen seconds to start talking once we got him away from Sylvia."

"Did he tell you he was the one to break into my house?"

Bobby nodded. "He said Sylvia made him do it. Had a whole tale about domineering matriarchs and familial obligation."

"He was more than a willing participant," I said. That all reminded me of Rick, though. "Did he say how Rick fit in all this?"

"No, Rick took care of that himself." He cocked his head toward my forehead. "How does that feel?"

I gingerly felt the bandages that covered my head. "It doesn't feel at all. I must be on some pretty good drugs." I cast a glance at Les. I wondered if he'd heard about my blood alcohol level.

"Don't worry; it's going to hurt plenty later on." Bobby sat in the chair at the side of my bed. "You were dead on, Salem. Rick was the key to the whole thing."

"I knew it." I didn't know if the smugness I felt was coming through all my stitches and bandages, but I did my best. "How?"

"He doctored a sales sheet for Rey to use as his alibi. Rey sells bottled water to businesses, and the All American Storage branch in Oklahoma City just happened to set up a new contract with Rey that day. Turns out Rick signed an invoice for the manager there, and he used their store number and dated it for the day before, so Rey could turn that in to his boss. So Rey's boss had the paperwork to say he'd made a sale that day. The boss didn't know the difference, and the store manager backed it up because he just thought he was helping Rey get a bonus for meeting his quota that day. He didn't know Rey from Adam and didn't see any reason not to help him out as long as it didn't cost him anything. But after you kept insisting, I had the OKC cops take another look at his alibi. When I found out it was an All American sale and Rick worked for All American here, I knew you had something." He reached over and squeezed my knee. "Maybe you do have an instinct for this kind of work."

"Maybe. I think from now on I'm going to stick with grooming dogs, though. I don't really like being tied up. Or hit in the head. Or beaten up. And I really don't like to have my dog kicked." I looked at Les. "I'm really sorry about your pi – your car."

Les, being Les, smiled and shrugged. "I'm glad it helped you get away."

"Yeah, sure, um...how exactly did it do that?"

"Viv told me that she was able to knock that guy out of the driver's seat and force him off the road. She wouldn't have been able to do that with a regular old car with a regular old driver's seat."

"I guess you have a point there." I waited for him to go on about how God had made sure I had that car so things could go down just as they did, but I guessed that was a stretch even for Les. "I'm sorry I was the one to finally put her down for good."

"Oh, she's not down for good. Randy's banging out the dents right now, seeing if he can get her back on the road. She'll be ready for you when you're able to drive again, if you need her."

"Oh good," I said. After everything that had happened, I should be grateful I was going to be driving anything.

"He found a bunch of stuff that he thought might be yours when he went to get the car. Pictures and papers and stuff." He pointed to a box by the door. "He put it in there."

I'd forgotten about that stuff. I guess it went all over the hill when we crashed.

Tony came in then. His eyes were red, and I don't think I'd ever seen him look so horrible. He was at my side in a heartbeat. "Salem! You're okay?" He reached for my hand, then pulled back. "I – where can I touch you that won't hurt?"

"I'm not sure right now. Ask again when the drugs wear off." I took his hand and squeezed it. "I'm fine, Tony. Are you okay?"

He shook his head. "It's – it's a shock."

I squeezed his hand again. Probably the relief of having charges dropped was dampened by knowing his own aunt and cousin had set him up on those charges to begin with. "Has Sylvia been arrested?"

Bobby nodded. "She's in custody now." He cast a glance at

Tony and at Les. "We'll talk more about it later."

I turned to Tony. "Remember Trisha Thompson? From school?"

"Of course."

"She goes by Patrice Watson now, and she's on the Channel 11 news."

"Ummm, yeah, I watch the news, Salem."

"Oh, well, of course you do. Can you give her an exclusive interview? She kind of helped me find the clue that broke the thing wide open." I glanced up at Bobby. "Solved the case. Before the police did."

I yawned, and they all three said they'd better let me get my rest. I held tight to Tony's hand for a second longer. "I'm sorry about sneaking out. Obviously, I didn't think it was going to turn into a life-or-death situation."

"I'm just glad you're okay," he said. His eyes told me, though, that he hadn't been at all surprised I'd snuck out; he'd expected me to do just that.

"Can I talk to Bobby for a second?" I asked.

"Let me pray for you first," Les said. He put a big warm hand on the back of my head and thanked God for saving me and Viv, and for making sure the guilty people were caught. He also asked that Sylvia, Rey and Thomas receive conviction from the Holy Spirit and repent so they could be forgiven and be reconciled. Personally, I just wanted them convicted by a court of law and to rot in jail for a couple of decades, but Les had a bigger heart than I did. Forgiveness was a lot easier for me in theory than it was in reality.

Tony and Les left with a promise of a visit later, and Bobby returned to his seat. "What's going to happen to them?" I asked.

"They'll be charged with murder, attempted murder, black-mail, and tampering with evidence. Anything I can convince the DA to pursue."

"What about Rick?"

"I'm not allowed to discuss Rick."

I gave him a dark look. "But you can tell me he's going to be okay, because whatever he did in this case he did because Sylvia was blackmailing him. You can tell me that since he's going to testify against Sylvia and Rey and since he worked so hard to help us get free from Rey and Thomas, he's going to get a very light sentence. You can tell me that much, right?"

Bobby just shook his head and tried unsuccessfully to hide a grin. "You remind me of this bulldog I used to have."

"Come on, Bobby, you have to give him a break. Stump might have died if it weren't for him. Heck, *I* might have died if it weren't for him."

"Plea bargains are not entirely up to me, you know. The DA and the judge do have some say in matters. Although I am flat-tered you seem to think I control the entire justice system."

"Bobby, please –"

"He's going to be okay, Salem. He's not going to get off com-pletely, but he's going to be okay, if he does what he says he'll do."

I remembered the best gift Rick had given me – after possibly saving my life – and knew right away I had to call Trisha. "By the way, how much am I allowed to discuss of all this?"

"Not a word."

"What do you mean?"

"I mean you're allowed to discuss anything and everything with me and me alone. No one else hears a word."

"Not even my best friend?"

"Who's your best friend?"

"Patrice Watson." Although she *did* hate me.

"Then *especially* not your best friend."

"If she guesses can I confirm it?"

Bobby sighed. "Am I going to have to get a restraining order?"

"Can you do that?"

He raised an eyebrow that said, "Just try me."

He left not long after, and I checked the clock. It was early; Trisha probably hadn't gone to work yet. I looked up their number in the phone book and, dialing with one hand, I waited for her to pick up the phone.

She didn't. Scott did. I panicked and started to hang up, but caught myself before I placed the receiver down. "Ummm...Scott?"

"Yes?"

I figured this was his business, too, so I might as well tell them both at the same time. "This is Salem. I need to talk to Trisha – I mean, Patrice – but it concerns you, too. So is there another line she can get on?"

He was quiet for a long time. "Look, why don't you tell me first and I'll tell her whatever it is you think you need to say."

What a guy. He wanted to protect his wife. Not exactly flattering that he wanted to protect her from *me*, but still...no wonder Trisha loved him so much.

"Okay. Here's the thing. You remember Ricky Barlow?" *And the time he stuck us in bed together?*

"Yes, I remember Rick."

I could tell in half a second he was going to slam the phone down.

"This is good news, Scott, I promise. I talked to Rick last

night, and he told me something I didn't know. Um, you remember that night, um, when you and I, um –"

"What is it, Salem?" Funny how you can hear things like a clenched jaw and a narrow stare over the phone.

"Well, the point is, we didn't. What you thought we did, and what Trisha thought and we did, and what *I* thought we did...we didn't."

He was really quiet. Deathly quiet. Then he said, "What?"

"Rick told me that night you passed out and I passed out and they just left us in bed together as a prank. It was all a joke."

"A *joke*?"

"I know, I know. Some joke. But I've been feeling really horrible about betraying my friend – and it's not as if I'm now totally proud of my behavior – but at least I'm relieved that we didn't really –"

"We *didn't*?"

"Didn't. Totally didn't."

The phone clattered and Scott screamed, "Trisha!"

So he called her that, too.

I couldn't make out any words. I heard Scott's voice, then Trisha's, then both of them at once, babbling, high-pitched. Then Trisha shrieking and Scott shouting and I freaked out for a moment till I realized they were overjoyed, rejoicing in the news. I could almost see them holding each other's' arms, jumping around in a circle, knocking over tables and lamps in their celebration. Kind of a like a very bizarre lottery win. Congratulations! You did *not* have sex with Salem Grimes!

I'd never had anyone be so thrilled to not have sex with me, and I could have been kind of offended except I knew exactly how they felt. A ton of guilt and regret was totally erased, wiped clean.

They kept up their noisy party and I finally left them to it, settled the phone back on the cradle, sighed, and snuggled down in the surprisingly comfortable hospital pillow.

I was amazed at how light I felt, thinking about Scott and Trish. According to Les, this is what repentance and forgiveness of sin was always supposed to feel like. Like you'd been completely cleansed from any wrongdoing, like you'd never screwed up or hurt anyone in your life.

But it hadn't happened that way, at least not for me. I *had* repented for sleeping with Scott, but I'd still felt plenty guilty. It wasn't until reality told me it hadn't happened in the first place that I felt this release.

I burrowed deeper in the pillow and wondered for the hundredth time in the past week what I was doing wrong with my faith. In so many areas, what Les and the church kept promising me just wasn't happening.

I was going to pray about it, I really was. But instead the meds kicked in and I fell asleep.

Trisha was there when I woke up. Her eyes were red, and she stood looking out the window by my bed, unaware that I was awake. I remembered a time when we were in junior high and Mr. Blackwell, the football coach who doubled as our world geography teacher, yelled at her for turning in her research paper on the Galapagos Islands a day late. He'd scared her so bad she'd cried then, too, and tried to cover it up by saying the blowing dust was bothering her allergies.

"I told you Tony didn't do it," I said. Croaked, actually. I should have cleared my throat before I tried to speak.

I sat up and did so, giving Trish a chance to wipe her eyes and gather her composure.

She shook her head. "You must have an instinct or something," she said.

"Or something," I said. "Is the dust blowing outside? I feel my allergies acting up."

"Me too," she said. She handed me the box of tissues on the rolling table and sat in the chair by my bed. "So he was innocent after all."

"That's right. And he's agreed to let you interview him first, as a personal favor to me."

She raised an eyebrow. "Seriously?"

"Sure. If you hadn't given me the tip about Ricky Barlow, I wouldn't have cracked the case." I wrinkled my nose. "How very Nancy Drew of me. Bobby would have figured it out eventually, but it does my pride some good that I was the one to steer him in the right direction."

"I hope this has taken him down a notch or two. He's as in love with himself as he ever was. Remember when you had that huge crush on him? Rode by his house on your bike five times a day –"

"Of course, I remember. I wrote Salem Sloan on everything I owned."

"You still have a thing for him, don't you?"

I shrugged. "I can't decide. I mean, he's still hot and there's just no getting around that."

"True."

"I don't know if I'm just reacting to his good looks, or if a part of me still carries a little torch. Not that it matters. I found out this week that I'm a married woman."

Trisha's jaw dropped. "You're kidding."

I shook my head. "Apparently, Tony and I weren't as divorced as I thought we were."

"Un-freaking-believable." She shook her head again. "This would only happen with you, you know, Salem."

She laughed, and for a second it was just like old times, the two of us giggling and talking about guys.

We got quiet, and she blinked a couple of times. "I have this bizarre urge to thank you for not having slept with Scott."

"I know. For some reason, I want to feel proud of myself, too. As if I have this wealth of new-found virtue I never knew about." I shifted in the bed and gave her a smile I hoped would tell her everything was okay. "We both keep the bar set pretty low where I'm concerned."

She dropped her gaze for a second then bit the inside of her lip. "Look, I don't really know what to say. I feel like I should apologize for doubting you were sincere when you said you were sorry, that you had –"

"You were never the one who needed to apologize," I said softly but firmly.

"Yeah, well, if you knew all the horrible things I was thinking about you, you might disagree. I wanted you to be wrong. I wanted to see you fail." She gave a short, humorless laugh and shook her head. "I acted like a complete witch at the restaurant the other night. I've been embarrassed about it ever since."

"Trisha, I'm telling you, you don't have to apologize. Your actions have been totally understandable."

"Yes, well..." She sighed and blinked fast. "For the past five years, I've told myself that I'd forgiven Scott. I saw just how phony that forgiveness was when I realized I didn't need it anymore."

I reached over and squeezed her hand. "Don't beat yourself up for being human, Trish. It's over. No, it's better than over; it never happened in the first place. And I think you can safely comfort yourself with the knowledge that you will never have to worry about that issue with Scott."

She stood and picked up her purse. "I'm glad you're okay, Salem. And I'm glad you've straightened up your act. I wish you all the best. And thanks for getting me the interview with Tony." She turned and headed for the door, then turned back. "Listen, I wasn't kidding about having a friends-join-free coupon for Fat Fighters. If you're interested," she quirked an eyebrow and flourished a hand along her side. "I could stand to lose a couple pounds."

"Thanks," I said. "Let me see how much all these stitches are going to cost and I'll let you know."

Chapter Seventeen

The doctor said I could go home later that afternoon. Les picked me and my box of random crap up at the hospital portico. Even after less than a full day in the hospital, the outside world seemed overly bright and unnecessarily loud, and I felt disoriented and a little loopy.

Feeling loopy reminded me of one thing I wanted to talk to Les about. "Did you hear about my blood alcohol level?" I asked when I was all buckled in.

He nodded and started the engine, pulling carefully out of the lot.

"I didn't drink. I mean, I did, obviously, but it wasn't my choice. Sylvia wanted to make it look like I was driving drunk, so she poured tequila into me while Thomas and Rey held me down." I had no reason to feel guilty. And I didn't, I supposed. But I did feel soiled, in a way. Like I'd worked really hard to keep the floor clean, and then someone else came along and tracked mud all over it. Except it was me, not the floor.

Les didn't say anything. Just nodded.

"I'm serious, Les. You can ask Viv."

"She already told me." He rolled his bottom lip through his teeth. "I'm glad you brought it up, though. I confess that when I heard you'd been drinking, I was disappointed."

"Yeah, well, that's okay."

"No, it's not. It's not okay for me to be disappointed when you fall. Because we all fall. It's my job to be there to help pick you back up; it's not now and never will be my place to judge you – not the kind of judgments I made when I heard."

"So what is it you're always telling me? Confess and believe God when He says you're forgiven? Practice what you preach, Preacher Man."

He smiled, and either because I was feeling a little sentimental toward Les just then, or because the drugs were clouding my rational thinking, I decided to broach the subject that had been bugging me. "Can we talk about that?"

"About the drinking?"

"No, about the forgiveness part. You remember when I told you about that friend of mine, the one who was mad at me because I slept with her fiancée?"

He nodded as he turned onto the loop. "Sure, I remember."

"It turns out, I didn't. I *thought* I'd slept with him, and so did he, and so did *she*, obviously. But that guy Rick, the one in the car with us last night? He was the one who'd set that whole thing up to begin with. He told me that nothing had happened between Scott and me."

Les gave me a brow-raised look.

"It was supposed to be a prank on Scott and Trisha. Come to think of it, it was probably less of a prank and more like a mean-spirited trick against Trisha, because Rick didn't like her and didn't want Scott to marry her. In any event, he stuck us in bed together and let us all think we'd betrayed Trisha. But we just passed out and nothing really happened."

"That is low."

"I know." I had to remind myself that in the first place, it wasn't my duty to judge Rick or anyone else. I'd certainly made enough mistakes, so I could understand the need for grace. And in the second place, he had brought Stump to me last night and stayed with us to help explain everything to the police. I think with his new marriage and family he'd made every effort to clean up his act, and I could easily empathize with someone who needed all the support they could get in that arena.

"But at least it's nice to know what really happened."

"Oh, man, I can't tell you what a relief it is. I even called Scott and Trisha and told them because they've had to go through all this process of forgiveness and working everything out. They were ecstatic."

"You did the right thing to tell them."

"Thanks. But here's the thing that's bugging me."

"Uh-oh."

"I'm serious. In fact, this has kind of been bugging me for a while now. You know how you're always talking about the spirit of God and how he filled your heart with joy, and you're always walking in love and peace and all that stuff? How come that's not happening with me? How come I prayed for forgiveness for doing that to Trisha, but I didn't feel any real peace until I found out it never happened? What am I doing wrong?"

"I don't know. What do you think you're doing wrong?"

"Huh-uh, nope, you're not doing that this time. I have a real question, and I want a real answer. You're the one who brought me into this following Christ thing. You're the one who made all the promises to me and told me how great it was going to be. I want to know what I'm doing wrong. How come my heart isn't full of joy? How come I'm not so full of love for God I'm doing the dance of joy everywhere *I* go? How come I still feel like a loser ninety percent of the time?" I was getting wound up. I'd just meant to talk to him about the thing with Trisha and Scott, but in typical fashion, once my mouth got going, it didn't want to stop. "What did you do that I didn't do? Did I not say something right, not say the right prayer?"

"You said the right prayer, Salem. I was there. God's not so much into semantics as He is into an honest heart. Did you have an honest heart when you prayed?"

"I meant it with everything in me." That much I knew for sure.

"Then you've got it. You've got the peace, you've got the joy, you've got the forgiveness."

I would have pounded my head against the dashboard if it wouldn't have hurt so much. "But I *don't*! I don't feel joy! I don't feel peace! Most of the time I walk around feeling like a big neurotic *mess!*"

We were pulling into Trailertopia now and I wanted to cry. Probably it was a combination of everything – the frustration I felt with God and with Les and the aftermath of almost being killed all coming together – but in any case I didn't want to start bawling because then I'd never get out what needed to be said. I took a deep breath and forced myself to speak clearly. "I'm serious. What you promised me, what you *have*, hasn't happened in my life. I would say it was because you are a more mature Christian than I am, but I know that's not it because you've told me you felt different from the moment you said the prayer."

He pulled in front of my trailer, killed the motor, and turned to me. "That's right. I did."

"You know what I felt? I felt fear. I felt worried that I was going to screw this up, too. I *wanted* to be happy, I wanted to feel something. But I have to tell you, Les, what was supposed to be the brightest moment in my life – and certainly in my *Christian* life – at this point it just feels like the moment when I first drank the Koolaid and tried to convince myself it was magic elixir."

I turned toward him in my seat, leaning my head against the headrest. I waited for him to say something, but he just sat silently, looking like he was mulling it over.

"I mean, if I could see something in my life, some kind of sign that there really is – is some kind of *power* there, maybe I'd be more encouraged. This week has been so awful, and I prayed and *prayed* for some way to make things better. And each time I prayed, it was like, instead of getting a miracle, I was faced with another horrible thing I'd done, thrown in my face. Like Trisha. Like Tony. Then I almost got killed? What good is the power of the Holy Spirit if it can't shield me from painful stuff like that?"

"And why do you think all these past mistakes came back up this week? Just the fickle finger of fate?"

I thought for a second. "Come to think of it, it feels more like the middle finger of fate."

He mashed his lips together in the way that I'd come to recognize was him trying not to smile. "Salem, remember the story of Peter and Jesus on the shore after the resurrection? When Jesus asks Peter three times if he loves him?"

"You know I do," I said softly. That story was probably my least favorite story ever. There was Peter, feeling battered and beaten after the crucifixion, knowing he'd screwed up, knowing he'd betrayed Jesus when he denied knowing him three times.

So here comes Jesus, asking him three times if he *really* loved him. As if he was telling Peter, "I know what you did. You said you'd never abandon me, but then first chance you get, you deny me three times." Like a bully, poking a stick at someone who was already on the ground. When Peter was at his lowest moment, Jesus stood in front of everyone and made sure all the disciples knew what had happened.

"I know how you feel about that story. But Salem, what if Jesus wasn't doing that to rub Peter's nose in his own mistakes? What if he did that because that was the only way Peter's wound would ever heal?"

I wasn't buying that, but since I couldn't think of a clear reason why not, I just shrugged.

"Salem, you know the kind of things that grow in the dark. More dark things. Secrets, shames. Those kinds of things can't survive in the light. You take a shame out into the light of truth, and it shrivels up. Jesus knew that. He knew he could have kept quiet, and the shame of Peter's betrayal would have hung like a stone around his neck for the rest of his life. He knew how awful Peter felt, and he knew the truth of what Peter really *was*. Each time he asked Peter, 'Do you love me?' he was saying to Peter, 'I know who you really are. I know you were scared, I know you panicked. I know you made a mistake. But I know what kind of man you *really* are.' He wasn't punishing Peter. He was holding up a mirror to show Peter his own true self. He was giving him a do-over."

I blinked, feeling off-kilter. I felt the urge to hold on to my grudge against Jesus for this scene from the Bible, even as I recognized that it didn't exactly serve me to do so. "You think that's what this whole week has been about?" I asked. "A do-over, for me?"

Les shrugged. "Could be. Sometimes you gotta rip it off like a Band-Aid."

I stewed about that for a while. I couldn't really wrap my mind around it all. It had been so hard, facing all those awful memories. "I don't know," I said. "Maybe. I just wish I could feel some of that joy you're feeling –"

"You know what your problem is, Salem? You're spoiled rotten."

I don't know what I had expected him to say. But it sure as heck wasn't that.

"And you're lazy."

"I – I am?"

"Absolutely. You expect God to do all the work."

That couldn't be true. And yet... "But isn't He supposed to? I thought it was through his grace that I was saved –"

"By grace, through faith. *His* grace, *your* faith. Your *faith* in his grace. That's where it's falling apart for you. You're not showing any faith. You want God to not just turn your life around, give you an eternity in His presence and a life with meaning and hope, but you want Him to come down and put a warm fuzzy in your heart so you can feel good, too."

"But – but –"

He was mad. He didn't sound mad. His voice was calm. But his eyes flashed and the more he spoke, the thinner his lips got. In the year I'd known Les, I'd said and done a lot of things that would have made most people mad, and he'd rocked along with that same steady smile and unflappable attitude. Apparently I'd hit his pet peeve: people who want a warm fuzzy from God.

"I could sit here for the next hour and tell you all the things

God has done for you. I could list for you all the blessings you have. But for you it wouldn't make any difference, would it? Because you're still sitting safely in your chair, refusing to stake anything, refusing to believe."

"I do believe —"

"What do you believe, Salem? That He's there? So what! 'You believe that there is one God. Good! Even the demons believe that — and shudder.'"

He was quoting scripture. I knew that, because he got his I'm-quoting-scripture voice on.

"It's not that —"

But he was on a roll now. "What you don't believe is that he loves you. Despite the dozens of times in the Bible he's told you he loves you, despite all the times *I've* told you he loves you, you refuse to believe."

"I believe it, Les, I do. I just don't feel it."

"Big freaking deal!"

I'd never heard Les yell before. I almost swallowed my own tongue.

"So you don't *feel* it. What difference does that make? Salem, only an idiot would prove things by what they feel. Remember how you used to *feel* like you could handle your alcohol? And remember how you used to *feel better* after you drank? Like you were more in control, like things were getting better? People *feel* things all the time. It's a feeling, Salem. It's not a fact. God's love is a fact. And when you're ready to quit playing it safe and believe that, despite what you *feel*, you'll get what you're looking for."

He turned and jerked open the car door and got out. He reached in the back seat and tugged out the box of pictures and junk and stomped up the steps of my trailer's front deck, dropping it by my front door.

I got out. I didn't know what else to do. Obviously he was done with me. I wondered if I should apologize. But to tell the truth, I didn't *feel* like it.

"Thanks for the ride," I said as I passed him on the deck. "I appreciate all you do for me. I mean that, Les. I really do."

I took the box inside and set it by the door of my prayer room. It took a good two hours for me to get over my mad at Les for being so rude to me. I didn't even try to figure out if he had a point or not, I just railed inwardly about how unfair he'd treated me and how a person would never grow into a mature Christian if *he* was going to be their role model and bite their heads off whenever they had a question. I felt good and sorry for myself for as long as I could.

Frank brought Stump home, and that helped a lot. She whined and whimpered, and I whined and whimpered and I thought I'd never been so glad to see anyone in my life. I told her that Thomas was going to prison, and if she wanted, she could attend his sentencing hearing and give a victim impact statement about the scars she would carry for the rest of her life. Obviously this wasn't a promise I would be able to keep, but how was Stump going to find out? It seemed to make her happy.

Actually, being home made us both happy. I never thought I'd be so glad to see my old trailer house, but after the past several days it was like a mansion to me. A mansion on wheels.

Les or his wife had brought over groceries while I was gone, and Frank and I made thick peanut butter and jelly sandwiches, and I poured two big glasses of milk. In the back of my mind was the possibility that Trisha and I really would go to Fat Fighters together, and I doubted PB&J would be on the menu after that, so I thought I should enjoy it while I could.

Frank left after two sandwiches and one grudgingly given Star Crunch, and I breathed a sigh of relief with Stump snuggled up on my lap.

I scratched her ears and thought about that terrifying ride toward what could have been a horrible death. In a strange delayed reaction, I grew a lot more afraid than I had been at the moment. My heart began to pound, and my breath came short. I went back over every second of that trip, my mind straying to what could have happened, what might have happened if Viv hadn't reacted, if things hadn't turned out the way they did.

"Please, God," I whispered, lost in a horrified trance, clutching Stump until she squirmed and grunted in irritation.

I blinked and shook my head. Crazy. I was safe now. I was begging God for something I already had, a prayer he'd already answered.

This called, I realized, for a real prayer of gratitude, an honest-to-goodness, on-my-knees prayer. I lugged Stump and her box into the prayer room and lit the candles.

Stump curled up in the box and fell asleep while I quieted my mind and tried to pray. My mind was a whirl of everything that had happened, everything I'd been struggling with, and everything Les had told me. I started off thanking God for saving us, for protecting me from Sylvia and Rey and Thomas, for seeing that all of us made it through alive. But my mind kept hanging on what Les had told me.

"Is that it, God?" I finally asked. "Is Les right? Is the love there and I'm just not letting it in?"

I crawled over to the box I'd brought in and pawed through

till I found the picture of me at five years old. *You never did want anyone to love you*, G-Ma had said. *Stubbornest thing you ever saw.*

"But that's not true!" I said to the picture. "Of course, I wanted people to love me. What kid wants to keep people at arm's length? What kid *wants* to distrust everyone they meet?"

I felt tears well for that poor little girl, who at five already knew too much about the ways people could hurt each other, could abuse trust and inflict pain. That little girl wanted love; she just didn't trust it.

"God, I want you to love me, I really do. I want to believe it. I'm sorry if I've been blocking you out. I'm sorry if I've kept you at arm's length. I never meant to, I swear it. It's just hard for me to believe, I guess, because no one ever has. If you need a leap of faith, this is it. You say you believe me, so I believe it. As of right now, I believe it."

I closed my eyes and swayed on my knees, willing myself to let my guard down, to open my heart and wait. I'd never felt so vulnerable. I felt a sliding away of a wall I hadn't even known existed.

"FINALLY."

I almost fell over backward. Then I thought, 'Oh, what the heck,' and I *did* fall over backward.

"Umm...God?" I thought, feeling like an idiot. Was that you?

He didn't say anything else, though. He didn't need to. What happened next kind of defied description, although thousands of people have tried to describe it. I felt awash, submerged, floating in love. I cried and rocked and blew my nose and laughed and cried some more. It was weird and goofy, and above all, it was real.

"What do you know?" I said in a wet, snuffly voice. "My heart is strangely warmed."

Stump didn't get it. She moaned and dragged herself over to the edge of the box so she should could lick my elbow, and I felt even more love. Love for her, *from* her, from God, for God, for everyone in this whole crazy world. My heart was so full I wanted to just lie there in the floor and soak in it.

I don't know how long I lay there, but I have to say it was miles better than any binge I'd been on, any party I'd ever been to, better by light years than any experience I'd ever had. I lay there, feeling it. Finally feeling it.

So this was the love of God. No wonder Les got so excited about it.

Les. I crawled back up and rubbed my eyes on my shirtsleeve. I had to call him. What was I going to say?

I went to the bathroom and blew my nose. My cell phone rang and, of course, it was Les.

"I'm sorry," he said.

"That's funny, because I was just about to call and tell you that you were right."

"I was?"

"Yeah. Les, listen, I prayed and I believed and I..." I had to stop because the tears were back and I couldn't get any words out. I cleared my throat. "Warm fuzzies!" I finally croaked.

"Oh, Salem," he said tenderly. He shouldn't have been so tender, because that sent me into fresh spasms.

He said a few other things but all I could do was sob and whimper and grunt occasionally. He told me to get some rest and he'd check back with me tomorrow. I hung up and cried again. I wondered vaguely if I should worry about dehydration, but it wasn't as if I could stop it.

I set Stump's box by the couch and lay down beside her, hanging my hand over the side so I could scratch her ears. She fell asleep and, after a while, so did I.

I woke up to knocking at the door. I'd been dreaming I rented a baseball stadium to tell everyone about how much God loved me. The place was packed. The more I tried to explain it, the more blank the stares seemed to get and the more enormous the silence became. And the more confused I became that I actually had something to brag about.

But when I woke up I remembered how I'd felt, and I thought, "Yeah. That happened."

I checked the clock and seeing as how it was dinnertime, I figured it was Frank knocking to get another free meal. If I'd known Bobby was the one knocking I would have checked my hair before I opened the door.

He wore a yellow golf shirt and jeans, and his hair looked a little damp around the bottom, like he'd just gotten out of the shower. "How ya doing?" he asked.

"Not bad, considering," I said. "Come on in."

"I can't stay, I was just in the area and I thought I'd check and see if you needed anything."

"Nothing right now. Les has pretty well fixed me up."

He stepped back onto the deck and I followed him. The sun was going down, yellow and purple streaks reaching far across the sky, black trees on the horizon. We stood silently at the rail and watched the darkness grow up from the ground, creep ever closer to us.

"So...you've had a busy week." He turned toward me, one hip against the rail.

"I can't claim I've been bored."

He lifted his chin. "How about you give boring a try for a while?"

I laughed. "I'll do my best, Bobby. I promise you that."

"Good, because..." He trailed off, his eyes suddenly intense on my face in a way that stopped my breath in my throat. He lifted a hand toward my face, then settled it on the rail.

Because why, I wanted to ask. But I froze there under the strength of his gaze, wondering what he saw, wondering why he looked so intense, almost captivated. Wondering what he had to look so conflicted about.

"You look different," he said finally.

"I feel different." I shrugged. I felt again that swelling of my heart. It had made a difference even Bobby could see.

"Peaceful. Happy. That's how you look now."

I felt myself smile, and thought he'd described it perfectly. "You're very perceptive," I said.

"Well, I'm glad everything worked out for Tony the way you wanted it to."

I blinked, lost for a second, then realized he thought that was why I looked different. I opened my mouth to tell him what had really happened, then remembered the dream about the stadium full of underwhelmed spectators and got scared. Instead, I shrugged. "Yes, well...I told you he was innocent. It feels good to be proven right."

"We would have found the truth, you know."

"I know."

"Eventually."

"Eventually. We're both big enough to admit that I just helped speed things up a little."

He gave me that crooked grin that used to send my heart soaring. Funny, you'd think I'd outgrow that by now.

"Yes, we're both big enough to admit that." He tapped the deck railing a couple of times and shifted his feet. "You did a good job, Salem. You really did."

I didn't know what to say because all I'd really done was be nosy, but at least I'd accomplished something. "So, this is what it feels like to help people. No wonder you like being a cop so much."

"Just leave it to us next time, okay?"

I saluted. "No problem. Tomorrow I go back to being the mild-mannered dog groomer by day, and the mild-mannered couch potato by night."

"That'll help me sleep better." Again, he tapped the railing and took a step back. "If you don't need anything, then, I guess I'll just head out..."

I nodded. "I'm fine. Thomas is behind bars, the fridge is stocked, Stump's on the mend. Life is good."

"Good, then I'll just –"

Suddenly he was back, right in front of me, and his hand was lifting my chin and his lips were on mine. I was so shocked that for a second I wondered if it was really happening, but oh, those lips were so real, firm and soft at the same time. It was a long kiss, still and captivating and wonderful. It didn't even occur to me that maybe I ought to pull away, not until the moment he did.

He looked almost as shocked as I felt, but a little defiant, too. Like he couldn't believe he'd done that but, by gum, he'd do it again if he wanted to. He took a step back, his hands in his pockets.

"Ummm..." I said. "Did you just kiss me?"

"There's room for doubt? It must not have been much of a

kiss."

"No, no, it was a good kiss," I assured him. "Spectacular. It's just that I have a really good imagination, and believe me, I've spent a lot of hours imagining you kissing me. And you know, I probably still have some meds in my system, so I had to ask in case it was just one of those..." I shut up.

He bit the inside of his lip. "So how was the reality, in comparison?"

"Far better," I said. Although we'd shared some pretty amazing fantasy kisses, too. But reality *was* better. "There's just this one thing..." Now, what was it? My mind was telling me I really shouldn't be kissing him because... "Oh yeah. I'm still married."

He had the decency to look a little embarrassed. "Oh, I know. I didn't mean anything by that, of course. I just –" He took a few steps back. "I knew you'd always wanted me to do that, so I thought I'd throw you one." He grinned to show he was kidding. Then he tripped over the top step and almost busted his butt all the way down the steps.

If he hadn't made that last crack I would have probably tried to hide my laughter, but I didn't. "Klutz. Trisha is so right about you. Huge ego."

He bowed and then saluted as he walked back to his car. "Take care of yourself, Salem. I hope next time I see you it's at the grocery store or something boring like that."

"I told you I'd try. That's the best I can do." I watched him drive away, then stood on the front deck for a long time, watching the stars come out and feeling the kiss of Bobby Sloan on my lips.

The End

TO GET TWO FREE SHORT STORIES
SIGN UP TO MY NEWSLETTER!

I'm so excited to offer two free short stories available only to the lovely, lovely people who sign up for my newsletter.

The first takes place immediately after The Middle Finger of Fate, called Fight the Fat. The second is Get the Dale Outta Here, and it takes place between Unsightly Bulges (Book 2) and Caught in the Crotchfire (Book 3).

Just go to www.FreeBooksFromKim.com to sign up!

Please consider leaving a review for The Middle Finger of Fate on Amazon, iBooks, Kobo, Barnes and Noble and Good-Reads.com. Thanks!

An Excerpt From

Unsightly Bulges

A Trailer Park Princess Cozy Mystery

Book Two

My friend and mentor, Les, is fond of telling me that I have to be careful what I pray for. "God just might give it to you," he says. Always with one eyebrow raised, like who knew what horrific pandemonium would inevitably ensue if God gave me exactly what I requested for a change. His ways were above my ways and all that.

But I didn't think even a God who works in mysterious ways would send a dead body to fulfill my request that he help me stick to my diet.

Excuse me. *Strat-EAT-Gic Plan.* In Fat Fighters, we were fined two units every time we said the "D" word. See, I had prayed for help not half an hour earlier, asking God to give me strength, willpower, discipline, a wired-shut jaw, *anything* to help me lose weight. Then I had driven straight to Sonic. It had been that kind of day. I knew I wasn't supposed to turn to food to relieve stress, but since I could no longer turn to alcohol, drugs, or wildly promiscuous behavior, that left either violence or fried foods. So, you can see how a double meat, double cheese burger with extra mayo and jumbo fries was actually a fairly sensible option.

I scrubbed my face with my hands and tried to convince myself that I deserved to be sitting there (at Sonic, America's Drive-In, where roller-skating carhops will bring your 237 grams of fat directly to your car window! You don't even have to get out from behind the wheel! I had no reason to feel guilty. I'd been pretty good, considering...well, considering how bad I usually was. I'd lost four pounds in the five weeks since my high school buddy Trisha and I had joined Fat Fighters.

Yes, I'd hoped to lose twenty. Or thirty. But four was nothing to sneeze at. My pants were still too tight, but at least I could sit down without feeling like I was going to sever an internal organ. This trip to Sonic was my first real binge. Then again, this was the first time a) my little dog Stump had coughed up something bizarrely shaped and of unidentifiable origin on my kitchen floor, b) I'd been bitten by a saber-toothed Pomeranian at work, and c) I had looming date with the husband. (That last didn't sound like a big deal for most people, but...well, I wasn't most people. Until the last few months, I thought Tony and I were divorced. Turns out, not so much.)

I sighed and leaned my head back against the seat, wishing the carhop would hurry up with my food. If I had too much time to think, I would freak out about the weekend with Tony, what I was going to wear, what I was going to say. Would he try to kiss me, for heaven's sake? If he did, how would I react? What was the protocol here? I mean, he was my husband.

I also reflected on the unfairness of a world that had no sympathy when you say you've been bitten by a Pomeranian. Those suckers might be small, but their teeth were like rattlesnake fangs.

And Stump. Good Lord. What could she eat that would look like *that* when it came back up?

I heard a rumble and looked up to see the garbage truck in the alley behind Sonic. I watched idly, my mind whirling as the metal dumpster rose into the air and spewed its contents into the truck, much as Stump had done just that morning on the kitchen linoleum. Crushed cardboard boxes, black trash bags, various papers and cups. Dead body.

I actually sat there for a few seconds, still worried about Stump, before it dawned on me that the dumpster behind Sonic is not our normal way of disposing of dead bodies. What my reaction lacked in timing, it made up for with intensity.

"Hey!" I shouted. Because that always helps.

Unfortunately, the carhop had just skated up to my window with my order, and she thought I was yelling at her. She jerked back, and my french fries went flying.

"Sorry!" I yelled. Because I was in yelling mode now. "Dead body! In the dumpster!"

She was too busy backing away, wide-eyed, to see the bigger picture.

The truck dropped the dumpster back down with a hollow thump and trundled on down the alley.

I cranked the engine over and swung out of the space. I should have looked back; I almost ran down another carhop behind me, but luckily, she was pretty quick with a dive. I steered with one hand and dug through my purse for my phone with the other. I bounced the car out of the parking lot and spun around into the alley at the same time my hand closed around my phone. I charged my rusty little bucket down the rutted dirt alley while I punched in 9-1-1.

"I need to report a dead body." Wow. Déjà vu. It was, what, three months since I had called the same number with the exact same message? Maybe I ought to put 9-1-1 on speed dial.

I was proud of myself, however, for not bursting into hysterical laughter this time. I had not wanted to do that last time, but I couldn't help it. I have issues.

It took a few attempts for me to convey to the dispatcher what was going on, and even then I don't think she completely understood the gravity of the situation. She seemed entirely too calm when she said, "Police are on their way."

But the truck was now stopped at another dumpster, so I hung up and jumped out of the car. I leaped onto the running board and shouted "Hey!" at the driver, slapping the window a few times.

He looked much the same as the carhop had when I'd shouted at her.

"You have a dead body in your truck," I mouthed through the closed window.

He stared at me.

"You *have*. A dead *body*. In your *truck*." I motioned for him to roll the window down.

After a second he leaned over, slowly, and inched it down, eyes wide.

"I was watching when you emptied the dumpster behind Sonic. There was a dead body in it!"

He looked confused. "There's a dead body at Sonic?"

"No," I said. I did not say, "you idiot," because I was trying very, very hard not to be that kind of person anymore. I took a deep breath. "There was a dead body in the dumpster. Now it's in your truck."

He threw the truck into park and said, "You're kidding."

"Ummm, no." Hopefully when I made jokes I was funnier than that.

I stepped back as he flung open his door and jumped up onto the seat. He braced his hand on the top of the cab and leaned, stretching on tiptoe to peer into the big bed that held all the garbage.

I circled the truck in time to see him inching, toes barely clinging to a metal seam along the side of the truck, toward the big bed. He held onto a pipe with one hand and leaned to look in. "Are you sure? I don't see – oh. Oh, good Lord. Oh, man."

He let go of the bar and dropped to the ground. "I saw a foot. Oh, man. Oh, man." His eyes rolled back in his head, and he staggered.

"I called the police. Hey, don't –" But it was too late. He keeled over.

I was holding his head in my lap and giving his cheek increasingly firmer "pats" when I heard sirens. The guy blinked a couple of times and looked up at me. "Oh man," he said again.

"Yes, I know." I scooted him off my lap and stood to wave at the squad car that was slowly making its way down the alley. I was happy to see a patrol officer I didn't recognize get out and do the cop-swagger toward me.

I knew it wouldn't be Bobby Sloan because he was a detective now. He had shown up at my last Finding-Of-The-Body, but that was a fluke. It could have been Watson, another cop with whom I was on more-familiar-than-was-comfortable terms. I would prefer not to see Watson again, and I was sure the feeling was mutual.

This guy looked young, probably just out of the academy. He was Hispanic, medium build with buzzed hair. He eyed the driver and me so suspiciously that I started to feel guilty, which was annoying.

He did just what the driver had done, hopping first onto the seat, then inching out far enough to see what the driver had seen.

I stood beside the alley and peered up at him. It was as if I could tell exactly the moment he realized he was going to have to climb into that truck to make sure the person attached to that foot was really dead. His mouth turned into a grim line and he looked down at us. "Stay right there," he ordered.

With a quick shake of his head, he hoisted himself up and straddled the side of the truck, then dropped into the truck.

The driver kept looking up at the opening of the hauler, as if the foot he saw was going to pop up any second.

After about thirty seconds the patrolman hauled himself back out. I guess it didn't take very long to establish the facts and get the heck out of there.

Bobby Sloan pulled up in a white sedan.

"You gotta be kidding me," he said as he got out.

I shrugged. "Wish I was."

He walked up and squeezed my shoulder. "Salem Grimes. Reporting a dead body. Now here's something you don't see every day. Every week, maybe, but not every day."

"I was minding my own business, Bobby, I swear. I just looked up and saw the body falling out of the dumpster. It was my civic duty to report it."

I crossed my arms over my chest and wished I'd been able to lose those thirty pounds already. I was never comfortable around Bobby, but he'd kissed me the last time I saw him, and I still didn't know why. The moment he stepped into the alley, that kiss was all I could think about.

Bobby ordered me to stay put and went over to talk to the

patrolman. I dropped onto the ground at the edge of the alley, beside the truck driver. He sat with his legs in front of him, arms on his knees, and shook his head every few seconds.

"Kind of weird, isn't it?" I asked, feeling sorry for him. The sight of that limp body tumbling into the truck ran over and over through my head, but, to be fair, the guy did look worse than I felt.

He turned to me. "You don't think there's any way I'd get fired for this, do you?"

"Why on earth would you get fired?"

He shook his head again. "I don't know, b ut I keep getting fired, and I was really hoping this job would last a while. I don't really know where I'd go from here."

I knew what he meant. Probably from driving a dumpster truck there weren't many places to go. "I work in a dog grooming shop. We're always looking for people to bathe the dogs. Maybe I could train you."

"I'd have to be trained to bathe a dog?"

"You'd be surprised." I stood and brushed the dried grass of my jeans. I held out my hand. "Come on. Let's just walk down to the other dumpster and back. Get some air." That truck was starting to reek.

And okay, here was the really bad part: I began to feel kind of sad about my double meat cheeseburger and fries. That was bad; I knew it was bad. More proof – as if I needed it – that I'd replaced my addiction to alcohol with an addiction to food. Out of the frying pan and into the fat pants. On the upside, I hardly ever picked fights with total strangers after I had a Stupendous-size order of fries and a king size Snickers bar. I was usually too sluggish.

Bits of trash littered the alley, and I realized that some of it could be evidence. "Some of this stuff could have blown out of the truck." I toed what looked like a cash register receipt.

"Yeah, we leave crap all over town," the driver said. "It blows out all over the place."

We walked slowly up and down the alley, but I had no way of knowing what was a clue and what was just regular old garbage. I saw two crushed soft drink cups, four more receipts, a diaper, a torn piece of orange t-shirt with "acon" written in a font that looked like bacon, and a Nerf bullet.

"That guy was naked," I said, bending to pick up the fabric. "I wonder if this was his shirt."

"Hey!"

I sprang back like I'd seen a snake.

The patrolman stomped down the alley toward us. "I told you two to stay beside the truck. Don't touch anything out here. We have to get forensics out here."

"We were just looking for clues," the driver said. He pointed to the Nerf bullet. "Could be something."

The patrolman jerked his head toward the truck. "Get back over there."

"Grump," I said under my breath as we walked back. I had mixed emotions – I wasn't sure if I should be upset or relieved that I had not ordered bacon on that burger, since it had ended up on the ground anyway. I wondered if I could go back and tell the manager what happened. Maybe they would give me a free Sympathy Bacon Burger, like a hero, kind of.

But then again maybe they wouldn't, since I'd almost mowed down one of their carhops. Probably better to go to a different Sonic from now on.

Bobby finished talking to new people who had shown up and came over to me and the driver. "Tell me again what you saw."

I took a deep breath. "I was sitting at Sonic, waiting for my order, and I saw the truck pull up. The dumpster lifted up and the body came tumbling out with all the trash. So, I followed him down the alley to tell him." I jerked a thumb toward the truck driver. "That's all I did."

He stuck his hand out to shake Bobby's. "Dale Coffee. Nice to meet you, sir."

"Dale, I'm Bobby Sloan. Sorry we have to meet under these circumstances."

"Me too," Dale said sincerely.

"Tell me what you saw."

Bobby had on his cop face. The thing about Bobby is, he's always had a cop face. Maybe that was one of the things that fascinated me about him.

Other Titles in the Trailer Park Princess Series
The Middle Finger of Fate (Book One)
Unsightly Bulges (Book Two)
Caught in the Crotchfire (Book Three)
'Tis the Friggin' Season (Short Story)
The Power of Bacon (Short Story)
Mud, Sweat, and Tears (Short Story)

Coming in 2017
Knickers in a Twist

ABOUT THE AUTHOR

This is me. I bought this outfit
and got my roots done for this picture. You can't tell, but I also got
a pedicure. It was a big day for me, let me tell you. My hands are
curled up because I didn't want to spring for the mani.

The award-winning author of the Trailer Park Princess comic mystery series. Kim Hunt Harris knew she wanted to be a writer before she even knew how to write. When her parents read bedtime stories to her, she knew she wanted to be a part of the story world. She started out writing children's stories, and her stories grew as she did. She discovered a gift for humor and a love for making people laugh with her tales, and the Trailer Park Princess series was born.

Kim loves to not only make her readers laugh and entertain them with a good mystery, but also to examine the issues the everyday people face...well, every day. Issues like faith and forgiveness, perseverance, and tolerance. Set in Lubbock, Texas, the fun books feature a cast of quirky characters, outrageous situations, a drama queen of a dog, and from time to time, a tear or two.

Kim lives with her husband of more than thirty years and two kids in West Texas.